About the Authors

Lynne Graham lives in Northern Ireland and has been a keen romance reader since her teens. Happily married, Lynne has five children. Her eldest is her only natural child. Her other children, who are every bit as dear to her heart, are adopted. The family has a variety of pets, and Lynne loves gardening, cooking, collecting all sorts and is crazy about every aspect of Christmas.

Jackie Braun is the author of more than thirty romance novels. She is a three-time RITA® finalist and a four-time National Readers' Choice Award finalist. She lives in Michigan with her husband and two sons.

Catherine George was born in Wales, and early on developed a passion for reading which eventually fuelled her compulsion to write. Marriage to an engineer led to nine years in Brazil, but on his later travels the education of her son and daughter kept her in the UK. And, instead of constant reading to pass her lonely evenings, she began to write the first of her romantic novels. When not writing and reading she loves to cook, listen to opera, and browse in antiques shops.

Latin Lovers

Latin Lovers: Under the Latin Sun

LYNNE GRAHAM

JACKIE BRAUN

CATHERINE GEORGE

MILLS & BOON

First Published in Great Britain 2021
By Mills & Boon, an imprint of HarperCollins*Publishers*
1 London Bridge Street, London, SE1 9GF

LATIN LOVERS: UNDER THE LATIN SUN
© 2021 Harlequin Books S.A.

Duarte's Child © 2001 Lynne Graham
Greek for Beginners © 2013 Jackie Braun Fridline
Under the Brazilian Sun © 2011 Catherine George

ISBN: 978-0-263-29888-8

MIX
Paper from
responsible sources
FSC
www.fsc.org   FSC® C007454

Printed and bound in Spain
by CPI, Barcelona

DUARTE'S CHILD

LYNNE GRAHAM

CHAPTER ONE

'WHAT action do you want me to take?' the private investigator enquired.

Duarte Avila de Monteiro let the silence linger and continued to gaze out at his stunning view of the City of London. *She'd been found.* Sudden success after so many fruitless months of searching felt intoxicating. He would retrieve his son. Her too, of course. She was still his wife. He refused to think of her by name. He refused to personalise her in any way.

'Do nothing,' Duarte responded without expression.

His wealthy client was a total emotion-free zone, the investigator decided in fascination. He'd just given the guy the news that he had finally traced his runaway wife and the infant son he had still to meet—and yet nothing was to be done?

'Leave the file on my desk,' Duarte continued in a tone of dismissal. 'There will be a substantial bonus when you present the bill for your services.'

On his way past what he assumed to be the secretary's desk in the ante-room outside, the investigator paused: the secretary was the most stunning Nordic blonde he had ever laid eyes on. 'Your boss is kind of chilling,' he murmured confidentially.

'My boss is a brilliant financial genius and also my lover,' the blonde whispered in a voice as cutting as slashing glass meeting tender skin. 'You just lost your bonus.'

Rearing back in startled disbelief at that poisonous response, the young investigator stared at the beautiful blonde, aghast.

'Shall I call Security to have you removed?' she added sweetly.

Within his imposing office, Duarte was pouring himself a brandy and contemplating the immediate future. He had an overwhelming desire to muster his entire security team and spring a middle-of-the-night assault on his estranged wife and child's accommodation. He *had* to move fast before she disappeared again with his son. His mobile phone gripped between lean brown fingers, he tensed and then frowned. For an instant, he could not believe that he had even contemplated such an act of madness. He could wait until morning... Well, he could wait until dawn at least.

He stabbed out the number for the head of his protection team. 'Mateus? You will proceed to the address I am about to give you. There you will find a caravan—'

'A *caravan*...?'

'Which contains my wife and my child,' Duarte admitted with a grimace at the sheer incredulity he could hear in Mateus's voice. 'You will ensure that if that caravan moves so much as an inch it will be followed. You will also be discreet while treating this as a matter of the utmost urgency and importance.'

'We'll leave immediately, sir,' Mateus confirmed, sounding shaken. 'Your faith in us won't be misplaced.'

'Discretion, Mateus.'

Duarte made a second call to put his private jet on standby for the next day. Was he planning to kidnap them both? She was his wife. Kidnapping was a crime. *She* had kidnapped his son. *Inferno!* A bloody caravan! Duarte gritted his even white teeth, a flash of white-hot rage threatening his hard self-discipline. She was bringing *his* son up in a caravan while she mucked around with horses. Who was looking after their child while she devoted her attention to four-legged animals?

Emily—safe, quiet, humble and as easily read as an open

book—a young woman unlikely to rock any boats. How had he *ever* thought that? With a raw-edged laugh, Duarte drained the brandy. He had picked her quite deliberately for those unassuming qualities. He'd given her everything that would have kept most women purring with delighted contentment. Fabulous wealth, a selection of luxurious homes and glittering social occasions at which she could show off her equally fabulous jewellery. His reward for his unquestioning generosity? She'd betrayed her marriage vows and his trust: she'd got into bed with another man. Obviously quiet women needed to be *watched*.

One of his medieval ancestors had murdered his unfaithful wife and got off scot-free because it had been regarded as an act of cleansing the family honour, rather than a crime. Duarte could not contemplate ever laying rough hands on any woman, even his estranged wife, no matter how enraged he was by her shameless behaviour. Then, Duarte never lost control in any field. He would deal with the situation as he saw fit. Walling her up alive would not have given him the slightest satisfaction and he could only assume his ancestor had been a seriously sick pervert.

There were other infinitely more subtle ways of controlling women. And Duarte knew *all* the ways. Duarte had never practised those arts on his seemingly innocent and shy little wife. So she was in for a surprise or two in the near future…

'I just don't understand why you have to move on,' Alice Barker confessed. 'I can drum up enough eager learners to keep you employed right through the year.'

Stiff with tension, Emily evaded the older woman's questioning gaze. Small in stature and slight of build, she wore her long curly red hair in a sensible plait. 'I don't usually stay anywhere for long—'

'You have a six-month-old baby. It's not so easy to stay

on the move with a young child,' Alice pointed out. 'I need a permanent riding instructor and the job's yours if you want it. My stables would profit from you staying on just as much as you would—'

Feeling the dialogue had gone far enough when there was not the smallest chance of her changing her mind about leaving, Emily lifted her bright head. Her aquamarine eyes were troubled and embarrassed, for she hated to turn down an offer that she would have loved to accept. However, telling the truth about why she had to refuse wasn't an option. 'I'm sorry, but we really do have to leave—'

'Why?' The older woman's weathered face was set in stubborn lines.

Emily's fair complexion was flushed with discomfiture. 'I guess I'm a rolling stone—'

'I don't believe that. I know travelling folk and you don't have that restlessness. You could have a comfortable home and job here with friends—'

'You're making this very difficult for me, Alice—'

The older woman tilted back her greying head and studied Emily with wry eyes. 'Maybe I'm hoping that you'll come clean and admit that you're running from something or somebody...and that the *only* thing keeping you on the road is fear of that somebody or something catching up with you!'

Emily turned very pale at that disturbingly accurate assessment.

'Of course, I suspected that you might be in some sort of fix,' Alice Barker admitted with a sympathetic look. 'You're too reserved and, by nature, I'd say you were a much more relaxed person. You're also too nervous of strangers.'

'I haven't broken the law or anything,' Emily responded in a strained undertone. 'But I'm afraid that's as much as I can say.'

But even as she made that assurance, she wondered if it was *still* true. Had she broken any English law in what she had done? How was she to know when she had not taken legal advice? She'd been on the run for eight months and she'd not got back in touch with her family or indeed anyone else during that period.

'Are you trying to shake off an abusive boyfriend?' Alice was keen to get to the root of Emily's problems. 'Why don't you let me help you? Running away never solves anything.'

Dismayed by her companion's persistence, Emily muttered in a rush, 'You've been really great to us. I'll never forget that but we *have* to leave first thing tomorrow.'

Recognising the sheen of tears in Emily's eyes, Alice sighed and gave the younger woman an awkward hug. 'If you change your mind, there'll always be a bed here for you.'

Closing the caravan door behind her, Alice trudged back down the lane to the stable block to lock up for the evening. Emily drew in a slow, deep, shaken breath. One thing that Alice had said had hit Emily on a very tender nerve. *Running away never solves anything.* That was so horribly true, Emily conceded heavily. Nothing had been solved or settled. It was eight months since she had left Portugal. She had run home to her family for support but her family had treated her like an escaped convict.

'Don't think that we're going to get involved!' Emily's mother had pronounced in furious dismissal. 'So please don't embarrass us with the details of your marital problems.'

'Go home to your husband. You're not staying here with us,' her father had told her in outrage.

'Have you gone out of your tiny mind?' Her eldest sister, Hermione, had demanded. 'What do you think your walking out on your marriage is likely to do to the family business? If Duarte blames us, we'll *all* be ruined!'

'You really are an absolute idiot to come here,' her other sister, Corinne, had said with stinging scorn. 'None of us are going to help you. Did you really expect us to react any other way?'

The answer to that frank question would have been yes but Emily had been too devastated by that mass rejection to respond. *Yes*, time and time again through childhood and adolescence and indeed right up to the age of twenty when she married, Emily had fondly hoped to receive some small sign that her family loved her. That blind faith had sunk without trace for the last time. She'd finally accepted that she was the cuckoo in the family nest, an outsider who was both resented and unwelcome and that nothing was *ever* likely to change that reality.

Why it should be that way she'd never understood. Yet she was painfully aware that had she got the chance to sit down and tell the honest truth about why her marriage had fallen apart, she would undoubtedly have been shown the door by her family even more quickly.

She'd had to face the fact that, whatever she chose to do, she was on her own. So she'd sold her engagement ring. With the proceeds, she'd bought an old car and a caravan and she had hit the road to make a living the only way she could. Travelling around the countryside from one stables to another, she offered her services for a few weeks as a riding instructor and then moved on to pastures new. The longer she stayed in one place, the greater the chance that she would be tracked down.

Of course, Duarte was looking for both her and his child. Duarte Avila de Monteiro, the terrifyingly powerful and even more terrifyingly wealthy banker she had foolishly married. His brilliance in the world of finance was a living legend.

When Duarte had asked Emily to marry him, she had been stunned for she hadn't been beautiful, sophisticated or even rich. Furthermore, her relatives might like to give themselves airs and graces in polite company but, though her family could not bear to have it mentioned, Emily's grandfather had been a milkman. So, understandably, Emily had been overwhelmed that Duarte Avila de Monteiro should decide to marry her humble and ordinary self. That he didn't love her…well, so nothing was perfect, she had told herself. At the outset, she'd been full of cheerful and trusting hopes for the future. Adoring him like a silly schoolgirl, she'd simply marvelled at her own good luck.

Although she had been in awe of her husband, she had never feared him, not the way others did. People were afraid to cross his reserve and offend him. People were afraid of his unapologetic ruthlessness. She'd been stupid *not* to fear him, Emily conceded heavily with the knowledge of hindsight. A wretched light in her troubled eyes, she reached into her son Jamie's cot and lifted his warm, solid little body up into her arms. Eight months ago, Duarte had threatened to take her baby from her as soon as he was born and raise him without her. Within days of being told of that appalling threat, Emily had fled Portugal in a panic.

But unhappily there was no escape from the reality that she had destroyed her own marriage. She had been the guilty partner. It was *her* fault that Duarte had demanded a separation, *her* fault that Duarte had ultimately decided that she ought to be deprived of their child as well. Indeed, in recent months, Emily had started feeling even worse over the fact that Duarte was being deprived of the right to even *see* his own son. Only her terror of losing custody of Jamie and her fearful awareness that she had neither Duarte's money nor influence had triumphed over her guilty conscience.

Now, however, Emily was finally facing the immaturity

of her own behaviour. It was time that she went to see a lawyer and found out exactly where she stood. It was time she *stopped* running…

Yet how did she deal with Duarte? And how would Duarte now deal with her? In spite of herself, she shivered as discouraging memories engulfed her. During their separation, Duarte had exiled her to the country house in the Douro for the winter. She had lived there alone for three months, hoping against hope that he would eventually agree to see her and talk to her again and that the great divide between them might somehow be miraculously mended. But that had been such a naive dream.

For Duarte, Emily thought painfully, would be happy to acquire a son and dispense with the baby machine who had produced that son. For really that was all she had ever been to her gorgeous husband…a baby machine. For what other reason had he married her? Certainly not for love, lust or loneliness. Childlessness was a disaster to the average Portuguese male and Duarte had an illustrious name. The Monteiro family could trace their aristocratic lineage back to the thirteenth century and, naturally, Duarte had wanted a child to carry on into the next generation.

Accustomed to early rising, Emily was up before dawn the following morning.

She'd packed the night before. After feeding Jamie and making herself some toast and tea, she collapsed his cot and stowed it safely away. Living in a small caravan had taught her to be tidy. As she slid into a pair of old navy jodhpurs and pulled on a voluminous grey sweater to combat the early morning chill, she watched her son. Sitting on the carpet in the compact seating area, Jamie was chewing industriously on the corner of a horse magazine.

Emily darted over and detached the magazine from his mouth. 'No, Jamie…here's your ring.'

Presented with the teething ring which had been chilled specially for his use, Jamie dropped it again and his bottom lip came out, brown eyes filming over with tears as he tried without success to reach for the magazine again. Sweeping her son up into her arms, Emily cuddled him and wondered why he loathed the teething ring which would have been so much kinder to his sore gums.

As always the warm baby smell of Jamie sent a great wave of love through her and she hugged him tight. He had Duarte's black hair and golden skin and the same shape eyes as her. Right now, because he had another new tooth on the way, he had pink flushed cheeks and he looked absolutely adorable in his red sweatshirt top and tiny jeans.

Checking that she had secured everything moveable, Emily decided to put Jamie out in his car seat. She had said her goodbyes the night before and all she still had to do was hitch up the caravan to the car.

It was a fresh spring day and the breeze blew back the Titian red curls from her brow. With Jamie balanced on her hip, she unlocked the passenger door of the car. Strapping her son into his seat and stowing the baby bag of supplies that went everywhere with them, she chatted with greater cheer than she felt to him. 'I timed this so that we would see the six o'clock train passing at the crossing. Choo-choo, Jamie—'

'Choo...' he seemed to sound out but she was prepared to concede that it might have been the wishful thinking of a proud mother.

Another day, another place, Emily reflected wearily and it was no longer the smallest thrill to contemplate the unknown that lay ahead. She had stayed longer than was wise at Alice Barker's stables, not only because she liked the older woman but also because she had been in dire need of a period of regular employment and earnings. Running even an old car was expensive; she had recently had to renew her insurance and replace the whole exhaust system. So, once again, she had little cash in reserve.

As she stuck her car keys in the ignition and turned, intending to hitch up the caravan, she heard an angry shout and then another. It sounded like Alice. Frowning in dismay, Emily hurried past the caravan to see what was happening. At the rear entrance to the stables, she saw a sight that shook her. Alice Barker was standing with a shotgun trained on a man.

'Just you tell me right now what you were doing!' Alice was demanding furiously.

As Emily rushed automatically to support the older woman, she heard the man speak and she caught several words. Alice's trespasser was striving to apologise in Portuguese. Emily froze in her tracks. *Portuguese?*

'I caught this chappie trying to creep up on your caravan!' Alice called to Emily with patent disgust. 'One of the peeping Toms, one of those filthy perverts…that's what I've caught. Just as well he doesn't seem to speak a word of English. I shouldn't think he's saying anything any decent woman would want to hear! Reach into my pocket and get my phone, and we'll ring the police!'

But Emily did not move an inch. Every scrap of colour draining from her slanting cheekbones, she stared at the stocky, well-built Portuguese male in his smart city suit. It was Mateus Santos, Duarte's security chief. Her tummy churned, her brain refusing to move at speed. The older man was as white as his own shirtfront, evidently not having expected to be greeted by a very angry woman with a shotgun when he came snooping.

'*Emily!*' Alice barked impatiently.

Mateus's strained gaze swerved to Emily's stilled figure with perceptible relief. '*Doña Emilia…*' he greeted her and followed that up with a hasty flood of Portuguese.

Emily understood a little more of the language than she

could actually speak and she caught the gist of his appeal. Mateus was asking her to tell Alice that he was no danger to anybody. Only that wasn't quite true, Emily decided in sudden total panic. If Mateus was at the stables, it meant that Duarte had tracked *her* down and that Duarte now knew where she was. 'I know this man, Alice. He's no threat, but please keep him here until I can get away—'

'Emily…what on earth is going on?' Alice demanded in bewilderment.

But Emily was already speeding back towards her car. Where Mateus was, Duarte would soon follow. She jumped into the driver's seat and then realised that she had still to hitch up the caravan.

With a gasp of frustration, she began to reverse the car and then dashed out again to haul at the caravan with frantic hands. The task accomplished, she was in the act of swinging back into her car when she saw the bonnet of a big silver vehicle filter into the mouth of the lane she needed to go down to make her exit.

Heart thumping somewhere in the region of her convulsing throat, Emily stared in absolute horror at the limousine. Duarte! It could only be Duarte behind those tinted windows. Just as suddenly, she unfroze again and flung herself into her own car. The ground siding the lane was unfenced and reasonably level. She could drive *around* the limo! Firing the engine, she slammed the door. Within six feet of the long luxury vehicle seeking to block her escape, she turned the steering wheel and took her car off the lane on to the rough grass verge. The caravan bounced in protest and the vibrations shook the car but, within the space of thirty seconds, she was back on the concrete lane again, the caravan still in tow.

She would go to a lawyer, Emily told herself frantically. She would stop at the first legal firm she saw and beg for an appointment and advice. She was not going to risk facing Duarte alone in case he simply took Jamie from her and flew him out to Portugal. Hadn't she read horror stories about disaffected foreign husbands taking that kind of action when their marriages to their British wives broke down?

And, worst of all, wouldn't Duarte have grounds to argue that *she* had virtually pulled the *same* stunt on him? Jamie was six months old and his own father had yet to meet him. What right did she have to keep them apart? An agony of conflict and guilt in her gaze as she questioned what she was doing, Emily pulled out of the lane on to the twisting country road that lay beyond.

Duarte would attempt to follow her but she was at an advantage for she knew the area. How could she take the chance of trusting Duarte when he might take Jamie away from her? She would be lucky to ever see her child again. Where she was concerned, her estranged husband would not be feeling the slightest bit sympathetic or reasonable. Why, oh why, oh why had she waited this long before acknowledging that it was past time she sorted out the whole mess?

Rounding a corner on the road, Emily had to start immediately slackening speed. A shaken laugh shorn of any humour was torn from her tight throat. The railway crossing lay ahead. The warning lights were flashing and the automatic barriers were coming down signifying that a train was about to pass through. She was trapped for a good five minutes by the very train she had promised Jamie he would see as a treat. By the time the express finally thundered past the barriers, Emily was studying her driving mirror and watching the silver limo appear behind her on the road. Caught! Fate had not been on her side. In a gesture of frustrated defeat, Emily lifted one of her hands from the steering wheel and struck it down on the dash board.

She felt a prick like a sharp stinging needle in the side

of her hand. Blinking, she glanced down and gaped in dawning horror at the big bee crawling away. It wasn't the season, a little voice screamed inside her, it wasn't the season yet for bees! She hadn't replaced her allergy kit when she had mislaid it over the winter. She dropped her hand down to open the driver's door. Already she felt like she was moving in slow motion; already she could feel the sensation of her heartbeat starting to race.

She lurched out of the car. She struggled to focus on the formidably tall and dark male striding towards her but she raised her hands to her face instead, feeling the tenderness and the heat there, knowing that her skin had probably begun to swell and redden. 'Sting…bee!' she framed jerkily.

'Where's your adrenaline kit?' Duarte demanded, instantly grasping the crisis and reacting at speed.

With enormous effort she blinked and connected momentarily with stunning dark golden eyes that she would never have dared to meet had she been in full control of herself. 'Lost…'

'*Meu Deus!* The nearest doctor?' Duarte caught hold of her as she doubled over with the pain piercing her abdomen and vented a startled gasp. 'Emily…a hospital…a doctor?' he raked down at her with raw urgency. '*Where?*'

It was such an effort for her to concentrate, to speak. 'Village through the crossing,' she wheezed.

She was conscious of movement as he carried her, the roar of car engines and raised voices in Portuguese but she was in too much pain to try to see what was happening. She opened her swollen eyes with a grimace of discomfort, for her whole body was hurting. She registered that she was lying in Duarte's arms inside an unfamiliar car and was suddenly terrified that everyone had forgotten about her baby. 'Jamie…?'

'*He* will be OK…'

Even in the state she was in, the sense that she was now

hearing his voice from the end of a long dark tunnel, she picked up on that stress. *She* might not be OK. She had been fifteen years old when it was impressed on her after an adverse reaction to a bee sting that she must go nowhere without her adrenaline kit. She had been too scared not to be sensible but, as the years passed without further incident, she had gradually become rather more careless. 'If I die…' she slurred with immense difficulty because the inside of her mouth and her tongue were swollen, 'You get Jamie…only fair—'

'*Por amar de Deus*, you are *not* going to die, Emily,' Duarte cut in savagely, lifting up her head, rearranging her with careful hands because she was starting to struggle for breath. 'I will not allow it.'

But before she lost consciousness, all she could think about was that it *would* be only fair if Duarte got Jamie. It was a punishment for her to be near Duarte again. It made it impossible for her to evade her own tormenting memories. Eleven months ago, one instant of hesitation had cost Emily her marriage—Duarte had found her in the arms of another man.

She'd let Toby kiss her and she still couldn't explain why, even to herself. At the time she had been desperately unhappy and Toby had astonished her when he had told her that he loved her. In her whole life, nobody had *ever* told Emily that they loved her and she had never expected to hear those words. Certainly, she'd given up hope of ever inspiring such high-flown feelings in her gorgeous but essentially indifferent husband.

While she'd been frantically wondering what she could say that would not hurt Toby's feelings, Toby had grabbed her and kissed her. Why hadn't she pushed him away? She'd not been attracted to Toby, nor had she wanted that bruising kiss. Yet she'd still stood there and *allowed* him to kiss her. She'd been unfaithful to her husband and there was no justifying that betrayal of trust to a male as proud and uncompromising as Duarte. In the aftermath, she'd been so distraught with shame that she had made a total hash of convincing her husband that that single kiss had been the *only* intimacy she had ever shared with Toby. Convinced that she'd been having an affair, Duarte had demanded a separation, even though she was four months pregnant with their child.

Emily's eyes opened and she snatched in a great whoosh of oxygen to fill her starved lungs.

The injection of adrenaline brought about an almost instantaneous recovery but she was severely disorientated and she didn't know where she was. As she began to sit up, scanning the unfamiliar faces surrounding her and recognising a nurse in her uniform, she gasped, 'What...*where*?'

'You just had a very narrow escape. You were in anaphylactic shock.' The older man gave her a relieved smile. 'You're in the cottage hospital. I'm the duty doctor. We administered the adrenaline jab in the nick of time.'

'Take it easy and lie down for a minute,' the nurse advised. 'Do you feel sick?'

As Emily rested back again, she moved her swimming head in a negative motion. After that initial buzzing return of energy which had revitalised her, she now felt weak as a kitten. She was on a trolley, not a bed, and as the cluster of medical staff surrounding her parted because the emergency was over she saw Duarte looming just feet away. She raised trembling hands to her still tender face, felt the swelling that was still there and knew that she had to look an absolute fright. In addition, the very minute that foolish thought occurred to her, she became aware of her own demeaning vulnerability.

For a split second, it was like time stood still. Her dazed aquamarine eyes wide above her spread fingertips connected with his spectacular dark golden gaze. His eyes were rich as the finest of vintage wine but utterly without expression. She could feel her heartbeat quicken, the wretched inescapable burst of liquid heat surge between her slender thighs. He came, he saw, he conquered, she misquoted, shaken to her depths by her own helpless response. From the first moment it had been like that with Duarte.

There had been a wild uncontrollable longing that had nothing to do with sense or caution. Something that had come so naturally to her, something that had been rooted so deep in her psyche that only death could have ended her addiction to him. He'd drawn her like a magnet and, what was more, he had known it from the first instant of their eyes meeting.

But their marriage had been a disaster for both of them, she reminded herself miserably. The more she'd loved him, the more she had become agonised by his inherent indifference. Impervious to her every attempt to breach that barrier, he had broken her heart. She had even been hurt by his satisfaction when she fell pregnant, for it was a satisfaction he had never shown in her alone. The old sick shame filled her as she recalled that fatal kiss which had cost her everything that mattered to her. She had finally broken through Duarte's reserve only to discover that *all* she could touch was his pride and his honour.

'I could strangle you for your carelessness, Emily...' Duarte breathed in a curiously ragged undertone.

'What *you* need is a good cup of tea. You've had a nasty shock too,' the middle-aged nurse informed Duarte in a brisk and cheerful interruption. Unaccustomed to being addressed as if he was a large child, he looked sincerely startled.

A porter began to wheel out the trolley on which Emily lay. As the nurse had spoken, Emily had finally recognised the ashen quality of Duarte's usually vibrant skin tone and the sheen of perspiration on his sculpted dark features. She closed her eyes, acknowledging the truth of the older woman's assurance. She had almost died on him. Evidently, he was relieved that she had survived. Maybe he did not hate her *quite* as much as she had assumed he did.

But then hatred meant a strong emotion where the target was concerned, didn't it? And Duarte had never felt *any* particularly strong emotion in her direction. A pain that felt almost physical enclosed her and she shut her eyes in self-defence. She knew that she had never had the power to hide her feelings from him and she had not the courage to meet his eyes levelly.

'Your husband has had the fright of his life,' the kindly nurse soothed her in a small empty side ward. 'When your child runs out in front of a car, you shout at him afterwards because you're angry and afraid that you almost lost him.'

'Yes…' Emily was rolled gently into a bed. She did not like to say that Duarte's most likely feeling now was one of complete exasperation and contempt. In her position, he would never have made the mistake of being without that life-saving adrenaline kit.

'Why am I being put to bed?' Emily asked, finding herself being deftly undressed.

'The doctor wants us to keep you under observation for a few hours just to be sure that you have no adverse reactions.'

Helped into a hospital nightdress in a faded print and left alone, Emily lay back against the pillows, anxiously wondering who exactly had charge of Jamie and how her baby was coping with her sudden disappearance. Almost at the same moment as she was thinking that the nurse reappeared, cradling Jamie, who was howling at the top of his lungs. 'I believe this little soul is yours and he wants his mum!'

Emily opened her arms and Jamie grabbed on to her the

instant he was brought within her reach. 'Who was looking after him?'

'The older man, who arrived just after your husband brought you in. He doesn't speak any English. He was out at Reception trying to calm your little boy down.'

Mateus Santos, she assumed, a committed bachelor who was probably pretty useless with young children. Jamie snuffled into weary silence against her shoulder just as Duarte appeared in the open doorway. He stilled when he saw the child in her arms and the nurse slipped out, leaving them alone.

Her tummy twisting, her eyes veiled, Emily muttered awkwardly, 'Have you seen Jamie yet?'

'No...Mateus brought him here in your car. My time was taken up tending to you,' Duarte admitted curtly.

Jamie had a death grip on her. He was going through that stage of disliking strangers that many babies went through around his age. He resisted being turned round and pushed his dark head under her chin. He'd had quite enough of excitement and strangers for one morning. It was anything but the best moment for Duarte to meet his son for the first time.

'Duarte...I'm *so* sorry!' Emily heard herself admit with her usual impulsiveness, a sob catching in her aching throat. 'I am so very sorry for everything...'

'That cuts no ice with me,' Duarte responded with eyes that were as hard and bright as burnished steel, cold derision etched in every line of his starkly handsome features as he studied her shaken face. 'How dare you drag my son round the countryside in a caravan like a gipsy? How dare you put me in the position where I have to answer to the police merely because I attempted to *see* my own child? And how dare you look at me now and insult my intelligence with that pathetic excuse of a word, ''sorry''?'

CHAPTER TWO

'THE... police?' Emily stammered even more aghast.

'Since I married you, you have brought me only shame and dishonour.' Duarte breathed starkly, his controlled lack of volume far more dramatic than any shout.

'The police?' Emily whispered again shakily, her sensitive tummy tying itself into sick knots.

'Your employer, Mrs Barker, reported your great escape from her property *and* my natural pursuit. She expressed concern for your safety. Two police officers are now waiting outside for my explanation.' Duarte drew himself up to his full imposing six-foot-four-inch height and squared his broad shoulders with all the fierce pride of his ancestors in his bearing, but sheer outrage glittered in his condemning gaze.

'Duarte—'

'If you dare to lie and suggest that I have abused you or mistreated you in *any* way whatsoever, I will fight you for custody of my son! Is that quite clear?'

As crystal. Chilled to the temperature of ice by that announcement, Emily trembled. Her arms wrapped more tightly still round Jamie. Impervious to that old chestnut that children were always disturbed by maternal tension, Jamie had dropped off to sleep against her shoulder. With that single threat, Duarte had deprived Emily of voice, breath and hope that their differences could be resolved. She was in shock and could not have said why. After all, if Duarte had been prepared to separate her from her child the instant he was born, he could only be even keener to do so after the months that had since passed.

But then, eight months ago, Duarte's words of threat had *not* been spoken to her face. It was only thanks to her friend, Bliss that Emily had learned of Duarte's plans. Bliss had overheard Duarte state his punitive intentions to his lawyer and had forewarned Emily of her estranged husband's intentions.

Now quite unable to dislodge her arrested attention from Duarte, she scanned his fabulous bone structure for some sign of softening and found none. He meant what he was saying. Standing there straight and tall and unashamed and more beautiful than any male had the right to be. Like a dark angel. Even emanating aggressive vibrations, he was absolutely gorgeous, possessed of the kind of sleek, dark, bronzed good looks that turned female heads wherever he went. Why the heck hadn't she smelled a rat the size of the Titanic when he proposed marriage to someone as ordinary as she was? And why on earth had he neglected to mention his tragic first marriage? For any heart that Duarte ever had was buried in the grave with his childhood sweetheart.

'Is that understood, Emily?' Duarte prompted lethally.

Dully she nodded, dredging her attention from him in shrinking apprehension. To think that on several occasions recently she had anxiously wondered if she had misjudged him! No, there was no room to suspect *now* that Bliss might have misunderstood what she'd overheard or that Emily herself had overreacted to something said in anger and never ever intended to be acted upon. After the way she'd behaved, Duarte did not believe she *deserved* to have their child.

'Yes…' Emily turned her pinched face away and rested her cheek against Jamie's soft, sweet-smelling baby skin to comfort herself. Every which way she looked, she had done wrong, and there was no point offending even more by seeking to defend herself.

'I have no wish to part you from our son,' Duarte stated in a grim undertone. 'He needs you very much.'

'Do you really think that?' she whispered shakily.

'I say nothing that I don't mean. Give me Jamie now that he is asleep,' Duarte urged moving forward. 'Mrs Barker followed my security team here. She has offered to take care of our son until you are released from hospital. I understand she is familiar to him.'

Taut with suspicion, Emily held fast to Jamie's precious weight, but then she saw Alice appearing in the doorway with a look of discomfiture on her face. The older woman was carrying Jamie's baby bag. 'I'll look after Jamie, Emily. It's the least that I can do.'

'I will leave you both and deal with the police,' Duarte delivered coolly.

Alice grimaced and sank down at the foot of the bed. 'How was I to know he was your husband? I thought Mafia hitmen were descending on us and I was really frantic when they took off after you!'

'You didn't know what was happening…and I was totally stupid,' Emily groaned in remorse. 'I made things even worse by trying to run again. I just panicked and then I got stung—'

'And your husband, whom I thought was a dead ringer for the Godfather at his most glamorous, *saved* your life.' Alice winced. 'I feel so awful now for calling in the police and now they *won't* go away until everyone's explained themselves about twenty times over.'

'It's OK… It's all my fault. I always do the wrong thing,' Emily mumbled heavily. 'Particularly around Duarte—'

'Not much of a husband if he makes you feel like that. Maybe, to make me feel a little more relaxed about all this, you could tell me that he is really wonderful.'

'He *is*... I was the one who wrecked everything.' Emily sighed.

By wanting more than Duarte had ever offered, she'd made herself unhappy. She'd had a hunger to be loved and, if not loved, at least needed. But Duarte had not needed her either. She had just felt like another one of his many possessions with no true existence or purpose without him. She had never had much confidence but, flung in at the deep end of a world so very different from her own, she had sunk like a stone, becoming even more shy and awkward. By the time of their separation, she'd gone from having low self-esteem to having no self-esteem at all.

Alice left with Jamie. Then a very weary-looking police sergeant made a brief visit to Emily's bedside to confirm that she had no complaint to make against her husband. Having made that assurance while cringing at the thought of what Duarte must have undergone, Emily fell asleep and did not awaken until lunch arrived on a noisy trolley. The doctor called in to have a brief word with her and tell her that she was free to leave. As she had no appetite for food, she slid straight out of bed. Removing her clothes from the cabinet, she got dressed again.

Mateus Santos was waiting at Reception to escort her out to the limousine.

Duarte was seated in the back of the limo. Emily climbed in and sat down at the furthest point from Duarte that she could contrive. 'What now?' she asked tightly.

'We'll pick up Jamie and then we're going home.'

The silence lay between them, deep as a swamp and twice as treacherous.

Emily swallowed hard. *Going home?* She had not yet given him a direct look. Now she turned her head, her throat tight, her sea-green eyes strained. 'Just like that?'

'Just like that,' Duarte confirmed, skimming her a veiled glance from his dark, deep-set eyes. 'I had your possessions cleared from the car and the caravan and packed. I also told Mateus to dispose of both vehicles as you will have no further use for them.'

That was the moment that Emily appreciated that she now possessed only the clothes she stood up in. Her fingers closed over the ragged cuffs of her old sweater in an effort to contain an almost overwhelming sense of being trapped. 'It would have been nice if you had asked me what I wanted to do with them.'

'But then, all that concerned me was what I wanted,' Duarte murmured with velvet soft cool, reaching forward to sweep up the car phone as it buzzed.

Going home? He was taking them straight back to Portugal. From below her lashes, she studied him, nervous as a cat on hot bricks. The hard smooth line of his high cheekbones in profile, the classic perfection of his arrogant nose, the tough angular jawline slightly blue-shadowed by the hint of returning stubble. He was incredibly good-looking and sexy and she found it very difficult to resist the urge to stare when his attention was distracted from her. She listened to him talk in Portuguese, as smooth and cool as if he had not just dramatically reclaimed his runaway wife and child. No, indeed, it might have been any ordinary day and she might have been any woman.

'Duarte…' she framed jerkily as soon as he had replaced the phone. 'I'd like to stay in England—'

'That's not possible unless you insist on a divorce.'

Emily did not feel that she was in a position to insist on anything. Duarte had slaughtered all the protest in her the very instant he had threatened to fight her for custody of Jamie. She'd already spent far too many months fretting about how poor a parent she might seem in comparison to him in any courtroom. Her evident lapse in fidelity, her flight to England, her fear-inspired failure to deal with matters like an adult which had forced Duarte to mount a search. Nothing that she had so far done would impress a judge. Nor would her case be helped when it came out that she had been raising Jamie in a caravan while she roved around taking casual employment. In a Portuguese court, she had not the slightest doubt that Duarte would win custody of their child.

She curved her trembling hands together to steady them. 'I thought you would want a divorce.'

'Not at present.'

Emily wanted to scream. He was shutting her out. He had always done that, depersonalising every encounter, holding her at a distance...except in bed. Her fair complexion reddened to ferocious heat at that inadvertent thought. Just then, she could not bear to recall the physical intimacy which she had once cherished as evidence that he must care for her to some degree. Now it pained her to recall her own humiliating naivety. They had had separate bedrooms from the start. Sex had always seemed to have a faint aura of the forbidden. But it also had been wildly exciting...for *her*. The only time she had dared to touch him had been in the privacy of her own bed. In daylight, Duarte had been way too intimidating.

In a fierce struggle to control her wayward mind, Emily made herself focus on the child's car seat anchored opposite. Jamie's seat. Duarte was taking them both back to Portugal. Duarte was not thinking of a divorce. Duarte was not currently planning to deprive her of her son. Those facts were the *only* facts that mattered right now, she told herself urgently. She was tired of running and exhausted by living on her nerves. All these months, she had had no real life. What lay ahead could surely be little worse than what she had experienced in the past...

'Are you going to have other women...again?' Emily heard herself ask and almost died on the spot because that dreadful question had just come out of nowhere and leapt on to her unguarded tongue.

The silence seemed to flex like a stranglehold ready to tighten round her slender throat.

Slowly, Emily looked up, aquamarine eyes aghast.

Duarte gazed back at her as if she had just dropped down through the car roof, a fully fledged alien with two heads. 'What do you mean by...*again*?' he prompted very softly.

Emily connected with electrifying dark golden eyes and gulped. 'I didn't mean anything...I...I just wondered.'

'You made an accusation,' Duarte contradicted with razor-edged cool. 'A specious feminine attempt to justify your own behaviour by implying that *I* played away—'

Emily was backtracking so fast she was literally into full-throttle reverse. Not because she was a coward but because she could not afford to antagonise Duarte, lest he change his mind and decide that Jamie did not need his mother as much as he believed he did. 'No, I didn't...I didn't—'

'Don't try it again,' Duarte warned steadily, shimmering eyes resting on her like a slowly uncoiling whip lash.

Turning away in turmoil to stare fixedly into the middle distance, Emily only then appreciated that the car had already pulled up outside Alice's farmhouse. The chauffeur opened the passenger door and she leapt out like a rabbit with a fox on her tail. The older woman was already coming outside with Jamie clasped in her arms. 'Will you and Duarte join me for coffee?'

Emily reclaimed Jamie, her heart beating very fast. She didn't want to get back into the limo. She wanted to run again and she knew that this time there was no place to run. 'I'll ask Duarte if we've got time—'

But Duarte was right behind her. He greeted Alice with a courteous charm which Emily had only got to enjoy briefly during their even more brief courtship. Emily stared at her husband, marvelling at the tone of regret he contrived to employ as he refused an invitation he could not have had the slightest desire to accept. She said goodbye in a dulled little voice and got back into the car to fix Jamie into his seat.

'Stop cringing around me,' Duarte instructed grittily as the chauffeur closed the door on them again.

At least the previous unfortunate subject which she had opened was forgotten. But she noted that he had given her no answer. Not that she cared any more, she told herself. They would hardly be living together again but wasn't it peculiar that he wasn't talking about what they were going to be doing? Or was exerting that kind of power over her part of the punishment?

Becoming only slowly aware of the silence, Emily turned her head. Only then did she recall that Duarte was really only now having his first meeting with his son. Duarte was studying Jamie with an intensity she could feel. Jamie was kicking his feet, smiling and in the mood to be admired. Emily watched Duarte. The tension etched in his bold bronzed features, the movement of the lean brown hand he semi-raised and then settled back on a long powerful thigh again.

He wanted to touch Jamie. He wanted to connect; naturally he did. Her throat thickened in the weighted quiet. She slid Jamie's little blue teddy towards Duarte, nudging his braced fingers with the toy. 'You could give him that—'

'When I need your advice, I'll ask for it.' Lean strong face clenching hard, Duarte dealt her a flaring glance of bitter hostility. 'It's not a lot of fun wondering whether my own child will scream if I try to touch him.'

Emily paled. 'I know…I'm sorry—'

A tiny muscle pulling tight at the corner of his hard jaw-line, Duarte thrust his broad shoulders back against the seat.

'I've got plenty of time to get to know him. I'll do it without an audience.'

He was so incredibly proud. Had she not seen the yearning in Duarte's body language as he contemplated his infant son, she might have believed that he felt nothing.

'I was scared to get in contact with you…I was scared of losing him—'

'I'm not about to discuss your behaviour in front of him. You're his mother. You sound distressed. Look at your son…he's listening to your voice and watching your every move and you're *scaring* him,' Duarte condemned.

Emily saw the truth of that censure in Jamie's anxious air and her strained eyes stung, forcing her to blink rapidly. She compressed her lips on all the words that wanted to spill out of her but which Duarte did not want to hear. And could she really blame him? She *was* making excuses again. Right at that moment, Duarte's sole interest was in his son. She was just an adjunct, along for the ride because Jamie needed her. However, it was painfully obvious to Emily that Duarte was barely tolerating her presence.

From the instant they entered the crowded bustling airport, Emily became conscious of her scuffed shoes, faded jodhpurs and ancient sweater. The outfit had been practical for the long drive she had expected to have but she felt like a tramp beside Duarte, immaculate in a charcoal grey suit exquisitely tailored to his tall athletic physique.

'I could have done with getting changed,' she said uneasily. 'But I don't really have anything suitable.'

She had left all her expensive clothes behind in Portugal. Not that that much mattered, she conceded ruefully, for that wardrobe had rejoiced most in fashion accidents. If she got the colour right, she invariably got the style wrong. Growing up, she had been a tomboy, living in jeans and riding gear. Her attempt to experiment with a more feminine look had been squashed in her sensitive teens by her

sisters' scorn. It had been poor preparation for marriage to
a rich man and entry into a daunting world in which her
appearance really seemed to matter.

'You can buy an outfit here and change,' Duarte pointed
out.

To Emily those words were confirmation that she looked
an embarrassing mess. Her throat thickened and her eyes
stung and she reddened fiercely for she had no money either. She hovered over Jamie's buggy with a downbent
head.

Through swimming eyes, Emily focused on the gold
credit card extended in silence by her husband. The most
enormous bitterness and pain seemingly rose out of nowhere inside her and she whispered helplessly, 'You
should've married some fancy model, a real fashion
plate…not someone like me!'

'It is a little late now.' Duarte's deflating tone was more
than equal to capping even the most emotional outburst.
'And this is not the place to stage an argument.'

Emily swallowed hard. When had she ever had the nerve
to argue with him? Yet it was odd how much she now
wanted to argue but she was far too conscious of being in
public where angry words would be overheard. Accepting
the credit card without looking at him, she released her hold
on the buggy and headed for the closest dress shop. There
she scanned the packed displays. Choose really bright colours, Bliss had once advised Emily, saying that such shades
flattered Emily's pale skin tone and balanced her red hair.
Emily sped over to a rack of cerise dresses but they were
way too plain in design to conceal a figure that Bliss had
gently pointed out was more boyish than lush. Browsing at
speed, she picked a jazzy orange handkerchief top with bell
sleeves and a big glittery lime green motif on the front.
Nobody was likely to notice her lack in the bosom depart-

ment under that, Emily thought gratefully. She teamed the
top with a long orange skirt that had the same fancy hem.

Both garments matched in colour and style, she reflected
with relief, thinking that that should definitely ensure a pre-
sentable appearance. She picked up a pair of high-heeled
leopard-print mules because she knew they were the height
of fashion. Her purchases made, she made harried use of a
changing cubicle. Emerging from the shop again, hot and
breathless, she saw Duarte and his security men standing
around Jamie's buggy in the centre of the wide concourse.

Mateus and the rest of his team focused on her and momentarily stared before lowering their heads. Then Duarte
glanced in her direction and froze. Not a single betraying
expression appeared on his darkly handsome features but
he seemed to breathe in very deep and slow. And she knew
right then that she had got it wrong again. Her heart sank
right down to the toes of her horribly uncomfortable mules
and she despised herself for her own weakness, her pathetic
attempt to please and win his approval in even the smallest
way.

'Sorry I took so long,' she mumbled, reclaiming the
buggy without glancing back up at him but conscious of
his brooding presence with every fibre of her wretched being.

'No…problem,' Duarte sighed.

In the VIP lounge, she caught an involuntary glimpse of
herself in a mirror and she was startled. She looked like a
fluorescent carrot, she decided in stricken recoil. Flinching,
she turned away from that mortifying reflection. Sitting
down, she tried to disappear into herself and her own
thoughts in the manner she had begun to practise within
months of marrying Duarte. He never had been any great
fan of idle chatter. She just wanted to sink into the wood-
work, sitting there in an outfit that he most probably

thought was ghastly. So why did she care? Why did she *still* care?

Emily had always been conscious that she was neither pretty nor beautiful. Her mother and both her sisters were tall shapely blondes with classic bone structures. Even in appearance, she had not fitted her family. At the age of ten, she had asked her mother where her own red hair came from in the family tree as even her father was fair. Her mother had dealt her a angry look as if even asking such a question was offensive and had told her that she owed her 'unfortunate' carroty curls to the genetic legacy of her late grandmother.

Seeing no point in bemoaning what could not be altered, Emily hadn't ever really minded being short, red-haired and small in the chest and hip department. But the same moment that she first saw Duarte Avila de Monteiro, she had started minding very much that she would never have what it would take to attract him. Of course, it had not once occurred to her that a male of his calibre and wealth would look twice at her anyway but she still remembered her own foolish feelings of intense sadness and hurt that it should be that way. That Duarte should be so utterly detached from her when her own senses thrilled to even his presence a hundred feet away.

And she still recalled the very first moment she had laid eyes on Duarte and very much doubted that *he* did…

CHAPTER THREE

By the time she was nineteen, Emily had qualified as a riding instructor.

Her two older sisters had found lucrative employment in their father's wine-importing business but Emily had not been offered the same opportunity. Indeed, urged by her mother to leave home and be independent long before she was earning enough to pay a decent rent, Emily had finally given up on the job she loved. She had taken work as a live-in groom at Ash Manor, Duarte's English country house.

The stable manager had hired Emily and, working at the manor, she had had an interesting insight into the lifestyle of a super-rich and powerful banker. Aside from his private jet, his fleet of helicopters and luxury cars, Duarte owned half a dozen palatial homes, superb horseflesh and a priceless art collection. He was the guy with everything, the target of endless awe, speculation and envy. But the one thing Duarte Avila de Monteiro did not have, it seemed, was the precious *time* to enjoy his innumerable possessions.

It had been weeks before Emily actually saw her wealthy employer in the flesh but she had already been told what he was like. Cool, polite, distant, formal, not the type to unbend with lesser beings, very much the product of a Portuguese aristocratic lineage said to stretch back to the thirteenth century.

His incredible silver sports car pulled up one afternoon while Emily and another female groom were cleaning tack. The stable manager hurried from his office to greet Duarte.

'That car's a MacLaren F1, worth six hundred grand,'

Emily's companion groaned. 'And just wait until you see *him*. When I first came here, I assumed the banker boss was some old geezer, but he's only twenty-eight and he's pure sex on legs. If you got him on his own without his bodyguards, you'd lock him in your bedroom and throw away the key!'

Even more than two years on, Emily still remembered that first shattering sight of Duarte. Sunlight gleaming over the luxuriant black hair stylishly cropped to his proud head as he climbed out of his car, a crisp white shirt accentuating his bronzed complexion but most of all she had noticed his stunning eyes, deepset and dark as sable at first glance but tawny gold as a hunting animal's the next. She was shocked and bemused by the unfamiliar leap of her own senses and the quite ridiculous stab of loss which assailed her when he turned away to open the passenger door of his car.

In place of the beautiful woman she had expected to see in Duarte's passenger seat was an absolutely huge shaggy dog curled up nose to tail into the smallest possible size.

The other groom backed into the tack out of sight. 'I'm not going to get stuck with that monster again. That dog's as thick as a block of wood, won't come when you call it and it's as fast on its feet as a race horse!'

Before the other girl even finished speaking, the stable manager called Emily over and told her to exercise the dog.

It was an Irish wolfhound. Unfolded from the car, it had to measure a good three feet in height and Emily was just one inch over five feet tall herself. But although Emily had not been allowed to have a pet as a child, she adored dogs of all shapes and sizes.

'Be kind. Jazz is getting old,' Duarte's rich, dark, accented drawl interposed with cool authority.

Emily angled a shy upward glance at him, overwhelmed by his proximity, his sheer height and breadth and potent masculinity. She had to tip her head right back to see his

lean, dark, devastating face. She collided with sizzling dark
golden eyes and for her it was like being knocked off her
feet by a powerful electrical charge. She trembled, felt the
feverish heat of an embarrassing blush redden her fair skin,
the stormy thump of her heartbeat and the most challenging
shortness of breath. But Duarte simply walked away from
her again, apparently experiencing no physical jolt of
awareness, feeling nothing whatsoever, indeed not really
even having seen her for she had only been another junior
employee amongst many: faceless, beneath his personal notice.

And, no doubt, had not fate intervened, her acquaintance
with Duarte Avila de Monteiro would never have advanced
beyond that point. However, in those days, Duarte had left
Jazz behind at the manor when he was out of the country.
The dog should have stayed indoors but the housekeeper
had disliked animals and as soon as Duarte departed, she
would have the wolfhound locked in the barn. Exercising
Jazz fell to Emily for nobody else wanted the responsibility.

'The boss is fond of that stupid dog. If it gets lost or
harmed in some way, well it'll cost you your job,' the stable
manager warned Emily impatiently. 'That's why we just
leave it locked up. I know it seems a little heartless but the
animal's well fed and it has plenty of space in there.'

But Emily was too tender-hearted to bear the sound of
Jazz's pathetic cries for company. She spent all her free
time playing with him in a paddock and she gave him the
affection he soaked up like a giant hungry sponge. So, the
evening that the barn went up in fire, when everyone else
stood by watching the growing conflagration in horror,
Emily did not even stop to think of her own safety but
charged to the rescue of an animal she had grown to love.

Although she contrived to calm Jazz's panic and persuade him out of the barn, she passed out soon afterwards
from smoke inhalation. Surfacing from the worst effects,

she then found herself in a private room in the local hospital with Duarte stationed by her bedside.

The instant she opened her eyes, Duarte sprang up and approached the bed, his appearance startling her out of what remained of her scrambled wits. 'Risking your own life to save my dog was incredibly foolish *and* incredibly brave,' he murmured with a reflective smile that in spite of its haunting brevity had more charm than she had believed any smile might possess.

'I just didn't think,' she mumbled, transfixed by the drop-dead gorgeous effect of him smiling.

'You are a heroine. I contacted your family.' His strong jawline squared. 'I understand that they are very busy people and, of course, I told them that you were already recovering. I am not sure whether or not they will find it possible to visit.'

Paling at that sympathetic rendering of her family's evident lack of concern at the news that she had been hospitalised, Emily veiled her pained gaze. 'Thanks…'

'It is I who am in debt to you. One of the grooms had the courage to confess that, but for you, Jazz would have spent every hour of my absence imprisoned in that barn,' Duarte admitted grimly. 'You are the only one in a staff of almost twenty who had the kindness to take care of his needs.'

Embarrassed by that unsought accolade, Emily muttered, 'I just like animals and Jazz may be a bit daft but he's very loving.'

The forbidding look on his lean dark features dissipated and he vented a rueful laugh. 'Jazz has a brain the size of a pea. He was my sister's dog. After her death, he should have been rehomed but I did not have the heart to part with him.' His face shadowed again. 'Perhaps that was a selfish decision for I am often away on business—'

'No. He just adores you. I couldn't get him to settle at

night until I got the housekeeper to give me an old sweater of yours to put in his bed,' Emily volunteered in a rush.

There was an awkward little silence. Faint colour now scored his superb cheekbones. He studied her through black lashes lush as silk fans, palpably questioning why he had unbent to such an extent with her. A minute later, he had been the powerful banker again, politely taking his departure, having done his duty in visiting her. A magnificent bouquet of flowers and a basket of fruit had been delivered soon after his departure. She had not expected to see him again except at a distance when he was at the manor.

But the next day when she was released from hospital, Duarte picked her up and insisted on driving her home to convalesce with her family. She spent the whole journey falling deeper and deeper in love with a guy so out of her reach he might as well have come from another galaxy. There was only a little conversation during that drive for Duarte was often on the phone.

Her family took one astonished but thrilled look at Duarte and his chauffeur-driven limousine and invited him to stay to dinner. Billionaire single bankers were hugely welcome in a house containing two young, beautiful single blondes. Indeed, her sisters Hermione and Corinne had competed for Duarte's attention with outrageous flattery and provocative innuendoes. Sunk in the background as usual by their flirtatious charm, Emily had felt painfully like the ugly duckling amongst the swans.

Emily was sprung back to the present by the necessity of boarding the jet. Soon after take-off, she realised that Jamie was overtired and cross. The steward showed her into a rear compartment where a special travel cot already waited in readiness for its small occupant. It took Emily a good twenty minutes to settle Jamie and then, with pronounced reluctance, she returned to the luxurious main cabin again.

Duarte rose from his seat and straightened to his full commanding height. 'Is Jamie asleep?'

Emily nodded jerkily, her tension rising by the second.

'Verbal responses would be welcome,' Duarte added drily.

Encountering brilliant dark golden eyes, she reddened hotly. 'Yes, he's asleep but maybe I should sit with him for a while in case he wakes up again.'

'Trying to impress me with maternal overkill? Tell me, who looked after Jamie while you were giving riding lessons?'

'Nobody—'

'*Nobody?*' Duarte queried with hard emphasis.

Emily frowned in surprise. 'It really wasn't a problem. I was only instructing a couple of hours a day and I would park Jamie's buggy outside the paddock. He was never more than a few feet from me and he usually had the company of parents watching their child's lesson.'

As Duarte listened, his lean powerful face tautened, his wide sensual mouth compressing. 'Usually? A working stables is no place to leave a baby unattended. You know as well as I do that riders can't always control their mounts and that your attention must've been on your pupil—'

Under that attack, Emily had stiffened and lost much of her natural colour. 'Jamie was always safe. I did the very best that I could—'

'But your best wasn't halfway good enough,' Duarte cut in with biting derision. 'You left my son at the mercy of passing strangers instead of ensuring that he received proper care—'

'I wanted to spend every minute with him that I could and you're making this sound much worse than it was,' Emily protested defensively. 'Everywhere I worked, Jamie got loads and loads of attention. Most people like babies, especially happy ones—'

'That's not the point,' Duarte said coldly.

Emily worried at her lower lip and then said heavily, 'Even if I had wanted to, I couldn't have afforded to pay someone to look after him—'

'And whose fault was that?'

As her tension climbed, Emily trembled and her tummy churned. Thinking straight had become a challenge; she had never been much good at confrontations. However, on this occasion she found herself struggling to speak up in her own defence. 'Whose fault was it that I left Portugal in the first place?'

Far from looking impressed or indeed startled by that comeback, Duarte inclined his arrogant dark head to one side and levelled his incisive gaze on her in the most formidable way. 'Presumably you are about to give me the answer to that strange question?' he prompted.

'I only left Portugal because I thought that you were planning to try and take my child off me the minute he was born!' Emily countered in an accusing rush.

Duarte angled an imperious brow. 'What kind of a nonsensical excuse is that? Before this morning, I never made a threat in that line. To be frank, my patience with you came to an end today. But who or what gave you the idea that I might have been considering such a dramatic move last year?'

Emily flinched and dropped her head, shaken at how close she had come in her turmoil to revealing Bliss's role in events eight months earlier. Had she done that, she could never have forgiven herself. Bliss had been the truest of supportive friends during Emily's troubled marriage, cheering Emily up when her spirits were low while offering helpful advice and encouragement. Although Emily had not contacted the other woman since leaving Portugal, she assumed that her friend still worked as Duarte's executive assistant. Bliss had eavesdropped on that confidential dia-

logue between Duarte and his lawyer and had forewarned
Emily. Were Duarte ever to discover that a member of his
own staff had been that disloyal, Bliss's high-flying career
would be destroyed.

'I just got the idea…at the time, the way you were treating me—well, er…it seemed to make sense to me and I
was afraid that you were planning to separate me from my
child—'

'So you chose to separate our son from *me* instead. Is
that how this sorry story goes?' Duarte dealt her a look of
shimmering challenge that made her breath trip in her already tight throat. 'This convenient angle that continually
seeks to turn you into a poor little victim? Well, I have
news for you—I'm not impressed, *querida.*'

'I'm not trying to impress—'

'No?' Without warning, Duarte sent her a sudden slanting golden glance as hard and deadly as an arrow thudding
into a live target.

Feeling the sudden smouldering surge in the atmosphere
but unable to comprehend what had caused it, Emily un-
twisted her laced hands and made a jerky move with one
of them as if she was appealing for his attention. 'I know
I've made mistakes—'

'Mistakes?'

'—but now I'm just being open and honest—'

'*Open*…and *honest*,' Duarte repeated with a brand of
electrifying soft sibilance that danced down her rigid spine
like a fullscale storm warning. '*Que absurdo!* An honest
whore you were not!'

Emily's lips parted company and she fell back a faltering
step in dismay at the proclamation and that particular word
being aimed at her. Even in the aftermath of finding her in
another man's arms, Duarte had not employed such an
emotive term. 'B-but—'

'But what? You were carrying my baby when you slept

with another man. How many women have affairs while they're pregnant with their husband's child?' Duarte demanded in a derisive tone of disgust that nailed her to the spot. 'But no such fine sensibilities restrained *you*. You even dared to introduce me to your lover. You also brought him into my home. Only a whore would behave like that.'

Forced to recognise the extent of the sins being laid at her door, Emily gasped strickenly, 'Duarte, it wasn't like that and Toby was *never* my—'

'Do you really think I'll listen to your pathetic excuses? You are nothing to me.' Duarte made that wounding statement with a savage cool that bled all remaining colour from her shaken face.

You are nothing to me. That he should feel that way was hardly news but spoken out loud that acknowledgement cut Emily in two.

'But you belong to me. *Minha esposa...* you are my wife,' Duarte completed with sardonic bite.

Under the onslaught of that ultimate putdown, Emily felt something curiously akin to a re-energising flame dart through her slim tense body and she flung her head back. 'No...I don't belong to you like your cars and your houses and your wretched art collection,' she heard herself asserting. 'I may be your wife but I'm not an object without any thoughts or feelings or rights—'

Although she had no recollection of him moving, Duarte was now a step closer, threateningly close. Even as she was still fighting to understand quite where her own unusually spirited defence had come from, she was awesomely conscious of the expanse of all that lean, taut masculinity poised within inches of her own much smaller frame.

In the electrifying silence that had fallen, shimmering golden eyes sought and held her scrutiny, all the powerful force of will he possessed bearing down on her. 'You have no rights in this marriage.'

'I don't believe you mean that…you couldn't,' Emily reasoned, tearing her gaze hurriedly from his as her heart rate speeded up. 'You're just very angry with me—'

'I am not angry with you,' Duarte growled like a leopard about to spring on an unwary prey. 'But I cannot and will not trust you with the kind of freedom I gave you before.'

'*That*…was freedom?' A startled laugh empty of humour was wrenched from Emily's working throat, for she had found her duties as a Monteiro wife as rigid a constraint to her days as a prison cell. Every daylight hour had been rigorously organised for her with a weighty yoke of responsibilities that took no account of her own personal wishes.

Hard dark colour scored the hard set of Duarte's proud cheekbones. 'So you find my former generosity a source of amusement?'

'Oh, you mean your money…' Emily very nearly let loose a second nervous laugh as comprehension finally sank in and her soft mouth tensed. 'Well, it wasn't much consolation when you were never around and I never did take to shopping, although I did try hard to like it. You see, I wasn't the sort of woman you should have married and I still can't really understand why you *did*…'

Duarte stared down at her with eyes as dark and fathomless and deep as the midnight witching hour. As he ensnared her fraught gaze afresh, she forgot what she was saying at the same time as she forgot to draw another breath. The atmosphere surged around her like a slow smouldering fire closing in, using up all the oxygen. But still she stood there, plunged without warning into a welter of physical sensations she had never been able to fight. As a wave of excitement as terrifying as it was thrilling washed over her, her heart thumped like a frantic bird trapped inside her, every tiny muscle tensing in reaction to the rush of liquid heat burning between her slim thighs.

'Can't you?' he murmured huskily.

The very sound of that silken dark drawl sent a responsive shiver down her spine. She snatched in a stark audible breath to flood her depleted lungs. She was tormentingly aware of the stirring heaviness of her small breasts and the painful sensitivity of her swollen nipples pushing against the bra she wore beneath her top.

'Aside from my wealth, I had nothing to offer you but you appeared to want very little.' Duarte studied her with spectacular dark golden eyes that had the most scorching effect on her already heated flesh. 'Apart from me…and you wanted me like you wanted air to breathe. At the time it seemed a fair exchange.'

Her mind a mess of jumbled and inane thoughts, Emily quivered as she literally struggled to concentrate on what he had just said. Understanding came in a trickle and then a gush and almost washed her away in a floodtide of pain and humiliation. Like an accident victim, she reeled back a step from their proximity, aquamarine eyes shattered, shame over her own weakness where he was concerned following fast.

You wanted me like you wanted air to breathe…

It was the most hurtful but demeaning truth she had ever had to swallow. Momentarily it threw her back into the past and a time when she would have done anything, accepted anything on any terms just to be with him. And all this time *he* had known that, a little voice of horror wailed inside her head. She was appalled and then shaken by her own refusal to accept that he had recognised from the very outset just how deep his hold over her was. All the shameless heat he had awakened without even trying drained away, only to be replaced by a fiery surge of hot colour that dwindled equally fast.

'You shouldn't have asked,' Duarte murmured, smooth as glass.

'Once…you wouldn't have answered,' Emily parted
numb lips to respond and her own voice emerged all bumpy
and broken.

'That was then. This is now and much has changed.'
Duarte surveyed her with hard dark eyes of satisfaction.
'But, sadly for you, not, I think, your hunger for me.'

'Well, that's where you're dead wrong…' A sudden re-
vivifying burst of bitter anger powered through Emily's
quivering length. 'As you said, that was then and this is
now and I got over my stupid crush when you got me
pregnant and then decided to forget I even existed!'

'Did you really get over it?' Duarte reached for her with
such a complete lack of warning and such shattering cool
that she stared up at him in a wide-eyed daze, a frown just
beginning to form between her brows. Before she even had
the chance to blink, his hard sensual mouth came down on
hers with all the explosive force and expertise of a heat-
seeking missile.

Since that onslaught was the very last reaction she'd expected, she had no time to even try to muster her defences.
She was blasted from angry shame straight into stunned
and helpless response, a muffled gasp torn from her throat
as he crushed her into the steely contours of his hard powerful physique. She couldn't breathe, didn't want to,
couldn't think, didn't want to. Her whole body seemed to
surge up and into his, instantly fired by the burning heat of
desire he could unleash. He pried her lips apart, let his
tongue delve in carnal and provocative exploration of the
tender interior of her mouth and she shuddered and moaned
as the upswell of electrifying sensation became more than
she could bear.

'Duarte…' she gasped feverishly. 'Duarte—'

'Jamie's crying. You should go to him.'

Like a woman lost in a dream she let him set her back
from him. Her brain felt befogged and her body was still

gripped in the talon claws of an excitement she had never expected to feel again.

'Jamie...' Duarte said again.

And, in the same instant, her wits returned and she emerged from the grasp of the sensual world which had betrayed her with a sudden nasty jolt. Blinking rapidly, she pressed a trembling hand to the tiny pulse flickering like mad above her collarbone and she stared up at Duarte in resounding shock. His lean, dark, devastating face was cool as ice, his brilliant dark golden eyes challenging.

Jamie! Finally recognising the faint cry that she normally reacted to within seconds, Emily hurried away, pale as death and all knotted up inside with maternal guilt and self-loathing. Jamie had mislaid his teddy but he calmed down the instant his mother reappeared. The teddy restored to his grasping hand, his sleepy brown eyes pinned to her face and then slowly began to drift closed again. Emily sat down on the bed by the cot.

She was still trembling and her body ached from that elemental surge of hunger which she suppressed for so long. Of course, it had been so much easier to deny that side of her nature when Duarte was not around. Reliving the immediacy with which she had fallen into his arms, she squirmed and hated herself. She should have had more pride. But on another level she was simply stunned that Duarte should actually have *touched* her again. Duarte who, eleven months ago, had said he could not even stand for her to remain beneath the same roof.

Yet, he had touched her again and she had made a fool of herself. But then, she ought to be used to that by now, she conceded heavily. Hadn't her gorgeous sophisticated husband always specialised in running rings around her be-sotted self? And her mind slid back again into the past when just a glimpse of Duarte had lit up her world...

A month after the fire in the barn, Emily had been informed that Duarte wanted to see her. Fresh from the morning exercise run with the horses, Emily had been cringingly conscious of her messy hair and muddy clothing but too worried about *why* he should want to see her to waste time getting changed.

For the first time, she set foot *inside* Ash Manor to see the beautifully restored Georgian interior that lay beyond the imposing front door. Jazz raced across the hall to throw himself at her with his usual exuberance. She got down on the floor to give him a hug that turned into a mock wrestling session—and then discovered that Duarte was standing watching her childish antics with his dog.

Momentarily his rare smile glimmered on his lips and he said something but she didn't catch what he said. The visual effect of Duarte after four weeks of deprivation had bereft her of all rational thought and concentration. In strong embarrassment, she'd scrambled up and he had shown her into a library where he invited her to sit down.

'I'm pretty dirty.' Emily had scanned the watered silk covering the indicated chair, preferring to look at it rather than at him as her wretched face burned scarlet. 'I'd be better standing.'

'As you wish. I won't be keeping you long.' Duarte lounged back against a polished desk, the very picture of polished elegance in his tailored business suit. 'When I entertain here, my friends and business associates often bring their families with them. I believe you're a riding instructor. I'd like you to start giving lessons to my younger guests. Naturally I'll raise your salary. Are you interested?'

Emily glanced up with a surprised but pleased smile. 'Very much.'

That winter, Duarte spent a remarkable amount of time at Ash Manor. Her duties gradually extended to generally supervising and entertaining any visiting children. At the end of the first month, Duarte said that it would be more convenient if she moved out of the flat she shared with the other grooms and into the manor itself. Dismayed to then be told that she was expected to take her meals in the dining room, she had ducked that challenge on the first night. Settling down to her evening meal in the kitchen, she had been aghast when Duarte strode in.

'What are you doing in here?' he had demanded in exasperation, startling her half out of her wits. 'You eat with my guests now.'

But everyone but Duarte and the children had ignored her in the dining room. Content to be ignored in a gathering of so many wealthy and important people, she had been taken aback when Duarte continually attempted to drag her into conversations.

'I heard Mr Monteiro tell Mum that you're marvellous with children and animals,' one of her temporary charges told her chattily one rainy evening while they worked on a horribly complex jigsaw. 'And very kind… Can I stay up until we finish this?'

Crumbs to a starving heart, she'd thought at the time, hugging those few words of approval to herself but secretly wishing that those words had been more personal. But much much later, when she was Duarte's wife, she had finally grasped that she had been under observation during that period, marched out like a reluctant-to-perform animal so that he could see how she behaved, how she thought, how she reacted in different situations. And quiet and shy had ultimately been fine with him. After all, what qualities does a male look for in a low-maintenance wife?

For that was the starring role for which she had been carefully picked with the minimum of required effort on his part. A low-maintenance wife, dead keen on soppy things like kids and dogs, unlikely to require much attention.

'You've done a terrific job,' Duarte informed her some weeks later. 'Let me take you out to dinner.'

Paralysed to the spot, she had stared at him. 'Oh, there's no need for that—'

'Emily—'

'Really, I wouldn't be comfortable imposing on you like that,' she had gabbled, distressed and embarrassed at the idea that he believed that he owed her some sort of treat for admittedly working very long hours.

'But I insist. Dinner... Eight,' Duarte had stated curtly.

So he took her out to dinner and she sat looking at him like a hypnotised rabbit, mumbling responses, spilling her wine and, due to the fancy menu couched in French, ending up with raw steak when what she had really wanted was a well-done one.

'Why are you so nervous?' he had finally asked with an air of imperturbable calm that just might have been laced with concealed exasperation.

'I'm just not comfortable,' she told him miserably.

'But we have often talked before this.'

'This is different—'

'So it is...' Duarte had given her a wry look. 'I don't believe I've had a date this disastrous since I was a teenager.'

'A...a *date*?' she had stressed in considerable shock.

'Why not? I like you, Emily. What more is required?'

After marrying him, she could have told him exactly what was required. But that evening, offered the substance of her wildest fantasies she had had no such caution and commonsense. She had simply gazed back at him, transfixed by a sensation of wondering joy and gratitude. 'I like you too,' she'd said inanely.

'Excellent,' Duarte had pronounced as the plate of raw steak was discreetly removed at his instruction to be replaced some timeless period later by a cooked one.

'In fact, I like you a lot,' Emily had heard herself adding like an eager schoolgirl.

'Even better,' Duarte had asserted valiantly.

But he hadn't kissed her that week or the next. In fact if she hadn't hovered one night during the third week in the most humiliatingly suggestive way, she honestly believed that he might not have bothered to kiss her at all until he married her. Evidently registering that some lusty enthusiasm was required to impress even the most shy and inexperienced of women, he had got it all over with at once. He had taken her to bed the same night. In the dawn hours, while she was lying on the far side of the bed, wondering frantically whether she ought to be sneaking back to her own room, Duarte had opened his stunning dark golden eyes and rested them on her blushing face and murmured with grave quietness, 'Will you marry me, Emily?'

And she had not asked why. Nor had she or he broached a single one of the questions that she imagined people usually exchanged on such a momentous occasion. She'd just nodded like a marionette having her strings pulled by expert hands. And those expert hands had reached for her again in reality as he breathed lazily, 'I may already have got you pregnant. We'll get married very soon.'

Emily was sprung from her introspection by an announcement over the tannoy that the jet was soon to land. With a groan at the necessity, she lifted her sleeping son from the cot and returned to the main cabin.

CHAPTER FOUR

WHEN Emily emerged from the jet with Jamie in her arms, she saw two limousines waiting on the tarmac to greet them. A slim svelte female, clad in an elegant suit the shade of eau-de-nil alighted from the first car. As the woman's pale golden hair glinted in the evening sunlight, a warm smile relaxed Emily's tense mouth and she hurried down the steps in Duarte's wake.

Bliss was *still* working for Duarte! As Bliss finally spotted Emily and the baby she was carrying, her face froze and she momentarily stilled. Naturally Bliss would be stunned to see her back in Portugal, Emily reflected, and then hurriedly ditched her own smile in an effort to be more discreet. Bliss had said that Duarte would never approve of his wife embarking on a close friendship with one of his personal staff and, naturally, Bliss had not wanted to risk damaging her career prospects.

'Mrs Monteiro...' Bliss acknowledged coolly, her clear blue eyes skimming off Emily just as quickly again, her exquisite face expressionless.

Bliss was being really discreet, Emily decided but she felt just a bit cut off by that greeting and anxiously wondered if she had offended the other woman with her silence in recent months. If she had, it would be ironic for she had stayed out of touch rather than subject her friend to the stress of further divided loyalties.

'Wait in the car, Emily,' Duarte instructed in an arctic tone.

Reddening as Mateus surged ahead of her to open the passenger door of the rear limousine, Emily climbed in and gazed back out at her husband and his executive assistant where they remained about thirty feet away. Duarte looked very grave but, as always, stunningly handsome. All tall and dark and sleek and bronzed, command and authority stamped into every hard line of his lean powerful face. Bliss, who had always reminded Emily of a fairytale princess brought to life, looked curiously frozen and a bright swathe of pink now burned over her delicate cheekbones.

Striding over to the limo, Duarte swung in beside Emily and the car moved off. Surprised that the jet had landed at Lisbon rather than at Oporto, Emily wondered if Duarte was heading to a business meeting. Certain that Duarte intended to send both her and his son back to the house in the Douro, Emily contemplated the very long car journey which lay ahead for her and Jamie.

At least it was spring, she thought ruefully. She had spent the winter of their separation in the country house and it had been dismal. These days the Monteiros only ever used the property for a rustic summer break or during the *vindima*, the grape harvest when the Portuguese enjoyed getting back to their roots. In winter, the villa had been shrouded in the thick grey mists that rose above the dramatic high banks of the Douro river and day after day it had rained heavily and got colder. Emily shivered at those depressing recollections.

'Perhaps I could spend the winters in England,' Emily proposed in a small taut voice.

Duarte moved a lean, silencing hand for he was talking on the car phone. He frowned at her, winged black brows drawing together above clear golden eyes. Biting at her lip, Emily turned away again. The limo had already left the motorway. They were on the outskirts of the pretty hilltown of Sintra and within a startling stone's throw of her former marital home, the Quinta de Monteiro. She assumed that Duarte was being dropped off home first.

Dense forest covered the hills above the ancient winding streets of the tiny village below the *quinta*. The verges of the road were carpeted with a colourful riot of naturalised crocus and scilla blooms. It was beautiful. But gooseflesh rose on Emily's arms as she found herself studying the narrow corner building where Toby had once had his artist's studio. The window shutters now bore a faded 'for rent' notice.

'I assure you that you won't be spending the winters or indeed, any other season in England,' Duarte imparted that news with a gritty edge to his dark deep drawl. 'I could not trust you that far from my sight.'

Emily twisted her head back with a bemused look. 'I beg your pardon?'

'From now on, everywhere you go you will be accompanied,' Duarte murmured.

'Wh-what on earth are you talking about?' Emily stammered as the opulent car glided below the imposing turreted entrance of the Quinta de Monteiro.

'You heard me.' Spectacular golden eyes tough as granite settled on her with unnerving force. 'If you go riding, you will take a groom, and for all other outings, you will have a driver and a bodyguard. At any hour of the day, I will expect to know where you are and what you are doing—'

'But I never went riding in the Douro...' Emily was having huge difficulty in comprehending the necessity for such excessive arrangements and her bewilderment was visible.

'I spend precious little time at our country house,' Duarte said drily. 'I was merely pointing out that there is a price to pay for my generosity in taking you back.'

'Taking me back...' Emily mumbled in repetition. 'Taking me back...*where*?'

'If I did not know you better, I would believe you were drunk,' Duarte delivered a split second before his chauffeur opened the door beside her. 'We will continue this discussion indoors.'

With an enervated flick of her eyes in the direction of the Quinta de Monteiro, a vast sixteenth-century building as monumental and impressive as a castle, Emily repeated uncertainly, 'Indoors? You want me to come inside?'

'No matter how much one might feel like it, one does not leave one's wife to sleep in the car,' Duarte framed with considerable sarcasm.

Emily sat bolt upright, finally pausing to consider that phrase 'taking you back' in a different light. Not just back to Portugal, it seemed, but back to sharing the former marital roof. True, it was an exceptionally large roof, beneath which the most bitter enemies could probably live separate lives, but even so Emily was shattered by the concept. With an effort, she parted her lips, keen to clarify the matter. 'Duarte...I—'

Springing out on to the gravel, he swung back and grasped her hand in an impatient movement to urge her on. 'Come on... Victorine is waiting to welcome us.'

Emily ducked down her head and peered round him in dismay. There stood Victorine like a door sentinel, a middle-aged woman clad from head to toe in unrelieved black, her face set like an ancient Egyptian grave mask. Welcome? Victorine *welcome* the head of the family's unfaithful wife back to the hallowed ground of the Monteiro ancestral home? Was he joking? Even in the early days of their marriage, Duarte's former mother-in-law had been unable to conceal her antipathy towards Emily.

'I'm not going in,' Emily argued in a feverish undertone. 'I had no idea you were bringing us here. I thought I was going back to the house in the Douro—'

'Then a geography lesson would appear to be in order,' Duarte gritted without hesitation. 'Get out of the car, Emily.

For once in your life behave as I might reasonably expect my wife to behave.'

Every scrap of colour drained from her complexion at that wounding statement which reminded her of her every past failure. Then redemption and release came from a new discovery deep within her pain. 'I'm sorry...I really don't want to be your wife any more,' she whispered and her voice might have shook but somehow that admission made her feel stronger than she had felt in a very long time.

'*Meu Deus!*' Duarte bent down and scooped her out of the passenger seat with powerful and angry hands. 'That I should lower myself to the dishonour of taking back an adulterous wife and that you should *dare* to display such ingratitude in response!' he growled down at her with enraged golden eyes.

Emily gasped in disbelief when Duarte lifted her bodily from the car with the ease of a male sweeping up a small recalcitrant child. She could not credit that her controlled and reserved husband, who was no fan of public displays, should behave in such a way while Victorine was watching them. But then, never had she seen Duarte's anger before, for he'd not allowed her to see it, and what he'd just said to her was burned like letters of fire into her memory banks. 'Put me down,' she gasped in stricken recoil but her request was ignored.

When they were still several feet from the tall front doors which were spread wide on the huge hall behind her, Victorine spoke. 'I am sorry to say it but if that trollop enters the *quinta*, I will leave, Duarte.'

'That would be a great pity,' Duarte murmured without expression as he lowered Emily down on to the step in front of him. 'But this is my home and within my home no one will tell me what I may or may not do, nor will anyone abuse my wife.'

Emily was as shattered by that tough comeback from

Duarte as the older woman appeared to be. Victorine's thin features betrayed incredulous resentment.

'Duarte...' Emily began in an agony of discomfiture.

'If my daughter Izabel could see you now with *her*...' Victorine condemned with a bitterness she could not hide.

Every muscle in Duarte's big powerful body went rigid and his dark deep voice carried an edge of reproach. 'Let your daughter rest in peace.'

As Victorine stalked back indoors in high dudgeon, it was Emily who broke the strained silence that she had left in her wake. 'Jamie's still in the car—'

'He's asleep. The staff will see to him for the moment.' Signalling the housekeeper hovering at the back of the hall, Duarte gave an instruction to that effect. Then, resting a hand to Emily's taut spine, he pressed her into the superb salon with its tall gothic windows and thrust the door shut behind them again.

The wall at the foot of the room was dominated by a huge full-length portrait of Izabel, an exotic brunette in a fabulous blue ball gown. Emily tore her gaze from that familiar but oh, so daunting image. Izabel, Victorine's beloved only child and Duarte's first wife. Five years earlier, Izabel had died in a ghastly car wreck that had also claimed the life of Duarte's twin sister. *Rest in peace?* Emily's sensitive tummy clenched. One way or another, she had been haunted every day of their marriage by Izabel, the ultimate of impossible acts to follow. Even now, Duarte could not bear to mention her name and the Quinta de Monteiro remained stamped by the spectral presence of its former mistress.

'Please go and speak to Victorine before she does anything foolish,' Emily urged wearily. 'I don't want to stay here anyway, so there's not much point giving her the impression that she has to move out to avoid me.'

'This is my home. Here you will stay.'

That abrasive intonation made her lift her head again and she clashed with smouldering dark golden eyes that could have splintered a lesser being at a hundred paces. She gulped. 'I *can't*... If that's how Victorine feels, what about the rest of the family and your friends?'

Duarte flung back his arrogant head and vented a harsh laugh of derision that ripped through the tense atmosphere like a knife blade. '*Inferno!* Do you think I took out a full page ad in the newspapers to spread the word that the village layabout had been screwing my wife?'

White as milk, Emily stared back at him and cringed. He'd never used such language around her before but in its use she finally recognised the savage anger he was containing and she quailed from it. 'But I never slept with him,' she argued in desperation. 'All that *ever* happened between us, you saw for yourself—'

'Saw and will never forget.' Duarte swore with a raw force that chilled her. 'Don't insult my intelligence. While you were in the Douro, I was foolish enough to reconsider your explanations—but then I received confirmation of your guilt from a third party. It was not *only* I who saw you acting like a slut.'

Emily had backed away several steps. Rigid with stress, she could not stop trembling. 'What third party? How could there be a third party who witnessed something that *never* happened?' she exclaimed in appalled protest. 'Was it your mother-in-law? I don't think Victorine would lose much sleep over lying about me.'

'You wrong her.' Duarte's contempt at that suggestion was unconcealed. 'She may not like you but she was not involved. Nor is your sordid affair common knowledge. Fortunately, that third party I mentioned is not a gossip.'

Emily lifted unsteady hands to her drawn face. It was a warm evening but her skin felt like ice and she dimly registered that she was suffering from the effects of shock. She was devastated to learn that, during their separation eight months earlier, Duarte had been fair enough to think over afresh whether or not she might have been telling the truth about Toby. Then, sadly, he had had his mind made up for him by some hateful person, who had either lied or seriously misinterpreted something they had seen. But who?

But just as suddenly the identity of that mysterious third party no longer seemed of immediate importance to Emily. She had let Toby kiss her and it was little wonder that, having seen that display, Duarte should have no faith whatsoever in her pleas of innocence. 'Obviously you're going to think what you want to think…'

Duarte strode forward and reached for her arms to hold her still when she would have spun away. '*Meu Deus!* What I *want* to think? Do you honestly believe that any man wants to think of his wife in another man's bed?' he raked down at her with charged incredulity, his lean, powerful hands biting into her elbows before he thrust her back from him.

Rage and aggression. That's what she was seeing. Two traits that Emily had once believed that her immensely wealthy, cool and sophisticated husband did not possess. Was he not one of the legendary *baroes*, a baron of Portuguese industry? Not just a banker alone. Duarte had interests in biotechnology, textiles, timber and cork, not to mention ownership of a world famous vineyard that produced wine to die for. One of the old money elite, it was true, but also innovative, tenacious and ruthless as all hell let out. Not a male with a problem in the realm of self-control.

Duarte thrust splayed brown fingers through his luxuriant black hair and breathed in slow and deep. His stunning eyes were veiled by spiky black lashes almost long enough to hit his superb cheekbones which were now scored with faint colour. 'If I frightened you, I'm sorry. It is difficult for me even to look at you in this room.'

Her face flamed and she studied the exquisite handmade pastel rug that adorned the polished floor. The night of that dreadfully boring dinner party she had walked out through the French windows on to the terrace with Toby to enjoy the breeze. How could she have forgotten that location? It did not suggest that she was the world's most sensitive person. *He* remembered—of course he did. But then she had greater cause to want to forget. Her strained eyes burned with tears and she mumbled, 'What can I say?'

'Nothing. The more you say the angrier I become. It is like a chain reaction.'

She couldn't look at him but there was no escape from her own despairing regret. One brief moment in time, one failure to react as her husband had naturally expected her to react with instantaneous rejection, a fatal hesitation that had cost her everything she had, everything she valued. And what a terrible truth it was that people never really appreciated what they *had* until it was taken away without any hope of return, Emily acknowledged painfully.

'I must speak to Victorine. She deserves greater consideration than I granted her on our arrival,' Duarte drawled with a grim lack of intonation. 'I lashed out at her then because I could not defend you against the charge of being what she calls a trollop.'

'You called me a whore…' Emily squeezed out the word from between compressed lips and swallowed hard.

'If I apologised, I'm afraid it would not be with sincerity,' Duarte admitted and the door thudded shut on his departure.

Emily snatched in an uneven breath. Sharing the same house with Duarte promised to be a nightmare, no matter how big the *quinta* was and no matter how infrequent their meetings. He despised her. He was never ever likely to believe that she had not been intimate with Toby. Indeed, Duarte could hardly stand to be in the same room with her. Yet he had kissed her on the flight—well, not at all the way he used to kiss her, she conceded wretchedly. There had been a dark, almost derisive lack of tenderness in that brief encounter and a cold calculated passion she'd never felt in him before. He'd sought out her weakness and exploited it without pity. Duarte had a streak of cruelty she'd never dreamt he possessed.

The housekeeper came to invite Emily to inspect Jamie's nursery. She went upstairs to find a whole bunch of admiring female staff gathered round a beautifully carved wooden cot in the centre of an airy room. Wearing an unfamiliar white sleepsuit, Jamie lay in his crisp blue and yellow bedding and continued to sleep like a log. Emily remained in the doorway, taking in surroundings in which she herself had had no input. Colourful ducks marched round the wallpaper border and bright curtains hung at the windows. The surface of every piece of nursery furniture was packed with waiting toys, many still in their packaging.

Her throat thickened as she appreciated that the room had been prepared long before Duarte had even found his son. Had he bought those toys himself? Gone into a shop, selected them in an act of positive thinking, determined to believe that he would eventually find them and get to bring his child home? Guilt ate her alive and she turned away shame-faced from the sight.

'It's a lovely nursery,' she said in careful Portuguese and she managed an appreciative smile.

The housekeeper led her further down the corridor and spread open the door of a large and beautifully furnished bedroom. Recognising the clothing being carefully put away by a maid as her own, Emily realised that she was now being shown her new quarters. On the other side of the *quinta* from the vast interconnecting bedroom suite she had once shared with Duarte. Just about as far as he could exile her and still keep her within the same walls—but at least she would be close to Jamie, she reminded herself, striving to keep up spirits sagging low enough now to hit the level of the wine cellars.

No sooner had the maid departed than a knock sounded on the door. Hurriedly composing herself, Emily opened the door to find herself facing a uniformed nanny, eager to proclaim her many childcare qualifications, her ability to speak English as fluently as she spoke Portuguese and her family's history of devoted service to the Monteiro family. Emily smiled and nodded repeatedly for not much else seemed to be required from her but she was taken aback and dismayed that Duarte should already have engaged a nanny for their son.

Jamie already had the entire household staff hanging over him like he was the seventh wonder of the world. But then, Duarte himself had been the last infant in the *quinta* nurseries and the Portuguese adored children—her son's arrival was a major event. But Emily felt that the immediate hire of a nanny when she herself had now nothing to do *other* than look after their son was a clear demonstration that Duarte did not consider her responsible enough for the task. Using the internal phone by the bed, she requested her evening meal in her room. She might as well get used to staying out of Duarte's way. He didn't want to see her, speak to her, have anything to do with her—and, in the mood she was in, she did not feel she could even blame him.

It was not as if she had *ever* had any actual proof that Duarte had slept with other women when he was away on business. But he had not come to her bed again after her pregnancy had been confirmed. After a while, pride had demanded that she lock that connecting door between their bedrooms and let him think that she wasn't one bit bothered by his lack of interest.

He was the man who had once murmured to her in the dark of the night and in the oddest tone of self-discovery, 'I have to confess that sex is very important to me.'

The man who had stood straight and tall and said, the day after his marriage proposal had been joyously accepted, 'I'm not in love with you and it is only fair that I should be frank on that score.'

Even after almost two years, the pain of hearing that admission spoken out loud still hurt her. She hadn't wanted him to pretend but she hadn't wanted him to speak those words either. Knowing in her heart of hearts had been one thing, a stark confession almost too much for her to bear. She had adored him and *still* adored him but she'd been so miserable in their marriage that now she could no longer see any point in their continuing such a charade. Just for Jamie's sake? Jamie, the precious child whose father had broken her heart.

When her evening meal arrived on a tray, she ate with no great appetite. Then she freshened up in the en suite bathroom and unravelled her hair from its constraining plait to brush out the tangles. She searched her reflection in the mirror. Emily Monteiro, unwanted, unloved wife. Major failure in the wife stakes, she added fairly. And on *his* terms he had given so much. The wedding ring, the name, the wealth, the security. So what if he had never ever returned her phone calls? So what if he had muttered Izabel's name on several occasions while he slept by her side? So what if he had got bored with her skinny, flat-chested body and engaged in a little discreet infidelity with more exciting and beautiful women?

Well, actually, she registered in the midst of her growing turmoil, Duarte Avila de Monteiro might still be the love of her life but she had pretty much hated him as much as she loved him once it became clear that her pregnancy concluded his interest in her. Once he had impregnated her, that had been that. Duty done, mission accomplished. She closed her aching eyes. The low-maintenance wife project had gone belly-up when he least expected it.

Sick and tired of her own emotionalism, Emily headed for the nursery. Jamie was sure to be close to waking and hungry by now. The door stood ajar and, hearing Duarte laugh, Emily hesitated in surprise. Then she heard the nanny issuing serious advice on how best to hold a baby and just had to sneak a look. She saw Duarte sprawled in a chair, long powerful legs extended as he held Jamie cradled in his arms and struggled to coordinate a feeding bottle held at an awkward angle.

'I need another hand,' he groaned in Portuguese.

Yet his lean, boldly masculine profile was relaxed. There was even the hint of a rueful smile at the corner of his expressive mouth as he dealt with the unusual experience of not being an immediate brilliant success at something. Evidently, he did not mind the young nanny as an audience to his efforts to get acquainted with his baby son. But he would not have turned to Emily for similar advice and support. Cut to the bone by that humiliating awareness, Emily crept back to her room, feeling like the most hated woman in the world. Even Jamie wasn't crying for her, she reflected painfully.

An hour later when she dared to emerge from her room again, Jamie was sound asleep in his cot. Emily was dying to lift her son and hold him close but there was a baby listener beside the night light. If Jamie cried, the staff would come running and she would look like an irresponsible mother. That warning image sent her into retreat.

She was leaving the nursery when Victorine intercepted her.

'You have Duarte's son. You must be feeling very

pleased with yourself,' the older woman condemned bitterly.

'Please don't feel you have to leave. This is your home,' Emily pointed out, ignoring that opening sally.

The older woman pursed her lips. 'It hasn't been *my* home since you first came into it. When Duarte put someone like you in my daughter's place, he...'

At the sound of that all-too-familiar refrain, Emily suppressed a groan. Once the centre of her mother's world, the late Izabel had been a renowned beauty as famed for her style as her effervescent charm. Unable to come to terms with Izabel's premature death, Victorine had deeply resented Duarte's remarriage.

As the older woman paused for breath in what had grown into a rant freely interspersed with spiteful comparisons, Emily simply sighed, 'Your daughter is no longer here but you're still part of Duarte's family and he's fond of you.'

Frustrated by Emily's lack of reaction to her gibes, Victorine dealt her a look of boiling resentment and hurried back the way she had come. Sticks and stones can break my bones but words can never hurt me, Emily rhymed to herself. But, feeling in dire need of some fresh air, she went out to the charming courtyard at the back of the *quinta*. There she sat on a stone bench in rueful appreciation of the superb box-hedged herbal gardens designed by her talented predecessor. The light was fading fast and using the same service staircase she had employed earlier, she returned to her room to have a shower before bed.

She'd already shed her top and skirt when someone turned the handle on her bedroom door and partially opened it. Freezing in dismay, she heard Duarte's deep drawl as he addressed one of the staff in the corridor and she dived into the bathroom in a panic to snatch up a towel.

'Emily?' Duarte breathed, a raw edge to his dark, rich voice that sent a current of foreboding through her.

She emerged with pronounced reluctance from the bathroom. 'Yes?'

Shimmering golden eyes raked over her shrinking figure and the death grip she had on a towel that was just a little too small for its purpose. She had one unpremeditated clash with his smouldering gaze and she hastily looked away again, her heart jumping as if she had jammed a finger in a live electric socket. The anger she had seen in him earlier was no longer contained. It leapt out at her like a physical entity and radiated around him like a dangerous aura. From the fierce set of his lean dark devastating face, the rigidity of his broad muscular shoulders and the clenching of his long brown fingers into fists, she read a level of unholy rage she'd truly never ever expected to see in a male as self-disciplined as he was.

'How *could* you?' he demanded wrathfully.

'How could I…wh-what?' she stammered, tummy churning at the terrible tension in the atmosphere.

'Don't play games with me unless you want to get hurt…' Duarte ground out. 'Victorine came to me in great distress to tell me how you had taunted her with her daughter's death…'

Emily's knees were locked together and her legs gave an involuntary wobble, the high-heeled mules she still wore providing a far from stable support. 'I didn't taunt her. All I said was that her daughter was no longer here—'

'I don't believe you. It's a very long time since I've seen Izabel's mother in such a state and you cannot even look me in the face.'

Emily could feel herself beginning to *feel* guilty even though she knew that she had said nothing that could have upset the older woman. Nor could she help but recall how enraged Victorine had looked when she'd realised that Emily was no longer a soft target on which to vent her spleen. She lifted her chin, raising strained aquamarine eyes to meet a gaze as stormy as the threatening glow inside a volcano about to erupt. 'She can only have misunderstood what I said—'

'Don't push me on this. Shock is written all over you. Shock that Victorine told tales and your unpleasantness has been exposed for me to deal with—'

'I did not taunt her with Izabel's death. Why would I do that, for goodness' sake?' Emily prompted on a rising note of protest.

'Because, as the mother of my son and my wife, you might well feel that you have a great deal of power in this house.'

A nervous giggle bubbled up out of Emily's constricted throat. 'Power? *Me?* I was less important than the most junior housemaid the last time I lived here! Victorine was always picking out my mistakes in front of the staff, embarrassing them, humiliating me…' As Emily's voice ebbed in recollection, it then gathered renewed steam. 'Nothing I ever did pleased her *or* you. I spent hours trying to make up menus, only to have them rejected. I got to the stage where I didn't care if you never ate again! I let her march me out to the endless coffee mornings, the polite social visits, the charity functions, the dinner parties for which you never turned up and I changed my clothes at least four times a flippin' day—'

'Emily,' Duarte gritted.

'Do you know something?' Emily proclaimed with the fierce bitterness that assailed her when she recalled how desperately hard she had worked to fill her role as a high society wife. 'I'd have had an easier ride down a nineteenth-century coal mine than I had being your wife!'

That last phrase dropped into a silence so deep that a feather could have fallen and sounded out a resounding crash. Duarte surveyed her with hard dark eyes. 'You condemn yourself with every word you say. It's obvious that you've *always* resented Victorine's presence here and would very much prefer to see her move out.'

Emily's lips opened and then very slowly closed again, her eyes widening in dismay as she realised what Duarte had extracted from her unfortunate outburst. Suddenly she could have bitten out her own impulsive tongue but innate honesty prevented her from lying. It was true—no way could she put her hand on her heart and say that she had *not* resented his mother-in-law in the past. Regimented by Victorine into a lifestyle she loathed and then continually criticised and shown up in front of others as she failed to fill the hallowed shoes of her superhuman predecessor, Emily had often wished that Victorine would magically vanish from her horizon.

'But it wasn't like that tonight, Duarte,' she argued vehemently. 'I *know* you're fond of her and I reminded her of that and asked her to think again—'

'I have more trust in her ability to tell the truth than I have in yours. If you ever do anything like this again, you will pay a high price. *Don't* turn away from me like that!' Duarte raked at her, making her flinch.

So now as well as being the most hated person in the house and a trollop and that other word which she could bear to recall even less, she was also a nasty shrew and an outright liar. Emily kept on turning away, for she had too much pride to let him see how savaged she was by his refusal to place even the smallest trust in her word.

Long powerful fingers settled on her slight shoulder and flipped her back again with a masculine strength that was far from reassuring. 'When I say jump, now you say, ''How high?'' Haven't you got that message yet?'

'No…and I won't,' Emily told him, her gaze glimmering with angry tears. 'You are not going to make me feel any worse about myself than I already feel!'

'So *you* feel bad?' Duarte loosed a derisive laugh that

broke the surging tension with the disturbing effect of shattering glass. 'But I bet not one tenth as bad as *I* felt about bringing you back into my home this evening…'

Emily dropped her head and tried to swallow the great fat lump of guilt in her throat. She was in turmoil, wanting to scream and sob and attack him all at one and the same time. Once again she'd been her own worst enemy. Why, oh why had she been foolish enough to even *speak* to Victorine? Why hadn't she just minded her own wretched business and walked away? But she knew why, didn't she? She had not wanted to feel that the older woman's departure was yet one more sin to be piled up at her door.

'But now you're about to make me feel much better about that difficult decision,' Duarte completed in a charged undertone that sent the oddest tremor down her responsive spine.

'Oh…and how am I going to do that?' she prompted chokily, fighting to hold the tears back until he left her again. He hated her, he absolutely hated her and she could not imagine how she had ever managed to persuade herself that Duarte had no truly strong emotions where she was concerned.

'Sex.'

Engaged in an apparently enraptured scrutiny of his soft leather loafers, Emily blinked rapidly in receipt of that explanation. Mentally she strained to persuade herself that he had not uttered that single unexpected word with the smooth cool of a male who had already overcome his anger while she was still struggling even to *think* like a rational being.

The silence seemed to rush and eddy around her like a high wind.

She raised her gaze to the well-cut beige chinos sheathing his long, long powerful length of leg and lean hips, up more slowly still to the belt encircling his narrow waist and the casual white shirt open at his bronzed throat.

'Sex...?' Emily almost whispered as if it physically hurt her to say the word.

Duarte lifted a lean hand and pushed up her chin. Volatile golden eyes set between spiky black lashes inspected her disbelieving face. *'Sim, querida.'*

Yes, he said in confirmation but her brain refused to credit the evidence of her hearing.

CHAPTER FIVE

'S-SEX?' Emily stammered helplessly.

'The concept appeals and intrigues,' Duarte murmured silkily.

Emily drew in a very ragged breath but still her voice was faint. 'Does it really? Tell me, when did this sudden attack of lust occur to you? Is this like…your equivalent of that ancestor of yours who bricked his wife up alive in a wall?'

'Such a very insightful question, *querida*.' Duarte surveyed her with brilliant dark eyes alight with hard amusement. 'But rather naive. I don't need to explain myself to you and why would I?'

As Duarte narrowed the distance between them, Emily went as rigid as a porcupine going on the offensive. 'Don't you dare touch me!'

Duarte scanned the flushed oval of her delicate face, his strong jawline hardening. 'Perhaps I want to remind you that you're mine. Perhaps it *is* that basic…I don't care.'

'Basic's not me,' Emily framed unevenly because she trusted herself even less than she trusted him. She could feel his proximity with every skin cell she possessed. In her mind's eye she could even visualise every shameless skin cell sitting up and begging and that made her cringe. For what had always lain at the very heart of Duarte's total irresistibility had been the simple truth that her *own* resistance was nil.

He hooked a lean brown finger into the towel she was still clutching. 'Overkill, don't you think?'

She trembled, a liquid sensation of heat pooling deep

inside her, her legs welding her to the spot. He was so close she could smell the warm male scent of his sunwarmed skin, so close she could feel deliciously threatened by the sheer size differential between her and the potent masculinity of his lean hard physique.

'You signed up for your own personal punishment plan while we were still airborne,' Duarte delivered in a tone as smooth as silk.

She was staring up at him, wholly enveloped in her own growing reaction to him. It had always been that way, which was why when things were wrong between them she just never looked directly at him, out of fear that he would guess how great his power was. Only now, she'd reached the point where she could not stop staring, drinking in every taut angle of that strikingly dark and handsome face of his, the proud arrogant jut of his nose, the fabulous cheekbones that lent his features such pronounced strength and definition, the fine grain of his skin that roughened round his hard jawline. And still she was not satisfied; still it was not enough to satiate that need within her.

'S-sorry? Punishment plan?' she echoed a whole ten seconds after he had finished speaking and only after frantically plundering her memory.

'My kind of punishment,' Duarte spelt out with measured satisfaction.

Stunning dark golden eyes held hers as he finally jerked loose the screening towel so that it drifted down into a heap on the rug. Strong hands lifted to snap round her wrists and prevent her startled attempt to stoop and retrieve it.

'Duarte…?' Emily gasped, very much taken back by his behaviour.

He held her back from him and let his intent gaze roam at a leisurely pace over her slim, slight figure. She tried to curve away from him, curl in protectively on herself while still standing, but he held fast to her. Visually exploring the rise and fall of her small breasts beneath the barrier of her bra, his attention strolled down to her tiny waist and the swell of her hips where a pair of white cotton panties that were not of the diminutive variety shut off his view.

'The cotton look was fine when sweet and wholesome was the draw but it's not to my taste now,' Duarte confided while Emily's pale skin coloured up like the rising sun beneath an appraisal that was reducing her to agonies of embarrassment. 'And since pleasing me must necessarily *be* your top priority—'

'*Why*? Why would it be?' she broke in, wild in her humiliation.

'Security of tenure,' Duarte specified in cool warning. 'And please let's ditch the I'm-so-shy routine I used to respect because I don't respect it any more.'

Her heart was thudding so fast, she could hardly catch her breath. 'It wasn't a routine—'

'But it must have been,' Duarte asserted in interruption as he backed her inexorably in the direction of the bed. 'All those hot afternoons you spent in *his* studio in pursuit of a surprise portrait supposedly for me? At a time when you had locked the door between our bedrooms you were attending all those sittings purely for my benefit? And you're *still* trying to persuade me that the same lout that I personally heard swearing eternal devotion to you never laid a finger on you?'

Emily nodded jerkily, conscious of how very unlikely he made her being innocent sound but still ready to argue. 'I was hardly ever alone with him. He had a girlfriend—'

Duarte elevated a winged dark brow. 'Get a better story. Or even better, tell me exactly what you *did* do with him—'

As he swept her up into his arms and settled her squarely down on the centre of the big bed and stepped back from her, she said feverishly. 'Nothing, absolutely nothing.'

'I beat the hell out of him,' Duarte informed her with chilling exactitude.

Suddenly the atmosphere was sizzling like a stick of dynamite ready to blow. In considerable shock, Emily gazed back at Duarte, all her colour ebbing—for the very last thing she would have expected from Duarte was that kind of violence.

'That was my right,' Duarte stated soft and low and dark, watching her like a hawk ready to pounce, smouldering dark golden eyes welded to her sincerely shaken face. 'Do you think that I didn't know that he followed you to the villa in the Douro? That he repeatedly attempted to see you? And that when that failed, he kept on phoning?'

A pin could have been heard dropping in her appalled silence.

Duarte studied her with a hard force she could feel in every atom of her being. 'If you had encouraged him then, if you had *once* spoken to him or seen him, you would not be here now.'

So throughout that winter she'd passed at the country house, nothing that happened there had gone unreported to Duarte. Emily was genuinely shattered by that discovery. 'We…we were separated,' she whispered shakily.

Savage anger flared in his blazing look of challenge. 'You were still my wife and what is mine stays mine until *I* choose to relinquish it!'

Before her she saw a male with traits she had failed to recognise before. The male that existed behind the deceptive patina of sophistication and cool courtesy. A more primitive breed of male, every bit as aggressive and possessive of what was his as any backstreet fighter. She'd never been so shaken in her whole life—for only then it occurred to her that naturally, Duarte used the same forceful drives for his personal life that he used every day in a more civilised way in business—in that field his ruthlessness was a living legend.

'Turning him away in the Douro was the only thing you did right,' Duarte pronounced grittily.

Emily was now realising that the only reason that Duarte had left her alone on the bed was to undress. She lay there with the curious sensation of being weighted to the mattress while she watched him finish unbuttoning his shirt. As he bent to remove his shoes, the shirt hung loose, disclosing an enervating glimpse of a broad chest the colour of living bronze, with dark curling hair emphasising his powerful pectoral muscles and the hard flat contours of his stomach. Her breath locked in her throat. As he straightened to his full six foot four inches, she couldn't take her eyes from him. He was a stunning vision of raw masculinity and it had been so long since she had seen him like that. Indeed, it was over a year since they had shared the smallest intimacy, she reminded herself, dimly seeking excuse for her total absorption in him.

'There will be no separate bedrooms this time, *no* locked doors,' Duarte spelt out, sending the zip rasping down on his chinos, angling his narrow hips in a slight movement that she found inexplicably but hugely sexy.

Her fair skin coloured up hotly on that straying thought and, dredging her eyes from him in severe embarrassment, she focused on the edge of the linen sheet already neatly folded down by a maid in readiness for an occupant. *Two* occupants, she reflected, her brain moving at a tenth of its usual capacity. Duarte was going to make love to her. It occurred to her that saying 'no' was still an option and that she really ought to say something.

'I really don't want this,' Emily told him.

'Just who are you trying to kid?'

Aghast at that blunt comeback, Emily blinked in dismay and was betrayed into a sudden upward glance. Duarte surveyed her in flagrant challenge, sardonic amusement gleaming at her shaken expression. He stood there naked and magnificent, his hard shaft fully erect.

'You are not chained to the bed but you're not running anywhere. Why?'

For a timeless moment, she simply stared at him, seriously wrongfooted by that enquiry. Throwing her a look of irredeemably male logic, Duarte came down on the bed and reached for her so fast, she gave a stifled gasp of fright.

'Let me tell you *why*,' he urged, knotting long fingers into her tumbled red-gold hair as he brought her up against his hard muscular chest. 'I can turn you on just by looking at you!'

Crushed into the unyielding strength of him yet forced to maintain an eye contact that she would have done just about anything to avoid, Emily felt as if she was fighting for her last ounce of pride. 'No…not any more—'

He tugged her head back, shimmering eyes scorching down into hers. 'So what was that little demonstration of total surrender on the jet, then? One last fling?'

Her whole body was already reacting to the steely contours of his with insidious little quivers of heat and a drowning weakness that was even more dangerous to her self-discipline. The fresh warm scent of him was in her nostrils with every breath she drew, achingly familiar, achingly erotic. 'You…you took me by surprise—'

'*Não te acredito*… I don't believe you,' Duarte derided, his breath fanning her cheek and then his hot hard hungry mouth claiming hers with a raw assurance that made denial impossible.

It was a shattering kiss, full of explosive demand. His tongue stabbed into the tender moist interior of her mouth and plundered the sweetness with an invasive force that made her heart hammer as fast as if she'd run a three minute mile. She trembled beneath that onslaught, her hands clenching, nails biting into her palms as she attempted to withstand the raw sexual enticement of his expert mouth on hers. But the little kernel of nagging heat he had already awakened low in her belly was too seductive. She started shifting in his grasp, pushing into him in a helpless surge and all the time, Dear heaven, I want him, want him, *want him*, was running like a charged mantra through her mind.

'Indeed, belief would be a great challenge,' Duarte husked, ungenerous in victory as only a rogue male can be—and then he did something that truly shook her. Taking her hand, he curled her fingers round his bold erection. 'That's more like it...'

He felt like hot steel sheathed in silk. Her hand shook a little and her face burned scarlet at being asked to do what she had previously only done in darkness and beneath concealing covers. But an undeniable excitement gripped her and she stroked his hard masculinity, feeling the inexorable surge of answering heat between her trembling thighs.

In response, he caught her back to him and mated his mouth to hers with ferocious hunger. Then he drew back from her when she was clinging to him. Her hands dropped from him and she was disorientated by the sensation of her breasts coming free from her bra without her having had anything to do with it. She glanced down at herself to see that the front fastening had already been undone. Even as she whipped up her hands to cover herself, Duarte was ahead of her, imprisoning her fingers in his own, forestalling her.

'Stop it...' she gasped, embarrassed by the sight of her own bare flesh because she felt that she could not compare to other women with the small pouting swells crowned by rosy distended nipples.

Duarte used his superior strength to flatten her back on to the bed and stared down at her with hot hungry eyes of appreciation. 'You can't hide the evidence of your own desire,' he breathed, lowering his head to capture a swollen, throbbing tip between his lips.

Her entire body jerked, for she had always been almost unbearably sensitive there. Her hands flexed within the hold of his and he released them but she dug her fingers into the sheets beneath her instead. Excitement was like a damburst inside her, pressure building up with every second and she could not withstand her own intense need to be touched. A low keening sound was torn from her as he tormented the rosy crests with the kind of skill that drove her absolutely wild. So somehow they got to the stage where he was holding her down purely to keep her still and her hands had, seemingly without an input from her, risen to lace into his luxuriant black hair, urging him on in helpless writhing yearning.

'So tell me you're not mine now, *minha pequena esposa*,' Duarte invited, a roughened edge to his dark, deep drawl as he lifted his head from the glistening buds still begging for his attention.

'Don't stop…*please*,' she heard herself beg like a supplicant and even as she said it she knew she would cringe for herself later, but just then the sheer craving he had unleashed took precedence.

'Was it like this with Jarrett?'

For a split second she could not think who 'Jarrett' was. Toby, Bliss's cousin. Toby Jarrett. The name stood out in her mind's eye and made her tummy clench. She gazed up at Duarte, suddenly as terrified as an animal knowing it was about to be slaughtered, and knowing that there was absolutely nothing she could do about it because he wouldn't believe her.

'You are just sick with shame,' Duarte bit out, studying her as if he had her under a microscope and could read every nuance of expression.

She shut her eyes on the hot scorch of threatening tears.

Even while her wretched body leapt and burned for him and her every thought was at bay, *he* was still in sufficient control to attack.

'Much good that does either of us,' Duarte growled in an oddly ragged undertone and then suddenly he was gathering her back into his arms, reclaiming her mouth with a kind of blazing fiery desire that went through her quivering body like sheet lightning. He shuddered against her and then he stilled and, for a split second of horror, she thought he was about to pull free of her and instinctively she wrapped her arms round him as tightly as she could.

And then she felt a long forefinger stroking her cheek where a tear had escaped and left a telling trail and he cursed in Portuguese. He claimed her lips again at the same time as his exploring hand teased the aching points of her breasts. That instant of all too painful self-awareness was sent into oblivion by the renewed force of her own response.

'Duarte…' she moaned at the peak of an almost agonised gasp as his stroking fingers discovered the dampness of the triangle of fabric stretched taut between her restive thighs.

He stripped away that last barrier and found the hot moist core of her femininity. Her heartbeat seemed to thunder in her own ears as her body writhed without her volition. There was only wild sensation and overwhelming hunger for anything that would ease the tormenting ache of pressure clawing at her. She could feel him against her thigh, hot and hard and rampantly aroused and just knowing that she could still have that effect on him intensified everything that she felt.

'I can't be gentle…' he groaned, rising over her and parting her thighs with impatient hands to haul her back to him.

'Doesn't matter…'

Nothing mattered then but the driving thrust with which he entered her. Her body was just one gigantic source of longing and then he was there, dominantly male, stretching her with his strength and fullness and there was so much intense pleasure she cried out against it.

'Emily, *meu bonita…*'

My beautiful one, she savoured in stunned surprise and gazed up at him to register the hard-edged need etched into his lean dark devastating face but saw the concern in his hot golden eyes. 'I hurt you?' he prompted.

She shook her head, beyond speech, and even if she could have spoken she could not have thought of any way to tell him that that much pleasure came close to pain. But it seemed he understood, for a flash of raw male amusement flared in his spectacular eyes and he came into her again, hard and fast and not to be denied. She arched her hips up to him in helpless encouragement. He set a raw sensual rhythm that heightened her excitement to a level she could not control. There was nothing but him and the wild surging rise of her own excitement, her own primal delight in his erotic dominance. Every pulse racing, his name on her lips, she reached the dazzling instant of release and cried out in ecstasy at the explosive charge of sensation pulsating through her in waves. She clung to him as he shuddered over her and vented a ragged groan of intense satisfaction.

Happiness was bubbling up inside her now. To be so close to Duarte again, to feel so at home, to feel needed, wanted, *secure*. As he freed her of his weight, she followed him across the bed to stay close. She buried her face in a smooth brown muscular shoulder and drank in the hot, husky scent of him like an addict. One arm sliding round his neck, she lay across him, happy but engaged in frantic thought. Intimacy was the foundation stone of any normal marriage. My goodness, what had possessed her when she had briefly believed that she ought to be saying no?

In fact, so strong was her sense of joy and relief that she

had not made that foolish mistake, she found herself muttering feverishly, 'You're just so fantastic...'

Part of her cringed for herself even as she said it and then she noticed how rigid he was under her and how silent. Not that in the aftermath, Duarte had ever been exactly chatty. But she also became agonisingly aware that he did not have his arms round her and that she was the one making all the effort to be cosy and close and warmly intimate. About then, she just started wanting to die.

'And you're so affectionate, *querida*,' Duarte breathed a little stiltedly and then he finally curved an arm round her slim, still length and smoothed warm fingers down her taut spinal cord.

'Stop it...' she whispered.

'Stop what?'

'I can feel you thinking,' she mumbled, sensing his mental distance from her with every atom of ESP she possessed.

'I am thinking that I need a shower,' Duarte said drily.

And why was he thinking that? A shower would get him back out of bed again, away from *her*, she reflected miserably, a mass of insecurities unleashed inside her again. But he couldn't stay in the shower forever, could he? Slowly she edged away from him again, hoping to be snatched back; it didn't happen. He rolled lithely over and sprang out of bed. All potent male, hair-roughened skin and rippling muscles. Absolutely gorgeous but never hers, never really hers even at the beginning and even less likely to be now after what had happened eleven months ago.

Emily pulled herself up against the tumbled pillows, reading the raw tension in his wide shoulders but unable to silence her own desperate need to be heard. 'Duarte?'

'What?' he growled like a grizzly bear.

He was *so* volatile, she registered in amazement. How had she never seen that in him before? Had she been so wrapped up in her own self-pity that she'd never appreciated that she was married to a male who literally seemed to boil beneath the surface of that cool front with dark, deep, dangerous emotion?

'I've got to say it…I'm sorry,' she muttered feverishly, plucking nervously at the corner of the sheet beneath her hand. 'No matter how bad it looked, I never felt anything for Toby and I never had an affair with him either—'

Duarte swung back to her with the speed of a lion ready to spring. Angry golden eyes struck sparks off hers in a look as physical as a slap on the face. 'Don't you know when to keep quiet?'

Shrinking back into the pillows and pale as death, Emily whispered, 'I *need* you to listen—'

Duarte threw up both hands in a violent gesture of lost patience and strode on into the bathroom.

She listened to the shower coming on full gush and a sense of defeat engulfed her. It was swiftly followed by the conviction that she was the most stupid woman in existence. Why was she always so naive with him? *Sex*, he had said before she succumbed to her dream of how she wanted it to be. And so lost had she got in that delusion that, in the aftermath of passion, she had swarmed all over him as if nothing had ever been wrong between them, but it had been only sex as far as he was concerned, not making love, not a meeting of minds. Incredibly exciting sex, in her opinion, but then what did she really know about what it was like for *him*?

Just the slaking of a physical hunger on the nearest most available female body? Well, she'd certainly made herself available. Exactly as he had expected. *I can turn you on just by looking at you.* She stuffed her hot face into the cooling linen. Her own personal punishment plan, he had said—and what had he meant by that? And why hadn't she asked? Her sated body told her where her mind had been. Lost. Wanting him, wanting him much more than common sense. She'd had no restraint. She had so desperately wanted to believe that physical intimacy could fill the terrible emptiness that losing him had filled her with, could provide the first bridge between them, could give her back *hope*. Her nails raked down the smooth sheet beneath the pillows, self-hatred burning her like poison.

Suddenly, she pulled herself up and back on her knees, thrusting her wildly tangled hair back over her shoulders. Her strained face taut, she leapt off the bed, looked around for something to pull on to hide her nakedness and snatched up his discarded shirt. She came to a halt on the threshold of the bathroom where Duarte was already towelling himself dry.

'I suppose you think everything you ever thought about me has been proven now...I suppose you think I *am* a whore!' she fired at him jaggedly.

Duarte raked a driven hand through his damp tousled hair and rested dark deepset brooding eyes on her in the tension-filled silence. 'Leave it,' he warned and tossing the towel aside, he strode past her.

Her legs felt horribly wobbly. She leant back against the bedroom wall to steady herself. A tight hard knot of pain was building inside her, threatening to take control of her entirely, no matter how hard she tried to get a grip on herself. 'Sleeping with me was like a power play, was it?' she mumbled sickly. 'A case of finding out how high you could make me jump? And just how desperate I would be to please you?'

'I told you to *leave* it...' Duarte ground out, the long sweep of his muscular golden back rigid with stormy tension as he hauled on his chinos.

Emily felt she'd already been reduced so low that nothing else could hurt her. However, it belatedly dawned on her that he was getting dressed again and that he wasn't staying the rest of the night and that seemed the lowest blow of all. 'Where are you going?'

Duarte swung back round to face her, his lean strong features ferociously set. 'Any place I don't have to listen to you getting it all wrong—'

'How am I getting it wrong?' she pressed in desperation. 'Duarte?'

Brilliant eyes grim, he let a harsh laugh escape. 'Do you think this is so easy for me? I'm thinking about you with Jarrett almost all the time. I can't get it out of my head...'

Her tummy twisted, her drawn face tightening.

'So all kudos to me for pulling off a fantastic performance between the sheets.' His derision, whether angled at her or himself made her flinch. 'Two years ago, I was your first lover and that meant something to me. Now it's all gone and I am just so bloody angry with you that I don't know why I brought you back here!'

She felt dead inside because he had killed her hopes. She was being rejected again. 'It was only a kiss and I didn't even like it...' she framed strickenly.

'If you open the subject one more time... Where the hell is my shirt?' he demanded in raw completion.

Realising that he had yet to notice what she was wearing, she peeled off his shirt and threw it back at his feet.

Duarte stared at her with pronounced intensity. She stood there like a statue, her hair falling round her like tongues of fire against her fair skin but for once she made no move to cover herself.

'Take your blasted shirt and get out!' she suddenly gasped.

He flicked it up, the movement all grace and derision somehow perfectly combined. She yanked open the door, spread it wide.

Duarte threw her a sardonic look. 'If you were looking

for a guy who turns the other cheek, you shouldn't have married a Monteiro.'

She slammed the door shut on his exit, turned the key in the lock and then ran all the way back to the bed to throw herself facedown on the mattress.

Almost simultaneously it seemed the noise of a sudden jarring crash sent her rolling over in shock to glance back in the direction of the door. She was just in time to see it smash back against the wall. She focused on Duarte, who had kicked it open, with shaken eyes of disbelief. He stood there with clenched fists, breathing heavily, all powerful and quite unashamed masculinity.

'You lock a door against me again and I'll break it down every time!' Outraged golden eyes assailed hers with pure aggressive force. 'Do you understand?'

Very slowly and carefully, she nodded.

CHAPTER SIX

HAVING scarcely slept during a night of emotional turmoil, Emily was up early the following morning and in the nursery with Jamie.

When his nanny found her there, the young woman smiled in understanding and left them in peace. Given lots of cuddles, Jamie was in the sunniest of moods, but soon his big brown eyes turned sleepy again. His every need met, Jamie had an enviable capacity to be as happy in Portugal as he had been in England.

Emily had a shower and put on a denim skirt and tee-shirt. A maid brought her breakfast and she had it out on the balcony—white coffee and wonderful fresh-baked bread served with home-made honey. She was told in answer to her enquiry that 'Don Duarte' had left for his Lisbon office shortly before eight.

It promised to be a glorious day. Surrounded by woods of pine, eucalyptus and oak, the gardens were lush and tropical, full of spiky palms and superb flowering shrubs, the extensive lawns already being industriously watered by the gardeners. Beyond the trees stretched the extensive *quinta* estate of orange and lemon and olive groves. Against the backdrop of the purple green mountains, the tiny village houses sprinkled the hillside like toys. In every direction the views were breathtaking.

Emily had missed Portugal so much during her absence yet, two years earlier, she knew she'd severely underestimated the challenges of marrying a male who not only did not love her but also whose world and expectations were so very different from her own...

Even their wedding had not been what she had wanted. Duarte had desired neither frills nor fuss and, as she loved him, she'd suppressed her longing for a wedding gown and worn a suit. Lunch had followed at an exclusive hotel but it had been attended only by her family and a handful of Duarte's business acquaintances.

'I'd call it a bit shabby,' her sister Hermione had said with a sniff. 'Are you *sure* this isn't a shotgun do?'

From the instant she'd told her family that she was marrying Duarte, the humiliating suggestion that he might only be marrying her because she had fallen pregnant had been repeatedly raised. When her denials were received with cynical disbelief, it had done nothing for her self-image.

Duarte had even been too busy for a honeymoon and they had been married for a week before she discovered that she was *not* his first wife. Studying their marriage certificate with dreamy eyes, she'd finally noticed that he was described as a widower.

'Why didn't you tell me?' she had asked in astonished hurt.

'It wasn't relevant,' Duarte had told her flatly.

Pressing for further details, she had naturally been shocked to learn of the car crash that had killed both Izabel and his twin, Elena. But she'd also noticed that that night, for the first time, Duarte didn't make love to her. Early on, she had learnt that trying to talk about Izabel drove Duarte from her. That same evening, sadly, Jazz, the dog she had adored and whom she had credited with bringing her and Duarte together, had passed away in his sleep and that concluded their stay in England.

Duarte had brought her home to the *quinta* and that very first day, Victorine had invited Emily to her private sitting room where there were framed photographs showing her late daughter Izabel, glorious in her fabulous wedding gown, Izabel on her Caribbean honeymoon, Izabel entertaining royalty...Izabel...Izabel...Izabel. Emily had learnt right then that she was a second-best wife.

A knock on the bedroom door forced Emily from her introspection. Victorine was trying not to look at the lock which Duarte had broken the night before. Emily flushed for naturally the older woman would know that she and Duarte had had a row. The whole household would be buzzing with the sheer shock value of Duarte doing something that much out of character.

'May we speak?' Victorine asked stiffly.

Emily was dumbfounded to see tears glistening in the older woman's shadowed eyes.

'I've seen your son. He is a very beautiful baby...' Victorine told her heavily. 'I feel great guilt that I lied about what you said to me last night and I could not sleep. I told Duarte the truth at breakfast.'

That astonishing confession froze Emily to the spot. At the same time, however, she could not help thinking that if what Victorine was telling her was true, Duarte had certainly not hurtled upstairs to offer *her* an apology for misjudging her.

'I am sorry for the way I have treated you,' Victorine continued doggedly. 'When I saw your son, who is the future of this family, I asked myself how much my unkindness might have contributed to your separation from Duarte last year—'

'Never mind, it's over...forgotten,' Emily broke in awkwardly, finally recognising that Victorine had indeed faced the results of her resentment and had emerged much chastened from the experience.

In revealing discomfiture, Victorine looked away from the damaged door. 'I've made trouble between you and Duarte but it won't happen again. The maids are packing for me.'

As Victorine turned away, looking old and frail and forlorn in her unhappiness, Emily touched her thin arm in a sympathetic gesture. 'You don't need to leave for my benefit.'

'Duarte said I must. He is very disappointed in me and very angry—'

'He'll get over that,' Emily asserted as Victorine began to sob, her fragile self-control splintering at the prospect before her. 'So you and I got off to a bad start but I just can't imagine this place without you and where are you going to go anyway?'

'Two years ago, Duarte said to me, "Emily is so sweet, so kind, you will love her"...and I *hated* you before I even met you!' the older woman wept.

Emily took Victorine back to her own rooms, knowing how much she would dislike any of the staff seeing her in tears. She began to understand that it had been her own change in attitude the night before which had ultimately led to the present situation. Unable to bully Emily as she had once done, Victorine had lied to Duarte and had then been horrified by her own behaviour. It was odd how good could sometimes come out of bad, Emily was thinking as she went downstairs after calming the other woman down.

It seemed to be a day for surprises: Bliss was in the main hall speaking to the *quinta* housekeeper. Clad in a simple navy dress that was a marvellous foil for her blonde beauty, Bliss moved to greet her.

'I had no idea you were here!' Smiling, Emily asked the housekeeper to serve coffee.

'Strictly in a business capacity, I'm afraid, so I can't stay for long.' Bliss sank down gracefully on a silk-upholstered sofa in the salon. 'Duarte has a big party arranged for this weekend. I was just checking the final arrangements. I've been acting as your husband's hostess since your departure.'

Unsettled by that news and quick to pick up on the brittle

quality of her friend's manner, Emily said in surprise, 'Didn't Victorine object?'

'That hateful old cow?' Bliss laughed. 'Oh, not being a softy like you, I soon settled *her*! I let her know that her ideas about entertaining were fifty years out of date and an embarrassment to Duarte. Ever since then, when there are guests, she takes an early night.'

That unfeeling explanation filled Emily with uneasy distaste. Victorine had her flaws but Emily would never have dreamt of referring to the older woman in such terms. 'Bliss—'

Bliss merely talked over her. 'Mind you, I never thought I'd see *you* back here again either. I was very annoyed when you did your vanishing act last year.'

Grateful for that honesty, Emily spoke up immediately. 'I'm really sorry I didn't keep in touch but—'

'That's not what I'm talking about. When I told you about that little chat I overheard between your husband and his lawyer, I was warning you to get your own legal advice instead of sitting on the fence, hoping all that nasty divorce stuff would go away. I wasn't expecting you to flee the country and put everybody into a loop trying to find you!'

Emily paled at that censorious clarification.

'In tipping you off, I felt like I had *personally* deprived Duarte of his child,' Bliss admitted in no more comforting continuance. 'What on earth possessed you? And now to come back here, regardless of how Duarte feels about you—'

'What are you saying?' Emily faltered in growing shock at what she was hearing.

'Come on, Emily…all Duarte cared about was getting his son back and resident in Portugal. Now he's got him, he won't let you take him away again. In a marriage that was failing from day one, where does that leave you?'

'I've never discussed Duarte or our relationship with you,' Emily reminded the other woman uncomfortably.

Her exquisite face an icy mask, Bliss rose to her feet. 'Well, excuse me for presuming on our former friendship—'

Emily flew upright in distress. 'No, Bliss...I didn't *mean*—'

'Don't come crying to me when you find yourself divorced and without your precious son!' Bliss told her scornfully. 'Can't you see the bigger picture here? Doesn't it occur to you that Duarte may already have another woman in his life?'

Emily's tummy gave a sick somersault and she could barely credit that the blonde was a woman she had once believed was a true friend. 'Why are you behaving like this?'

'Maybe you should have settled for my cousin, Toby, while you had the chance,' Bliss derided dulcetly before she departed, leaving Emily standing in the salon in a stricken daze.

Had Duarte met someone else? Well, why not, a little voice demanded. Wouldn't he have felt he had every excuse to find solace elsewhere? She could feel herself inwardly coming apart at the seams under the new stress which Bliss had imposed on her already overwrought system.

She'd just heard Bliss's car driving off when a phone was brought to her.

It was Duarte on the line. 'Will you meet me for lunch?'

Emily blinked in disconcertion. Duarte was neither in the habit of phoning her during his working day nor of inviting her to meet him for lunch.

'I have something to tell you,' he murmured tautly.

A woman who drove him to smashing locked doors open was *not* for him. He regretted bringing her back to Portugal, recognised his mistake. No, more probably he planned to tell her that he had met someone else. Slow, agonised tears started trekking down her cheeks.

'Emily?' he prompted. 'I'll send a car for you. Please come.'

He rang off without another word. She went upstairs to see if the more dressy clothes which she had left behind when they separated were still intact in the room she had once occupied. They were. She fingered through the many options available. Cerise pink, fire-engine red, fluorescent orange, traffic-stopping purple. Picking the jazzy pink which hurt her aching eyes, she got changed. He was going to dump her again. She *knew* he was. Last night, he had more or less said right out how hard he had had to push himself to go to bed with her again. Mind you, at the time, he'd *seemed* fairly enthusiastic!

The car ferried her the thirty-odd kilometres into Lisbon. Duarte had a superb apartment on the Avenida da Libertade and, as she ascended from the car in the long tree-lined boulevard, sick butterflies were dancing in her tummy.

Ushered into the imposing drawing room where she'd once fallen ingloriously asleep during a supper with his friends, following an evening at the opera, she focused on Duarte. Her heart started behaving as if someone was playing football with it and her mouth ran dry.

Poised by one of the tall nineteenth-century windows, black hair gleaming in the sunlight, his elegant light-grey pinstripe suit cut to fit his broad shoulders and long powerful thighs, Duarte looked absolutely spectacular. Studying those lean, darkly handsome features of his and hurriedly evading those all-seeing, all-knowing, stunning golden eyes, she ran out of breath. Suddenly, all she could think about was the passion of the night hours and all she could feel was the intimate ache that still lingered at the core of her own body as a result.

'Thank you for coming,' Duarte said with grave quietness.

'I'd never have the nerve to stand you up,' Emily confided, her fingers biting so hard into the clutch purse she was holding that her hands were hurting. 'Where are we going for lunch?'

'I thought we could eat here.'

Instantly, she felt trapped. True, a public place was hardly suitable for the delivery of any revelation likely to *upset*. But couldn't he just have waited until he came home for dinner? Instead, she'd been summoned like a schoolgirl to hear her fate and that felt distinctly humiliating.

'Do I have to eat?' she enquired brittlely. 'I'm not hungry.'

'As you wish. Would you like a drink?'

'A brandy…' She glanced at him while he dealt with her request, seeing the tension etched in the hard cast of his bronzed profile. The atmosphere was so strained, she felt an unwary word might snap it in two.

Sitting down on the edge of an opulent antique sofa, she sipped nervously at the brandy.

'This morning, Victorine admitted that she'd deliberately mislead me about what you said to her—'

'I know. She also spoke to me and apologised,' Emily responded.

Duarte paced forward from the window and moved his hands in a very expressive gesture of regret. 'I misjudged you and I owe you a very big apology for I have never known you to be cruel.'

Emily shrugged jerkily, unable to reap the smallest satisfaction from that acknowledgement. 'It was just another metaphoric stick to beat me with, wasn't it?'

Dulled colour rose to accentuate the strong slant of his high cheekbones. 'You may be right. However, when my former mother-in-law then went on to confess that she'd resented you from the very hour that I married you, I was very much shocked.'

Surprised though Emily was that Victorine had gone that far in her need to ease her conscience, Emily simply sighed. She was more concerned about what he might have to say next.

'I was foolish to believe that Victorine would easily accept another woman as my wife,' Duarte stated with a harshened edge to his dark, deep drawl. 'Had I not had a board meeting early this morning, I would've come to speak to you immediately.'

'Well, business first and last,' Emily breathed helplessly. 'There's nothing new in that.'

'No…but I think today business came first because it was easier to handle,' Duarte conceded, startling her with that frank admission. 'Naturally I feel guilty. Our home should have been the one place where you could feel relaxed and content but Victorine's spite must've made you very unhappy.'

Emily felt like a stone. Old resentments and bitterness had hardened her usually soft heart. 'I always blamed *you* more than I blamed her…'

Duarte's golden eyes zeroed in on her and narrowed. The taut set of his jawline revealed his surprise at that condemnation. 'But you never once complained about Victorine—'

'And why would I have?' Emily got up in a sudden movement, powered by angry defensiveness at that suggestion that she ought to have spoken up sooner. 'Why would I have thought that complaining would have got me anywhere with you? After all, you are not the world's most sensitive person either, are you?'

A sardonic black brow quirked. 'Meaning?'

'Those portraits of Izabel in the salon, the dining room and the main hall…' Emily illuminated tightly. 'I could've understood that if you'd had children with her but you didn't. How was I supposed to feel that the Quinta de Monteiro was *my* home?'

Duarte was studying her with frowning intensity but a faint perceptible pallor was spreading round his taut mouth. 'I never *thought*…I was so used to them being there—'

'Well, you know…your first wife may have been a great beauty and the paintings may be wonderful art, but you should've had them moved to less prominent places. I felt intimidated by them. And although I'm not terribly interested or indeed gifted in any way at fancy interior design and stuff like that,' Emily admitted flatly, 'I would've appreciated the freedom to redecorate just one room and feel that it, at least, was mine.'

Every bone in Duarte's lean dark devastating face was rigid by the time she had finished speaking. 'I cannot excuse myself for my lack of sensitivity.'

'No, you can't,' Emily agreed with very little in the way of satisfaction. Then nothing he said could touch or ease the hard knot of pain inside her. Even while she railed at him, she was thinking how pointless her reproaches were. Those oversights had merely spelt out his basic indifference to her feelings. He'd never been in love with her and only a man in love would have considered such things. But she'd said enough, knew that if she said anything more, he might realise just how jealous she'd been of his first wife. Not very nice, she reflected guiltily. Izabel had proved to be an impossible act to follow.

'It's all water under the bridge now.' Emily drew in a slow steadying breath, for she knew exactly what she needed to find peace of mind—her freedom. Freedom from such demeaning comparisons between herself and a dead woman. Freedom from wanting the love she could never have because that wanting was self-destructive. 'So, before you start telling me things you would much prefer not to tell me, *I* have something to say.'

'You have my full attention,' Duarte drawled in the most insidiously discouraging way.

'How do you do that?' Emily found herself asking. 'How do you manage always to make me feel that I shouldn't say what I'm about to say? I mean, you don't even *know* what I'm about to say!'

Duarte reached for her tense hands and unlaced them to hold her taut fingers in his. A bleak look had darkened his amazing eyes to a midnight glimmer of light as he gazed down at her. 'I'm not planning to smash any more doors down, *minha esposa*. Is that what is worrying you?'

The warmth of his hands on hers was a subtle enticement, as was the endearment. Pinned to the spot by those brilliant, dark, sexy eyes of his, she shivered, every tiny muscle she possessed tensing. That close, she could feel the heat of his lean powerful body, smell the evocative scent of him, composed of warm male laced with a faint hint of some exotic aftershave. All so familiar, all so devastatingly familiar that her senses reacted to him no matter what she did.

'I'm sorry if I frightened you. I lost control of my temper but it will not happen again,' Duarte intoned huskily, the very sound of his dark, deep voice setting up a quiver at the base of her spine.

'Stop it...' Emily urged shakily, desperately seeking to muster her defences against that wholly seductive onslaught of sensations.

'Stop...*what*?' Duarte probed with a sincere incomprehension that infuriated her.

Her teeth gritted behind her compressed lips. She saw just how weak she was. It seemed she never learnt where he was concerned. He got close and her brain seemed to go into free fall—and yet he was still being cool and precise and he was not deliberately striving to set her wretched body alight. That knowledge just made her feel so horribly humiliated by her own lack of control that she dragged her hands free of his and stepped back.

'What's wrong?' Duarte murmured levelly. 'Are you still angry with me?'

Angry? Was she *still* angry? Mulling over that question, Emily conceded that she'd started being angry with Duarte within weeks of marrying him. Even while loving him to distraction, she'd been angry from the instant she laid her devastated eyes on Izabel's gorgeous photogenic face. Angry because she wasn't loved the same way, angry that her only value to him seemed to lie in supplying him with the child he wanted but angrier still that she was so hopelessly and helplessly obsessed with a man who neither needed nor loved her. In one way or another, she'd been made painfully conscious of that reality almost every day of their marriage.

'There's nothing wrong...' Emily said, not quite levelly. 'I just want a divorce.'

Duarte stilled the way people did when they got an entirely unexpected response. 'And you don't think that comes under the heading of there being something wrong?'

'Right now...' Emily breathed, colour highlighting her heart-shaped face, 'I do not want you getting clever with me.'

'Clever...' Duarte flung his proud, dark head back.

Her fingers coiled into fists by her side as she forced herself on. 'I told you yesterday...I told you I didn't want to be your wife anymore—'

'Last night...' Duarte trailed out those two words until she felt like her face was burning, 'you gave me a rather different message.'

'I didn't know what was going on last night. I wasn't myself,' Emily stated between compressed lips of mortification. 'But that mistake is not going to make me change my mind about what's best for me—'

'Jamie?' Duarte slotted in, smooth as a stiletto.

Emily paled. 'I'm willing to live in Portugal so that you can see as much of Jamie as you like—'

'All right, you move out and I keep Jamie.'

Emily's lower lip parted company with her upper in sheer shock.

'Now I wonder why you aren't into that solution when it is only the reverse of what you are suggesting that *I* should accept,' Duarte pointed out without remorse. 'Only twenty-four hours after I get to meet my son, you want to deprive me of him again and you somehow expect me to be cool about it?'

'All right, you're making me feel horrible…' Emily muttered, unable to avoid seeing the unlovely comparison he'd put before her. 'But feeling as you do about me, you have no right to expect me to live with you just for Jamie's sake.'

'Haven't I? You were perfectly happy last night until I blew it,' Duarte reminded her without hesitation. 'Now, had you said then that you could not bear me to touch you, I would have agreed that at the very least we should separate.'

Emily caught on fast to that argument. Hugely aware that he could talk semantic circles round her and tie her into knots to the extent that she would soon not know where she was in the dialogue, she grasped hurriedly at the get-out clause he had put before her. 'Well, I'm saying it *now*. I can't bear for you to touch me!'

'Where do you get the nerve to say that to me?' Duarte derided, reacting to that statement with a level of incredulity that was seriously embarrassing.

Flushed to the roots of her red-gold hair, Emily backed off several steps. 'I'm not taking back a word of it…'

Like a leopard on the prowl, Duarte followed her retreat.

'I don't have to justify wanting a divorce—'

'Yes, you do,' Duarte overruled with infuriating logic.

'OK...' Trapped between the wall and Duarte's lean powerful physique, Emily came to a halt with her shoulderblades up hard against the plaster. 'When I married you, I was too young to know what I was doing. You took advantage of the fact that I was in love with you. I had a lousy hole-in-the-corner wedding and I didn't even get a honeymoon!'

Duarte elevated a winged black brow with pronounced disbelief. 'That's...*it*?'

'That's only to *begin* with!' Emily slung, her temper firing up fast at his refusal to take her seriously. 'Then you brought me home to a house ruled by your ex-mother-in-law, who hated me on sight. After that, you hardly bothered to notice that I was alive—'

A charismatic smile began to form on Duarte's wide, sensual mouth. 'I seem to recall noticing that you were alive so often and with such frequency that I once fell asleep in a board meeting!'

Chagrinned by that literal interpretation of her words, Emily changed tack to suit that line of argument as well. 'So you *admit* that all you ever shared with me was a bed—'

'If you wanted to share the board meetings too, you should have mentioned it.'

Pure rage filled Emily. 'When I phoned you during the day, you never once returned my calls!'

Duarte frowned. 'What calls?'

'I daresay there was a time or two when you were much too busy to speak to me but there is just no excuse for you never once phoning me back—'

'I never refused a call of yours in my life,' Duarte interrupted with a palpable edge of masculine annoyance. 'I have better manners. We Portuguese are not so taken up with business that we overlook either courtesy or family during working hours.'

'Well, I was overlooked time and time again until I got the message!' Emily raked back at him in a growing fury at her inability to make any charge stick and draw blood. 'And where were your precious manners when you failed to turn up for the dinner parties I arranged in my deadly boring, dutiful role of being your wife?'

'Again you are making false accusations, not one of which you have ever mentioned before,' Duarte condemned with chilling bite. 'Where is all this nonsense coming from and why have you wandered from the point?'

'*My* point is—' Emily stabbed the air between them with a raised hand and, even in the grip of her temper, was rather pleased with the effect.

Without warning, Duarte moved forward and brought his hands up to plant them on either side of her startled face, long fingers meshing into the strands of her fiery hair. Shimmering golden eyes that had the flashfire charge of lightning clashed with hers. '*Your* point is non-existent or else you might have said something worth listening to by now,' he grated rawly, half under his breath, as he gazed down at her. 'I asked you here so that we could talk in private and I could express my regrets for my behaviour last night. But you have refused to listen. Instead you have done nothing but sling lies at me!'

'Lies…?' Intimidated in a very physical way by the manner in which he had her cornered, Emily was nonetheless conscious of a sudden maddening and truly insane need for him to touch her in exactly the way she had told him minutes earlier that she could not *bear* to be touched.

'Desire is not a one-way street. I know when I am wanted by a woman,' Duarte spelt out in the same dark dangerous undertone that was playing merry hell with her awakened senses.

'Really? Absolutely always?' Emily framed doggedly but no longer quite sure of what she was saying and why.

Other reactions were taking over at mind-bending speed: the steady acceleration of her heartbeat, an alarming shortness of breath, a sensation of exhilaration and awareness so intense it was like standing on a razor edge.

Duarte laced his hand into a whole hank of fiery redgold strands to hold her fast and then he brought his hot hard mouth crashing down on hers. Fire in the hold, she thought crazily, every inch of her jolted by the surge of wild excitement charging her. He dropped his hands and inched up the skirt of her dress, long sure fingers gliding up over her slender thighs with a knowing eroticism that only added fuel to her response.

She was shaking, clinging to him. She did not know how or when her hands had crept up to grip his wide shoulders but only by holding on to him was she staying upright. With a sudden hungry groan, Duarte cupped his hands to her hips and lifted her against him, pushing her back against the wall, letting her feel the full force of his arousal. Any grip Emily had on reality vanished at that point.

She heard herself moan under his marauding mouth like an animal. With every invasive stab of his tongue he mimicked a infinitely more primal possession and stoked her desire to more electrifying heights.

'Duarte… Please,' she gasped.

'Please what?' Duarte probed huskily, pushing her thighs further apart, letting his expert fingers linger within inches of the throbbing core of her shivering body.

'You're torturing me!'

Duarte let her slide down the wall on to her own feet again and one of her shoes had fallen off, making her blink in confusion at the lopsided effect of her own stance.

'If I was a real bastard, I'd make you beg,' Duarte spelt out in a roughened undertone, spectacular golden eyes scorching over her as she struggled somewhat belatedly to haul her dress back down from her waist. 'But I'm far too excited to deny myself that long!'

'What are you *doing*?' Emily squeaked as he swept her up into his arms with more haste than ceremony.

'Emily…' Duarte groaned as he strode out of the drawing room and down the corridor towards the bedrooms. 'What do you *think* I'm doing?'

CHAPTER SEVEN

'BUT we were talking about getting a divorce!' Emily protested, sufficiently reanimated by the change of surroundings to say what she should have said five minutes sooner.

'Correction, *you* were talking on that subject. When you can put up some convincing resistance to my advances, I'll consider talking about it,' Duarte proffered with a wolfish and very male downward glance of challenge.

'I am not getting into bed with you again… It would be wrong!' Emily argued frantically as she shouldered open the door in a luxurious bedroom.

'Wrong at this juncture would be playing the tease and why should you want to?' Duarte enquired, lowering her to the carpet, bending down to pluck off the remaining shoe she wore so that she could stand normally and then spinning her round to unzip her dress.

As he spun her back like a doll and gave the sleeves of the garment a helpful tug to assist it on its downward journey, Emily stood as though transfixed. 'Duarte…I'm being serious—'

'So am I,' he swore, watching the dress slide down with satisfaction and shrugging out of his beautifully tailored jacket to let it fall on the carpet as well. 'I want you. Here. Now. Fast…'

'But you haven't even told me yet what you brought me to tell me…' her voice faltered and trailed away altogether as she thought of that 'here…now…fast' bit he had threatened and a truly unforgivable dart of liquid heat forced her to lock her knees together.

'I've done all the talking I want to do for one day. I've

apologised. I've owned up to gross insensitivity. You were as receptive as a rock-face but you didn't complain about anything I can't fix,' Duarte asserted on a very single-minded tack as he shed his tie and wrenched at his shirt with pronounced impatience.

'All right, I was lying when I said I didn't want you to touch me,' Emily owned up in desperation. 'But please keep your shirt on. If you take it off, I'm lost.'

Momentarily, Duarte paused and cast her a gleaming glance of vibrant amusement. He slid out of the shirt with the fluid grace of a matador in the bull ring. 'This is one battle you're destined to lose—'

'But I can't… We can't. This…*this* is not the answer!' Emily surveyed him with guilt-stricken intensity as he stood there poised, all hair-roughened bronzed skin and lean hard muscle. Him looking like a Greek god was not exactly the biggest help she'd ever received in her belief that she had to put a lid on what was happening between them.

'Isn't it?' Duarte reached out and hauled her into his arms, smouldering dark gaze roaming over the rise and fall of her breasts. He unclipped the bra, found a pouting swell of tormentingly sensitive flesh and rubbed his thumb over the throbbing tip. 'I want you so much I'm in agony…'

She leant into him even though she tried to stop herself. She could feel the same want mounting like a hungry, conscience-free flood inside her. Last night might never have happened. She was shocked at the strength of her own yearning, shocked by the overpowering surge of excitement awakened by the sight of his lean hand cupping her breast.

'This is what we need now, *minha esposa*,' Duarte asserted, pulling into him and lifting her to bring her down on the side of the elegant sleigh bed. 'Talking is too dangerous. Talking when there is no solution is just stupid.'

Hearing those sentiments pronounced with such unquenchable masculine conviction should have sent her leaping from his arms in angry frustration. But he was arranging her on the bed with the care of a male about to extract the utmost from the experience and she could not take her eyes from his. Dear heaven, those wonderful eyes. He just had to look at her and her own thoughts just dwindled and yet somehow she felt secure about that, safe. That was all wrong and she knew it was but when Duarte loomed over her like every fantasy she'd ever had, self-control was not an option her overheated body wanted to consider.

'Talking is supposed to *be* the solution,' she murmured in a last attempt to place head over heart.

'It put us in separate beds last night. It made me kick in a door. You think that's healthy?' Duarte challenged as he stripped down to a pair of black silk boxer shorts that were the very last word in sexy apparel. 'No, my way is better.'

My way is better. Not exactly the last word in compromise, was he? But she gazed up at him and the most enormous swell of love surged through her and, all of a sudden, nothing else mattered.

'Once, you used to look at me like that all the time.' Duarte came down on the bed like a predator, taking his time, and a helpless little shiver of anticipation rippled through her taut and restive limbs. 'I became accustomed to it…'

Most men would be pretty content to be uncritically adored by their wives, Emily reflected. And the ironic truth was, while she'd remained content to settle for less on her own behalf, she had been happier. Whether he knew it or not, the wild card that had upset the balance had been the very unsettling discovery that he had loved Izabel. No, nobody had told her that; even at her worst, Victorine hadn't been that cruel. She had seen it in that wedding photograph of Izabel and Duarte together, the love, pride and satisfaction he had had in his acquisition of his beautiful bride.

'I want it back,' Duarte said lazily and he pressed his wide, sensual mouth to the tiny pulse below her ear, a sensitive spot that seemed to overreact with blinding enthusiasm and sent her momentarily haywire with hunger.

Gasping for breath and trying to sound cool, Emily looked up at him and trying to sound dry but actually sounding very stressed, she said, 'I don't do adoration any more. I grew up.'

Duarte let a provocative hand roam over her distended nipples and her back arched as if he had burned her. 'But you can regress,' he murmured smooth as silk.

Regressing felt so darned good, she thought helplessly. He pushed her flat again with a husky laugh of amusement and lowered his carnal mouth to her tingling breasts where he turned torment into a new art form. Control evaporated about there for Emily. Her body was all liquid burning heat powered by a hunger that was steadily overwhelming her.

'You want me?' Duarte demanded, fierce control etched in his dark features.

'Now…' she begged.

He spread her thighs like a Viking invader set on sexual plunder and it still wasn't fast enough for her. He came over her, into her, in a shocking surge of primal male power and she almost passed out at the wave of intense pleasure.

'You feel like hot silk,' he groaned with raw sensual appreciation, plunging deeper still.

And from then on in, she gave herself up to voluptuous abandonment. The hot sweet pleasure just took over and she could only breathe in short agonised gasps. In the steely grip of that mounting excitement, her heart thundering, her blood racing like wildfire through her veins, she whimpered and arched her hips to invite his urgent thrusts. She cried out at the peak of a climax of breathtaking power, her entire body wrenched into the explosive hold of that erotic release.

Afterwards, it was like coming back to life after a long time somewhere else. Where else, Emily could not have specified at that precise moment, but it didn't seem to matter for she felt this glorious sense of unquestioning contentment and delight. Her needs felt few; she was with Duarte and Duarte was with her. Life felt wonderful.

Duarte rolled over, carrying her with him, and gazed down at her passion-stunned face with brilliant golden eyes of satisfaction. 'I think that settles the divorce question for the foreseeable future.'

Disorientated by that sudden descent to the prosaic and the provocative when her own brain was still floating in euphoric clouds, she blinked and stared up at him. Duarte pushed her head down into his shoulder, dropped what felt like a kiss on the crown of her head and held her close in silence.

'Duarte?' she mumbled, trying to ground her brain and focus.

'I'm going over to London on business next week. You and Jamie can come and we'll visit your family…OK?'

Thrown by that suggestion, Emily began to lift her head.

'I was bloody furious when I discovered you'd gone there and they'd thrown you out again,' Duarte stated, startling her even more, his strong jawline clenching. 'Not very sympathetic, were they?'

Emily had paled. 'I hadn't got around to telling them about us being separated…or anything else,' she mumbled, shrinking from any mention of that episode with Toby. 'Mum and Dad just didn't think it was right that I had left you and they probably thought that showing me the door again would send me back to Portugal more quickly.'

'Or maybe they thought that helping you might offend *me*,' Duarte drawled very quietly. 'And that if they offended me, I might not be just so generous in putting new business in the way of the family firm. Have you even considered that angle?'

Emily regarded him with shaken reproach. 'Is that how you think of my family? That's an *awful* thing to suggest!'

'I'm an appalling cynic but, obviously, you would know your own flesh and blood best...' Duarte murmured, relieving her with the ease with which he made that concession.

Emily relaxed again.

'It's just that most parents would think twice before they threw a married, very pregnant and distressed daughter back out into the snow,' Duarte continued, dismaying her with his persistence. 'They also took my side. They didn't even *know* what my side was but they took it all the same—'

'People don't always react the way you expect them to...especially when you take them by surprise, as I did,' Emily pointed out defensively.

'I can certainly second that.'

He didn't like her parents. Why had she never realised that before? Emily lay there in his arms, forced to reluctantly concede that, if anything, the emotional distance between her and her parents had only grown since her marriage and had been almost severed altogether when she turned up on the doorstep without her husband in tow eight months earlier. Her family had visited her only once in Portugal. Although Emily had bent over backwards to ensure their every comfort and provide every possible entertainment, true enjoyment had seemed to elude her relatives. Her mother and her sisters had seemed to band together in a trio of constant criticism which had made Emily feel about an inch high. The couple of invitations she had made after that had been turned down with no great effort devoted to polite excuses.

'Let's have lunch and then go home and spend the rest

of the day with Jamie,' Duarte suggested, taking her mind off her regret over her uneasy relationship with the family she loved.

'That's a lovely idea,' she said warmly.

Only then did it cross her mind that she'd come to the city apartment expecting to hear some ghastly revelation that had never transpired. Desperate to conserve her own pride, she'd started rambling on about getting a divorce when a divorce was probably the very last thing in the world that she wanted. Sometimes, she worked herself up into such a state, she acknowledged shame-facedly. Duarte had made passionate love to her twice in twenty-four hours. Was that the behaviour of a man interested in another woman? And wouldn't she have made the biggest mistake of her life in saying no? They had achieved a closeness that had entirely eluded them the night before.

They lunched in the elegant dining room and were just finishing their coffee prior to departing when the door opened without any warning and Bliss strolled in carrying a document case.

'I'm sorry, Duarte. I didn't realise that your wife was here. Mrs Monteiro…'

'Miss Jarrett,' Emily muttered, barely able to look at the blonde after the unpleasantness of their meeting earlier in the day.

But Duarte was already rising from his chair, his charismatic smile lighting up his darkly handsome features. 'My apologies, Bliss. I changed my plans and neglected to inform you.'

A dewy smile free of her usual mockery fixed to her exquisite face, Bliss sighed softly, 'I really ought to be used to that by now.'

'I'm going home for the rest of the day.'

Emily watched the little tableau playing out in front of her with wide eyes of disconcertion. She saw Duarte stride to greet Bliss and receive the document case rather than wait for her to come to him as he once would have done. Duarte was, as a rule, formal with his employees and ungiven to addressing them by their first names. When had he decided to relax his formidable reserve with Bliss?

'I'll see you out,' Duarte assured Bliss.

As they left the room together, Emily sat like a stone in her chair for several seconds. Just when had such a staggering change taken place in Duarte's relationship with his executive assistant? Unable to sit still, she found herself getting up and walking restively over to the window. She recalled Bliss's low soft voice, a tone she'd never heard the blonde employ before and she'd never seen her smile like that either, like an infinitely more feminine version of the harder-edged Bliss she herself had got to know. Out of nowhere, a tension headache settled round Emily's temples like a tightening circle of steel. Thump, thump, thump was her body's enervated response to the mental alarm bell going off at shrieking decibels inside her head.

Duarte and Bliss? Were her suspicions insane? Was she even thinking straight? But hadn't Bliss carefully ended their friendship only a few hours earlier? Hadn't Bliss made it clear that her sympathies now lay squarely with Duarte? And, finally, hadn't Bliss venomously pointed out that Duarte might already have another woman in his life?

Was Bliss that other woman? Her tummy churning at the very thought of such a development, Emily struggled to get a grip on her flailing emotions. She felt like a truck had run over her. She felt cold inside and out. Why shouldn't Duarte be attracted to Bliss? Bliss was beautiful and witty and clever. Bliss was exactly the kind of wife Duarte should have picked to replace Izabel. Was he sleeping with her? *Had* he slept with her? Exactly when had his relationship with his executive assistant become so familiar that he smiled at her like that? Smiled with warmth and approval and intimacy?

Was she crazy to be thinking these kind of thoughts? There they were, calling each other by their first names and exchanging smiles, and suddenly she had them tucked up in bed together? She was not going to leap in and say anything to Duarte. She was *not*. Any such questions would be very much resented.

And while she stood there, fighting to put a lid on her emotional turmoil, she found herself thinking back to her friendship with Bliss Jarrett. Within months of her marriage to a male who worked very long hours, Emily had become very lonely. Although she'd been dragged out everywhere by Victorine on social visits and had met several women whom she might have become friendly with, the language barrier had reigned supreme. She'd met very few people who spoke fluent English and it had taken her a long time to master even the basics of Portuguese.

When she had phoned Duarte's office, she had always been put through to Bliss. She would leave a message with Bliss but Duarte would never call back. Once or twice in those early days, she had phoned just to check that her message had been passed on to him. With an audible suggestion of embarrassed sympathy on Emily's behalf, Bliss would gently assure her that her husband had received the message.

Eventually they had begun chatting and Emily had confided that she hated shopping alone. Bliss had offered to accompany her and then hastily retracted the suggestion with the apologetic explanation that Duarte would not approve of his wife socialising with a mere employee. Desperate for company, Emily had pointed out that what Duarte didn't know wouldn't hurt him.

And so the friendship that she had valued had begun, a friendship that was a breath of fresh air to someone as lonely and insecure as she had been then. Shopping trips, lunches and, on several occasions when Duarte was abroad on business, Bliss had invited her to her apartment for a meal. There she had met Toby and there she had come up with the stupid childish plan to have her portrait painted in the forlorn hope of displacing an image of Izabel from even one wall of the *quinta*.

'Are you ready?' Duarte asked from the dining room doorway, making her jerk and return to the present.

Emily breathed in deep, steadying herself. She would make no comment; she would say nothing. There was probably nothing whatsoever in what she had seen. It was only her own insecurity playing tricks on her imagination. Crazily she pictured herself standing up at a divorce hearing and saying 'Duarte *smiled* at her…that's my evidence.'

In the lift that took them down to the ground floor, Emily stole a glance that spread and lingered to encompass every visible inch of her tall, dark and absolutely gorgeous husband. She loved him. They were back together…weren't they? He was making an effort to repair the great yawning cracks in their marriage, wasn't he? So what if most of the effort he was putting in was bedroom-orientated? Did that matter? Did that make him less committed? Had he *ever* been committed to her?

Engaged in such frantic and feverish thoughts, Emily tripped over a metal bin to the side of the exit, skidded across the floor and came down on her bottom.

'Meu Deus!' Duarte exclaimed and immediately reached for her to help her to her feet again. 'Are you all right?'

'So…s-so,' she stammered, refusing to massage the throbbing ache assailing her bruised hip.

'Didn't you see it?' Smoothing her down, Duarte focused on the bin which was about four feet tall and hard to miss.

Emily clambered into the limousine on wobbly legs. She would keep her tongue between her teeth for the whole drive home. Just then, she recalled that odd little scene she had witnessed at the airport between Duarte and Bliss. The way he had taken a few extra minutes to speak to Bliss in private before joining Emily in the car, the tension she'd witnessed between them. What had he been saying to Bliss to make her freeze and turn red? Exactly how intimate were they?

'When did you get so friendly with Bliss Jarrett?' That demand just erupted out of Emily's mouth and she was horrified at herself, at the clumsiness of that leading question, not to mention its undeniably accusing tone.

There was one of those truly awful laden silences.

Duarte elevated a sardonic brow and his spiky black lashes partially screened his dark deepset gaze. 'I don't think that's a subject we should open.'

What the heck was that supposed to mean? An evasive response was the very last thing she needed, in the mood she was in, but she really did try very hard to let the subject stay closed. She bit down on her tongue so hard, she tasted her own blood. She told herself that she ought to trust him but, the trouble was, she knew she no longer trusted Bliss. And even though Duarte was emanating sufficient vibes to warn her off, she ignored them.

'It's natural for me to be curious.'

'I'm not sure that you'll be grateful for my explanation. Bliss was very embarrassed when she realised that you had had an affair with her cousin and she offered to resign,' Duarte advanced in a glacial tone.

'Did she really?' Emily whispered shakily, feeling like he had just dropped a giant suffocating rock on top of her.

'After those developments, it would have been a little difficult for us to return to our former working relationship as though nothing had happened. I have great respect for Bliss both as an employee and a personal friend. I would appreciate it if you would keep that fact in mind.'

'I'm not really sure what you're saying,' Emily mumbled although she was dreadfully afraid that she did. She was also horribly tempted to say that, in terms of personal friendship, Bliss spread herself around behind other people's backs, but it sounded mean and petty and she stopped herself just in time.

Duarte angled his proud dark head back and viewed her with chilling dark eyes without the smallest shade of warmer gold. 'You have no right to question me. You had an affair. You broke up our marriage. You then vanished and it was seven months before an investigator even picked up on your trail—'

'Duarte...' she broke in jaggedly, her voice breaking under that onslaught.

'Throughout those months I didn't know whether you were dead or alive or even whether or not I *was* actually a father. It was a very difficult time for me. During that period, Bliss became something more than just an employee—she became a supportive friend.' His beautiful dark eyes were like a card-player's eyes, remote, cool, but disturbingly challenging.

She wanted to kill him. Then she wanted to strangle herself. He was telling her the cruellest thing. He was telling her that her own behaviour, her stupid immature vanishing act and all those months of silence had laid the foundations of what he termed a 'friendship'. Was he telling her that Bliss was his mistress and that he wasn't giving her up? And was it unjust and melodramatic of her to suspect that Bliss might have a far more ambitious agenda than mere friendship in mind? Hadn't Bliss frightened Emily into leaving Portugal and then made use of that opportunity to increase her own standing with Duarte? Or was, Emily asked herself, she trying to justify her *own* mistakes and blame Bliss for the fall-out?

At that point what felt like the last piece of a bewildering puzzle seemed to fall into dismaying place and Emily stared at Duarte in sudden horror. 'Bliss is that third party you mentioned, *isn't* she? That discreet person who confirmed that I was carrying on with Toby when I *wasn't*—'

'I won't dignify that accusation with an answer,' Duarte countered drily.

It was as if he was slamming a door in her face without conscience. She wanted to ask him how intimate his relationship with Bliss had become but was not entirely sure she could stand to hear an honest answer at that moment. He would not feel that he had to defend himself. After all, didn't he believe that she had betrayed him with Toby first? She could feel his anger, contained but always there between them, awakened by the reminder of her supposed affair, his attitude hardened by the manner in which she had questioned him about Bliss.

'Tell me,' she muttered dry-mouthed, feeling that no matter where she turned she was in a no-win situation and always in the wrong, 'would you even have considered bringing me back to Portugal had I not had Jamie?'

'The jury's still very much out on that one,' Duarte drawled with freezing cool. 'Right now, I'm changing direction like a metronome.'

Neither of them said another word for the remainder of the drive back to the *quinta*.

After they arrived Duarte strode off with the terse explanation that he had an important call to make, Emily went upstairs to fetch Jamie and scooped him out of his cot with eager hands. After stopping for a chat with the nanny and discussing at some length the reality that her son needed more clothes, she cuddled Jamie all the way down to the ground floor again. There she set him on a rug in the salon to talk to him.

'Your father doesn't like me very much right now but that's OK,' Emily informed her six-month-old son with a rather wooden bright smile, destined to reassure him that she really wasn't sad. 'I'm just warning you that whenever you do anything stupid, it will come back and haunt you for a good hundred years. It will smack you in the face at every turn and leave you feeling awful—'

'I think you're taxing his concentration span...' Duarte murmured from somewhere behind her at the same time as she noticed that Jamie was kicking his feet and demonstrating definite signs of excited welcome at the approach of someone he liked.

'I didn't know you were there!' Emily was seriously rattled by his appearance.

'Put on the fake smile again. Jamie's not very discerning.' Duarte hunkered down by her side to grasp their son's extended chubby fingers. 'He wouldn't know a pity-fest from a celebration.'

'If that's supposed to make me feel better—'

'No...but *this* is...' Anchoring one powerful hand into her tumbling hair, Duarte tugged her head around and captured her startled lips under his. Instinctively, she began to tip towards him. That slow-burning kiss awakened a bone-deep yearning inside her for the pure reassurance of physical contact and acceptance.

And then something funny happened. Her memory threw up a perfect recollection of his last words before they vacated the car. Just as quickly, she found herself pulling back from him for the first time in her life and she caught the flash of surprise in his stunning gaze before he veiled it.

'If I'm only here for Jamie's benefit, we'd better not stretch me too thin,' she said tightly.

Duarte reached forward and lifted their son with the same carefulness he might have utilised in handling a bomb. And her heart twisted because she knew it was her fault that he was still afraid of being rejected by Jamie. Emily being

Emily, she then felt immediately horrible for not allowing Duarte to kiss her as much as he wanted to.

'Victorine tells me that you invited her to stay on,' Duarte murmured while he struggled to get Jamie into a comfortable position on one raised, lean, powerful thigh. 'In the circumstances that was extremely generous of you. However, she's asked me if she can move into a house on the outskirts of the estate which is currently unoccupied. I've agreed.'

'With me in charge, prepare yourself for a sudden slump in staff efficiency,' Emily told him apprehensively.

'If there's a problem, you come to me and I will deal with it.'

Meanwhile Jamie chortled and dug delighted hands into Duarte's luxuriant black hair and pulled hard.

'He's not scared of me any more,' Duarte breathed with a sudden grin.

Duarte took Jamie upstairs to the picture gallery which was lined with distinctly gloomy canvases of Monteiro ancestors and gave their infant son a potted history of the family with a perfectly straight face.

'Don't you think he's just a little young for this?' Emily remarked.

'This is our family. Nothing comes before family. Not business, not anything,' Duarte imparted with considerable gravity. 'My earliest memory is of my father bringing me here and telling me what it means to be a Monteiro.'

Not noticeably impressed, Jamie went to sleep draped over Duarte's shoulder. When Emily came back downstairs from settling their son for a nap, three estate workers were engaged in removing Izabel's giant portrait from the wall in the salon. The whole room would have to be redecorated. She wondered where the painting was going, looked at that gorgeous sultry face and sighed to herself. For so long, she had tormented herself with pointless comparisons between herself and Duarte's first wife. Now she was receiving what would seem to be her just reward. She now had live competition that struck her as much more threatening.

Nothing comes before family, Duarte had stated with unequivocal conviction. Finally he had answered that loaded question she had shot at him in the car. Jamie came first, so therefore Jamie's needs would take priority over more personal inclinations and mothers were not interchangeable. But where did Bliss fit into that picture?

That night she lay in her bed watching the door which had been expertly repaired stay resolutely closed. She was not one whit surprised. Duarte had been angry when she turned away from him during that kiss. Duarte would sooner burn alive than give her a second such opportunity. He was so damnably proud and stubborn.

So there you are, once again you did the wrong thing, Emily told herself wretchedly. Here she was worrying that the man she loved might be, at the very least, seriously attracted to a woman who was on convenient call for him throughout his working day. And what had Emily done? Angry with him, striving to protect her own pride, she had rejected him and she could not have picked a worse time to do it...

CHAPTER EIGHT

FIVE days later, on the afternoon of the party which Bliss had organised, Emily was fiddling in desperation with a vast floral arrangement in the main hall.

Victorine had been creative with flowers. Emily was not. In spite of all her efforts, the blooms looked like they'd been dropped from a height into the huge glass vase and persisted in standing like soldiers on parade when what she really wanted them to do was *bend*.

The past five days had been an ongoing punishment. The long-awaited removal of Izabel's portraits had left ghastly marks on the panelling in the main hall and on the wall-paper in the dining room and the salon. As there wasn't time for redecoration, she'd attempted to move the furniture around, which hadn't worked very well. In the end she'd taken paintings from other places to try and cover up the damage. At one stage she had been tearing her hair out to such an extent she had even seriously contemplated approaching Duarte and begging for Izabel's wretched portraits to be brought back from wherever they had gone...on a temporary basis. Only the prospect of his incredulity at such an astonishing request had prevented her.

Her mood was not improved by the reality that she and Duarte were existing in a state of armed neutrality in which her bedroom door stayed closed and might even be left to gather cobwebs. That was not good for her nerves. Last night she'd decided that even having it smashed down in what now seemed like true *heroic* style wouldn't make her bat an eyelash and would indeed be welcomed.

Meanwhile, Duarte was being teeth-clenchingly courteous and charming, his entire demeanour that of a male wholly untouched by anything so uncool as a desire for the smallest physical contact with his wife. She knew he would not break...at least, not in her direction. At the same time she had the dubious comfort of knowing that Bliss was rarely out of his reach. At her lowest moments, Emily wondered if he was already slaking his high sex-drive with the glamorous blonde and even if Duarte and Bliss could have been secret lovers long before Toby came into Emily's life...

Indeed, her imagination had taken her to the outer reaches of her worst nightmares. In those worst-case scenarios, Duarte figured as the biggest four-letter word on planet Earth and behaved with Machiavellian cunning and cruelty to deceive his dumb, stupid wife. Now she was finding herself recalling her own trusting friendship with Bliss's cousin, Toby Jarrett.

'It's so simple,' Bliss had laughed. 'You want Izabel's portraits out of the way, you have yourself painted and present your husband with the canvas as a gift. He is certain to take the hint.'

But Bliss had had an uphill battle persuading Emily that she was worthy of being painted. To sit for her own portrait had required a level of self-esteem that Emily did not possess. However, in the end Emily had allowed herself to be convinced and, by then, Toby had already been renting a tiny house and studio in the village below the *quinta*.

They had first met at Bliss's apartment. He'd had his girlfriend with him, a wealthy and possessive divorcée who did not trust other women within an inch of Toby's blond good looks and easy boyish charm. But Toby had never flirted with Emily when she went down to his studio for sittings. His lady friend had soon tired of superintending Emily's visits like a suspicious chaperone.

With Toby living so close to the Quinta de Monteiro,

Emily had felt it was only polite to invite him to dine with her and Duarte one evening. So she had told her first lie to Duarte and had pretended that she had just got talking to the young Englishman in the village. Prevented from revealing her friendship with Bliss, how could she possibly have told the truth? And, since she'd wanted the portrait to be a big surprise, she had had to keep her visits to Toby's studio a secret.

After a meal during which her husband and Toby seemed to radically disagree on virtually every subject under the sun, Duarte had drawled, 'Try to bury him in a larger gathering of guests if you invite him again. He's as argumentative as a rebellious teenager and, if he's such a wonderful artist, why did he drop out of his art college in England?'

Duarte had been extremely unimpressed by Toby. Emily, by then in the early stages of pregnancy and suffering from horrible morning sickness and a distinct feeling of abandonment because Duarte had not made love to her in weeks, had felt defiant. Whatever else, Toby might be, he was, in Emily's humble opinion, an incredibly talented painter. As far as she was concerned, any artist who could make her look almost beautiful was gifted beyond belief. She'd looked forward to the prospect of Duarte being forced to eat his own words.

Nobody had been more astonished than Emily that fatal night when Toby suddenly broke into an impassioned speech on the terrace beyond the salon. Telling her that he loved her, that Duarte did not deserve her, that if she ran away with him, he would cherish her forever and never neglect her as Duarte did. Since Emily had seen no warning signs of Toby falling in love with her, she'd been transfixed by shock. The most enormous self-pity had engulfed her when she appreciated that, for the very first time ever, someone was telling her that they *loved* her. Duarte, she'd thought in an agony of regret that evening, would never

ever look at her that way or speak to her as though she was some unutterably precious being whom he could not live without.

'*Meu Deus...*' Duarte breathed without the smallest warning from behind Emily.

Dredged at dismaying speed from her miserable recollections of the past, Emily turned scarlet because even *thinking* about Toby made Emily feel ultra-guilty. She spun round to find Duarte, sleek and sophisticated in a superb dark business suit, engaged in studying her floral arrangement with raised dark brows.

'Was the vase knocked over?' Duarte enquired.

Emily paled and surveyed the results of her creative efforts with tragic eyes and a sense of injustice. Bad had gone to worse. Several stems had broken beneath her too-rough handling and the blooms now hung forlorn.

'No, the vase didn't fall,' Emily admitted in a small, wooden voice devoid of any human emotion. 'I was trying to arrange the flowers.'

Beside her, she heard Duarte draw in an audible breath. 'I was looking at it from the wrong angle. It's one of those trendy displays...right?'

'Oh, shut up!' Emily launched at him, shocking him as much as she shocked herself with that outburst that rejected his face-saving excuse. She dashed a defensive hand across eyes that were now filled with stinging tears. 'It looks blasted awful and you *know* it does! I'm no good with flowers—'

'Why should you be?'

'Because other women are and I'm no good at *anything*!' Emily lamented bitterly and went racing for the stairs before she broke down altogether. On the first wide landing, she glanced back over her shoulder. Towards the back of the hall, Duarte's uniformed chauffeur, who was holding a pile of fancy-looking gift boxes, stood like a graven image.

Duarte was just staring up at her with stunned dark eyes that seemed to suggest that not only was she lousy in the feminine creativity stakes but also decidedly unhinged.

Emily fled on up the stairs like a lemming gathering speed to jump off a cliff. Why not? A night of horrible humiliation stretched before her. Playing hostess with Bliss smirking on the sidelines at her awkwardness. The even more horrendous challenge of choosing what to wear. The crazy but superstitious conviction that having her predecessor's portraits banished had been the kind of move calculated to bring serious bad luck.

Therefore, it was decidedly disorientating for Emily to race for the sanctuary of her bedroom and find the bed stripped, the wardrobe doors hanging open on empty spaces and two maids engaged on a thorough clean-up. Slowly she backed away again, only to find something or someone very solid blocking her retreat. She whirled round, trembling, shaken, bewildered by what she had just seen.

'Calm down,' Duarte spread eloquent hands in a soothing motion.

'Calm down? Where am I being moved to now? Out the front door? Or down to the cellars with the rats?'

'Let's not get totally carried away, Emily. There are no rats in the Monteiro wine cellars.' Duarte made what she considered to be a totally unnecessary contradiction.

'But there *is* one upstairs!'

Duarte frowned. 'You are joking, I hope—'

'Why are you always so literal? I'm referring to you!' she hissed in frustration.

Duarte tried to reach for her hand. She folded her arms but he was persistent. Unfolding them by the means of gentle pressure, he imprisoned one of her hands in his. Then he dragged her down the corridor, across two landings and all the way over to the other side of the house. Nothing short of thumbscrews would have squeezed a demand to know where he was taking her from Emily's mutinously compressed lips.

Duarte cast open the door of his own bedroom, indeed threw it dramatically wide. Emily stalked in, seething with so many uncontrolled emotions she was afraid she might explode.

'Now look around you,' Duarte suggested, sounding just a little taut.

Her teddy nightshirt was spread across one corner of his bed like a major statement. 'But...b-but, we've *never* shared a room—'

'Any reason why we shouldn't?'

Straying away from him, thrown into a loop by this unexpected development, Emily plucked her nightshirt off the bed, embarrassed that it had been put on show when it was so very unworthy of public display.

'Is that a...no?'

Emily shrugged and rubbed the fringe on the rug with the toe of her canvas-shod foot. But in the depths of the eyes she kept tactfully lowered lurked surprised satisfaction. Indeed, it was amazing how powerful she felt at that moment. He would have done *anything* sooner than ask up front. She could feel his tension. A non-verbal invitation to share a marital bed was quite a proclamation of intent on his part and a none-too-subtle step in the right direction. Suddenly the past five days of dreadful stress she had suffered while attempting to seem unconcerned by the divisions between them seemed very worthwhile—ultimately, *he* had come to *her*.

'It's a big bed,' Emily acknowledged softly. 'I suppose we can be as frigidly polite in that bed as we are at the dinner table.'

'OK,' he murmured with a level of cool that almost made her smile. 'By the way, I've bought you a present.'

Emily was stuffing the nightshirt into as small a ball as

possible and endeavouring to lose it discreetly by pushing it with a prodding toe below the bed. 'A...*present*?'

Duarte indicated the gilded boxes now stacked two feet high on the dressing table.

'For...*me*?' Emily hurried over to the stack to investigate with great curiosity. Never before had Duarte given her a surprise gift.

She hauled all the boxes over to the bed. The lid of the biggest one went flying and she ripped into the tissue paper and was astonished to emerge with some sort of garment. 'You bought me...something to wear?'

'For the party tonight.'

'Why would you buy me something to wear?' Emily asked in sincere bewilderment.

Duarte elbowed back his well-cut jacket and dug two lean hands into his trouser pockets and shifted a wide shoulder in an understated shrug. 'A whim...'

She shook out the incredibly tiny garment. 'But it looks like...' She bit back the tactless word, 'underwear', and studied the fine glistening fabric with wide questioning eyes.

'A dress?' he suggested.

'A...d-dress?' she stammered, striving valiantly to conceal her horror at the prospect of appearing in public with bare arms, legs on display and nothing whatsoever to draw attention away from her non-existent bosom. 'But it's too small to be a dress...'

Duarte breathed in deep.

'And it's so *pale* in colour.' A sort of delicate palest blue that was certain to make her naturally fair skin look washed-out and ghostly.

'Maybe this wasn't one of my better ideas,' Duarte remarked in a rather strained undertone.

Dear heaven, she was being so cruelly tactless! He finally made the effort to go and buy her an unexpected and personal gift and she stood around moaning about it like an ungrateful brat. If he wanted her to appear with every skinny bone accentuated, she would do so. If he wanted her to wear a dustbin bag, she would try to wear it with a smile. It was the thought which counted, not the actual gift.

With forced enthusiasm she dug into the remainder of the boxes, terrified of what other horrors awaited her. Shoes to match but so flat, she would disappear; only two-inch high heels, she noted in dismay. Lingerie fine enough to flow through the proverbial wedding ring alongside the dress but at least while she was shivering, she would be benefiting from an extra layer. An unpadded bra...how *could* he? Was nothing sacrosanct?

Strolling over, Duarte extended a large jewel case. 'Sapphires to go with the dress.'

She froze as if a spectral hand had danced down her spine. As he flipped open the case to display a gorgeous necklace and drop earrings, Emily exuded discomfiture rather than pleasure. 'Did Izabel...ever wear them?' she whispered haltingly.

'No...I have *never* asked you to wear anything worn by Izabel!' Duarte grated in a seriously rattled response.

'But I thought...you know? All that jewellery you shoved at me just after we got married...I thought it had belonged to her.'

Duarte looked heavenward as if praying for self-control. 'Izabel only ever wore diamonds and Victorine has them now. I gave you the family jewellery, not one piece of which Izabel liked.'

'Well, I wish you'd told me that a long time ago...' Emily admitted tremulously, now willing to stretch out a shy fingertip to touch the gleaming beauty of a single sapphire. For her, just for *her*. She could hardly believe it. She swallowed the great fat lump forming in her throat and blinked back tears.

'I may have my flaws but I am not *that* insensitive.'

They were talking about Izabel quite naturally, Emily registered in surprise. He was finally talking about Izabel instead of going horribly silent and bleak and avoiding the subject.

'I'm really touched that you should go to all this effort just for me,' Emily said chokily but she hoped, where the dress and the bra were concerned, he wasn't planning to make a habit of spontaneous shopping trips on her behalf.

'It's an effort that I should have made a lot sooner than this,' Duarte breathed almost harshly.

'Better late than never...' Emily mumbled, pretty much stunned by that admission of fault. She felt even guiltier that she had never worn any of the jewellery he had given her after their marriage because she'd honestly believed it had all been Izabel's. She must have seemed so ungrateful, she thought now.

She took a deep breath. 'I think I ought to admit that I've always been terribly jealous of Izabel.'

'Jealous?' Duarte awarded her a startled look.

Emily winced. 'She got the wedding dress and the honeymoon. She was so beautiful and really gifted at decorating—'

'She hired top designers—'

'And being a hostess—'

'She hired the best caterers—'

Emily frowned, for he was denting the mystic myth of Izabel and she could not understand why he should be so disloyal to her predecessor's memory. 'Obviously, she was special. You fell in love with her when you were only a teenager—'

Duarte vented a grim laugh that silenced her. 'Please don't tell me that you listened to Victorine's story about Izabel and I having been childhood sweethearts!'

'Well, yes...but—'

Seeing her confusion, Duarte groaned out loud, his lean strong face bleak. 'You really don't know the truth even now, do you? But then, who would go out of their way to tell you the sordid details? I didn't want to relive them and Victorine always preferred to inhabit a dream world where her daughter was concerned.'

'Sordid details?' Emily queried in bewilderment. 'What are you talking about?'

'Izabel was a drug addict and not one who had any desire to be cured.'

Feeling the bed hit the back of her knees, Emily dropped down on it in a state of shock. 'You're not serious...'

Recognising her disbelief, Duarte expelled his breath on a hiss. And then he told her about Izabel. Yes, he had first met her when he was sixteen but Izabel had been five years older and quite out of his reach. Indeed he had not met her again until he was in his twenties. An heiress in her own right, Izabel's father had died when she was a child and she'd been raised by her adoring mother and allowed unlimited freedom from an early age.

'Unfortunately, I didn't move in Izabel's world, nor did I know her circle of friends. While they were partying, I was studying and then working eighteen-hour days in the bank. When I met her again six years later, I was mad for her,' Duarte admitted bluntly. 'I couldn't believe that she was still single. I couldn't wait to marry her; I just couldn't believe how *lucky* I was...'

Emily studied the rug at her feet. She really didn't want the intimate details, but they washed off her again because her mind was still fighting to handle the concept of the glamorous Izabel as an addict.

'I caught her with cocaine on the second day of our honeymoon. She just laughed, called me a killjoy and said I had better get used to it because that was how she lived. I was shattered,' Duarte confessed with grim exactitude. 'Before the wedding, I *had* seen her in a very excitable state but I didn't recognise her behaviour as abnormal or suspect the truth. She did have a very lively personality…and she was a tremendous show-off.'

'A…show-off?' Emily's own misconceptions about Izabel were sunk into final obscurity by that almost wry label.

'Izabel craved attention and publicity. No matter what it took, she had to be noticed and admired. She was the ultimate party girl.'

'Couldn't you persuade her to accept professional help?'

'Four times in three years she was rushed into hospital with overdoses. Neither the doctors, nor I, nor even her mother could talk her into entering a rehabilitation clinic or even considering a treatment plan. Mentally, she went downhill fast—but addicts have a distorted grip on reality—'

'Surely other people must've realised she was taking drugs?'

'When she did anything crazy, her friends would cover up for her because they had the same habits to protect and conceal. She had her own money, dealers in every port of call and any relationship we had fell apart within months. My sister Elena died because I was unable to control Izabel.'

Duarte's restive hands moved in a small silent motion that just screamed guilt and more pain than Emily had ever witnessed in another human being.

'I don't believe that. I *don't* believe it was your fault!' Emily protested fiercely.

'When I was abroad, Elena would try to watch over Izabel, for Victorine was quite unequal to the task. My twin made the fatal mistake of getting into Izabel's car and letting her drive. The car went off the road at the most phenomenal speed…' he completed thickly.

'Please don't think of this or talk about it any more,'

Emily begged, humbled by the agony he could not hide and appalled by what she had learnt. She was devastated that he had contrived to bury what could only have been a three-year-long nightmare behind that formidable reserve of his.

'Not exactly a story calculated to put either of us in a party mood,' Duarte remarked broodingly.

'If you would like to put her pictures back up, you can,' Emily mumbled, that being the biggest sacrifice and apology she could conceive at that particular moment.

Duarte dealt her a look of sheer bewilderment.

'I feel sad for Izabel and you now. Poor Victorine too...all those pathetic tales she fed me about her perfect daughter and I can even understand why she did it now—'

'An alarming inability to deal with reality?' Duarte suggested.

'No, she wanted to remember Izabel as she might have been without the drug abuse—remember the good things, not the bad. Maybe you would feel better if you copied her a little...' Emily muttered awkwardly.

'There *were* no good things,' Duarte grated with sudden savage impatience. 'Why do you think I married you?'

'I'm not sure I want to know, in the mood you're in,' Emily said gently.

But Duarte was determined to tell her. 'After Izabel, I swore that no woman would ever have that kind of power over me again,' he breathed with stark bitterness.

Oh, well, that was really not news, Emily reflected, understanding that he was in an explosively emotional frame of mind after finally rising to the demeaning brink of admitting that his first marriage had been a disaster. Perhaps he might eventually reach the healthy point of wondering why his second marriage had run into rough waters as well.

For Emily could now see that *she* had paid the price for the amount of pain, humiliation and disillusionment that the self-destructive Izabel had inflicted on Duarte. Once bitten, forever shy. She also understood there was much that he'd *not* said, for she could read between the lines. He had really loved Izabel because he had not given up on her. How many times had he struggled to help Izabel and had his efforts thrown back in his face?

Somewhat put out by Emily's stoic and seemingly unresponsive silence, Duarte drove a not quite steady hand through his black luxuriant hair. Baulked of a further outlet, he said bossily, 'You should be getting ready for the party.'

And display body parts she much preferred to conceal beneath long skirts and sleeves and loose tops that hinted at more than she possessed. Like a lamb to the slaughter, she gathered up his gifts and went for a shower to freshen up.

When it crossed her mind that if she wore her hair down with that brief dress and low heels, she might look like she was mostly hair and vertically challenged, she decided to put her mane of red-gold hair up instead. Show off her neck. Why not? All else was going to be bared. Having donned the dress, an hour later, there was no temptation for her to examine her reflection in the mirror.

As she came downstairs she noticed that some gifted person had worked wonders with the floral disarrangement she'd abandoned earlier. Duarte strode out of one of the ground-floor reception rooms. Clad in a well-cut dinner jacket, he looked devastatingly male. Her heart skipped a beat but now there was a kernel of resentment.

Duarte focused on her with intent dark golden eyes and stilled as if someone had yanked an off switch inside him.

Emily started backing up the stairs again. 'I could have told you...I look like you don't feed me. Give me two minutes and I'll be covered up again!'

Duarte strode forward. 'You look breathtaking...'

Full marks for stunned stare of appreciation, she thought

and waited on the punchline that she was sure was about to come and then she would be a good sport and laugh.

'Gorgeous, *minha jóia.*'

Emily winced. 'No, I'm not.'

Duarte grabbed her hand and practically carried her over to the giant gilded mirror on the paneled wall. 'What do you see?'

'I'm not looking. I don't like my legs, my arms, my— er—other bits.'

'I love them,' Duarte husked bending over her. 'You have beautiful legs—'

'They're too short,' she hissed.

'Very shapely ankles, dainty arms, a neck like a swan's—'

'It's not long enough—'

'*Everything* in perfect proportion and you look distinctly ethereal in that shade of blue—'

'Spectral and gaunt?' She inched up her eyelashes.

'Ravishing. You grew up with two sisters jealous that you outshone them entirely in the looks department. Stop tormenting yourself with your non-existent flaws,' Duarte urged with a frank exasperation that had a much more powerful effect on her confidence than his compliments.

Finally studying her reflection, Emily saw herself as she had never seen herself. Elegant, slim and small it was true but not scrawny. Putting her hair up had been a good idea for now she could see that her face had a shape and her eyes looked all bright and starry. She turned ever so slightly sideways to check out the bosom profile. No improvement there but my goodness that dress flattered her, particularly the colour!

She looked in the mirror and met Duarte's intent gaze. He dealt her a hot, sizzling appraisal that spoke lustful volumes and made her quiver in helpless response. Well, she was ravishing him, anyway. 'My sisters aren't jealous of me—far from it,' she told him ruefully.

'Why else would they always be putting you down and cracking jokes at your expense?'

She sighed. 'It's just always been that way…their sense of humour, I suppose.'

'And your mother either acting as if it's not happening or even joining in. I know you care about your family but I think you need to assert yourself and make them treat you with respect.'

At that point the front doors were opened wide to greet the arrival of their first guests. There was no time for further conversation but she was disconcerted by what he'd said. It hurt that he had noticed her family's lack of respect but she was touched that he was concerned enough to advise her. Unfortunately, she could not imagine standing up to demand anything from her far more assertive elder sisters.

The party was in full swing by the time Bliss arrived and made an entrance. Every male head turned to watch Bliss glide across the room, her shapely figure enhanced by a scarlet silk sheath dress that was a far cry from her discreet business suits.

Her heartbeat accelerating, Emily watched Duarte cut through the crush to greet his executive assistant and she turned away again. There was *nothing* going on between Bliss and Duarte, she told herself firmly. They had become friends. She would just have to learn to live with that.

Duarte was not acting like a male involved in an affair. Duarte was behaving very much like a male who wanted to keep his marriage intact. She'd actually made it to that holy of holies once denied, a shared marital bed! He had told her about Izabel. He was entranced by their son. He had bought her a whole outfit and it did seem to do something special for her. Then there were the sapphires which had attracted many admiring comments and every time she said 'Duarte gave them to me,' she felt like a million dollars.

So she was looking on the bright side, refusing to dwell on murky suspicions for which she had no proof. Bliss Jarrett had always been a man's woman and very ambitious. It was hardly surprising that she should have ditched her covert friendship with Emily and chosen to shift her allegiance to Duarte instead. And, to be fair, Emily reflected ruefully, possibly Bliss *did* thoroughly dislike her now for what her foolish flight from Portugal had done to Duarte.

While she talked herself mentally into that state of calm and security, Emily drank her way through two glasses of wine. She rarely touched alcohol, for she did not have much of a head for it, but she felt in dire need of a little Dutch courage.

'Emily…?' called a bright familiar voice.

It was Bliss, all smiles and self-satisfaction. 'I've arranged a terrific party, haven't I?'

'Yes…absolutely.' Emily plastered what she hoped was a serene smile on to her lips and prayed for an interruption.

Across the room, she glimpsed Duarte, his brilliant eyes centred on both women. Emily smiled so hard at Bliss her face hurt.

'He's mine. Just you watch me in action,' Bliss invited.

'I trust him…' Emily didn't know if she did but it sounded good and strong. What she really wanted to do was lock Duarte up somewhere very secure, just to be on the safe side.

'When Duarte found you, he was about to instigate divorce proceedings.'

Emily widened her eyes in the desperate hope that that made her look incredulous. 'I asked for a divorce. He said no.'

'I don't believe that for a moment!' Bliss derided with

blistering scorn. 'We're lovers. Haven't you worked that out yet?'

Emily froze. Her heart divebombed to the soles of her feet. Her tummy performed a sickening somersault. 'I don't believe you.'

'Suit yourself.' Bliss simply laughed and walked away.

Emily finished her wine with a shaking hand. *Lovers!* That announcement was not a cue to panic, she instructed herself. In dismay, she watched Duarte move out on to the dance floor with Bliss. Emily wriggled through the clumps of chattering guests round the edge of the floor. Peering under arms for a better view and stretching her neck and standing on tip toe, she kept Duarte and Bliss under close surveillance.

She lifted another glass from a passing tray and watched Bliss press her lithe body into intimate connection with Duarte. But a moment later, Duarte backed off from that contact. Bad move, Bliss, he's not into intimate displays in front of audiences, Emily thought angrily. But then, when had Bliss ever been able to resist a challenge? Hadn't Bliss once told her that a clever woman could easily manipulate any man into doing her bidding? Now Bliss was whispering coyly into Duarte's ear. Duarte flung his arrogant head back and laughed and Emily felt stabbed to the heart and her bravado curdled at source.

If he fell for an Izabel, he could fall for a Bliss. *Lovers?* While she herself had been in England? Emily didn't know what to believe. One minute she was suffering agonies of jealousy but the next, she was telling herself that she could not trust anything that Bliss said. Forcing herself to stop spying on her husband and his 'friend', Emily turned on her heel.

Only minutes later, Duarte curved an imprisoning hand to her elbow and tugged her back against him to murmur ruefully, 'The one drawback of those shoes is that I can't see you in the crowd. Where have you been?'

'Oh…around.'

Now it seemed it was her turn to be whirled round the dance floor. She snuggled up so close to his lean hard body that a postcard could not have squeezed between them. Duarte tensed a little in surprise.

'If you push me away, you're *dead*,' Emily swore. 'It's bad enough having to smell *her* perfume on you.'

'Isn't jealousy hell?' Duarte imparted with a silken lack of concern that was just about the last reaction she had expected to receive.

'What would you know about it?' Emily snatched in a charged breath and then just stormed right to the heart of the matter. 'Bliss told me that you were lovers!'

Assailed by that dramatic contention, Duarte responded in the most withering of tones, '*Que absurdo!* Why would Bliss say such a thing? That is not my idea of a joke, Emily.'

'Are you saying you don't believe me?' Emily's voice rose in volume at the same velocity as her temper.

Duarte tightened the arm he had curved to her rigid spine like a restraining bar. 'No comment—'

'If you don't give me a straight answer, I'm walking off this floor!'

'You've been drinking…you're upset—'

Emily flung her head back and studied him with tormented aquamarine eyes. No. He didn't believe her. He was being smooth, evasive, possibly even extremely *cunning*.

'Bliss said that you weren't comfortable with her being here,' Duarte murmured very drily. 'Even at a distance of a hundred feet, I could see that too. You really don't need to make up childishly silly stories as well.'

Emily wrenched herself free of him with a sudden movement that took him by surprise. She felt violent, furious, incredibly bitter. Bliss and her games, always one step ahead. Duarte? If he was innocent, nothing short of a tape-recording would convince Duarte that Bliss had said such a thing. If he was guilty, all he had to do was accuse his wife of being intoxicated and jealous!

Concentrating on avoiding Duarte, Emily circulated. Every time he came within twenty feet of her, she moved on and plunged into animated conversation with someone else. At last their guests began to take their leave but it was a slow process. Then an elderly woman announced that her handbag had gone missing and immediately became very upset. Emily could have done with her husband's calming presence—her own level of Portuguese was unequal to the challenge of soothing the poor woman. Unfortunately, Duarte was nowhere within view and Emily had to martial the anxious and weary staff into an ordered search. The bag was finally found intact in the cloakroom. Telling the servants just to go to bed and clean up the party debris in the morning, Emily ushered their volubly apologetic guest out to her limousine with great relief.

As Emily walked back indoors, the big house felt eerily silent and empty. Had Duarte just gone up to bed? From the amount of light reflecting on the landing window, Emily realised that the lights had been left on outside in the court-yard garden. With a groan, she went back downstairs to switch them off. She frowned when she saw that the garden doors were still open and then she stopped dead in her tracks: Duarte and Bliss were outside.

Even as Emily looked, Bliss made a sudden almost compulsive movement and tipped forward into Duarte's swiftly extended arms. They were locked together like two magnets in the split second it took Emily to surge forward and gasp strickenly, 'You rotten, lying bastard!'

CHAPTER NINE

DUARTE thrust Bliss hurriedly back from him and wheeled round, his lean strong face startled, his whole demeanour one of almost exaggerated incredulity.

'Did you think I'd gone to bed?' Emily's voice broke on that rather meaningless demand but her brain was locked on that intimate image of them together and the sheer horror of the discovery that her very worst fears should have been proven right before her eyes.

Bliss strolled forward, her scarlet dress shimmering in the lights, her exquisite face offensively cool and collected. 'This is rather embarrassing but I do assure you that you misunderstood what you just saw. I simply stumbled and Duarte saved me from a nasty fall—'

'Do you honestly think I'm s-stupid enough to swallow that old chestnut?' Emily stammered, half an octave higher, utterly thrown by the blonde's reaction until she worked out that Bliss was assuming yet *another* role and this time for Duarte's benefit. That of supportive lover engaged in a tactful cover-up!

Duarte studied Emily's drawn and accusing face and he squared his broad shoulders. 'Don't be silly, Emily,' he urged in the most galling tone of authority. 'It's a warm night and Bliss was feeling faint. She almost fell and I steadied her. *End of story.*'

Duarte rested expectant dark deepset eyes on his wife.

Instantly, Emily looked away, away from both of them. She was trembling and sick with shock at their behaviour. Why were they doing this to her? Couldn't Duarte, at least, have come clean? Instead, they stood united against *her*, both of them making the same stupid excuse and both of them treating her as if she was an hysteric making wild childish allegations!

'I think I ought to go home, Duarte. I'm so sorry about this,' Bliss sighed with regret.

Enraged by the other woman's composure, Emily spun back. 'Tell me, what role are you playing now, Bliss? You're a very good liar but I have to admit that my head's spinning tonight!'

'Get a grip on yourself, Emily,' Duarte grated.

Emily couldn't bring herself to look at him. She kept on staring at Bliss. 'Have you told my husband about what a great friend you were to me before I left Portugal?'

'I really don't know what you're referring to,' Bliss responded drily.

'Oh, really?' Emily marvelled that she herself did not simply spontaneously combust with rage and sheer violent frustration. 'You mean you don't remember all those cosy lunches we shared at the Faz Figura restaurant in the Alfama? You don't recall the dozen shopping trips either? Not even my visits to your apartment?'

Bliss directed a marvellous look of sublime discomfiture at Duarte as if she was listening to the ravings of a very confused and drunken woman.

'Well then, if I never *visited* your apartment, tell me how I know that you have your dining room chairs covered in fake zebra skin?' Emily asked fiercely, determined to corner and entrap Bliss in her own lies. 'How come I know that you have a grandfather clock that belonged to your parents in your sitting room? Leather seats, glass tables—?'

As Emily's desperation to expose the blonde's lies rose to a charged peak, Bliss expelled a weary sigh. 'Well, I *do* have a leather suite but then so do many people and I would *adore* a grandfather clock but I've never owned one. As for the fake animal fur seats?' Bliss grimaced. 'I have rather better taste.'

Emily's rigid shoulders slumped. Evidently it would take someone a great deal cleverer than she was to catch Bliss out.

'Please go home, Bliss,' Duarte urged in an electrifyingly quiet request. 'I'm sorry you had to witness this.'

Bliss strolled past Emily like a queen and walked back indoors.

Duarte swore in driven Portuguese, and strode over to Emily, who was staring emptily into space. He gripped her by the arms to force her round to face him. 'What the hell has got into you? A friendship with Bliss? Since when? Are you paralytically drunk and delusional? How could you make such an ass of yourself?' he demanded with savage incredulity.

Emily was in a daze. 'Bliss *does* have a grandfather clock,' she protested shakily. 'And we were friends and I'm not drunk but I'm beginning to *feel* delusional!'

His smouldering dark golden eyes narrowed and he converted his hold on her limp arms to a supportive soothing hold. Looking distinctly at a loss, Duarte expelled his breath in a slow hiss. 'Look, I think you need to get some rest…OK?'

'You think I'm crazy. Or do you? Maybe you're as big a deceiver as *she* is! If that's how it is, fine. I don't care any more.' Emily raised her arms in an abrupt movement to shake free of his lean hands. Turning away from him, she set off down the corridor.

'I'll be upstairs in five minutes…' Duarte called after her. 'Do you want me to come up with you?'

'No, thanks.' If he thought she was going upstairs to share a bedroom with a male who thought she was only one mental step removed from a nervous breakdown, he had better think again.

Emily trudged back across the echoing main hall and out the front doors just in time to see the tail lights of Bliss's sleek silver sports car disappearing down the winding drive. Naturally one grandfather clock would now be speedily disposed of or possibly Bliss had got rid of that parental legacy months ago, Emily reflected numbly, for the clock had not suited the ultra-modern decor of Bliss's city apartment.

Unable to bear the claustrophobic silence of the house or the prospect of another confrontation with Duarte, Emily wandered out into the moonlit gardens. The dew-wet grass crunched beneath her feet. The palms cast spiky, mysterious shadows that faded the further she moved away from the house. She saw the domed bulk of the building the Monteiros called a summerhouse glimmering in the darkness beneath the trees. A grand eighteenth-century folly built of white marble, it was large enough to house a full orchestra. Mounting the steps, Emily dropped down on to a hard marble bench. Just then, the folly had a great deal more appeal than any bed containing Duarte.

Her husband thought she was nuts. He had gone from outraged disbelief to sudden grave concern. Right now, he was probably ringing one of his many medical friends to ask for some serious advice and book her an appointment with a psychiatrist.

In the quiet of the folly, Emily skimmed her shoes off to flex her crushed toes and willed herself to be calm. She saw that once again she had been set up by Bliss. Having seen Emily watching her with Duarte, Bliss had staged a pretend fall. No other explanation made sense. If Duarte wanted to snatch Bliss into a passionate embrace, he was highly unlikely to do so in a well-lit courtyard in full view of more than forty windows.

So, in that sense, she *had* made an ass of herself, Emily acknowledged grimly. But it was difficult to care when she was truly at the end of her tether. Bitterness was rising inside her like a dam surging to break its banks. Assert yourself, Duarte had told her when he was telling her how to deal with her own family.

But when had she ever asserted herself with *Duarte*? She was Mrs Doormat Monteiro and it was little wonder that Bliss was able to best her at every turn. Eleven months ago, Duarte had demanded a separation and he had dispatched her to the house in the Douro and she had gone without a murmur. She had behaved as if she *was* an unfaithful wife!

Why? She had been consumed with guilt over a kiss that she had neither invited nor enjoyed. Why had she beaten herself up for so long over that stupid episode? She had not been unfaithful and she had not betrayed her husband. But, totally intimidated by Duarte's chilling rage and his even more appalling conviction that she had actually been sleeping with Toby Jarrett, she had become so distraught that she had been incapable of offering a convincing self-defence.

As Emily sat there ruminating on her cold marble bench, she began to see that she had spent most of the twenty-two years of her life blaming herself for every bad and unlucky thing that had ever happened to her. When her parents didn't hug her as a child and her older sisters bullied her, she had assumed that the fault was in her and not in them. She had felt guilty and ashamed that she wasn't sufficiently loveable and had just tried harder and harder to please in the hope that somehow matters would improve. Only they never had improved, she conceded sadly.

Then she had married Duarte. Duarte with his domineering force of will and powerful personality. She had put up with everything thrown at her. Victorine, Duarte's endless absences on business, a lifestyle she disliked. Had she ever complained? No! She had blamed herself for not being content with what she had and for wanting too much.

Instead of putting the blame squarely where it belonged on Duarte's shoulders.

Hearing a twig snap somewhere nearby, Emily froze into stillness.

'Are you trying to play hide-and-seek now?' Duarte derided as he strode into view from below the screening darkness of the trees. 'It is three o'clock in the morning. Do you realise how long I've been searching for you? How concerned I've been? If I hadn't found your tracks across the grass, I'd have been turning the staff out of bed to look for you!'

Emily studied him with a glorious sense of calm and not the smallest desire to apologise for her lack of consideration. In moonlight, Duarte was a dramatic study in black and white. So tall, so dark, so handsome. Always in control, preferably in control of *her*—yet he was losing his reserve at a staggeringly fast rate this time around. Why? She wasn't the same woman she had been at the time of their separation, eleven months ago.

'You really have been a lousy husband,' Emily sighed. 'And I don't need to be hysterical or intoxicated or nuts to tell you that—'

'You can abuse me all you like *indoors*,' Duarte stated icily. 'I refuse to stand around in the garden at this hour listening to this nonsense.'

'Fine. Goodnight,' Emily said quietly.

'Look, you're overwrought—'

'You're not at the bank, Duarte…so drop the command tone of voice. I won't be bullied or browbeaten—'

'But you might just be strangled,' Duarte intoned, mounting the steps at an aggressive pace. 'Now, I understand that you feel threatened by Bliss and that it may even be my fault that you feel jealous and insecure—but no way are you going to make a major event out of that stupid incident in the courtyard!'

'Am I not?' Emily sat up a little straighter and raised her chin.

'It's outright nonsense for you to pretend that you suspect me of infidelity!' Duarte delivered in the same thunderous tone. 'And, in your heart, you *know* it is—'

'Do I?' was all Emily said and not in a tone that suggested she was greatly interested in the subject.

'I would not have an affair with an employee—'

'I thought she was your friend…and wasn't I once an employee? And in a much humbler capacity than Bliss has ever been.'

Duarte dealt her an electrifying look of smouldering frustration. 'That was different!'

'So maybe Bliss was what you call different, too—'

'Are you *trying* to wind me up?' Duarte demanded incredulously, staring at her expressionless face with probing intensity.

'Why would I do that? Bliss need not be a problem, Duarte…providing that you can prove to my satisfaction that you are innocent.'

'What the hell is that supposed to mean?' he launched at her.

'That this evening I witnessed something suspicious between you and Bliss,' Emily reminded him in the same reasonable tone that seemed to be making his even white teeth clench. 'I don't need to justify my expectation that you should now immediately convince me beyond *all* reasonable doubt that you are blameless.'

'And how am I supposed to do that?' Duarte bit out furiously.

Emily lifted a slight shoulder and dropped it again. 'I don't know. It's not my problem, is it?'

'I've had enough of this!' Duarte growled and, taking a sudden step forward, he bent down and scooped her off the bench and up into his powerful arms. 'You've gone haywire since last night! You're trying to play games with me—'

'By demanding that you prove yourself innocent? Was it a game when you did the same thing to me after seeing Toby kiss me?' Emily asked dulcetly.

Duarte froze. 'So *that* is what this is all about...'

Imprisoned in his arms and as limp as a rag doll, Emily looked up at him. 'And I've been much kinder to you than you were to me in the same circumstances—'

'Just keep quiet or I'll lose my temper!' Duarte seethed, arms tightening round her slight figure as he strode down the steps and headed back towards the house.

'I mean, you can't say that I sat you down, stood over you like a hanging judge and frightened you to the extent that you just fell apart at the seams...can you?'

'Shut up!' he roared.

'You see, I'm not a bully—'

'What did you say?'

'I think you heard me—'

'*Inferno!* I am bloody well not a bully!' Duarte raged, jawline rockhard. 'How dare you accuse me of being a bully?'

'Well, if carting me back indoors without my consent is *not* bullying, I don't know what is.'

Duarte jerked to a very abrupt halt. 'I'm looking after you, not bullying you,' he framed, in such a rage he could hardly get the words out.

'But I don't want to be looked after. I can look after myself and I can walk on my own legs.'

With hugely exaggerated care, Duarte lowered her to the grass. Only then did she realise that her shoes had been left behind in the folly. Duarte had been well aware of the fact. He gave her a sardonic smile.

'Thanks,' she said compressing her lips.

'That night I saw you in Jarrett's arms, I controlled my

temper. How many men would have done that?' Duarte demanded rawly.

'I was very upset and I felt guilty even though I hadn't done anything and you scared me—'

'I didn't lay a finger on you!' Duarte bit out.

'No,' Emily agreed unevenly. 'But I was scared that you might—'

'When have I *ever* hurt you?' His bronzed features very pale in the light still cascading from the *quinta*, Duarte stared at her in fierce reproach.

'Never. But that night I was scared—and, because I was scared and very upset, I made a hash of explaining myself to you. You didn't listen anyway. You were already convinced that I had betrayed you. Yet what did you see?' she prompted tautly. 'You saw him grab me and kiss me—'

'I was around long before that,' Duarte cut in grimly. 'I heard him begging you to run away with him and a whole hell of a lot of other juvenile rubbish!'

'Until Toby spoke, I had no idea that he believed that he was in love with me. I was in shock and I didn't want to hurt him and I didn't know what to say—'

'So you just stood there and let him kiss you. If that's as good as your story gets, don't waste your breath trying to raise the subject again!'

'Well, I'm looking forward to seeing how you plan to convince me that you have been one hundred per cent faithful to me for the whole of our marriage,' Emily countered in a slightly strained voice as she picked her way painfully across the gravel fronting the house in her bare feet.

'I expect you to trust me' Duarte informed her without the smallest hesitation.

'I expected you to trust me and look where it got me,' Emily countered without hesitation. 'So please don't expect me to be more generous than you were.'

On the steps of the house, she stopped to brush off the

gravel embedded in the stinging soles of her feet. That task achieved, she headed straight for the sweeping staircase.

'Emily…this is ridiculous,' Duarte breathed wearily. 'When you vanished for eight months, I thought it would serve you right if I did find another woman but I didn't *do* it!'

'Prove it,' she said without turning her head.

'How the hell can I *prove* it?' he raked at her rigid back. 'Call in character witnesses?'

Emily was so exhausted after the effort it had taken to stand up to Duarte's towering personality, she was beyond any further thought or action. In any case, since she had long since sent the staff to bed, Duarte was going to have to douse lights and lock up, which was likely to take him quite a while. In the bedroom that she'd never shared with him before, she dug her teddy nightshirt out from under the bed, padded into the bathroom and stripped where she stood. Donning the nightshirt, she freshened up and pulled the clips out of her piled-up hair, letting it fall round her in a wild tangle. On her passage to the bed, she remembered the sapphires she still wore. Setting the earrings and the necklace down on the cabinet, she slid between the sheets and lay there, barely able to keep her heavy eyes open.

Had she got anywhere with Duarte? Had he seen the point that she'd been trying to make? That he had judged *her* on superficial evidence? Where had his trust been? Had he ever trusted her? It was not as if she'd ever been a femme fatale, who flirted like mad with other men and gave him cause for concern.

Duarte strode into the bedroom like a threatening storm ready to rain down thunder and lightning. As his attention settled on the slight bump she made in his bed, some of his high-voltage tension visibly ebbed.

Emily sighed, tucked her hand under the pillow and

turned on her side to go to sleep. 'G'night,' she mumbled sleepily.

'Right...so now I'm getting the big freeze!'

She thought about that and sighed again. 'I'm just tired.'

Ten minutes later, he tugged her across the bed into his arms and she groaned out loud while surreptitiously snuggling back into the hard heat of him. He turned her round to face him, brilliant dark golden eyes still ablaze with vibrant energy.

'Bliss *did* have a grandfather clock,' he murmured with the air of a male expecting a burst of applause. 'And no, I have never been in her apartment but I do recall her telling me a long time ago that the only thing her father left her when he died was an ugly big clock. An appraiser had advised her to keep it as an investment and she had it shipped out here.'

'Congratulations,' Emily mumbled, eyes dropping closed again.

'You can't go to sleep now, *minha jóia*,' Duarte ground out incredulously. 'Did you hear what I said?'

'Talk about it in the morning—'

'It *is* the morning and we're flying over to London in precisely six hours' time,' Duarte reminded her with considerable impatience and he shook her shoulder slightly, lifted and dropped her limp hand, striving to rouse her again.

But nothing short of a fire alarm would have wakened Emily or persuaded her to take the slightest interest in anything other than sleep.

'Anyone ever tell you that you sleep like the dead?'

'You.' Glancing up from the magazine she was pretending to read, Emily noted anxiously that once again, Duarte was staring at her from his seat opposite. He had been doing that ever since she came down to breakfast two hours earlier and yet he had barely spoken to her. The drive to the airport had been similarly filled with unspoken tension and in half an hour the jet would be landing in London.

'Tell me, do you remember what I said to you last night just before you feel asleep?' Duarte enquired with studied casualness.

Emily chewed at her lower lip and silently shook her head. It was a lie. She did have a vague recollection of him accusing her of giving him the big freeze but that was not a subject she was particularly keen to reopen, for she was all too well aware that when she had wakened around seven in his arms she had *not* given him the big freeze. Reddening at that mortifying awareness of her own drastic lack of control, Emily returned to her fake perusal of the magazine and wondered why she'd dreamt about Bliss's grandfather clock during the night. Quite where and how the clock had figured in her dream, she could not recall.

'You're just so quiet,' Duarte remarked.

'Last night drained me,' she muttered honestly.

'You made your point. You more than made your point,' Duarte extended. 'But I assure you that I have *never* been intimate with Bliss Jarrett.'

Emily nodded, much as if she was listening to a weather report.

'At least *look* at me…' Duarte intoned in low-pitched frustration, evidently as aware as she was of the presence of the nanny nursing Jamie at the other end of the cabin.

Slowly Emily raised her head, aquamarine eyes full of strain.

She encountered stunning dark golden eyes that made her own instantly sting with tears and hurriedly she dropped her head again.

'Please don't cry…' Duarte leant forward and grasped her knotted fingers between both his hands. 'I feel enough of a bastard as it is.'

Emily gulped.

'I've really screwed up our marriage,' Duarte muttered half under his breath, startling her into looking up again—but there was nothing to be gained but a view of Duarte's gleaming dark springy hair bent over their linked hands. 'I don't want you to argue with me about that.'

Emily surveyed his bent head in growing wonderment. She had no intention whatsoever of arguing with him on that score. There was a moment of awkward silence while he gave her a chance to argue in his defence. His wide shoulders emanated ferocious tension when the silence remained unbroken.

'In the future I will do a lot of things differently,' Duarte swore, practically crushing the life out of her fingers, every word emerging stilted and raw with emotion. 'I'm not the most liberated guy around but I can change. Ordering people around just comes very naturally to me...'

'I know,' Emily whispered. 'It's just I'm not really sure why you're talking like this—'

Duarte lifted his proud head and his incisive dark golden eyes glittered over the bemused expression on her face. 'I didn't sleep last night. I kept on getting flashbacks of you cowering in a chair in front of me after I caught...*saw*,' he adjusted hastily, 'you in Toby Jarrett's arms that night. I don't think you got out a single sentence that I didn't interrupt—'

'I didn't—but maybe I was a bit tough on you last night because understandably, you were very, very angry with me after what you saw—'

'Emily, shut up,' Duarte groaned. 'You probably weren't tough enough. I need you to stand up to me—'

'I don't like confrontations but I'll try.' Emily watched Duarte breathe in very deep and slow. 'You don't need to say anything more. I know why you're saying all these things...'

'You *do*?' Duarte looked dubious.

'You're afraid that I'm planning to get off this plane and take Jamie and refuse ever to come back to Portugal but I wouldn't *do* that to you again,' Emily assured him heavily.

'Actually…' Duarte released her hand and flung himself back into his own seat. He surveyed her with bleak dark eyes. 'That *wasn't* why I was saying those things. For once in my life, you are ahead of me. Believe it or not, I hadn't considered that possibility.'

'I won't part you from Jamie,' Emily reaffirmed a second time.

'If you come back to Portugal with me this evening, you can have the dress, the honeymoon and the very moon itself if you ask for it,' Duarte asserted with brooding darkness. 'Whatever you choose to do, I will not issue any threats.'

Emily was hurt that he had so little faith in her promises. She just could not fathom what was going on inside that darkly handsome head of his. He was like a man suffering from ever-growing shock. His moods were all over the place. He was as tense as a rumbling volcano. He was talking like she had never heard him talk before in his life. Was he really so scared of losing Jamie? Then why wouldn't he be? Without very much thought at all, she had denied him any contact with his son for many months. How could she blame him for doubting her?

'Duarte…there's a couple of things I'd like to say,' Emily admitted in a rush. 'Please listen, even though you don't believe what I'm telling you…'

'I'm listening…'

'I never told you that I had become friendly with Bliss because she said that you'd think it was inappropriate and that it might damage her career prospects with you,' Emily related, deliberately not looking at him lest she lose her nerve. 'I met Toby in her apartment and she persuaded me to let him paint me. The portrait was supposed to be a present for you—'

'I don't really want to hear any more,' Duarte incised in a charged undertone.

Emily ignored him and started talking even faster so that she could finish. 'When I left the house in the Douro eight months ago, it was only because Bliss phoned me to warn me that she had overheard *you* speaking to your lawyer and discussing your chances of taking my baby away from me as soon as he was born.'

The silence simmered like a heatwave about to explode into violence.

Emily mustered her courage and glanced at Duarte. His attention carefully pinned to some point in the middle distance, his bronzed skin was stretched super-taut across his hard bone structure. Pallor was stamped round his set mouth, the pallor a male restraining and containing rage.

'Is there any more?' he almost whispered.

'Nothing important.' Shrivelled by his silent, smouldering reaction to her revelations, Emily grabbed up her magazine again, grateful the jet was coming in to land.

Thirty minutes later, in the crowded concourse inside the airport, Emily turned to say to Duarte, 'I'm leaving Jamie with you…OK?'

Her husband emerged from his extreme preoccupation and frowned at her. 'But we're going to see your family together—'

'I thought you had a business meeting—'

'I had it rescheduled.'

Emily interpreted that sudden announcement as confirmation that he did not trust even *her* out of his sight, never mind Jamie. 'It's just I'd prefer to see my family alone—'

'I'm coming with you,' Duarte informed her in a studiously level tone. 'We'll let Jamie and his nanny go straight to Ash Manor and join them there later.'

'You're not listening to me. I want to speak to my mother alone. I want to talk to her in private. I don't want company.'

'When I said I could make changes, I did not mean I could turn into New Age man overnight,' Duarte drawled. 'Your mother will walk all over you and upset you. She always does. If I'm there she stays within certain limits.'

'I don't want New Age man, Duarte...I just want you to respect my wishes.'

'Don't say you weren't warned, *minha esposa*.'

Odd how he could boss her about with such sublime cool himself but react like a caged lion at the mere prospect of anyone else taking advantage of her easy-going nature. It was a kind of territorial possessiveness, she supposed vaguely. Feeling sympathetic, she allowed him to arrange for a limo to take her to her family home when she could perfectly well have climbed on the train and got there much faster.

CHAPTER TEN

'I SUPPOSE you had better come in,' Lorene Davies said grudgingly when she found her daughter on the doorstep of her smart detached home.

Nervous as a cat, Emily watched her mother's slim, straight back disappear into the kitchen. An attractive blonde woman well into her fifties, she looked a good decade younger. Following her disinterested parent, Emily hovered in the kitchen doorway while Lorene continued to stack her dishwasher with plates. Not much of a welcome after her eight-month absence, Emily thought tautly. But then, had she really expected anything different?

'Been in touch with your husband recently?' the older woman asked with her first flicker of curiosity. 'He came here looking for you last year and he seemed to blame us for not keeping you here. It was really very embarrassing and, I can tell you, I was very annoyed about it. You've always been a problem, Emily.'

Emily stiffened, thinking she'd been the quietest, tidiest and most helpful child in the household but had only ever earnt criticism in return for her best efforts.

'Look, I'm sure you don't want me taking up your time when you're so busy. I won't keep you long,' Emily murmured, her nails digging into the palms of her clenched hands as she willed herself on. 'I'm only here for one reason. I hope you can give me an honest answer and I promise not to hold it against you—'

'What on earth are you rambling on about?' Lorene Davies demanded angrily, unaccustomed to her timid daughter addressing her in such a manner. Emily forced her

154

chin up and stood as tall as she could. 'I have a right to know why you don't like me—'

'Don't be ridiculous! Don't like you? What's that supposed to mean?' Her mother said scornfully. 'You have such odd ways, Emily.'

Emily lost what little colour she had. 'If I'm odd, you made me odd. I need to hear a reason from you and then I'll leave you in peace.'

Tight-mouthed, Lorene studied her for a long timeless moment of tension. 'All right. Before we moved up here from Cornwall, I had an affair and lived with another man for a while. That man was your *real* father...'

'What are you telling me?' Emily mumbled, her skin coming up in gooseflesh.

'What you said you wanted to know.' Lorene folded her arms, looking defiant and bitter. 'His name was Daniel Stevenson. He owned a big stud farm. Daniel said he was going to marry me when my divorce came through but he changed his mind when I was about seven months pregnant. He told me to go back to my husband and he slung us out—'

'My father—Peter Davies *isn't*...my father?' Emily said sickly.

'No, but when I went back to Peter he said he'd raise you as his child and we moved up here to make a fresh start. That's more or less it.'

'This Daniel Stevenson...I look like him, don't I?' Emily prompted chokily.

'You're the image of him,' Lorene confirmed grimly. 'He died about fifteen years ago. A riding accident. I can't say that I grieved when I heard about it. He was a creep. I really loved him but I was only one in a long line of foolish women—'

'I'm sorry...' Emily saw the core of her mother's hardness in the bitterness in her eyes. Lorene had been hurt, humiliated and abandoned.

'I'm sorry too,' the older woman muttered wearily. 'But I could never feel for you what I felt for your sisters. It wasn't your fault but I still can't look at you without remembering Daniel and I couldn't forgive him for what he did to me.'

'I can imagine. Thank you for finally telling me,' Emily managed to say and then she turned on her heel and walked straight back out of her childhood home. Her sisters had probably known the truth for years, she thought strickenly, possibly even recalling something of that time when their mother had taken them to live with Daniel Stevenson. Why had she been excluded from the secret?

For an instant she hovered on the outside step, struggling to get a hold on the shock consuming her. Duarte, where are you when I need you? The craving for Duarte was so strong she could've cried. Was she really going to tell him that sad little story? The unfaithful wife and the womaniser? Duarte with his incredibly respectable family tree and aristocratic background?

The front door behind her opened again. 'Would you like to come back in?' Lorene asked awkwardly.

'Thanks for the offer but no,' Emily muttered in harried surprise and without looking back she hurried back out to the limousine parked and screened by the high hedge.

Hurried steps sounded behind her. A hand briefly touched her arm. 'Emily, I'm sorry…' Lorene Davies suddenly sobbed.

In any other mood, Emily would have been astonished by that display of emotion in her direction but just then she could not deal with it and all she wanted was to escape. As she flew through the garden gate and back on to the pavement, the rear passenger door of the limousine opened and Duarte stepped fluidly out in front of her.

'What are you doing here?' she gasped chokily.

He scanned her pasty, white face and opened his arms and she threw herself against him with a strangled sob. She'd never been so glad to see anybody. It felt so good to be held. Nothing else seemed to matter. Nothing seemed to hurt so much. He lowered her into the car and nudged her along the seat to climb in beside her.

'How did you g-get here?' she stammered in bewilderment.

'Cab. I suspected that you were planning to confront your mother and I thought I should be within reach just in case it didn't pan out the way you wanted it to.'

She wiped her streaming eyes with the tissue he supplied. 'It didn't. I asked her why she didn't like me and I thought…I thought maybe she would deny it. Or say I had been an extra child she'd never wanted 'cos my sisters are so much older…or that I was a bad pregnancy or a very difficult baby—'

As the limo moved off, Duarte pulled her back against him and curved his arms lightly round her. 'And instead?'

'It turned out I'm the family's dirty secret—'

'Stop exaggerating,' Duarte urged, smoothing her tousled hair back from her damp brow. 'Come on…'

'Mum had an affair with a real creep and he was my father—'

'I suspected something of that nature,' Duarte confided quietly.

Emily tensed and tipped her head up to squint up at him in the most awkward way. 'You…*suspected*?'

'You don't resemble any one of your relatives, *minha jóia*. That in itself could have been simple genetics but, taken in tandem with the manner in which they treated you, it did make me wonder.'

Looked at from upside down, Duarte really did have the most incredible long lashes, Emily conceded absently. She sighed. 'I feel like I've just lost my whole life…like I'm not the person I thought I was—'

'You're Emily Monteiro,' Duarte reminded her instantaneously. 'We'll do some research on your true father if you like. A few details that did not relate to him being a "real creep" might help you come to terms with this.'

'My mother got so upset after telling me…but when she started telling me she was so hard about it.'

'She's probably been dying to get it off her chest for years but I'm sure she didn't get much of a kick out of confessing when it came to the point. Especially as, knowing you, you probably said thanks in your politest voice before tottering away.'

'Pretty much… How do you know that?'

'If you could thank me after I demanded a separation, you could certainly thank your mother for hurting you.'

Emily was so shaken by that statement that she pulled away from him and turned round to face him levelly. 'Did I say thanks that night after you had said you wanted a separation?'

Duarte nodded in confirmation. 'I took it to mean that you had decided that you *did* want to be with Toby Jarrett—'

'Oh, no…you misunderstood!' Aquamarine eyes aghast, Emily shook her head. 'How could you think that?'

'Emily…what I saw and heard that night was a major, not minor shock to my system and you weren't the only one of us saying things you hadn't thought through.'

'Oh… What did you want me to say?'

Duarte gave her an almost wry smile that tugged at her heartstrings for a reason she could not define. 'You were supposed to get down on bended knees and plead for a second chance. Instead you went upstairs and started packing.'

Emily shut her eyes and slumped back against the seat.

Duarte had just told her something she would rather not have known, for it tore her apart. She might have got all that nonsense about Toby cleared up there and then and they might never have separated at all!

'Why is it that you *seem* to be such a predictable woman and yet you never ever give me the response I expect?' Duarte demanded in rampant frustration.

'Sorry…'

'Forget it. I'll go back to my bad old ways. Easy as falling off a log,' Duarte assured her smooth as silk. 'We're going to embark on our honeymoon at Ash Manor. Agreed, it's *not* the Caribbean but the Caribbean does not have good associations for me—'

Duarte had her attention now. 'Honeymoon?' she parroted.

'Bliss and Toby are off the conversational agenda for the moment,' Duarte decreed, warming visibly to the bad old ways of command.

'How can they be?'

'I'm logical, *minha jóia*. No controversial discussions equals no arguments. We can have a church blessing in Portugal and you can trot down the aisle in a rainbow of clashing colours—'

Emily fumbled to find her voice. 'Are you sending me up with all this?'

'Trying to take your mind off your newly discovered family connections.'

'You don't need to go that far—'

Duarte quirked a sardonic black brow. 'I admit that giving you the moon, if you ask for it, is likely to prove a problem—'

'But why…why would you do all this for me?'

'I want to stay married, *querida*. Much as I would like to, I can't chain you to the marital bed or force you to live with me. Basically, I'm endeavouring to launch a rescue bid on our marriage.' Duarte rested his spectacular dark eyes on her shuttered and still tear-stained face. 'If, at any point, you feel moved to offer even an ounce of enthusiasm for that venture, feel free to speak up.'

Emily tore her gaze from the undeniable enchantment of his and thought of how much she loved him, even when he was being unspeakably smart at her expense. 'This is all about Jamie...can't you just admit that?'

Duarte settled himself fluidly back into the far corner of the limo and scorched her with his golden eyes in challenge. 'Is that what you want?'

'Yes!'

'OK...it's about Jamie. I won't tax your patience with all the pros and cons of a child having two parents.'

Given the honesty she had believed she craved, Emily felt dreadful. He was willing to do *anything* to keep their marriage afloat for Jamie's benefit. 'I appreciate your honesty,' she said woodenly.

'Happy now?' Duarte prompted with what she considered to be sheer cruelty.

'Ecstatic...' she mumbled.

It was so strange to be back at Ash Manor as Duarte's wife. Those few days after their wedding, two years earlier, she'd still not felt like his wife. Duarte disappeared into the library to make some phone calls and she went off in search of Jamie. He greeted her with a little shout of pleasure and held out his arms to be lifted.

'Because you're a Monteiro, I'm going to stay one too,' she told her son mournfully but she could not stay down for long in his company.

Duarte loved his son. Duarte had experienced instant love and acceptance where his child was concerned. What did she get in comparison? She got the name, the wealth and now she was going to have the stupid dress and the stupid honeymoon rammed down her throat, whether she wanted them or not! On the other hand, whatever else Duarte was doing, he was not pining for Bliss, was he?

Why did she always want what she couldn't have? Duarte valued their marriage and that should be enough for her now. She'd grown up a lot—she'd stopped living in cloud cuckoo and hoping he might suddenly fall passionately in love with her. But at the same time, she should also be making demands. He was never likely to be more approachable or more willing to listen to her again.

She took Jamie out for a walk in his pram. It was a high coach affair purchased in Lisbon and totally impractical for country conditions. But while she bounced the pram down a grassy laneway beneath the trees, she was considering the demands she felt she ought to make. Having returned to the house and passed her sleeping son over to his nanny, she went into the drawing room and found writing paper and a pen. Then she wrote and she wrote and she wrote.

Duarte was still on the phone when she entered the library. He gave her a slow smile, brilliant eyes roaming over her tense pink face, skimming lower, lingering in provocative places as though he was touching her. He filled her with an awareness that was so strong she was embarrassed by her own susceptibility.

'I want you...' he murmured huskily as he tossed the phone aside and reached for her.

'I think you should read this first...' Emily slid her demand sheets across the polished surface of his desk.

'What's this, *minha jóia*?'

'My blueprint for the rescue bid,' she told him tautly.

Duarte laughed with vibrant amusement, tugged her down on to his lap and started to read. Then he gently and firmly lifted her off him again. 'I work no more than eight hours a day, the only exception being an emergency? That's not possible—'

'You could try it.'

'If I go abroad, you come too?'

'You could try going less often—'

'"For every day you spend away from me, I will spend a day away from you,"' Duarte read out loud in disbelief. 'That's blackmail. We would never see each other!'

'I need a life too—'

'*Do homemes a praça, da mulheres a casa,*' Duarte quoted that well-known Portuguese proverb with gravity. Men out and about, women at home.

'The rescue bid is off—'

He paled. 'OK. You win but have you ever heard of the art of compromise?'

'I did nothing but compromise the first time around and I was miserable and lonely.'

Looking grim, Duarte made it on to the second sheet and then he smiled at her with that sudden flashing charisma that could make her heart sing. 'Truthfully—you don't really want me out of your sight for longer than eight hours at a time?'

'If you want to think that, that's fine by me.'

His smile vanished. He skimmed through all the minor requests, even chuckled a few times and then, without any warning, he suddenly slung the last sheet aside and sprang upright. 'You don't want any more children with me? What kind of a condition is that?'

He looked so hurt, so full of reproach and incomprehension.

'You made me feel that I had to give you a baby when we first married and the truth is, I felt too young and I wasn't ready to be a mother then,' Emily admitted awkwardly.

'I never ever demanded that you give me a baby—'

'No but you took if for granted that I would.'

'If that is how you feel…didn't you *want* him?' Duarte shot at her in sudden emotive appeal.

'I adore Jamie but if ever I have another baby, it has to be because *I* want another baby.'

'All I can say is that I believed you felt the same way as me about having a family…'

She saw the sincerity in his eyes as he made that claim and felt terrible.

'Obviously I won't make the same mistake again,' Duarte drawled flatly. 'No wonder you were so miserable when you were pregnant—'

Emily's eyes shimmered. 'I was unhappy because after I became pregnant you just…well, I mean, you never touched me again—'

'Did you expect me to disregard the doctor's advice?' Duarte demanded in astonishment.

'What advice?' Emily frowned.

'Emily, you were present when the doctor advised us to desist from marital relations for the first few months!'

'I never heard him say that…' She sank down in the chair behind her. Thinking back, she remembered that during the first antenatal examination she had had, she had refused to have Duarte present and the nurse had translated the doctor's comments because the older man had not spoken English. When Duarte had been called back in the nurse had gone out and the doctor had talked at length to them both, but Emily hadn't paid much heed for she had trusted Duarte to translate anything of any further importance.

'You honestly didn't know?' Duarte raked an impatient hand through his black hair and stared at her. 'If you didn't understand, why didn't you ask me to explain afterwards, if not at the time?'

'I couldn't wait to get out of there! The whole time the doctor was examining me he was telling me off for being so thin and underweight and he was upsetting me. You never even mentioned it to me,' she condemned in turn.

'What was there to mention? Who wants to discuss a blanket ban on sex?'

'I misjudged you. I'm sorry. I wouldn't have locked the bedroom door if I'd known we were supposed to be desisting, or whatever he called it,' she lamented, feeling foolish. 'I felt so rejected.'

'I wasn't exactly celebrating either.' Reaching down, Duarte tugged her upright, his lean, strong face taut. 'We were like strangers when we first got married. I believed I could take a wife and that we could be content without being very close—'

'You chose the wrong woman—'

'I deserved a gold-digger.' He gazed down at her with rueful, dark-as-midnight eyes. 'I made you very unhappy.'

'I need closeness…'

'I'm working on it—but I'm really good at the physical end of the scale…' Duarte cupped her cheekbones, spread his fingers and drew her mouth under his with a hot, hungry urgency that nonetheless contained a vein of tenderness she had never felt from him before.

And suddenly she was kissing him back with the most desperate surging need powering through her, her slim body quivering at every contact with his. Breathing raggedly, he lifted his head. 'Let's go to bed—'

'It's barely tea time—'

'Let's go to bed—'

'What about Jamie's bath?'

'Our son has a nanny, and I can't wait and neither can you,' Duarte assured her with mesmeric intensity, shifting against her to acquaint her with his bold arousal, cupping her hips in the same sinfully erotic way to pull her up to him.

They got to the bedroom without meeting anyone, which had been Emily's only fear. Duarte brought her down on the bed fully clothed and came down on top of her and kissed her breathless. The need in her was so intense she was raw with it, shaken by her own desire. She just wanted him so much and his passion more than matched hers. He was wild for her and the more she recognised that, the more she threw off her inhibitions. She raked her nails down his back at the height of fulfilment and looked in stricken dismay at the marks she had left on his beautiful back in the aftermath.

Duarte just laughed and hugged her to him with easy strength. 'You just used me, *minha esposa*. As a vent for a very upsetting day. I'm not complaining but if I ever call back home at lunchtime and grab you off your feet and pin you flat to the nearest horizontal surface, you have to promise to be equally understanding.'

As Emily could not picture him dragging himself from the bank at lunchtime, she just pressed a kiss to a muscular brown shoulder and drifted off to sleep, satiated and secure.

CHAPTER ELEVEN

EMILY spun slowly round in front of the cheval mirror, admiring herself from every angle.

It was the wedding dress of her dreams. Romantic, filmy, the colour of champagne and the most superb fit. Her tiny waist was accentuated which had the miraculous effect of lending her the illusion of a fuller swell in the bosom department. Not that it mattered to anyone but her, for Duarte seemed to have a genuine passion for her just as she was.

Humming under her breath, she feasted her eyes upon herself. He would love the dress. She knew he was bracing himself for the clashing rainbow of colours because he was not to know that dear Bliss had convinced her that that was what most flattered her. But it had only taken one glimpse of herself clad in palest blue for Emily to see the light.

They had spent three weeks at Ash Manor, returning to Portugal only the night before. Three of the happiest weeks of her life. There was a kind of magic in the air between them. No doubt that was her romanticising his erotic and intense absorption in making love to her at every possible opportunity but they had had a lot of fun out of bed too. With Jamie. Out riding together. And all the time she'd been learning that she had spent a long time married to and living with a male she had never really got to know. But then, Duarte had not really wanted her to get to know him then.

'I thought you would be the kind of wife whom I would always find in the stables with the horses,' he had confided only the week before. 'Instead you were always out socialising and shopping and, when you were at home, you threw constant dinner parties. It reminded me of life with Izabel. I hated it.'

Instead of pleasing him with her efforts to fit the role she had assumed he wanted her to occupy, she had actually been pushing him away. The more she discovered, the more she loved him for what he was really telling her was that they were much better matched than she could ever have believed. He liked to entertain friends and family at home but he very much preferred to keep business connections out of their home.

He gave her flowers every day and laughed at the way her arrangements turned out. He gave her true affection that did not always lead to passion. He gave her everything but his heart. And she had pretty much given up on his heart. As she finally came to understand just how much Izabel had hurt him, she knew why he had had the reserve and that desire to control. His heart had brick walls round it except where Jamie was concerned and if she ever told him that all that was wrong with him was his gigantic unconfessed fear of being hurt again, he would never, ever forgive her.

After all, she'd already hurt him with Toby, hadn't she? She had dwindled into a poor little victim instead of forcing him to recognise that she was telling the truth.

As for Bliss, well, Emily believed that she'd already worked out the most likely scenario on that score. Duarte was probably going to admit to her that he had slept with Bliss during the difficult months that he had been searching for his wife and child. She was going to have to deal with that and she didn't know how she would. But that explanation made sense as to why Duarte should have insisted on not talking about Bliss for a few weeks, didn't it? Duarte had decided that if he had risked telling her the truth first, their marriage had no hope of surviving.

An impatient knock sounded on the door. 'Emily…?'

She smiled, suppressing the pained regret roused by her most recent thoughts. She opened the door a chink. 'Close your eyes…'

'No. I want to see you,' Duarte overruled. 'I've waited long enough.'

She opened the door wide and let him look.

His brilliant eyes shimmered over her. 'You look amazing. I was a selfish bastard two years ago—'

'I don't think you meant to be,' Emily told him forgivingly.

'That's right, Emily. Encourage me to be like that again.'

'What time do we have to be at the church for the blessing?' she prompted.

'We've got plenty of time—'

'Why won't you tell me what time?'

'I have a couple of people waiting downstairs and we need to deal with them first.' Duarte banded an arm to her spine as they reached the first landing.

'What people?'

'Had I had the option, I would've staged this weeks ago but I couldn't track the guy down. He was hiking round South America.'

'Who are you talking about?' Emily frowned.

Dropping his hand to her waist, Duarte ushered her towards the salon. 'Toby Jarrett.'

'Toby?' Emily gasped in pure horror. 'I don't want to see *him* again!'

However, a bigger shock awaited her within the salon. Not Toby, whom she was expecting, but Bliss. Bliss turned from the window with a saccharine smile that froze when she registered in visible bewilderment that Emily was wearing a wedding dress.

'We won't keep you long, Bliss,' Duarte drawled. 'To save us all a long trawl through murky waters, you could just confess to being a scheming, vindictive woman.'

Bliss blinked and stared at Duarte. 'I beg your pardon?'

'You weaseled your way into a fake friendship with my wife so that you could cause trouble. You never ever told me when Emily called the office and tried to speak to me. You also forgot to fill in my diary for the dinner parties—'

'I don't believe I'm hearing these terrible accusations,' Bliss said in a mortified tone of reproach.

Emerging from her own shock that Duarte should even have made such very accurate accusations, Emily's head turned as the door that connected with the dining room pushed open and framed Toby Jarrett. Emily's face reddened fiercely. Tall and fair and lanky, Toby moved deeper into the room.

'What are you doing here?' Bliss demanded sharply.

'I'm here to call your bluff,' Toby sighed, his frank open features grim. 'You offered me several thousand pounds to try and seduce Duarte's wife last year. I was broke but even I wasn't that low. I was quite happy to settle for the portrait commission—'

'He's telling outright lies!' Bliss snapped. 'Surely you don't believe this rubbish, Duarte?'

'Why *should* Toby lie?' Emily murmured tightly, focusing on the blonde with shaken eyes of revulsion after what the younger man had revealed. 'What has he got to gain from lying now?'

Duarte studied his executive assistant with chilling cool. 'I cannot blame Emily for trusting you when I made the mistake. You're sacked, Bliss—and, by the way, if you keep on telling people that I slept with you, I will take you to court for slander—'

'And how are you ever going to prove that you *didn't*?' Bliss slammed back at him and she gave Emily a cold look of triumph. 'You're never going to know for sure, are you?'

'I think the fact that you pulled the same stunt with your

last employer would go a long way to vindicating me,' Duarte remarked very quietly.

Stilling at that response, Bliss turned white and then she stared at her cousin in furious condemnation. *'Toby?'*

'Sorry—but when you came out to Lisbon to work on the strength of a fake reference issued by one of my father's friends, you promised that you were making a fresh start.'

'You did something like this *before*?' Emily demanded of Bliss.

'Her last boss was married, too. She told a couple of people in confidence that they were lovers and got the rumour mill going,' Toby explained ruefully. 'Then she tried to blackmail him by threatening to lie to his wife as well. But he went to the police. Bliss got off with a police caution but only because she managed to convince a doctor that she had had a nervous breakdown.'

'Were you planning to blackmail Duarte too?' Emily asked the blonde in horror.

Bliss seemed oddly diminished in stature but her eyes were as hard as ever. Without troubling to respond—indeed, accepting that her every malicious act had been exposed—she just walked out of the room.

'I think she was hoping to *marry* Duarte,' Toby told Emily gently. 'But to achieve that, she had to get you out of the picture. She went mad with rage when Duarte remarried—'

Duarte looked shaken by that information.

'I'm sorry I was such a jerk last year, Emily.' Toby shrugged awkwardly and hovered in front of her where she could no longer avoid looking at him. 'But to know you is to love you and I'm a hopeless romantic. There you were, the neglected wife—'

'She's not neglected any more,' Duarte slotted in faster than the speed of light. 'And you told me that you fall in love *very* easily—'

'I suppose that's true. Blame the artistic temperament.' Toby grinned at both of them, quite untouched by the smallest shade of embarrassment.

'I just wish you'd come clean with me about what Bliss was up to,' Emily censured helplessly.

'He wanted you for himself. Why would he have told you the truth about his cousin?' Duarte remarked flatly.

'I was ready to talk about Bliss after you and Duarte separated because that did make me feel bad, as it was pretty obvious that you weren't remotely interested in me. But you wouldn't talk to *me* when I trekked out to the Douro to try and sort things out,' Toby reminded Emily.

'And then I beat you up to make you stay away from her,' Duarte conceded in the thwarted undertone of someone trying to regret an action but not succeeding that well. 'You did try to get me to listen to you but I wasn't prepared to give you a hearing.'

'And after that,' Toby said with a feeling shudder, 'I was totally out of charity with you and too scared to try and talk to Emily again.'

Duarte thanked Toby for lending him his support and in doing so, ushered the younger man to the door where he urged him to enjoy his flight back to Peru.

'You're darned right I will—in your jet!' Laughing, Toby strolled out looking as if he hadn't a care in the world.

Emily watched Toby depart and felt very much like taking him by the collar and shaking him. He had caused so much trouble but it had really washed right back off him again. Easy come, easy go, that was Toby. Yet, in spite of that, Toby *had* made the effort to try and set her straight about Bliss. It was just unfortunate that she had refused to speak to him.

'I'm grateful that Jarrett was willing to provide the back-up for exposing Bliss.' Duarte shot her stilled figure a veiled glance. 'I was afraid that, without his support, you would remain suspicious.'

Emily coloured and spun away, afraid that what she was thinking would show in her face and rub salt in the wound. Duarte was so proud. Yet he had tracked down Toby and asked him for his help. She cringed inwardly at what that approach must have cost Duarte in terms of pride.

'When did you realise that Bliss was lying?' she asked uncomfortably, in one way feeling guilty that she had forced him to such lengths but in another feeling hopelessly upstaged. She had demanded proof and, no matter what the cost to himself, Duarte had supplied her with proof of Bliss's true nature. It might have taken him three weeks to track down Toby but Duarte had not called off the search. Nor had he hesitated to confess that he had been equally taken in by the other woman. Emily was extremely disconcerted by his behaviour.

'The grandfather clock...I did tell you that I had a vague recollection of Bliss once telling me about the clock—'

'No, you didn't,' she argued.

Duarte awarded her a wry smile and reminded her of how tired she had been at the end of that party three weeks earlier. 'You didn't take in what I had told you. As soon as I recalled the clock reference, I appreciated that if Bliss could lie about that, she was most probably lying about *everything*—'

'So why didn't you tell me that, the next morning?' Emily demanded.

'I still had no proof to offer that I hadn't had an affair with her,' Duarte pointed out. 'And, to be frank, I had shot myself in the foot, trying to make you jealous of her—'

'Say that again...' Emily was frowning at him, struggling to understand that sudden confession.

Duarte moved expressive and fluid hands. 'I—'

'Tell me that bit again about trying to make me jealous,'

Emily cut in a second time. 'I just want to be sure that you actually *said* that—'

Duarte was very taut. 'That conversation we had in the car after you had come to the city apartment. You had been talking about divorce again. I was angry with you. It was the impulse of a moment to exaggerate the less formal terms of my relationship with Bliss—'

'To…make…me…jealous,' Emily echoed afresh as if she was having a great deal of trouble coming to terms with that concept. 'You mean, you *lied*—'

Duarte winced at the bluntness of that term. 'At that stage, I didn't think it would do you any harm to wonder exactly what I *might* have been doing while you were staying lost in England for months on end—'

Emily folded her arms and stared at him with accusing aquamarine eyes. 'I don't believe I'm hearing this—'

'At that stage I was still suffering from the conviction that I was making a very generous gesture in trying to put our marriage back together again—'

'So you told me what was most likely to undermine it? You let me think you had got so close to Bliss—?'

'*Meu Deus*…I lived to regret my impulse, didn't I?' Duarte countered with feeling fervour. 'All I did after you went missing was work and search for you—but to confess that seemed weak!'

Emily pivoted away from him to hide a sudden helpless smile. He'd wanted to make her jealous. He had not had a clue what a nest of intrigue he was naively stirring with his behaviour. His pride had been hurting. He had been foolish but in a manner that now struck her as quite ridiculously sweet. Where was the man whom she'd once believed was so utterly indifferent to her feelings? It occurred to her that that man had never existed.

Bliss had found a fertile playground in the emotional distance between Duarte and his new wife and Emily's own shy insecurity had been the other woman's greatest aid. The blonde's first tentative efforts to cause trouble would have been swiftly concluded had Emily ever turned round and asked her husband why he never returned her phone calls.

'I have never found Bliss attractive. I was always aware of her cold nature but I did not require anything warmer from an employee whom, even now, I must concede *was* an exceptionally efficient assistant,' Duarte asserted heavily.

'When I began telling you on the flight to London about the other things she had done, you were furious with her, *not* with me...' Emily registered, turning back to look at him again, relishing that reference to Bliss as being cold.

'Of course I was furious—but more with myself even than Bliss, *minha jóia*' Duarte admitted with bleak, dark eyes of regret. 'I was bitterly angry that you had been manipulated to that extent and that I had exposed you to her malice. If I had treated you as I should have treated you, Bliss would have been powerless.'

'Yes. Just one more thing,' Emily framed with curiosity. 'The first day I came back. At the airport, you stayed with Bliss to talk to her...what about?'

'I took exception to the way in which she looked at you and spoke to you,' Duarte admitted without hesitation.

'You were telling her off.' Emily tried very hard not to laugh but for a few seconds, it was a fight she thought she would lose. She swallowed hard. She thought back to some of the things he'd said to her that same day and compared it to the speed with which he had turned on Bliss to rebuke her for what he had evidently seen as a lack of respect; she could only be amused.

'I assure you that I never ever discussed either you or our marriage with Bliss. Our more relaxed working relationship did not embrace any true confessions. I do not discuss private matters with anyone—'

'I know…' Emily conceded, fully convinced. 'Until recently, not *even* with me.'

'Right…OK, I walked right into that one,' Duarte agreed, but dark colour had risen to outline his high cheekbones.

'I just want you to appreciate that not telling me the truth about Izabel was taking confidentiality a giant step too far,' Emily murmured gently.

Duarte snatched in a sustaining breath and squared his broad shoulders. 'I believed you would think a great deal less of me if you knew what a mess my first marriage had been.'

Distressed by that patently honest admission, Emily closed the distance between them and reached for one lean brown hand. 'It wouldn't have been like that. I would have understood you much better—'

Duarte gazed down into her hugely sympathetic aquamarine eyes and murmured with brilliant golden eyes that had a rueful tinge, 'I should admit that I also rather enjoyed being treated like an omnipotent god.'

Emily blinked in disconcertion.

'It enabled me to feel in control…and I'm not in control at all!' Duarte groaned out loud with startling abruptness as he glanced at his watch and registered the time. 'We're running late for the church!'

Emily sighed. 'Look, you don't have to go through with this simply to please me. When it comes down to brass tacks, stuff like this dress and the church blessing, well…I'd much rather not have them if you really don't want them.'

'Of course I want them, *minha esposa*…' Tightening his hold on her fingers, Duarte hurried her out to the waiting limousine with quite indecent speed. 'This blessing will signify a new beginning to our marriage and a proper commitment on my part to make you happy—'

'You mean you *never* had any intention of making me happy two years ago?' Emily muttered painfully.

Duarte tucked her and her skirts into the car with careful hands and sank down beside her. 'Then the only thought in my head was making *me* happy.'

'Oh…' Only somewhat soothed by that contradiction, Emily decided that she would have to think that confession over in greater depth. 'You're saying you were totally self-ish…'

Duarte vented a reluctant laugh and closed his hand over hers again. 'I was striving to evade using exactly those words.'

The limousine drew to a halt mere minutes later outside the little village church. As Emily stepped out of the car, she was taken aback to find Victorine moving forward to present her with a beautiful bouquet of flowers and proffer stilted but evidently genuine good wishes. Emily smiled with true pleasure and thanked the older woman.

'That was so sweet of her, Duarte,' Emily enthused as her husband led her into the church, which was filled to overflowing with more flowers and lit only by candles. 'Oh, this is really lovely…'

The blessing was simple but sincere. Emily listened to every word with the happy and grateful sense that indeed she and Duarte had already found their new beginning. Her eyes damp with unashamed tears of emotion, she was startled when Duarte closed his arms round her and kissed her breathless in the shadowy darkness of the tiny church porch.

Emerging from that unexpectedly passionate clinch, Emily was flushed and in need of being guided back to the car.

'I want you to know that I have rearranged my work schedule and delegated a good deal of the business that formerly took me abroad,' Duarte informed her, studying her with intent dark golden eyes. 'This is the optimum right moment for you to make further demands, *querida*.'

Emily's mind was a terrible blank. She was in awe of this male so determined not to fall into the mistakes of the past again. Indeed, she felt just a little like a new project being enthusiastically attacked and could not help but worry about the effect of what so many sacrifices would be on him in the future. Would his first fine flush of courageous effort wear off and leave him feeling that life with her was just one big pain?

'You really don't need to *do* any more to please me. I'm not going anywhere. I'm not going to leap on the first plane back to England when we have some stupid row,' Emily assured him carefully. 'You can stop worrying.'

'I also want to admit that I totally overreacted over Toby Jarrett because, from my point of view, there was some horrible truths in what he said about my not deserving you,' Duarte ground out like a male set on an unstoppable course to tell all whether he wanted to or not. 'It was bad enough seeing him kiss you but it was worse thinking that I drove you into his arms!'

'Oh, dear...' Emily glanced at his darkly handsome profile as they walked back into the *quinta*, registering his pronounced tension with dismay.

'In fact, the weeks you were in the Douro were not exactly the best weeks of my life,' Duarte framed with charged difficulty, striding straight past the assembled household staff apparently without seeing them and carrying her with him towards the stairs. 'You see, you were still in Portugal. I had seen off Toby, dealt with him. You were still within reach...'

'Hold it a minute...' Emily urged weakly and hurried back a few steps to accept the flowers that the housekeeper was proffering and thank the older woman and their staff for the kind chorus of best wishes being offered.

Darting back to Duarte's side, breathless with her arms full of flowers, Emily prompted him helpfully, 'You were saying that while I was still within Portugal you thought of me as being still within reach…?'

Lean, powerful face rigid with tension, Duarte frowned and carried on up the stairs with Emily scurrying in his wake. 'Duarte?'

'When you vanished I was on the brink of coming to see you and asking you to come home,' Duarte completed in a charged admission.

'Please don't tell me any more…' Emily urged in a wobbly voice as tears clogged her throat. 'It's only going to make me hate myself for running away even more than I already do—'

'No. I think you had to do a vanishing act before I could admit to myself how much I loved you. And, having admitted that to myself, it sort of got it out of the way and you can be sure I didn't think about it again until very recently,' Duarte confided.

On the threshold of their bedroom, Emily surveyed him with very wide eyes of shock.

Duarte removed the flowers from her arms and settled them on the nearest piece of furniture.

'You can't leave them lying there. They'll die out of water,' Emily mumbled, no longer sure what she was saying. 'You just said that you loved me…'

Duarte closed both hands over hers and pulled her over the threshold and closed the door with a well-aimed kick.

'That is so bad for the wood,' Emily rebuked, feeling distinctly dizzy.

Duarte drew her close and splayed his fingers to her cheekbones. 'I wanted you the minute I laid eyes on you—'

'I bet you don't even *remember* the first time you laid eyes on me!' Emily objected, regarding that lesser claim as an equally contentious subject and wondering dismally if he thought that he needed to pretend that he loved her to make her happy.

A winged dark brow climbed. 'Don't I?'

'No way do you remember,' Emily told him a second time.

'You were wearing ancient jeans with holes in the knees and an old green sweater,' Duarte recounted with a certain amount of self-satisfaction. 'Your gorgeous hair was tied back with a piece of baling twine—'

'You remember…' Emily acknowledged in open disbelief at the accuracy of that description. 'But you didn't even seem to look at me—'

'So I'm subtle, *minha jóia*,' Duarte teased with glancing amusement brimming in his gaze as he absorbed her continuing shock. 'I thought you were very fanciable but I wasn't planning to do anything about it—'

Emily was hanging shamelessly on his every word. 'What changed your mind?'

'You dragged my dog out of a barn on fire and I was hugely impressed. There you were, not only sexy but nice into the bargain and so modest. Then I took you home to your family and realised you were Cinderella in disguise. All my protective instincts were roused—'

'Were they?'

Having begun, Duarte was now eager to tell all. 'I thought up that job so that I could get to know you better—'

'Without committing yourself to anything more,' Emily slotted in helplessly. 'And after you had looked your fill on me being kind and helpful with little children and animals, you asked me out to dinner with a view to what?'

'Marrying you. What's wrong with that?' Duarte went on the defensive, bright golden eyes clinging to her taut expression and troubled eyes with forceful intensity. 'OK, so I was terrified of making another mistake and I didn't rush in to asking you out—'

'It's all right. You may not have rushed in to asking me out but you did rush in to asking me to marry you,' Emily conceded but somehow still contrived to make it sound as if she had received the consolation prize.

Duarte hauled her into his arms, troubled eyes colliding with hers. 'And doesn't the fact that I couldn't wait to make you my wife tell you something?'

'You decided you'd wasted enough time observing me?'

'*Inferno!*' Duarte groaned as he stared down at her in frustration. 'I was in love with you. I just didn't want to admit that even to myself!'

She searched his lean powerful face and the intensity she met in his stunning eyes set her free forever from the belief that he did not love her. Her heart went off on a roller-coaster ride that left her breathless. 'So when did you appreciate how you felt?'

Perceptibly, Duarte winced. 'When we were separated and I started thinking that maybe I should give you a second chance—'

'It took you that long?' Emily probed unimpressed.

'Slow learner...' Possibly feeling that they had dwelt enough on his reluctance to face the strength of his feelings for her, Duarte claimed a slow deep kiss that made her pulse race.

'Just one thing you haven't explained,' Emily recalled as she surfaced. 'I assume Bliss *was* the third party who confirmed that I was supposedly having an affair with Toby—'

Paling, Duarte gave her a look of deep regret. 'Who else? She said that Toby had confided in her and that she had urged him to break off the relationship—'

'That conniving little shrew—and you couldn't see the wood for the trees!' Emily condemned hotly.

'If it hadn't been for that kiss I witnessed, I wouldn't

have been so easily convinced,' Duarte argued. 'But, at the time, as far as I was concerned, Bliss had no axe to grind and every reason to avoid referring to the fact that her cousin had seduced my wife!'

'You should have had more faith in me—'

'After Izabel, trust was a problem for me. As for having more faith,' Duarte continued, deftly closing his hands to her waist and lifting her off her feet to deposit her down on the bed. He followed her down with easy grace and studied her. 'I still haven't heard an explanation of why you asked me the day I found you and Jamie if I was intending to have other women *again*?'

'Oh…that!' Her own ire doused by a dose of the same medicine, it was Emily's turn to look uncomfortable. 'Bliss never once said that you had other women but she used to sort of hint that she suspected that you strayed when you were away on business—'

'Never *once*,' Duarte delivered. 'I always valued our marriage. I would not have risked it—'

'Even when the bedroom door was locked?'

'I put that down to your being pregnant…just not being in the mood,' Duarte confided huskily. 'But when I saw you with Toby, I put a very different construction on that locked door.'

Raising a newly confident hand, Emily let her fingertips stroke down over one hard sculpted cheekbone in a loving caress. 'I love you loads and loads and loads but please don't ask me why it took me so long to decide I wanted a divorce.'

'Are you kidding?' Duarte groaned, the last of his tension dissipating as he heard those words and studied her hectically flushed face with intensely appreciative eyes of gold. 'Every time you mentioned divorce, I went into panic mode. I thought I was going to lose you again. When we were flying into London and I was facing the fact that Bliss was lying and I had got everything wrong, I felt like I was fighting for my life—'

'So that was why you were behaving that way. Sort of desperate…' Emily recalled with a heady sensation of having more power than she had ever dared to hope over the male she loved.

'And you were *so* convinced that my sole objective was hanging on to Jamie, I saw that if I told you I loved you then, there was no way on earth you were likely to believe me,' Duarte confessed with a ragged edge roughening his dark deep drawl.

'You're probably right. On the other h-hand,' Emily stammered slightly as a lean hand glided in a possessive sweep from her waist to her breast.

'You were saying, *minha jóia*?'

'I forget…' And she looked up at him, her fingers lacing into the thick black hair she loved to touch, her aquamarine eyes shimmering over him with wondering satisfaction while he slowly lowered her down on to the pillows.

Duarte frowned and abandoned her with startling abruptness. 'That reminds me.'

Emily sat up in shock and watched him stride through to his dressing room. 'Reminds you of what? Where are you going?'

Duarte emerged again with a large parcel which he balanced on the foot of the bed while he ripped off the packaging.

As Emily focused on the painting of herself which she had last seen at Toby's studio, her soft mouth opened in considerable shock.

'You were right. Toby *is* one hell of an artist. I took the painting from him because I felt that he had no right to keep an image of my wife,' Duarte informed her loftily, a possessive glow in his gaze as he surveyed her. 'I intended to destroy it but, when I looked at the canvas, I could not bring myself to commit such an act of destruction.'

Emily's eyes stung. 'Now I *truly* believe that you love me—'

'Never doubt it, *minha esposa*. I will never stop loving you,' Duarte swore, abandoning the canvas to gather her back into his strong arms and claim her mouth with hot and wholly appreciative fervour.

Eighteen months later, Emily tucked Jamie into his bed. Their son had learned to walk early and at supersonic speed he'd demonstrated extraordinary persistence at escaping from his cot. A little bed shaped like the toy cars he adored had seemed a safer option for their miniature mountaineer.

Smoothing his tumbled black hair from his brow, she watched him slide into the sleep of exhaustion, contentedly clutching his faded blue teddy and looking impossibly angelic. Throughout the day Jamie ran on pure livewire energy and Emily was very grateful to have not only the assistance of a nanny but also of Victorine, who had become one of Jamie's most devoted slaves. Emily adored her son too but she was already recognising many of Duarte's traits in their son. The try, try again determination, the bone-deep stubbornness and the hot temper—and she was equally grateful that Jamie had a father willing to exert loving but firm control.

There had been quite a few changes in their lives over the past eighteen months, she reflected with the lightness of heart that had become second nature to her. No longer did she worry herself sick about imminent disaster. Knowing that she was loved and valued and very much needed by Duarte had made a huge difference to her self-esteem. Even her Portuguese had improved by leaps and bounds, enabling her to overcome her former shyness and enjoy company and make proper friends.

After exchanging stilted taut phonecalls with her mother the year before in an effort to ease the tension between them and visiting again, Emily had finally acknowledged that she and her mother were never likely to be that close. Her mother's husband, Peter Davies, had never had any interest in her and that had not changed but, now that she understood why that was so, it no longer hurt her.

However, it had been a very welcome surprise when both her sisters, initially shaken by the effect of Emily finally asserting herself, had slowly come round to seeing her as she *was* rather than as the illegitimate kid sister whom they had pretty much been taught to despise. Only then had she realised how easily families could all sink into the same bad pattern of behaviour. She had finally appreciated that neither Hermione nor Corinne were that close to Lorene either but over the past year her sisters had steadily become closer to Emily.

'They just copied your mother. It wasn't until you made them stand back and question their attitude that they saw how it had been. They're adults now and they've started thinking for themselves,' Duarte had asserted with immense approval, no longer referring to them as the ugly sisters and indeed making much-appreciated efforts to introduce them to eligible men.

And Duarte? Emily crossed the corridor into their bedroom—the nursery had been moved to a more convenient location. Emily smiled as she noticed the adrenalin kit in the bedroom—Duarte had insisted they had one in every room.

Duarte strolled out of the bathroom, still wet from the shower, only a towel wrapped round his lean hips. 'Is Jamie asleep?'

He still took her breath away, Emily conceded, striving not to stare like a teenager at all that potent masculinity on display. 'Out like a light—'

'It'll be the five o'clock start he had today.' Duarte gave a slight shudder at the memory of being bounced into rude wakefulness at dawn by his energetic son.

'Oh, well,' Emily said wickedly. 'You are the man who once wanted a really big family and I have reached a decision—'

Duarte had tensed. 'What about?'

'I want another baby—'

'Two to bounce on us at dawn?' Duarte tried to tease but shock was written all over him at that announcement. 'Emily, you really *don't* have to make the kind of sacrifice for me. There's a lot more to family than numbers. I'm perfectly happy with Jamie—'

'But I'm not and this has very little to do with you,' Emily told him with dancing eyes, touched by his efforts to dissuade her when she knew how much he regretted never having had the opportunity to really share her last pregnancy with her. 'I just have this yen for another child—'

Duarte searched her smiling face with a frown and he argued, 'I don't want you being sick and miserable—'

'But it's not going to be like that again—'

'How do you know?'

'I *know*,' Emily told him with an air of feminine superiority. 'I just know…OK?'

He reached for her and drew her lazily up against his big powerful body, sending her temperature rocketing. Stunning golden eyes glittered over her with possessive heat. 'It's just we come first and I want you to be happy—'

'You're the man who promised me the moon,' Emily said plaintively, lashes cast down. 'I'm *still* waiting…'

Duarte vented a deeply appreciative laugh and backed her down on the bed. 'Are you ever going to let me live that down, *minha esposa*?'

'Probably not.' She smiled up at him, her heart in her eyes, luxuriating in the adoring look he could not hide, thinking how lucky she was and how gloriously happy. It had not taken the gift of the moon to bring about that transformation. All it had taken was love.

'I love you more every day,' Duarte groaned hungrily against her extended throat, feeling her quiver and arch in instant encouragement. 'You've got me flying home for lunch now. You make me insatiable—'

'Hear any complaints?' Emily teased, inching off his towel like a shameless woman set on seduction. 'Instead of some boring working lunch, you get me—'

'And the more I get of you, the more I want you,' Duarte confided, stringing a trail of tormenting kisses across her delicate collarbone. 'OK...we'll think about another baby when we've really talked over the idea in depth.'

Arabel Monteiro was born nine months and two weeks later and their daughter's conception never was discussed in depth. Emily was neither sick nor miserable during her second pregnancy and Duarte presented her with a very beautiful diamond-studded moonstone pendant and earrings.

'You're not getting off the hook that easily,' Emily warned him cheerfully.

'I think you finally know me, *minha esposa*,' Duarte pronounced with loving eyes and his wonderful smile.

GREEK FOR
BEGINNERS

JACKIE BRAUN

To Roma Costanzo
with thanks for all of her love and support!

CHAPTER ONE

IF DARCIE HAYES had any lingering doubts about her decision to call off her wedding a week before the "I dos" and end her engagement to her longtime beau, they were eradicated the moment she stepped off the plane in Athens and scanned the crowd.

A driver was supposed to meet her at the airport. That was part of the nonrefundable, all-inclusive Greek tour package that her spendthrift fiancé had booked for their honeymoon. The honeymoon she had decided to take alone.

Tad got their Buffalo, New York, condominium and their antisocial cat in the breakup. She'd figured a couple of weeks away from her well-meaning friends and family in sun-drenched Greece was a fair trade since she'd never liked the condo, and the cat had never liked her. Now, she had the sinking feeling that Tad had gotten the better end of the deal.

She saw no hand-printed sign bearing her name. Nor was anyone smiling in welcome and waving to gain her attention. For a brief moment, a handsome man on a cell phone stopped talking and their gazes met.

Her best friend Becky's last text played through Darcie's head.

Meet a man. Have a fling. Get ur sexy back.

Becky had wanted to come on the trip, but she hadn't

been able to get the time off work on such short notice. That wasn't stopping her from giving Darcie all sorts of advice on how to spend her time, including having a fling. Well, if Darcie were going to cast caution to the wind, this would be exactly the sort of man she would pick to do it with. He was so gorgeous that her mouth threatened to fall open. It settled for watering, and she was forced to swallow or she would have drooled. The crowd of departing passengers surged around him then, obstructing her view. When the travelers cleared, he was gone.

After that, the only person who made eye contact with Darcie was a portly porter who approached with a trolley as she waited for her bags at the luggage carousel. It was just her luck that only one of the designer knock-offs showed up. It was the smaller of the two—the bag in which she'd packed her "second-string" outfits, the first string being the new clothes she'd bought especially for the trip. The bag sported wheels and a retractable handle, but the handle was out and dangling uselessly to the side. As for the wheels, one had been sheared off somehow.

The porter pointed to the missing wheel and busted handle, and then pointed to the trolley. Darcie nodded. Even though the bag was only one size up from a carry-on, when she'd hefted it onto the scale at the airport in Buffalo, she'd nearly given herself a hernia. She was more than happy to have someone else do the heavy lifting now.

The porter was old enough to be her father, but nothing about the smile he gave her was paternal. After loading her bag onto a cart, he winked. Then his gaze skimmed down and he said something in Greek that, even though she didn't know what it meant, had her checking the buttons on her blouse to be sure they were fastened.

"I, um, can take it from here," Darcie said, handing him

a couple euros for a tip and then making a shooing motion with her hands.

Alone again, she heaved a frustrated sigh. So much for the part of her itinerary that read, "You will be met at the airport by a member of our friendly and efficient English-speaking staff and taken directly to one of Athens's finest hotels."

But then what her near-miss of a husband considered "sparing no expense" on the trip of a lifetime and how the majority of people would define the concept were two different things entirely. Tad had never earned a penny that he hadn't pinched mercilessly afterward. Darcie was all for getting a good deal, but more often than not, you got what you paid for. She had a bad feeling this trip was going to be a case in point. The plane ride had been her first clue, wedged as she'd been for the long, transatlantic flight into a coach seat so narrow that even a runway model would have found the dimensions unforgiving.

Darcie wasn't a runway model, nor would she ever be mistaken for one, even if at five foot eleven she had the height. She also had curves, the kind for which words such as *big-boned* and, her personal favorite, *full-figured* had been strung together. She'd long ago reconciled herself to that fact that no amount of dieting was going to result in her being considered dainty. Instead, through hard work and an amount of discipline she hadn't known she'd possessed, she'd toned her body into its best shape ever for her wedding day. She'd planned to rock the church wearing a fitted white mermaid gown, but she'd never walked down the aisle.

That had been her choice, but still…

She headed for the nearest counter, putting her back into steering the trolley, which, she discovered, had an annoying tendency to veer to the right. All the way there, she prayed that one of the two uniformed men standing behind the counter would speak enough English to understand her.

"Excuse me," she began, smiling at both. *"Yia sas."* That meant "hello" and pretty much measured the extent of her Greek.

Luckily, one of the men replied in English, "Hello. How can I assist you?"

"Someone from my tour was supposed to meet me here and take me to my hotel, but I don't see anyone. I was hoping you might know where I should wait for them."

The man nodded. "What is the name of the company?"

"It's Zeus Tours." She rifled through her purse and produced a full-color brochure and a printout of her itinerary, which she handed to him.

The mouth under his thick moustache twitched with a smile and he nodded again. "Zeus Tours. *Ne.*"

"You know of them?"

"Ne," he said again. It meant "yes," but his amused expression didn't leave her feeling relieved. Next to him, the other man had started to chuckle.

Oh, this didn't bode well, but she forged ahead. "Um, so are they here?" She gestured to the busy terminal at large.

He glanced around. "I do not see Stavros."

The other man said something in Greek that had them sharing a laugh.

"Stavros." She repeated on a nod. "Am I supposed to meet this Stavros somewhere other than here?"

"Here. There." The man shrugged. "I suggest you have a seat and make yourself comfortable." He handed the papers back to her and pointed to a nearby bank of chairs. "It could be a while."

"A while?" Her stomach dropped.

"Stavros keeps his own schedule. If he owns a watch, he never consults it."

At this the man's coworker hooted with laughter.

Darcie was tired and growing irritable. She wanted a shower, a nap and something to eat, not necessarily in that order. It wouldn't hurt to throw in a drink somewhere, either. A nice glass of chilled white wine, perhaps. Or a shot of ouzo…straight from the bottle. What she didn't want to do was spend any more of her first day in Athens in the airport as the punch line for a joke. But she worked up a smile and offered her thanks.

She was attempting to wheel the trolley away when someone tapped her on the shoulder. Darcie turned to find the gorgeous man she'd spied earlier. Her stomach took another dive, but this time for reasons that had nothing to do with disappointment.

Up close, she realized that he was taller than she was. Darcie actually had to look up. Even if she'd been wearing the highest pair of heels she owned, she only would have been on eye level. Six foot three, she figured, and every last inch of him was packaged in firm muscle beneath an untucked white linen shirt and a pair of designer jeans that fit snugly across the thigh.

His skin was tanned, his jaw subtly shadowed. His hair was nearly black and fell across brows of the exact shade. The eyes below those brows were a rich chocolate-brown and smiling even though his mouth held only the faintest curve.

"Hello," he said.

Her tongue untied long enough for her to manage a basic greeting. "Hi."

"I could not help but overhear your conversation. Maybe I can be of help," he said in gorgeously accented English.

"I hope so." It came out on a sigh and Darcie came to her senses. "What I mean is, my fi— Um, friend booked an all-inclusive vacation package with Zeus Tours. I was

promised that someone would meet me at the airport, but…"
She lifted her shoulders in a shrug.

"Ah, Zeus Tours." Like the pair at the counter, the man
apparently was acquainted with the company, but he didn't
laugh. Rather, the corners of his mouth turned down in a
frown. "May I ask why you decided to book your trip with
that particular company?"

"My, um, friend found them on the internet and got a
really good deal."

It sounded like he said, "I am sure she did." He glanced
around then. "And where is your friend?"

Tad was probably with his mother, Darcie mused. It had
taken her six years to accept the fact that an engagement
ring was no match for the tight knots in Evelyn's apron
strings.

"Couldn't make it," she replied, leaving off the telltale
pronoun.

A pair of dark brows rose. "So, you came to Greece by
yourself?"

Even a man who looked like a Greek god could be a psychopathic killer. So, Darcie said carefully, "Yes, but you
know, it's a guided tour and they're expecting me."

The man glanced around and then back at her.

"Well, I'm sure someone will be here…any minute." She
pulled out the brochure again and tapped the front of it with
the tip of one finger. "I've been assured a *safe* and *super-
vised* good time over the course of the next two weeks."

This time the man's mouth joined his eyes in smiling.

"I apologize. I am making you nervous when I am only
trying to help. Here." He pulled out the cell phone she'd
seen him talking on earlier. "If you give me the number, I
will call the company for you. I know the owner. He and I
went to grade school together."

A psychopathic killer wouldn't offer to make phone calls, she reasoned. She handed him the brochure.

Darcie could hear only one side of the conversation and it was in rapid-fire Greek, but she could figure out easily enough that the handsome stranger was irritated on her behalf. Whoever was on the other end of the line was getting an earful. When the man concluded the call, he returned the phone to his back pocket.

"Well?" she asked.

"Unfortunately, your ride has been delayed. I will take you to your hotel."

"You…but…" she sputtered and glanced around, torn. She was eager to leave the airport, unpack and unwind in the comfort of her hotel room, but… "I don't even know your name."

He smiled. "I am Nick. Nick Costas. The men at the counter can vouch for me, if you would like. I fly in and out of this airport often enough. Or I can show you some identification." Without waiting for a reply, he pulled out his wallet and produced his driver's license.

"The State of New York?" She glanced up. "You're American?"

"Yes, for the past five years, but much of my family still lives in Athens. Between business and family, I am here often." He pocketed his wallet. "And you are?"

Single now.

She cleared her throat and in a demure voice managed to respond, "Darcie Hayes of Buffalo. We're practically neighbors."

It was a stretch given that his address was on Park Avenue in Manhattan and she lived upstate, several hours away. They shared a time zone but were worlds apart based on the designer watch strapped to his wrist.

Still, he was attracted to her.

She may have been long out of practice when it came to flirting, but she knew male interest when she saw it. For a woman who'd spent several years waiting to walk down the aisle while her boyfriend deferred to his mother's wishes, it was heady stuff indeed.

"It's good to meet you, Darcie Hayes of Buffalo."

He offered a hand and their palms met briefly. The simple contact managed to make her insides quake. Of course, they were shaky to begin with as a result of exhaustion and the fact that she'd bypassed the in-flight meal of mystery meat coated in unappetizing neon yellow gravy. Still, she pulled back her hand, worried she might make a fool of herself.

"It's nice to meet you, too. And I really appreciate your help." She tucked a hank of hair behind one ear. "Um, what did the tour company people say?"

"Stavros is…indisposed."

Stavros, there was that name again. Nick said he'd gone to school with the man who owned the company, but she asked hopefully, "Is this Stavros the driver?"

"The driver, the tour guide and the owner of Zeus Tours."

"Oh, boy. A real multitasker, hmm?" She blew out a breath. "When you say indisposed, what does that mean exactly? Has he fallen and broken his leg? Or contracted a nasty virus and is racked with fever?"

Nick shook his head. "Stavros is still lying in bed. He told me that he had a late night out with his friends and overindulged."

"He's h-h-hung over?" she sputtered incredulously.

"I am afraid so."

Darcie gritted her teeth. She should have known. The moment Tad bragged that he'd gotten a great deal, it should have been abundantly clear that the dream Greek honeymoon trip he'd booked was too good to be true for a reason.

"I was really hoping this Stavros had a stomach bug,"

she muttered. This surprised a laugh out of Nick. She asked him, "How familiar are you with Zeus Tours?"

Nick wasn't laughing now. "I am familiar enough to know that Stavros pours more money down his throat than he puts back into his company. He took over when his father died two years ago. In that time, he has had to let go more than half of his employees. He is not a bad man, but neither is he a good businessman."

Although she wasn't normally one to air her complaints to a stranger, weariness had her muttering, "Terrific. Just terrific. I'm here for a vacation. God knows, I'm due for one. I haven't had a day off work in two years. I've worked overtime and taken every crappy assignment I was handed without complaint so I could save up money for…for…" She waved a hand and tried to reel in her emotions. "Anyway, I was counting on the vacation described in the brochure—first-rate accommodations, air-conditioned motor coaches for sightseeing with a knowledgeable guide, authentic Greek cuisine at some of the country's best restaurants. Is this company going to be able to deliver on *any* of its promises?"

"No." He didn't hesitate at all, making that one word all the more damning.

Darcie closed her eyes briefly. "Of course not. Half of my luggage is missing. What showed up is, well, the half I wish were missing. Not that it really matters, given that my dream vacation is turning out to be a bust and I haven't even gotten out of the airport yet." She sighed. "I should have taken the condo and Rufus."

"Rufus?"

"Also know as the spawn of Satan. He's a cat," she added when Nick continued to frown. Not that her explanation made anything clear. She shook her head. "Never mind. Trust me when I say, this is the story of my life."

"Come." Nick smiled. "You can share this story of your life on the drive to your hotel."

Why not?

Darcie decided to listen to the little voice telling her that Nick Costas wasn't a threat. After all, it was the same little voice that had told her to cut all ties and run where her ex-fiancé was concerned, so she figured it knew what it was talking about. It had taken her several years to pay attention the last time. She only had two weeks in Greece. She was going to make the most of them. Starting now.

"In the mood for a good laugh, are you?" she asked wryly.

Nick smiled again. Oh, he was in the mood...for something. A diversion at the very least, and he figured he'd found one. A pretty one, too, given the woman's tumble of chestnut hair, wide-set Aegean blue eyes and a body that would have made the ancient goddesses green with envy.

He'd come to the airport that day with every intention of leaving Greece and returning to his home in Manhattan. He'd booked a flight to New York, a flight that would be boarding shortly without him. Just as well. He'd been angry with his family and their unabashed matchmaking and had allowed his emotions to cloud his judgment.

Of course, he would have to be back in Greece within a fortnight anyway. No amount of irritation would cause him to miss his brother's wedding. He would never live down the talk otherwise. And there was plenty of that already since Pieter was marrying Nick's childhood sweetheart, Selene.

Half of Athens was gossiping about it, waiting for a fight to erupt between the brothers. Nick was determined not to indulge the gawkers, as awkward and, yes, painful, as the situation was. He lamented the strain between him and Pieter. He regretted the division in his once unified family. But neither could be helped. The best he could do was to gather up his dignity and feign indifference.

"Allow me," he told Darcie and took over pushing the trolley. Five steps later, he nearly took out a bank of unoccupied chairs.

"It wants to go in circles," she warned.

She was shaking her head and smiling. He liked her smile. Her lips were inviting even without any added gloss. A lovely diversion, he thought again.

And why not? He was entitled. He had no strings to tangle him up. He hadn't had those since Selene. That was the way he preferred it, too, as he'd pointed out to his grandmother that very morning when Yiayia expressed concern about his ongoing single status. Nick had no such concerns. What he had was a plan, a meticulously crafted five-year plan to grow his auction business. After that, he might start thinking about settling down, but never again would he allow his heart to be broken. Once was enough.

"Is this part of the story of your life?" he asked Darcie, motioning to the wayward cart.

"That's right." She lowered her voice to a confidential whisper. "I probably shouldn't tell you this, but since you're being so nice, I feel I owe you the truth. I'm a magnet for bad luck."

"Really?"

"Really. Swear." She traced a cross over her very impressive chest.

Nick followed the progress of her fingertip before allowing his gaze to lift to her lips again. "Perhaps your luck is about to change."

CHAPTER TWO

WHILE SHE WAITED for Nick to retrieve his car from the long-term parking lot, Darcie called Becky. Even if she didn't think Nick was a psycho, she decided it would be wise to let someone know she had arrived safely in Athens and was now in the hands of a stranger. Calling her parents was out of the question. Ditto for her sisters. That left Becky, who answered on the fifth ring.

"Someone had better be dying," her friend muttered ominously, and Darcie realized it was the middle of the night in Buffalo.

"I'm not dying, just checking in," she said. "Sorry I woke you, Becks. I forget about the time difference."

"Darcie? Oh. Hey." She pictured Becky struggling to a sitting position on her bed and trying to force the cobwebs from her head. "Is everything okay?"

Darcie scuffed the toe of one shoe against the pavement. "Sort of."

"What does that mean?"

"Well, my flight arrived on time, but I'm missing half of my luggage. The good half."

Becky had helped her pack, so she commiserated. "That stinks. On the bright side, now you have a valid excuse to buy more clothes."

"Yeah." Like Darcie could afford to do that. She coughed

and continued. "Oh, and there's been one other small glitch. No one from the tour company was at the airport to meet me."

"What? That's ridiculous. You need to report them to the Better Business Bureau or something."

"I know. Apparently, the owner of the company is a lush." She forced out a laugh. "Figures, right? I mean, Tad got such a good deal on this vacation there was bound to be a catch."

Becky muttered something obscene about Tad. It wasn't anything Darcie hadn't heard before. Her friend had been quite vocal in her dislike of him. That had been a source of contention between the two women in the past, but no longer. She found herself wondering what Becky would make of Nick.

"I hope the rest of the trip goes smoothly," her friend said.

Unfortunately, based on what Nick had told Darcie, she had her doubts. She told Becky as much.

"What are you going to do? Can you get a refund and hook up with a different company?"

"I don't know." The fine print on the package said the price was nonrefundable, but Darcie planned to try anyway. She figured she had nothing to lose. "In the meantime, I have a ride to the first hotel on the itinerary. The tour group is supposed to stay there for a couple of nights. That should give me time to see if the company is going to be able to deliver on any of its promises and, if not, make other arrangements." At least she hoped it would.

"Good. Darcie, if you need money—"

"No. I don't. But thanks." Not only could Becky not afford it, but she'd also been generous enough already, letting Darcie crash at her apartment until she found a place of her own. That certainly beat moving back in with her parents, even temporarily. What thirty-year-old woman wanted to do that?

Darcie took a deep breath then and, keeping her tone nonchalant, said, "You're going to love this. The person who agreed to drive me is this insanely gorgeous man with an accent that is to die for."

There was a slight pause before Becky asked, "You're taking a cab, right?"

"No. Actually, I met this man in the airport and he... offered to drive. He showed me identification," she hastened to add. "His name is Nick Costas. He lives in Manhattan, but he's from Athens originally."

"Darcie, I don't know," Becky began, worry evident in her tone.

"What happened to, 'Have a fling and get ur sexy back?' Hmm?"

"Well, I didn't actually expect you to take my advice! When do you ever listen to me? I mean, if you listened to me, you never would have given Tad the time of day, much less wasted six years of your life engaged to him."

Point taken. Becky had told Darcie from the start that Tad was a first-class mama's boy and would stay that way.

"Relax. I'm not having a fling. It's only a ride to a hotel. Nothing more." Except maybe in her fantasies.

"Okay, but call me when you get there."

"I will."

"Promise me, Darcie. I'm not going to be able to go back to sleep until you do."

"I promise. I'll call."

She hung up just as Nick's car pulled to the curb. Unlike the other boxy subcompacts parked nearby, it was a sleek, low-slung convertible.

"Nice car." She tapped a finger to her lips as she studied its graceful lines. "A 1963 Porsche, right?"

He nodded slowly. "A 356 Super 90 Cabriolet, to be exact."

"Fully restored?"

"Yes, but with original parts. And I have a certificate of authenticity from the manufacturer."

"Ooh. That pushes up its value."

"It does." Nick tilted his head to the side. "How is it that you know so much about automobiles?"

Darcie chuckled at his incredulous expression. "I work for a classic car magazine. I guess I picked up a few things along the way."

"You're a writer."

She frowned. Not for lack of wanting, she thought. "No. I just check the facts of articles other people write."

"Which magazine might that be?"

"*Automobile Enthusiasts Monthly.* It's relatively small and based in Buffalo. You probably haven't heard of it." Darcie hadn't until Tad's friend had offered her the job just before her engagement.

"I have a subscription. I find it very *factual.*" He got out of the car and stood beside her. "What else can you tell me about this particular model Porsche?"

"Well, as I recall, it was very popular in America when it first came out."

"It still is among collectors."

"And you're a collector." It made sense. A man with a Park Avenue address likely would have the disposable income to indulge his whims, even ones that ran into six figures.

But Nick was shaking his head. "I collect for others. As much as I like this automobile, I will not be buying it. It will go to whoever pays the most to possess it. It is what I do for a living." He pulled out a business card, which he handed to her. It read, Costas Classic Auto Sales and Auctions.

"Impressive."

"It would appear that you and I have two interests in common."

"Two?"

"Classic cars and…" His smile could have melted a glass and made it clear what that other interest was. She smiled in return and hoped the laughter that followed came off as worldly rather than the sort fueled by giddiness and nerves.

"Let me take your bag," he said.

The Porsche had a rear engine, meaning its trunk was in the front. When Nick opened the compartment, Darcie eyed the small space.

"Gee, maybe it's just as well the airline lost one of my bags. I don't think both of them would fit in here. I guess when you own one of these babies you have to travel light to travel in style." She glanced at Nick, a question forming. "Where's your luggage?"

The left side of his mouth rose. "On a plane bound for New York." At her puzzled expression, he added, "I was planning to fly back today."

"Why did you change your mind?"

"I decided I was being rash."

"So you missed your flight and offered assistance to a perfect stranger instead," she replied dryly. Talk about rash…and flattering. Just wait until she told Becky *that*. Her friend was going to hyperventilate. As it was, Darcie's breathing was a little uneven.

"A stranded stranger," Nick corrected. His smile was full-blown this time and very effective. "One who is also very beautiful."

Her heart fluttered and she blinked. "Oh."

"You are blushing."

"I, um…" She waved a hand, not certain how to reply.

"Surely, you have been told before that you are beautiful?"

"Of course I have." She rolled her eyes. "All the time, in fact. We're talking daily. It gets old."

The truth was no, at least not in the past several years. Tad wasn't one for compliments. Even during the courtship phase of their relationship, pretty words had been few and far between. After he'd slid an engagement ring on her finger? Forget about it.

You know how I feel about you, Darcie. That should be enough.

Maybe it should have been. But it wasn't. Every now and then, especially when she was PMSing and feeling bloated and unattractive, a compliment would have been nice.

And then there was his mother. Evil Evelyn, as Becky had dubbed her. The older woman was quick with thinly veiled digs about Darcie's appearance, including her good "birthing hips."

"You are beautiful," Nick said again. "And your blush only makes you more so."

This time, Darcie accepted the compliment with what she hoped was a gracious smile. *Beautiful.* Why not? Wasn't beauty in the eye of the beholder? And what a beholder.

Nick opened the car door for her before heading around to the driver's side. It was another small courtesy that made her feel like she'd stepped into some sort of fairy tale.

"Shall I put up the top?"

"No," she told him. "Leave it down. I can use the fresh air after all those hours in a stuffy airplane."

And, okay, in her fairy tale, a ride in a Porsche convertible only added to the romance.

He was seated behind the wheel now. "Even if it means tangled hair?" He reached over and coiled the end of one lock around his index finger. If he wound it any tighter, she would be forced to lean closer to him.

While their gazes held, she blindly plumbed the depths of her oversized purse until her fingers encountered an elastic band. Pulling it out with the same verve a magician uses to produce a white rabbit, she announced, "I believe I have a solution for that."

Nick eyed the elastic band a moment before uncoiling the lock, and she hastily tugged her hair into a ponytail.

"Very clever, but you missed some."

This time, he made contact with more than her hair. His fingertips were warm against her cheek as they corralled the wayward strands and tucked them behind her ear. The gesture might have been construed as friendly if not for the gleam in his dark eyes or the Richter-scale-worthy effect it had on her pulse.

A car horn blasted behind them. Its driver yelled something in Greek. Nick yelled something back in the same language, but his tone was more circumspect than annoyed, and his expression could only be described as pleased.

To Darcie, he said, "People are in too much of a hurry. I prefer to take things slowly. Rushing is no good."

With that, he turned the key in the car's ignition. The Porsche's powerful engine growled to life and they were off.

Nick wasn't familiar with the hotel listed on her itinerary, but he plugged the address to The Santor into his cell phone and downloaded directions as he merged into traffic.

"It should take about forty minutes to get there," he said as they left the airport behind.

Darcie settled back in her seat, determined to take in the sights along the way. Not only was this her first time in Greece, but it was also her first trip abroad. Indeed, other than a couple of weekend jaunts to Toronto with Becky, she'd never been outside the United States. Despite the passing scenery, however, she remained almost painfully aware of the man seated next to her, and her gaze kept returning to his profile. God, he was handsome and he'd made it plain that their attraction was mutual. This might not be a fling exactly, but it was awfully damned flattering to have such a good-looking man paying attention to her.

When he turned and caught her staring, she blurted out, "Were you always so buff? I mean, a car buff. Were you always a car buff?"

"Car buff?"

"Interested in cars," she clarified, relieved that her slip of the tongue hadn't made it past the language barrier.

He nodded. "My uncle raced them for a time, and the summer I turned sixteen, I traveled with him on the European Grand Prix circuit."

"That sounds exciting."

Nick smiled in agreement. "It was. Very."

"Did you ever race?"

"I considered it at one point, but no." He shrugged. "Ultimately, I was more interested in the cars—that is to say their overall design—than how fast they could travel on a closed course. So, when I was eighteen, I bought a 1957 Porsche Speedster I found advertised in the newspaper."

"Wow. Nice first car." Hers had been her grandmother's ancient sedan. It was the size of a small country and guzzled fuel like a college student guzzles coffee while studying for final exams. Darcie had happily traded up to the decade-old compact she still owned.

Nick was chuckling. "Not really. It needed a lot of work, which is why I could afford it. I spent the entire summer tracking down all of the parts to rebuild its engine." His smile was both nostalgic and proud.

"And you were hooked," she guessed.

She'd felt that way the first time she'd composed an article for her high school's newspaper. Three paragraphs on changes to the lunch menu and she'd known what she wanted to be when she grew up. Now, eight years after earning a degree in journalism, she could barely claim to be a journalist.

Nick was saying, "Hooked. Yes, I was. Especially after I decided to sell the Speedster at auction in Kalamai two summers later. Collectors came not only from all over Greece, but from other parts of Europe to bid on it. I loved the excitement. So, I used the money from the sale to buy another car, fix it up and auction it off. Later, I decided I did not want to go to the auctions, I wanted to run them. So, that is what I do."

She heard satisfaction in his tone. Pride. How long had it been since she'd felt either of those emotions when it came to her own job? How long had it been since she'd dreamed of bigger and better things for herself when it came to her career? Her life? Settling. Darcie had done so damned much of it.

"Did you come to Greece on business then?" she asked.

Nick shook his head and some of his dark hair fell across his forehead. It lent an air of recklessness to his already pulse-pounding good looks.

"Not this time. I came for a family wedding."

Wedding. Even spoken with Nick's gorgeous accent, the word brought Darcie up short, reminding her as it did of her recent close call with "I do." How different her life might be right now if a week ago she hadn't finally found the courage to act on what her heart—and, well, Becky—had been telling her for so long. Tad wasn't the right man for her.

"Yet you were going to leave today."

"I would have been back. The ceremony does not take place until the Saturday after next."

His response had her blinking in surprise. "That's more than two weeks away, and you're already here?"

"It is expected," he replied.

Darcie detected a slight edge to his tone and thought she understood its source. She knew all about family expectations. She had three sisters, two older, one younger, all of them happily married and busily procreating as if the survival of the human race depended on them. Meanwhile, Darcie had passed the big three-oh mark in the spring and the only thing that remained of her eagerly anticipated nuptials was the stack of gifts that would have to be returned when she got back.

A groan escaped. At Nick's quizzical glance, she said, "I feel your pain. My family can be, well, difficult to please at times. So, who's getting married?"

"My brother Pieter."

"I take it he lives here."

"Yes. As does my entire family."

Yet Nick made his home in a city across the Atlantic. Interesting. "No apron strings for you," she murmured.

"Apron strings?"

"Nothing. Are you and your brother close?"

"We used to be closer."

At that, his lips flattened into a grim line, leaving her with the distinct impression there was much more to the story. Still, she kept her curiosity in check and changed the subject. They engaged in polite small talk until they arrived at their destination. Even before she saw the hotel, she knew it would be a dive. The oath that slipped from Nick's lips told her as much.

Luxury accommodations? Right. The squat, two-story building looked like it should have a date with a wrecking ball, despite the sign out front printed in Greek and English that announced it was Under Renovation. It was more rickety than some of the country's ancient ruins. Glancing around, Darcie realized The Santor wasn't located in the best of neighborhoods, either. As hungry as she was, she didn't think she would be comfortable hoofing up the block to the restaurant she spied there. At the moment, two men were loitering out front, smoking cigarettes and passing a liquor bottle back and forth.

With her earlier hysteria threatening to return, she muttered, "Rufus really wasn't so bad."

Nick's brows drew together. "Your cat?"

"No longer. I was thinking good riddance after what he did to my favorite silk dress. But now…" She shrugged.

"Has anyone ever told you that the story of your life is very confusing?"

"Only all the time."

"I'll walk you in and see you settled."

No protest passed Darcie lips. Since it would have been token at best, she didn't see the point. No way did she want to go inside that death trap by herself.

"Thanks. I'd appreciate it."

Nick retrieved her sorry-looking bag and they made their way to the entrance on a makeshift walkway of cardboard that had been placed over mud puddles. On either side of the door were potted palm trees whose fronds were coated with thick, grayish construction dust.

Nick held open one of the grimy glass doors. "After you."

"Gee, thanks."

She took a halting step inside and waited for her eyes to adjust to the dim lighting. Once they did, she wished they hadn't. The lobby was filled with an assortment of power tools and building supplies, and every last inch of the place was as dust-coated as the palms outside. Her apprehension kicked into high gear as she imagined the condition the rooms would be in.

As if sensing her hesitation, Nick placed a hand on the small of her back and propelled her toward the reception desk. A woman stood behind it. Darcie pegged her to be about forty-five and a chain smoker. A lit cigarette dangled from her lips and a second one burned merrily in the ashtray on the countertop. The woman squinted at them through the haze created by both dust and smoke.

"Good afternoon." The greeting was offered in Greek as she set the cigarette in the ashtray.

"Good afternoon," Nick replied. His gaze flicked to her name badge and he added, "Pesha. How are you today?"

He said this in English, which Pesha apparently understood and could speak, because she switched to English as well.

"I am much better now." Her smile was flirtatious and made it clear why. Darcie couldn't fault the woman for that. Nick had certainly brightened her day. "How can I help you?"

"My friend has a reservation."

"Friend." Her smile widened and she exhaled. Residual wisps of smoke curled out from the woman's nostrils. Not terribly attractive, but they did distract one from the tar stains on her teeth. "What is the name?"

"Darcie Hayes," Nick said.

There was no computer to consult, only a thick, leather-bound book through which Pesha began flipping. Finally, she glanced up.

"Sorry. I have no one by that name registered here this week."

"Um, what about for a Darcie Franklin." It would have been her married name. She avoided meeting Nick's questioning gaze.

More page flipping ensued before Pesha shook her head. "*Oxi.* I cannot find that name among my guests, either."

"There must be some mistake. The tour package was booked months ago and paid in full."

"Tour package?" Pesha said slowly. "Which tour package might that be?"

"A multicity, sightseeing excursion that was booked through Zeus Tours."

"Stavros!"

The woman spat out the name with enough force to turn the two benign syllables into the vilest of curses. But she wasn't done. She continued in Greek, gesturing wildly the entire time. Darcie was left with no choice but to grit her teeth and listen. By the time Pesha switched to English again, she had worked up a good head of steam.

"That man owes me for the last three tour groups that stayed here. I have told him, no more! I have been turning his customers away all day."

She selected one of the cigarettes from the ashtray and took a long, lung-blackening drag.

"Um, when you say no more," Darcie began.

"I will not honor any more of his bookings unless he pays me in advance." Pesha stamped out the cigarette for emphasis.

"I can understand your annoyance with Stavros." Darcie was pretty annoyed with the man herself. "But I paid in full for a room at The Santor."

Sure, the accommodations were crap, but it was the principle of the matter. They were crap for which Tad's credit card already had been hit.

Pesha picked up the second cigarette and inhaled deeply before blowing out a stream of smoke that shot past Darcie's left shoulder. Even so, wisps of it lingered and stung her nose.

"No, you paid Stavros in full, but he has not paid me. He has not paid me for too long!" Pesha chopped at the air with the hand holding the cigarette, sending ashes flying. Darcie was only glad the woman wasn't clutching a sharp object. "And until he does, I will not be putting up any more of his tour customers. Now, if you wish to pay with cash, I will be happy to give you a room."

Darcie could see the woman's point. Pesha had a business to run and Stavros had stiffed her more than once. Still, it left Darcie in a bind, and if she had to shell out more money for a room, it sure as hell wasn't going to be in this fleabag establishment. She turned to Nick, who apparently read her mind.

"I will take you to another hotel. Perhaps something that is closer to shopping, restaurants and nightlife."

Darcie cleared her throat and added, "But reasonably priced. My budget is limited."

Pesha bristled as they turned to leave.

"You will not find a better bargain than The Santor," she insisted.

Since so much of Darcie's life was left to fate at the moment, it was with a sense of destiny that she replied, "I'll take my chances."

Mindful of what Darcie had said about her budget, Nick took her to one of the chain hotels in the city, even though it offered neither the charm nor the ambience of the nicer and pricier establishments he would have preferred. But it was conveniently located and tidy, with a smoke-free lobby and a concierge who appeared eager to please.

After she booked a room, they lingered near the bank of elevators. He wasn't in a hurry to leave. In fact, he almost regretted having to say goodbye. Darcie didn't seem eager to end their association, either.

"How good are the chances that Stavros will refund the money for my trip?" she asked.

"Not good. My guess is he does not have the money to refund."

She made a humming sound. "That's what I was afraid of. At this rate, I will be on a flight back to New York before the end of the week."

Her budget, Nick assumed. He meant it when he said, "That would be a shame. Greece is a beautiful country with so much to see."

It might not have any effect, but he planned to call Stavros on her behalf and apply a little pressure. Darcie Hayes and unsuspecting travelers like her shouldn't have to pay for the man's bad business decisions and personal habits.

Nick's reasons, of course, weren't all pure. His gaze took in the long line of her legs. Even in flat shoes she was a tall woman. *Statuesque* was the word that came to mind. Sexy applied, too, given her well-rounded curves and the toned backside he'd glimpsed. Why did he get the feeling she was unaware of the power of her allure? In his experience, most women who looked like she did weren't. They flaunted their looks, used them to get what they wanted. The fact that Darcie didn't made her not only refreshing, but also a puzzle.

Nick liked puzzles. They ranked right up there with games of chance when it came to guilty pleasures.

"I can't thank you enough for all you've done," she was saying.

"I have done nothing."

"I disagree. You've acted as my personal driver for the past couple of hours. I'd probably still be sitting in the airport with my busted-up luggage waiting for a ride that wasn't coming if it weren't for you."

She was all but tipping over on her nose. The signs of exhaustion were unmistakable, from the shadows under her eyes to the droop in her shoulders. He doubted that she would last an hour in her room before sleep claimed her, and knew a moment of regret that he wouldn't be there when she awoke.

"I am happy I could help. I would hate for a visitor to my homeland to go away with an unfavorable impression of Greek hospitality. Stavros Pappanolos's poor example notwithstanding, you will find that the people here are very generous and helpful."

"Oh, you've more than made up for Stavros."

She cleared her throat. There was that becoming blush again. Nick leaned forward, drawn by her reserve. Before he could kiss her, she held out a hand that poked into his solar plexus. Her cheeks flamed bright red now.

"Well, I guess this is where we say goodbye," she said.

Was it? Nick didn't think so. But she was tired and he had fences to mend with his family.

He took her hand and meant it when he said, "It has been entirely my pleasure, Darcie Hayes."

CHAPTER THREE

DARCIE WAS STILL on Nick's mind the following day as he sat in his grandmother's kitchen having a midmorning snack of freshly baked *koulourakia portokaliou*. The sweet, orange-flavored cookies were a staple in Yiayia's house, precisely because they ensured company.

His parents were there as well. George and Thea Costas lived right next door. In fact, Nick's entire extended family was clustered together in a small geographic area on the western edge of Athens. True to tradition, Pieter already owned a house just down the road. In two short weeks, he and Selene would live in it together as husband and wife.

Even the sweetness of the cookie wasn't enough to wipe out the bitter taste in Nick's mouth.

"Your tea is growing cold," Yiayia said, interrupting his thoughts. The snow-white hair coiled on her head made a striking contrast to her usual black frock. Sophia Pappas had been a widow for twenty-three years and still wore the color of mourning. She also considered it her duty as the family's matriarch to meddle as she saw fit. "And you are frowning, Nikolos. Is something wrong with my cookies?"

"Nothing is wrong with your cookies." He took another bite and smacked his lips for emphasis. "I just have a lot on my mind."

"This is a difficult time for you." His grandmother nodded sagely.

"Only because everyone insists on making it so."

"Have you given any more thought to Pieter's request?" his mother asked.

It took an effort not the crush the cookie that remained in his hand. Pieter wanted Nick to be his *koumbaro* or best man at the upcoming Greek Orthodox ceremony. As such, it would be Nick who put the crowns on Pieter and Selene's heads and switched them back and forth three times to symbolize their union.

Nick wanted no part of that. He couldn't believe his brother even had the nerve to ask.

"I have said no too many times to count, Mama."

She frowned. "I wish you would reconsider. He is your brother, Nick. Your *only* brother."

"Pieter conveniently forgot that when he started seeing Selene behind my back."

"You were gone, Nick. You went to America to start your business," Thea reminded him unnecessarily. "You told Selene you understood when she said she did not want to move to New York, too."

What Nick understood was betrayal. Despite what he'd told Selene at the time, he'd held out hope that she would change her mind. In his heart, he'd believed that the two of them would marry eventually. Until Pieter.

"I will not be his *koumbaro*. Be happy that I have agreed to attend the wedding at all."

"Be happy, be happy," Yiayia chided with a shake of her head. "You would do well to listen to your own advice, my boy. You will not find a bride of your own if you do not look."

"I can assure you, I do not lack for female companionship."

"Take care how you speak around your grandmother," George interjected gruffly.

Nick recognized the tone. It was the same one his father had used when Nick stepped over the line as a boy. He was over the line now, too. And so he apologized.

"I am merely trying to point out that if I wanted a wife I would have one."

He wouldn't call himself the black sheep of the family, but his wool was definitely dyed a different shade than his brother's, much to his mother's and Yiayia's regret. In addition to his Manhattan apartment, Nick kept a house just outside Athens near the Aegean. His whitewashed home was situated on a hillside and boasted panoramic views of a harbor that was dotted with yachts and fishing boats. His mother claimed the view soothed his restless nature. In some ways, watching all of those boats sail out into open waters only fed it.

"The women you know in Manhattan are not proper wife material," his mother said.

This was true enough, in part because at this point in his life, with a business to build and the related travel taking up so much of his time, he wasn't ready to settle down.

Still, he couldn't resist asking, "How do you know this, Mama? You have not met any of the women I have been with since Selene."

"I do not need to meet them. I am your mother. I know." Thea folded her arms.

He loved his family. He loved Greece. But ever since he'd sold that first automobile to a collector living in the United States more than a decade earlier, he'd known that he would never settle for the quiet and predictable life he would have endured living here and working with his father.

His family had never understood Nick's obsession with classic cars and his desire to see them restored, much less the pleasure he took from connecting a collector with exactly what he or she sought. They were proud of him, certainly. Through hard work, shrewd investment and a little bit of luck, Nick had managed to turn his passion into a multimillion-dollar enterprise. They just wished he'd decided to base it in Athens rather than New York.

"Besides, those women are not Greek," Yiayia said.

It boiled down to that for his grandmother. His mother, too, though she was less inclined to say so out loud. Both women wanted Nick to marry a nice Greek girl, preferably one from a family they knew, so that he would return home, buy a house nearby and settle in. It wasn't going to happen, but that didn't keep them from trying.

Sure enough, his mother was saying, "I saw Maria Karapoulos at the market yesterday. Her daughter Danika was with her. She has moved back from London. Her job there didn't work out."

"Just as well. They don't know how to make a proper cup of tea in England," Yiayia observed. Both women laughed. "How does Danika look? As pretty as ever?"

"Prettier," Thea said. "She has lost some weight, and I think she has contacts now. She wasn't wearing her glasses. She has such lovely eyes."

"And she comes from a nice family," his grandmother noted.

Nick sipped his tea and said nothing. The eyes he was thinking about were blue and belonged to Darcie.

His mother went on. "I invited her to the wedding. Her parents were already on the guest list. It seemed rude not to extend an invitation to her as well."

"Good. Good. She will have fun at the wedding," Yiayia said. "Especially if she has someone to dance with."

Even though his tea was plenty sweet, Nick added a little

more honey and tried to ignore the conversation going on around him. But he knew what was coming.

Sure enough, his grandmother added, "Nick could be her escort."

He gave his tea a vigorous stir. "No."

How many times must they go through this particular exercise before his mother and grandmother accepted that he didn't need or want their help to find a date? He'd considered asking one of the local women to come with him just to get Thea and Yiayia off his back, but that posed a problem of its own. Thanks to all of the gossip, the single women in his social circle saw Nick as a challenge or as an object of pity. He didn't want to be viewed as either.

He glanced over at his father, hoping for an ally, but George pushed his chair away from the table and rose. Motioning over his shoulder, he said, "The drain in the bathroom sink is running slow. I promised your grandmother I would take a look at it."

"I will give you a hand," Nick offered.

But George shook his head. "No. You finish your tea. I can manage on my own."

"Thank you, Papa," Nick drawled sarcastically.

His father stopped at the doorway. "You might listen to your mother, you know. I remember this Danika she speaks of. The girl comes from a good family. You could do worse."

Now there was a recommendation. The room was quiet after his father's exit. Nick was just starting to think the topic had been dropped when his mom said, "You are not going with anyone. It would be a shame for two young, single people to attend alone."

Yiayia clapped her hands together. "So it is settled. Nikolos will take her."

"No. I will not take her."

"No?"

Nick blotted his mouth with a napkin and worked to keep his tone civil. "I am not going to take Danika or any of the other women you two have suggested to the wedding. I have said no and I mean no."

"No! No! Always no!" His grandmother gestured with her arms before demanding, "Give us one good reason why not."

A curvy young woman with deep blue eyes, killer legs and a thick, wavy mane of hair came to mind and inspiration struck.

"I have a date."

Both older women blinked in surprise. His mother was the first to find her voice. "You have a date?" she asked skeptically.

"For the wedding?" Yiayia added, her tone equally dubious.

Lying did not come easily to Nick, no matter how good he considered the cause, so he answered her question with one of his own. "Is that so hard to believe? I am not repulsive, you know."

"You are as handsome as Adonis," his mother affirmed, undeterred. "But just yesterday you stormed out of here after the grocer's daughter happened by and your *yiayia* invited her in for a cup of tea."

"Happened by?" His brows rose. "She was dressed for cocktails, not tea. It was a setup. I do not appreciate your matchmaking. Nor do I need your help, as well-intentioned as it may be."

Thea sighed. Nick hoped that was a sign that the matter would be dropped, at least for now. Unfortunately, his grandmother wasn't done.

"Who is this woman you have invited to your brother's wedding? When did this happen? You have not mentioned her before."

Since nothing had actually happened yet and very well might never, Nick decided to answer Yiayia's other question first. "You do not know her. She is an American."

"American." His grandmother put a hand to her chest and frowned.

"It is not a disease, you know." He chuckled, hoping both to lighten the mood and to divert the conversation. Neither woman cracked a smile, however.

"You know her from New York?" Thea asked.

"Actually, I met Darcie in Greece." Which wasn't a lie. He saw no need to mention when or where.

"Darcie. What kind of a name is Darcie?" Yiayia's frown deepened. "It does not sound like a Greek name."

His mother had other concerns. "Does she live in Athens?"

"No. She came here on holiday."

When his conscience bucked, he rationalized that he wasn't lying to his mother and grandmother. He was merely offering a selective version of the truth.

"What does she do for a living?" Yiayia inquired.

"She works at a car magazine." Beyond that, Nick knew precious little about Darcie Hayes other than the fact that he found her very attractive. At the moment, he also found her his ticket out of a tight spot. "I tell you what. I will bring her by some time and you can ask her all of these questions yourselves."

He thought he was off the hook, or at the very least had delayed his day of reckoning. Yiayia dispelled that notion.

"Good. I will set an extra plate for supper."

"S-supper?" he sputtered. "Tonight?"

"We will eat at seven."

"Come early," his mother added with an eager smile that sent his insides churning.

What had he gotten himself into?

* * *

Darcie had forced herself to stay awake until 9:00 p.m. the previous evening. She'd called Becky as promised and explained about her changed itinerary, after which she had collapsed face-first on the bed and slept like the dead. When she awoke just before ten o'clock the following morning she had a deep crease from the sheets across her right cheek, but after nearly thirteen hours of uninterrupted slumber she felt almost human. She also was starving again.

If the tour had panned out as advertised, she already would have enjoyed a buffet breakfast with her fellow travelers and been boarding an air-conditioned motor coach headed for the Parthenon on the Acropolis. She showered and dressed, donning tan shorts and a fitted white T-shirt before lacing up a pair of sneakers. For one moment she allowed herself to picture the floral sundress and new sandals in her missing luggage. Shaking off her wistfulness, she headed for the door, eager to leave the hotel and start exploring. The day before, she'd been too exhausted to do more than walk up the block from the hotel to a small market that the concierge had recommended. She'd bought bread and fresh fruit. Today, she was in the mood for a real meal and ancient ruins.

It came as a total surprise when the first sight to greet her when she entered the lobby was Nick Costas striding purposefully through the main door. He broke into a smile that made her knees weak. It buoyed her ego that he appeared so pleased to see her.

"Darcie. Excellent. You are still here."

"Hello, Nick. Is something wrong?"

"Wrong?" He shook his head. "Not at all."

She narrowed her eyes. "Why do I sense a *but* coming?"

"Because you are too perceptive." He laughed. "You were on your way out."

"Yes. To eat."

"May I join you?"

"Okay. I should warn you that I'm not sure exactly where I'm going. I was just planning to wander around until I found a restaurant that looked appealing."

"May I make a suggestion then?"

"By all means."

"I know a wonderful spot not far from here that makes the best moussaka."

"Moussaka. My favorite," she said, although she had no idea what it was. Intrigued by both the meal and the man, Darcie agreed.

Nick took her to an out-of-the-way café that made her feel as if she had stepped back in time thanks to the building's neoclassical architecture. Conversations stopped as they wound their way to a table in the back of the small, crowded establishment. Darcie got the feeling she was the only tourist among the patrons. After giving her a cursory glance, however, the other guests returned their attention to their own tables.

A waiter appeared not long after they settled in their seats and took their order. She asked for the moussaka, in part because Nick had recommended it, and because she was unfamiliar with the other items on the menu. He ordered the same, as well as coffee for the pair of them and a bottle of sparkling water.

"I get the feeling I'm in store for an authentic Greek meal," she said once they were alone.

"You are. I hope you like it."

Her stomach was growling loud enough to be embarrassing. "I'm sure I will," she told him. "Um, what exactly is moussaka?"

His rich laughter rumbled. The sound was pleasing, especially since she didn't feel his amusement came at her expense.

"It is a dish made with eggplant. Do you like eggplant?" he asked.

"I love it. Yum."

She'd eaten it…once. It had been breaded and pan-fried, and then slathered in Evelyn's homemade tomato sauce and melted parmesan cheese. The indigestion Darcie had experienced afterward likely had been the result of Tad's mother's fault-finding throughout the meal rather than the food itself.

Nick apparently wasn't fooled. "You are an adventurous one, I see. Willing to try new things."

She liked his assessment, even if the speculative gleam in his eye gave her pause.

"I believe in being open-minded. Why not take a few chances?"

Nick smiled. "Why not indeed?"

A moment of silence passed as he studied her. She found it hard not to fidget given the intensity of his gaze. Was he picturing her naked? Darcie sucked in her stomach just to be on the safe side and found the courage to ask, "Perhaps you should tell me what's on your mind."

"A favor."

"Oh." She stopped holding in her stomach.

"You look disappointed?"

She brushed her hair back from her face. "Not at all. Ask away. Ask for anything. I owe you."

This time his laughter was low, intimate and ridiculously arousing. "That is not the sort of thing you should tell a man, *agapi mou*. If I were without scruples, you could find yourself in trouble after making a statement such as that."

Darcie was too intrigued and too attracted to Nick to be alarmed. Maybe it was the warmth that radiated from his dark eyes, or the slightly self-deprecating quirk of his sensual lips. She was sure he posed no threat to her safety. To her sanity? Well, that remained to be seen.

"But you do have scruples."

"How can you tell?"

"A man without them would not have bothered to help me yesterday without asking for anything in return."

"Yet here I am one day later, begging a favor." His lips quirked again.

"Begging is different than demanding. A man without scruples would demand, I think."

"I am glad you see it that way." His expression sobered then. "You are certainly under no obligation to agree to my proposition. I want to make that perfectly clear from the outset."

Proposition? The mere word, said as it was in that delicious accent, caused heat to curl low in Darcie's belly. Sitting with Nick inside the little café, she felt worldly, sophisticated and a lifetime removed from the awkward young woman from Buffalo who had allowed herself to be browbeaten into inertia by Tad's overbearing mother.

Darcie was pleased to find her voice was magnificently matter-of-fact when she replied, "It's clear, Nick. So, what is this proposition of yours?"

"I would like to invite you to dinner tonight."

"Dinner?" She blinked.

Maybe she'd heard him wrong. Darcie wasn't disappointed, but she was somewhat surprised. Sharing another meal seemed, well, a little mundane given his dramatic lead-in. Maybe *proposition* had a different meaning in Greece than it did back in the United States. Or maybe she'd imagined the speculative gleam in his eyes. Or maybe she was just too long out of practice with members of the opposite sex to be able to figure out their intentions beyond mere flirting.

"Dinner. Yes." He hesitated then before adding. "With my family."

Her mouth fell open at that. She knew she was gaping, yet it was a full thirty seconds before she could force her lips to close. She'd dated Tad for more than a year before he'd taken her home to meet his mother. Little had she known then that he'd been doing her a favor. Still…

"Are you going to say anything?" Nick asked at last. A grin lurked around the corners of his mouth.

"Sorry," she mumbled. "I'm just a little surprised by the invitation."

"I have no doubt of that. We have only just met, after all. And it is a big favor to ask."

The server returned with their bottle of water, a couple of glasses and two demitasse cups of coffee, forestalling her reply. Darcie took a sip of the coffee. It was stronger than she was used to, very sweet and hot enough that it burned her tongue. She barely noticed the pain. She was too preoccupied with the gorgeous man sitting across from her. Things like this didn't happen to her. There had to be a catch. Or a camera crew lurking nearby, waiting to jump out and tell her she'd been punked.

She glanced around, ruled out a hoax and asked, "Why do you want me to meet your parents?"

"Not only my parents. My grandmother will be there as well."

"Why not?" She lifted her shoulders. "The more the merrier."

"Yes." But there was nothing merry about his expression. He looked downright grim.

"So, um, why? Not that I'm not flattered by the invitation," she hastened to assure him. "But I'm curious."

"I told you that I was in Athens because my brother is to be married."

She nodded. "In two weeks."

"My mother and grandmother have had their heads together for months trying to find a date for me."

"You can't find one on your own?" Darcie winced as soon as the words were out. "What I mean is, so you are single." She winced again and picked up her coffee, braving a second burn on her tongue if it would keep her from blurting out any more embarrassing remarks.

"I'm not in a relationship at the moment." A pair of dark brows rose. "And you? I should have thought to ask if you are involved with anyone."

"Nope. No one."

And she had to admit, her emancipation—that was how she was coming to view it—felt pretty darned good right now. She was free. Free of Tad's lukewarm affection and his mother's passive-aggressive jabs. Free of her own mother's well-meaning interference and her married sisters' well-meaning advice. Free of self-doubt. Well, mostly free. Yes, Darcie was happily free to flirt, to enjoy the company of a handsome man and to accept, if she so chose, his invitation to dinner.

And she so chose.

His dark eyes warmed. "That is good. Very good."

"Oh?"

"It would not do for me to be propositioning a woman who is already spoken for."

"No worries there." Feeling emboldened, she added, "I speak for myself these days."

"Another reason to like you. Now, back to my predicament. My mother and grandmother mean well. They think I am pining."

"Pining?" She didn't like the sound of that. It implied another woman was in the picture.

He shook his head. "Perhaps lonely is a better word."

Better, but improbable. "I don't think so. You don't look lonely to me."

More to the point, men who looked *like* Nick Costas didn't tend to get lonely. They tended to have smartphones filled with the names and numbers of women who were eager to share meals and mattress space.

Nick took a sip of his coffee. "Lacking for companionship," he said at last.

Laughter bubbled out before she could stop it. "Sorry. I find that even harder to believe."

"Unfortunately, my mother and grandmother are less inclined to see the truth. So, they have been…matchmaking. I told them I have no need for their help."

"Because you can get your own dates."

"Yes, as our lunch proves. But…" The corners of his mouth turned down and he shrugged.

"How do I figure into this?"

Darcie thought she knew, and she was already flattered, but since jumping to conclusions was her specialty, she decided a little clarification wouldn't hurt. Besides, it would be really embarrassing if she was wrong.

"There is a woman who recently returned to Greece after living in London for a few years. My mother knows her mother, and has invited both of them to my brother's wedding. Now I am expected to be her escort. I told her and my grandmother that I already have a date. You."

The smile he sent Darcie could have melted a glacier. She shivered anyway and gooseflesh pricked her arms.

"Oh." Her mouth threatened to fall open again. She kept it closed by putting her elbow on the tabletop and propping her chin on her fist.

"What is this look?" he asked, his eyes narrowing as he studied her face.

She dropped the hand from her chin and busied herself

lining up the cutlery next to her plate. "I was going for non-chalant, but I suppose you could call it gobsmacked."

"Gobsmacked? I am not familiar with this term."

"Um, it means shocked."

"Because we barely know one another," he guessed.

"Sure." She moved the knife one-sixteenth of an inch to the right. "That reason will do."

"It is a lot to ask, but I was hoping you would agree." When she continued to fuss with her utensils, he reached across the table and settled his hand over hers. "I would be most grateful."

Darcie glanced up and moistened her lips. It was all Nick could do not to moan. That sexy mouth of hers was going to be his undoing. The table was narrow enough that it would take little effort to lean across it and kiss her. It was tempting. *She* was tempting.

"I don't speak Greek," Darcie said, interrupting his fantasy.

For a moment, he wasn't sure he could speak at all.

"Nick?"

He cleared his throat, bemused by the strange infatuation he felt. "That will not be a problem. Both of my parents are fluent in English, and my grandmother knows enough to get by. I can always translate if she does not understand something or if you do not."

"That's…good."

And still she hesitated. So, he decided to sweeten the deal. "Have you had any luck getting a refund on your tour?"

"No. I left a message last night and planned to call again today."

Nick had left messages as well. Stavros was either passed out cold or screening his calls. If Nick had to bet on one, he would put money on the former.

"What if I were to be your guide? In return for accompanying me to dinner, I will take you to the sites mentioned on the tour's brochure."

And why not? It would give him something to do for the next couple of weeks while he dodged his mother and grandmother's well-meaning mediation and Pieter's ongoing attempts to bury the hatchet. And he couldn't think of another woman he'd rather pass the time with than Darcie.

"That's very generous of you, but without a refund from Stavros I can't afford to stay in Greece much longer, let alone for the full two weeks."

"Leave Stavros to me."

One way or another, Nick would see to it that Darcie Hayes had her trip...and enjoyed it.

"You do realize I will be heading home the day before your brother gets married, right?"

"That is fine."

Nick did not need an actual date for Pieter's wedding. All he needed was a viable reason in the interim to avoid a setup. Once his mother and grandmother met Darcie, they would cease and desist in their matchmaking. As solutions went, it was perfect. Now if only his family would stop trying to force a reconciliation between him and Pieter.

"I don't know," Darcie began. "It sounds as if I'm getting the better end of the deal."

She only thought so because she hadn't yet met his *yiayia* or the rest of his kin, Nick thought wryly.

"Does that mean we *have* a deal?"

"I… Why not? Sure." She stuck out her hand just as she had the previous day.

Nick studied the long, unadorned fingers for a moment before giving in to his previous impulse. Bypassing her palm, he leaned over to kiss her full on the mouth. Her sweetness had him lingering and wishing for privacy. Unfortunately, there was none of that here. Sure enough, when he drew back, the restaurant erupted in applause and shouts of *"Opa!"*

Darcie's blush was becoming, if at odds with the frank interest evident in her eyes. Maybe she had gotten the better end of the deal after all. Not that Nick minded one bit.

Back at her hotel, Nick insisted on parking his car and walking her inside. Darcie thought she knew why. He wanted to kiss her again. Well, no problem. She wanted to kiss him again, too.

The lip-lock they'd shared in the restaurant had been amazing. On a scale of one to ten, Darcie would rate it a ten...thousand. That didn't even take into account the degree of difficulty involved. Nick had managed that score with a table wedged between them and a wide-eyed crowd of spectators, whose spontaneous applause afterward, by the way, had been entirely appropriate. Heck, that kiss had deserved a standing ovation. Darcie would settle for an encore.

Should she ask him to come up to her room? They would have privacy but it might seem too forward. He might think she wanted to sleep with him. Did she?

Why yes, she did. She was human and breathing and he was gorgeous and sexy beyond belief. But should she?

Probably not a good idea. She'd never been the sort of woman who slept with a man on the first date. Or the second. Or the third...

"Darcie—"

"Even the fourth would be pushing it."

Nick's brow wrinkled. "Excuse me?"

"Nothing." She waved a hand. "Just, um...here we are."

They had reached the elevator and Darcie still wasn't sure what she should do. He took the decision out of her hands by pushing the button.

"Are you coming up?" she asked casually.

"I would like to, but…" He shook his head.

"A gentleman," she mused.

It sounded like he said, "A fool."

"So, I'll see you to—"

He pulled her into his arms and kissed her with all of the passion and skill he'd shown in the restaurant, but with far less of the restraint.

"—night."

Nick's breath was sawing in and out, but he managed to mutter something in Greek that told Darcie he was every bit as turned on as she was.

Before the elevator arrived, he turned and walked away.

CHAPTER FOUR

DARCIE NEEDED AN outfit for dinner since nothing in her luggage full of second-string clothes seemed appropriate. But what did one wear to meet a man's parents when one barely knew the man?

She mulled that question as she wandered the labyrinth of streets near her hotel. Shops abounded, interspersed with cafés and taverns. The only problem was that the goods the stores sold were geared toward tourists: snow globes featuring miniature Parthenons, key chains and postcards. As for clothing, it fell into two categories: logoed T-shirts and the traditional Greek garb that she doubted anyone in Greece actually wore.

Two hours into her quest the arches of her feet were beginning to ache, but she decided to stray a little farther from the beaten path. After another half an hour, her persistence was rewarded when she arrived at the door of a small boutique that the owner of a nearby bakery had recommended. After licking the last crumbs of freshly made baklava from her fingertips, Darcie headed inside.

The boutique was small and totally kitsch-free. It also was expensive, with prices that reflected the quality of the garments on display. Darcie swallowed hard after glancing at the tag that dangled from a cap-sleeved cocktail dress made of red silk. She calculated the exchange rate in her head. It was far more than she felt comfortable spending, even though the dress was gorgeous. She moved on to another rack, but it was of no use. The garments there, while also lovely, were equally expensive. On a sigh, she turned to leave.

"May I help you find something?" a woman asked in English as she stepped out from behind the counter. She was about Darcie's age and nearly her height in a pair of killer high heels. The name tag pinned to her chest read Nerina.

Darcie shook her head. "I was just looking."

"For anything in particular?"

She started to say no only to admit, "I've been invited to dinner this evening."

The woman smiled knowingly. "With a man."

"Yes. He's taking me to meet his parents."

"Oh, this is serious. He is Greek?"

"No and yes." At the saleswoman's perplexed expression, Darcie added, "No, it's not serious. At least not how you mean. We've only just met and…it's not serious. But, yes, he is Greek. Well, I guess he's actually American now, but he's from Athens. Originally. You know, he was born here." She grimaced. "I'm probably not making any sense."

"I understand. You are nervous." Again, Nerina's knowing smile made an appearance. "Even though you have only just met, you like this man."

"I do."

It was the truth. What was not to like about a man who had been gracious and kind and treated her with respect, all while making it clear that he found her attractive and wouldn't mind seeing her naked?

Okay, so maybe Darcie had extrapolated that last part, but the kiss Nick had given her in the restaurant had made her toes want to curl. And the one in the lobby of her hotel?

She was surprised she hadn't spontaneously combusted in the elevator afterward.

"Then we must find you something perfect for this evening." Nerina turned to another rack and began flipping through the garments.

Darcie cleared her throat. "I'm afraid I'm on a limited budget. Actually, a very limited budget. I shouldn't be buying clothes at all, but the airline lost my luggage and…"

"And then you met this handsome man who has invited you to dinner to meet his parents, and you want to look stunning."

Darcie sighed. "That about sums it up." Placing a hand on her stomach to quell her nerves, she asked, "Do you take credit cards?"

Nerina nodded and then tapped her lips thoughtfully for a moment before bursting into a satisfied grin.

"I have just the dress."

Later that afternoon, freshly showered, Darcie took her time getting ready, shimmying first into a bra and panties that weren't likely to be seen, but made her feel sexy and sophisticated nonetheless. Both pieces were lacy and utterly feminine, and the only articles from her trousseau that had made it into the lucky piece of luggage that managed to arrive in Greece along with her.

Afterward, she studied herself in the mirrored door of the closet with a critical eye. Turning sideways, she sucked in her stomach until her belly was concave and the bottom of her rib cage became visible. Gee, as long as she didn't breathe, she sported measurements that the pinups girls of the 1940s would have envied. But Darcie was fond of breathing, so she let out her breath on a gusty sigh. Goodbye twenty-four-inch waist.

Still, she liked her curves and the muscle tone she'd

managed to carve into them thanks to six months' worth of grueling workouts with the personal trainer from hell. She reached into the closet for the dress she'd just purchased. She had to admit it showed off all of her assets to their greatest advantage.

Since the evening's dinner was at someone's home, Nerina had suggested a more casual wrap dress in a soft jersey fabric the color of ripe peaches. Both the color and the cut flattered Darcie. Best of all, she could pair it with flat shoes she already owned, saving her a second purchase. Nerina also had been generous on the price, declaring the garment on sale even though it was not marked as such.

"Enjoy your evening," she'd said as Darcie left the shop.

Looking at herself in the mirror now, Darcie grinned. Oh, she planned to.

Peach was his new favorite color, Nick decided, when Darcie stepped out of the elevator into the hotel lobby. As he eyed her curves, the air backed up in his lungs. The reaction wasn't entirely unpleasant, but it was unsettling and rare when it came to women. Except for this woman. Around Darcie, he couldn't seem to catch his breath at all.

From the first moment he'd spied her in the airport, he'd found himself drawn to her, interested in a way that he'd initially assumed was purely the result of sexual attraction. He'd gone on instinct when he'd approached her and offered his assistance. He'd followed his gut again when he'd come to her earlier in the day, asking a favor. Nick didn't regret his impulses, but he knew a moment of panic when she smiled at him now and his mouth went dry.

"I hope I'm dressed all right. I wasn't sure what to wear," she said.

"You look lovely." He kept his gaze locked on her face,

not trusting himself to take in those curves a second time without touching them.

"Thank you."

A pair of glossed lips parted in a smile that was nearly impossible to resist. He bit back a groan and asked, "Are you ready?"

"I am."

This time, instead of a Porsche, Nick was driving a 1965 Shelby Cobra.

"Very iconic," she murmured of the cobalt-blue car that sported twin white stripes up its hood and down its trunk. "One of the most sought-after cars as I recall from fact-checking an article about one. Is it the real deal?"

"If you are asking if it is one of the ten special racing editions, yes."

"Signed by Carroll Shelby?"

"Of course." Once again, Nick appreciated the depth of her knowledge. A woman who spoke car. He'd never met one before.

"I'm almost afraid to sit in it," she told him when he opened the door for her. "This baby goes for what? A couple hundred thousand American dollars?"

"Closer to three."

"Well, there, you've put my mind at ease," she replied dryly.

Nick chuckled. "Get in." Since the car had no roof and only a low, curving windshield, he handed her a scarf. "For your hair."

"Very thoughtful. Thank you. I feel Grace Kelly-ish. Or I would if I were a platinum blonde with classical features and a slimmer build."

"There's nothing wrong with your hair color, features or your...build."

She sent him a sideways smile. It sounded like she said, "I could get used to you."

The drive to his grandmother's house was relatively short. Still, as they cruised through the city, Nick used the time to prep Darcie on his life, starting with the basics such as his age and education.

"I have not told them very much about you."

"That's because you don't know very much about me," she pointed out.

"I am eager to remedy that." His tone hinted at something much more intimate than a family dinner. "I have told them that you are American and that we have not known one another for long. That way, they will not expect us to have all of the answers."

Besides, the sexual chemistry between the two of them was very real and would go a long way to making their relationship plausible in his family's eyes.

Darcie was nodding. "All right. So, how did we meet?"

"I think we should keep it simple and as close to truthful as possible. I do not usually lie to my family." He shifted his attention from the road to her when he added, "I do not usually lie to anyone."

"I figured that. Same goes for me." She took a deep breath. "So, we met in an airport."

"Let's make it Newark."

"I saw you across a crowded room, our eyes met and it was magic." She laughed, but something about her assessment struck Nick as disturbingly accurate.

"How about if we just say I offered to give you a ride when yours did not show?" He turned, found himself lost in the same blue eyes that had sucked him in across the airport terminal and added, "I was only too happy to come to the aid of a beautiful woman."

"The only problem with that is I do not live in New York City, but upstate in Buffalo."

"You were in New York on business then."

She nibbled her lip. "There's not much travel involved in my line of work. Not like yours. I can check facts over the phone or by computer. I've never had to hop a plane to do my job. Not that I wouldn't mind."

"On holiday then?"

"I guess that's believable."

"Have you ever been to New York?"

"Once. It was right after I graduated from high school. I went with my friend Becky and her family. We stayed at a hotel near Times Square and took in a Broadway show." Her smile was wide and nostalgic. "I loved it."

"The show or the city?"

"Both. All of that energy. I felt energized, too."

Nick heard awe in her voice and understood it. That was how he'd felt the first time he'd visited New York— absolutely blown away by the mania, yet eager to be part of it, too. Athens was hardly a small town, either in population or in feel, but no other place Nick had traveled, which he did extensively for business, compared to New York.

"You will have to visit again. I would be happy to show you around."

He meant it, he realized with a start. He could see her in his adopted city, enjoying the herb-crusted salmon at his favorite restaurant, sipping coffee at a sidewalk café near Central Park, window-shopping on Fifth Avenue. Most disturbing, Nick could picture Darcie in his apartment—his quiet and at times lonely retreat from the bustle of the city— curled up on his couch with a glass of wine in her hand, smiling at him in invitation.

She was smiling at him now when she replied, "Maybe I will."

He swallowed and forced his attention to the least erotic thing he could think of. "Tell me about your family. Do they also live in Buffalo?"

"For the most part. I have three sisters. Two older, one younger, all of them married. They're scattered in the suburbs with their husbands and kids, driving minivans and carpooling to soccer games and gymnastic classes."

"But not you."

"To my mother's everlasting regret."

"And your father? What does he think of your situation?"

"He tells me there's plenty of time to get married, have kids and buy a minivan." She frowned then. "But…"

"But?"

"He thinks I'm wasting my talent at my current job," she admitted quietly.

"Are you?"

Darcie made a sound that was halfway between a laugh and a sigh. "That's the subject for a very long conversation. Right now, I think we should stick to the basics."

She was right, of course, but Nick was too curious about her to let the matter drop. "What talent is it that your father feels you are wasting?"

"I have a degree in journalism from Buffalo State University. I enjoyed feature writing. Some of my professors told me I had a flair for it. My plan was to work at a newspaper and once I had enough decent clips—"

"Clips?"

"Copies of articles I'd written. Once I had enough of those, I was going to apply for a job at one of the large women's magazines headquartered in New York."

"So, you wanted to come to the big city?"

"I did," she admitted on a shy smile. "Once upon a time I thought I could make a name for myself in publishing."

"But?"

The smile vanished. Darcie shrugged. "Something came up and then the fact-checking job at *Automobile Enthusiasts Monthly* came along."

"Do you ever do any writing for that magazine? You certainly know enough about cars to do a credible job of it."

"The editor has let me do a couple of blurbs about upcoming car cruises, but nothing meaty or in-depth. He either tackles those himself—it's a small publication—or he farms them out to a freelancer. It doesn't hurt that the freelancer is a poker buddy." She sighed. "So, I check facts."

The more she said, the more questions Nick had. He contented himself by asking the one that cut straight to the heart of the matter.

"Do you enjoy your work, Darcie?"

"I suppose." She shrugged. "It pays the bills."

A tepid and telling answer, in Nick's opinion.

"You should do something you feel passionately about. Otherwise, what is the point?"

"I guess you would know, since you're obviously passionate about your work."

He glanced over and waited until he was sure he had her full attention. "I am passionate about much more than my work."

Nick's frank reply and the accompanying intimate smile sent a spurt of pure lust coursing through Darcie's veins. The excitement churning away inside frightened her a little. It was so foreign. It seemed forbidden. But it wasn't, she reminded herself. She was a single woman, a consenting adult. Heck, if she were being truthful, she was a parched patch of desert desperate for a good dousing of rain. Bring on the storm.

"If you continue to look at me like that, I will be tempted to forego dinner and return to your hotel instead," Nick told her. Once again, his words were blunt. His smile bordered on sinful.

She called herself a chicken, but decided to play it safe.

"Sorry, I was just thinking about…all of the changes that have occurred in my life recently. Maybe more are in order." Warming to the notion, she added, "God knows, the timing couldn't be better. I need to find a new place to live. Why not a new job, too?"

It wasn't as if anything tied her to *Automobile Enthusiasts Monthly*. The pay was mediocre, the benefits were crap. She'd only taken the position after she and Tad became serious. At the time, with some help from him, she'd convinced herself that a career in New York was a pipe dream. Settling down in Buffalo with reliable if tedious employment and a future with Tad—those were what had mattered, what she had wanted most.

"You are at a crossroads," Nick said. Up ahead, the light turned red and he slowed the Shelby to a stop.

Darcie gestured with her hand. "It's really more like this busy intersection, but with no working traffic light."

"Ah, then you need to take care in getting to the other side."

Treading carefully, that was how she'd spent the past several years. Feeling reckless now, she said, "Or I could just run like hell and hope for the best. After all, we've established that I am adventurous."

"I like your style." Nick's hand left the gearshift to caress her cheek. He was leaning toward her, eyes hooded with unmistakable intent, when a horn blasted behind them.

"The light is green," she said, suppressing a laugh.

"Yes. A green light. I believe I got that very impression."

The car shot forward. Darcie's pulse lurched as if trying to catch up. The scarf was in no danger of blowing off, but she pulled it snugger around her head, just to have something to do with her hands.

"Let's talk about you."

"All right. You know what I do for a living. You also know I have a brother who is to be married."

"A younger brother. Pieter."

"Very good. You pay close attention to details."

"It's what I do." She shrugged. "I check facts for a living, remember?"

"Or you did."

The seed, so recently planted, seemed to be taking root. But she forced herself to focus on the present. "Tell me about Pieter. How old is he? What's he like? Are you close?"

A muscle ticked in Nick's jaw, although when he spoke, his tone bordered on blasé. "He is a year my junior. As boys, we did everything together. Now…he works with our father at his shop. They are electricians by trade."

"The family business?"

Nick nodded. "My father had hoped I would follow in his footsteps as well."

"But you had other interests."

"Yes."

One syllable said without regret but full of sadness. More family expectations, Darcie decided. Hoping to lighten his mood, she shifted the subject. "Why don't you tell me about Pieter's fiancée?"

That muscle ticked in Nick's jaw again. "Selene."

The wind rushed past in the open car, but the tension grew thicker. "Um, that's a pretty name."

He snorted. "We grew up together, the three of us." Nick paused before adding, "Selene and I used to date."

Darcie blinked, too surprised to apply tact when she said, "You dated the woman your brother is marrying?"

"It would be more accurate to say that my brother is marrying a woman I dated," he replied tersely.

"Oh." More like *uh-oh*. Darcie had stepped into something unpleasant, and she had no clue how to scrape it gracefully off her shoe.

"You are wondering if I am heartbroken."

"Are you?" she asked bluntly.

"It was over a long time ago."

Nick might not be heartbroken—and the jury was still out on that as far as she was concerned—but Darcie didn't think it was as over as he claimed it to be. She heard another emotion in his tone. Anger? Betrayal? If it truly was over, he would feel nothing. She wanted to ask why he and Selene had broken up, but she sensed that topic wasn't open for discussion.

She said quietly, "It has to be awkward."

"It is."

Did this mean Nick was on the rebound, too? She wasn't sure how she felt about that or even if she had the right to feel anything. They had been driving in silence for a couple of minutes, when something occurred to her.

"Um, speaking of awkward, will Selene and Pieter be at dinner tonight?"

As it was, Darcie had enough to worry about what with convincing his parents and grandmother that she and Nick were an item without adding bad blood and an old lovers' triangle to the mix. Thankfully, Nick shook his head.

"They have other plans. Some last-minute meeting with the caterer about changes to one of the side dishes. Apparently, a cousin of the bride has a severe peanut allergy."

"Oh, thank God." Darcie closed her eyes and grimaced. "Not about the allergy. Those can be deadly. Anaphylactic shock and all. But—"

"I know exactly what you mean." His dry laughter served to put her at ease.

A few minutes later, they arrived at a two-story white stucco home surrounded by lush, terraced gardens.

"We're here."

Showtime, Darcie thought, as she removed the scarf and checked her appearance in the rearview mirror.

"You look beautiful," he assured her.

Even so, nerves fluttered in her belly. She offered up a prayer that in addition to passing parental inspection, she wouldn't humiliate herself by getting sick.

"This is my grandmother's house, but my mother and father live just there."

He pointed to the home next door that was similar in size and appearance and whose yard was equally well-landscaped. Concentrating on the details helped quell her nerves. As limited as her knowledge of plants was, she recognized geraniums spilling from the pots near the front door, as well as near the iron railing that girded a second-story terrace. And even without the assistance of a breeze, she could smell the heady scent of roses.

"Wow. Your mother and grandmother must have green thumbs. Everything looks so, well, *green*. My mom is like that. And my sisters. They can grow anything, anywhere. As near as I can tell, my thumb is black."

"Black?" He took her hands, studied the digits in question. "They look normal to me."

"It's just a saying. It means I'm a plant killer, which is why the only plant I own is a ficus whose leaves are made of plastic. There's no chance of killing that sucker."

"I see," Nick said patiently.

No, he didn't, because there was no point to this conversation, except for stalling. Darcie was babbling like an idiot, but she couldn't seem to stop herself. More words tumbled out. "Although the ficus still looks pathetic thanks to Rufus."

Nick's lips twitched. "The cat you referred to as the spawn of Satan?"

"That's the one. He used it as a scratching post."

Nick got out and came around the car to open Darcie's door. "Come." Suddenly he seemed so formidable, as though he were prepared for battle. The sudden change from playful to guarded did nothing to settle Darcie's nerves.

He led her to the door, entered without knocking. This might have been his grandmother's house, but he didn't stand on formality. She liked that. The foyer opened into a living room with a fireplace. It was a comfortable room, a place that invited one to sit and relax. Darcie wished she could, but she was wound up as tight as a spring. From the rear of the house, she could hear voices, although she couldn't make out anything that was being said since it was in Greek. She heard Nick's name mentioned and then she thought she heard her own. When she glanced at him, his expression was apologetic.

"They say they are eager to meet you."

Darcie doubted his translation was complete or completely accurate.

He took her hand. "This way."

The mingled scents of spices and roasting meat wafting from the kitchen should have had her mouth watering, but it was dry as sawdust. She stopped walking.

"I need another minute," she whispered and sucked in a deep breath.

"You are nervous. I understand."

Did he? It wasn't only her part in the deception that had her worried, but what his family would think of her. Her old insecurities bubbled up before she could stop them. What if they found her as lacking as Evelyn had?

"You will be fine."

"Fine," she repeated, feeling anything but.

"It is only one meal."

Yes, but it felt like her last supper.

"Darcie." Nick framed her face with his hands. His palms were warm, the pads of his thumbs slightly calloused as they brushed over her cheeks. "You…"

Whatever else he said, and she thought it might have been in Greek, was lost to the rushing in her ears. Besides, words, no matter what the language, were superfluous. He was going to kiss her again. That much came through loud and clear. And she wanted him to. So much so that she didn't bother to wait for him to lean in and claim her mouth. She clasped the back of his neck and closed the gap between them herself.

She'd always been a fan of fireworks, though it had been a very long time since she'd experienced any. This kind lit her up inside until she was sure her skin glowed from the heat. Someone moaned. She was pretty sure the sound came from her. Regardless, Nick took the opportunity to change the angle of their mouths. His hands no longer framed her face. His fingers splayed over the small of her back, exerting subtle pressure that brought her flush against his hard chest.

A woman's voice cut through the haze of hormones.

"This must be Darcie."

They sprung apart. Fireworks fizzled until they were but pesky smoke. Way to make a first impression, Darcie thought, giving herself a mental slap. Nick, meanwhile, offered the sort of charmingly sheepish smile that probably had helped him out of plenty of scrapes as a boy.

"Mama. My apologies. I seem to have gotten carried away."

"Yes. That much I could see for myself," she replied dryly.

But she was smiling. And so was the older woman standing just behind her in the doorway.

In heavily accented English, Nick's *yiayia* said, "Manners, Nikolos, manners. Introduce us."

He rubbed his hands together. "Of course. Darcie Hayes, this is my grandmother, Sophia Pappas, and my mother, Thea Costas."

Hands were shaken, greetings exchanged. Darcie knew she was being sized up. Funny, but some of her earlier nervousness had evaporated. Nick's mother and grandmother were curious about her, that much was very clear. But she sensed no antipathy, no animosity. She felt welcome if not accepted. And that was before his grandmother slid one of her boney arms around Darcie's waist and propelled her toward the kitchen.

"Come. I will pour the wine. You will tell us about yourself. Start with your ancestors. Might there be a chance some of your people came from Greece?"

CHAPTER FIVE

NICK'S FATHER ARRIVED just before the meal was served. By then, Darcie's nerves had calmed substantially. It helped that while seated in the kitchen watching Thea and Sophia finish the preparations she'd polished off a glass of a lovely dry red wine.

She refused a refill when Nick would have poured her one. It wouldn't do to get snockered. But she told them, "This was very good."

"It is bottled by Nick's uncle, my brother, and his sons," Thea said proudly. "They have a small vineyard in Thrace."

"Nick is the only one of his generation to leave Greece to work," Sophia lamented. "We keep hoping he will return for good one day."

"Yiayia," he said.

"What? I only say what is true. That is what we all hope will happen. Is it not, Thea?"

His mother flushed and was saved from answering by Nick's father, who said as he entered the kitchen, "He is here now. Let us enjoy our time together."

The older man wasn't as tall as Nick, but his shoulders were just as broad. Age had added more girth to his waist, deep lines to the corners of his eyes and gray hair to his temples. But he remained a handsome man. This is how Nick would look in thirty years' time, Darcie thought. Warmth spread through her. She chalked it up to the wine.

"This is my father, George Costas," Nick said.

"Darcie Hayes." When she would have shaken his hand, George kissed both of her cheeks.

"She is prettier than Danika." He winked at Nick.

"Danika?" Darcie mouthed.

"I will explain later," Nick mumbled.

"Stop flirting, *Baba*, and go wash up," Thea said with an exaggerated shake of her head. "Dinner is ready."

They ate *alfresco*, seated around a table under a pergola in Yiayia's backyard. Vine-covered trellises lined the pergola's sides, offering shade from the late day sun. The center of the table was heaped with enough food to feed twice as many people.

Darcie smoothed a napkin over her lap. "Everything looks wonderful, Mrs. Costas and Mrs. Pappas."

"Call me Yiayia. Everyone does."

"And you may call me Thea," Nick's mother said, passing Darcie a platter of sliced lamb. "You are not a vegetarian, I hope. A lot of young people are nowadays."

"No." Even if Darcie had been, the delicious-smelling meat would have tempted her to take a bite.

"That is good," Yiayia said. "Nick likes red meat."

"True." Thea nodded. "But he will fly home for dinner on a Palm Sunday if I promise to make *bakaliaros tiganitos*."

At Darcie's perplexed expression, he explained, "It is a salt-cured cod that my mother then batters and deep fries. It is very tasty, but it is the dipping sauce she makes to go with it that has me booking my flight."

"Here, we are so close to the ocean that the fish is fresh and plentiful," Yiayia said.

"Manhattan is next to the Atlantic," he pointed out patiently and Darcie got the feeling this was a long-standing argument.

"It is settled," George offered. "Water and fish are everywhere."

But Yiayia wasn't done. "Do they even know how to make *bakaliaros tiganitos* in America?"

"I will look on the menu at the next Greek restaurant I visit."

Sophia shrugged. "It does not matter. They will not cook it as well as your mama does. I taught her, just as my mother taught me. Just as your mother will teach your future wife." She glanced slyly at Darcie.

George apparently didn't get the memo about playing it coy. "Maybe you could teach Darcie, Thea."

Everyone at the table turned and gaped at him. Nick was the first to recover. There was a gleam in his eye when he said, "I do like Mama's *bakaliaros tiganitos*."

"Nick likes *all* of his mama's cooking," George said with a hearty laugh. "He gets that from me."

"If he is not careful, he will get this, too." Thea patted her husband's stomach. More laughter followed, chasing away a bit of the strain.

"If you would like, I could share some of my recipes with you," Thea said to Darcie, "including the one for *bakaliaros tiganitos*. It is not so hard to make, but you must soak the fish overnight or it will be too salty."

"Thank you. I would like that."

"Are you a good cook?" Sophia asked.

"Um, I…" Darcie had mastered the art of microwaving in college, and she knew how to whip up staples such as grilled cheese and spaghetti, as long as the sauce for the latter came from a jar. But her culinary skills didn't go much beyond that since, at Evelyn's insistence, Darcie and Tad had eaten most of their meals at his mother's. In Darcie's new home, wherever that might be, she was going to take the time to learn. "I plan to be."

Yiayia's eyes narrowed. Clearly, that answer hadn't won Darcie any points.

"Do you cook for Nick?"

Before she could formulate a response, he explained, "We eat out whenever Darcie comes to town."

"And where does she sleep when she comes to town?" Yiayia asked pointedly.

Darcie felt her face flame, but Nick took the question in stride. "She sleeps in a bed," he replied without specifying whose. Since his grin left little doubt, she kicked him under the table.

Earlier, in the kitchen, they had discussed how Darcie and Nick met. Now, the topic turned to what she did for a living, what her family was like and the names of her siblings, brothers-in-law, nephews and nieces. Yiayia, of course, snuck in a question about how many children Darcie wanted. By the time coffee and dessert were served, Yiayia had determined two things. One, Darcie was too thin and, two, she must have some Greek in her, if only because she liked the strong coffee.

"I like the cake, too," Darcie noted after taking a bite. It was topped with powdered sugar and lightly toasted almonds. "It's delicious. What's it called?"

"Revani," Yiayia said.

"Revani," Darcie repeated. Or so she thought. But Yiayia was shaking her head.

"No, no, no. Re-vah-*nee.*"

"Emphasis on the last syllable," Nick supplied.

Darcie tried the word again, this time earning his grandmother's nod of approval.

"I make this special for Nick. I will be sure to give you the recipe so you can make it, too."

Darcie sent him a smile and asked, "Is this another favorite of yours?"

But it wasn't Nick who answered.

"My brother is fond of all sweet things."

Pieter stood just outside the door that led from the house. At least, Darcie assumed the man was Pieter. The family resemblance was there in the shape of his eyes and the athletic build. And if he was Pieter, that would make the woman standing beside him Selene.

OMG!

Darcie set down her fork and blotted her mouth on the napkin. Then she sat up straighter in her chair and sucked in her stomach. Selene was slender and petite. Darcie felt like an Amazon in comparison. And the other woman was drop-dead gorgeous with high cheekbones, delicately arched brows and sleek black hair. In short, she was Aphrodite incarnate. A glance at Nick confirmed what Darcie already knew: if he was over what had happened, he was doing a poor job showing it. His eyes had turned as hard as stone.

"Pieter! Selene!" Thea smiled nervously. "We did not think you would be here."

"We finished our appointment with the caterer early and thought we would stop by for cake."

"How did you know about the cake?" Nick asked.

"Yiayia called earlier and mentioned it."

All eyes cut to Yiayia.

"I am an old woman," she muttered with the wave of an arthritic hand. "I cannot remember what I say, who I say it to."

Half of Pieter's mouth rose in a resigned smile. "The only reason you are here is because you did not think that we would be. I guess I was foolish to hope."

Nick said nothing, but that muscle started to tick in his jaw again.

"It does not matter. I am glad to see you, Nick. We both are." Pieter curved his arm around Selene's shoulders and she offered a tentative smile.

The tension built along with the silence. Darcie was the one who breached it.

"Pieter and Selene. Nick has told me so much about you both. It's so nice to finally meet you."

"And you are?" Pieter asked.

"Darcie Hayes. Nick's…Nick's girlfriend."

She'd already stepped in this mess with one foot. Why not both?

"You played your part well this evening," Nick told Darcie once the two of them were in the Shelby and heading back to her hotel.

At times he had forgotten their bargain and actually enjoyed himself. That was until Pieter and Selene's arrival. Seeing them together never put Nick in a good mood. This evening it had been tolerable. He had Darcie to thank for that.

"You weren't half-bad yourself," she told him. "If your car auction business doesn't pan out you might consider a career on Broadway."

She smiled, but her tone didn't match the lighthearted comment.

"Is something wrong, Darcie?"

She fussed with the scarf's knot under her chin. "Your family is really nice, Nick. I enjoyed meeting them all."

"And they enjoyed meeting you," he replied warily.

"I don't like lying to them, Nick. Even if most of our lies were ones of omission."

He nodded. "Most of them."

The one that stood out had come from Darcie at the end of dinner: *I'm Nick's girlfriend.*

Upon hearing that, Pieter's expression had reflected not only surprise, but also happiness and hope. More than anything else from the evening, it was the hope that bothered Nick's conscience.

"Sophia is something else." Darcie chuckled. "But she only has your best interests at heart. All of them do."

Nick saw his brother's hopeful expression again only to banish it. "If that is so, they should be satisfied now. You made quite an impression on them."

"I suppose." She cleared her throat. Her tone was tentative when she said, "Your brother seems nice. Selene, too."

Nick made a noncommittal sound and concentrated on driving, hoping Darcie would drop the subject.

She didn't.

"They both seemed genuinely happy for you...us...well, you know what I mean."

"Guilty consciences looking for absolution," he muttered. But was that the cause? He decided to change the subject. "Are you really going to try the recipes my mother and grandmother gave you? Or did you just say that to humor them?"

"Oh, no. I meant it. I'm not sure where I am going to get salt-cured cod, but everything else looks pretty manageable."

"They love to fiddle in the kitchen. I think they should have their own television program."

"Cooking with Thea and Sophia," Darcie offered. They both laughed. "I would watch it. I really do want to learn. I know the basics, but for the past six years, we pretty much ate all of our dinners at Evelyn's house."

"Evelyn?"

"Tad's mother," Darcie said quietly.

Nick glanced sideways. Darcie was staring at her hands,

which were now folded in her lap. "What is a Tad? Or should I ask who?"

She ran a tongue over her teeth. "He's my former fiancé."

Nick nearly blew through a red light. He brought the Shelby to a stop to the protest of skidding tires. Giving Darcie his full attention now, he asked, "How recently former?"

She wrinkled her nose. "Pretty recent. We were supposed to get married last Saturday, but I called it off the week before."

The breath left Nick's lungs in a gust as he added two and two together and came up with four. "He is the reason you are now looking for a new place to live."

"Yes. Tad got the cat and the condo in our breakup. I got...Greece."

Nick's eyebrows shot up in surprise. "So this trip was to be your..."

"Honeymoon," she finished for him. Her smile was tight, her laughter apologetic as he absorbed a second bombshell that he hadn't seen coming.

He should say something, he thought, although "sorry" didn't feel right, even if what she had just shared must have been painful. Endings always were. Briefly, he considered telling her about Selene and Pieter. She probably would welcome a little quid pro quo under the circumstances. But the words stuck in his throat. They drove the rest of the way in silence.

"Stop here," she said when they reached her hotel. "There's no need to park and walk me inside."

He wanted to disagree. But the evening was over and it was time to say good-night. It was just as well. His emotions were all over the place. He didn't care for the confusion. One thing he knew for sure, however, was that his interest in Darcie had not diminished one iota.

"What time shall we meet tomorrow?" At her puzzled

expression he reminded her, "I said I would act as your tour guide. I intend to live up to my end of the bargain."

"Oh. I'll leave the time up to you."

"I am an early riser, but how about nine o'clock?"

"All right. We can meet in the lobby again, if that works for you."

He nodded. "Where would you like to go?"

"The Parthenon."

Nick smiled. "Then the Parthenon it is." When she reached for the door handle, he said, "Aren't you forgetting something?"

She glanced around, her expression uncertain. "What?"

"A kiss good-night." Unable to resist, he leaned over the gearshift and captured her mouth. As the kiss deepened, he regretted the car's bucket seats. "Sleep well, Darcie," Nick said, pulling back.

"Right. As if…" she muttered, getting out.

The phone in Darcie's hotel room trilled at an ungodly hour. She pushed the pillow off her face and, eyes still closed, felt around on the nightstand until she found the receiver.

"'Lo," she mumbled.

"Are you alone?" It was Becky.

Darcie rubbed her eyes. "Yes, I'm alone. Why wouldn't I be alone?"

"You were supposed to call after your date with Mr. Tall, Greek and Gorgeous," her friend reminded her. "When you didn't, well, I thought…"

No need for Becky to fill in the blank. Darcie's imagination had been busy doing that very thing for most of the night.

"Nick dropped me off at the hotel just after ten. I fell asleep soon after. Alone. Sorry I didn't call. I was just too tired. Jet lag and all." It was a handy excuse, but not the whole truth. The whole truth was Darcie hadn't wanted to examine more closely the evening, its ending or the insane attraction she felt for the man in question.

But Becky wasn't giving her an out this time. "So, how was it?"

"Nice. I had a good time."

"Nice? A good time? Sheesh, Darcie. I called for details. Not the abridged version you save for your mother."

Darcie chuckled at that. "My mother is never going to hear any version, abridged or otherwise, where Nick is concerned. I think she still may be holding out hope that Tad and I will get back together and there will be no need to deal with the stack of gifts she promised she would help me return."

"Speaking of Tad, I ran in to him at our favorite coffee shop."

"Tad doesn't like coffee." He complained the beverage stained his teeth.

"I know. Even stranger, he made a point of coming over and saying hello to me."

That was surprising. Tad and Becky didn't like one another, but over the years, they had brokered a truce of sorts—a truce Darcie would have assumed null and void now that the wedding had been called off.

"He asked if I'd heard from you."

"He did not."

"Swear. He wanted to know how you were doing."

"What did you say?"

"I told him we'd talked and that you were having a fabulous time with a hot Greek man."

"You did not!" Darcie exclaimed.

"Okay, those weren't my exact words. But I did tell him that his bargain trip had turned out to be a bust and that you'd been stranded at the airport until a nice man came to your aid. Tad said he'd been trying to reach you on your cell. For that matter, I have, too."

Darcie glanced toward her discarded purse on the chair in the corner. "I silenced the ringer before dinner with Nick's family last night. I haven't turned it back on. Did Tad say why he was calling?"

"No. He looked, well, like he was kind of lost without you."

"Tad?" Darcie couldn't help but be surprised. "I didn't think he would notice my absence. He still has his mother, after all." She shook her head. "That was mean. I don't want him to be unhappy."

"That's because you're a nice person, Darcie. Too nice. Tad took advantage of that. So, are you going to call him? I don't think you should."

"I won't. At least not until I return home." When her friend started to object, Darcie pointed out, "We have to talk, if only so he knows where to forward my mail. Besides, I'm the one who called off the wedding, Becks. That makes Tad the injured party."

A snort came over the line. "Do yourself a favor, and don't feel too sorry for him. Remember, he's the reason you found yourself stranded in Greece."

"Yes, but that's turning out okay." A grin spread over Darcie's face.

"I knew it! Tell me everything about last night. And remember, no skimping when it comes to details."

She still wound up giving Becky an abridged version of events, leaving out completely the arrival of Pieter and Selene at the end of dinner, and the awkward tension that had followed. Darcie didn't want to more closely examine the feelings Nick stirred in her. It was easier just to leave it at mutual attraction. The timing for anything else was completely wrong—apparently for both of them.

As their conversation wound up, Becky said, "Have fun exploring the Parthenon. Hey, take a picture of Nick with your phone and send it to me. I want to see your hot man for myself."

After they said goodbye, Darcie had less than an hour to get ready. The elevator doors slid open at the lobby with five minutes to spare. When she stepped out, the hot man in question was standing to one side of the reception desk. His mouth curved into an appreciative smile that turned her insides to mush. With one look, he made her feel beautiful, desirable and once again ready to toss caution to the wind. That was enough, she decided.

"Kalimera su," she said when she reached him.

His brows rose.

"One of the few Greek phrases I know. Did I say it right?"

"You did. Good morning to you, too." He kissed her cheeks, lingering long enough to make the greeting less platonic. "You look lovely, by the way."

"You do, too. Not lovely, but…" Good enough to gobble up in a T-shirt that fit snugly across his chest. She coughed and forced her gaze back to his. "Um, ready to take in the sights?"

By way of an answer, he took her hand.

Growing up in Athens, Nick had been to the Parthenon dozens of times. He experienced it anew seeing it through Darcie's eyes. She was in total awe.

"It's hard to believe something built more than four hundred years before the birth of Christ is still standing."

"Not all of it is," Nick pointed out.

"But enough of it remains to hint at its former grandeur," she argued. "Those columns are massive. Haven't you ever wondered how the ancient Greeks managed to get them up without modern tools and machinery?"

He grinned. "I am now."

"I'm serious, Nick."

"So I see."

"There's very little in the United States that dates back more than a couple hundred years. Yet here stands a temple, a stunning example of Doric-style architecture, I might add, that was designed by Phidias to honor Athena, the patron goddess of your city, and constructed more than two thousand years ago."

"Your knowledge of the Parthenon is impressive," he said.

"I read about it." She started to laugh. "Over there."

Nick turned to find a large sign listing the same facts Darcie had just spouted. He started to laugh, too, and then pulled her into his arms. He didn't let her go. Both of them sobered.

"I like your sense of humor," he said.

"It's one of my better attributes."

"I can think of other attributes that I prefer even more." He slid his hands down her back and, even though he wanted to place them elsewhere, he forced them to stop at her waist. They were in public, after all, and surrounded by camera-toting tourists.

"You must mean my eyes." She batted the lids. The eyes in question were laughing at him. "I've been told they're a pretty color."

"You are enjoying this," he accused.

"Enjoying what?" she asked a little too innocently. "I don't know what you mean."

"I do like your eyes," he agreed. "But they aren't what kept me awake last night." As intended, his bald assertion wiped the smile from Darcie's face. Then he asked, "How did you sleep? Did you toss and turn?"

"I...I..." She swallowed.

"That is what I thought."

Those blue eyes narrowed. "That's not fair."

"Why?"

"I did toss and turn, but I'm still suffering from jet lag."

"You are full of excuses."

"It's true."

"All right. I have a cure for that." His voice was low and for the briefest moment his hips bumped against hers as he spoke. "Would you like to know what it is?"

"Right now? Right here?" She gave a panicked glance around.

Nick brushed the hair back from her cheek and leaned closer. His lips purposely grazed her ear when he whispered, "Warm milk."

"Warm—" Darcie dissolved in a fit of laughter that drew curious stares from passersby. When she composed herself, she accused, "You set me up."

"I cannot be responsible for the thoughts you entertain." His voice dropped an octave. "Although I would not mind hearing what they are."

She put a hand on his chest and playfully pushed him backward half a step. "Oh, no. I'm not walking into a trap a second time."

Just that quickly, he erased the distance she'd created, and pulled her close. "Now I *really* want to hear those thoughts. Over dinner, perhaps? Say yes."

"Well, when you put it that way. Yes."

CHAPTER SIX

NICK CHANGED HIS mind several times before settling on a restaurant. Even then he wasn't sure he'd made the right choice. He had no doubt Darcie would enjoy the food and the ambience. They were what made it so difficult to get a table at Moscophilero…unless one had a long history with the owner, as Nick did. But the restaurant's location gave him pause. It was in Piraeus and, as such, much closer to his house above the harbor than anything in Athens would be. Within fifteen minutes of his paying the check, he and Darcie could be ensconced in his living room sipping a nightcap. As for what they could be doing within an hour, that gave him pause.

Where was this heading? Where did he want it to head? Such questions had never arisen with the other women he'd dated, but Darcie was…special. In addition to turning him on to an extent he'd never experienced, she also brought out his protective instincts. Add in her recently ended engagement and Nick didn't want to rush her. But he did want her. So, he needed to be sure they were both after the same thing: a mutually satisfying, albeit short-term, sexual relationship. Recriminations afterward wouldn't do.

Ultimately, he decided to tell her their destination and see if she would prefer to stay in Athens proper.

"I wouldn't mind seeing the seaside," she told him when they met in the hotel lobby.

Her assent did little to quell his nerves. But when they stepped outside, her laughter did.

"Nick Costas, man of many cars. I never know what you'll be driving next." Her lips curved.

Earlier, when he'd taken Darcie to the Parthenon, he'd been driving an Aston Martin coupe. He liked to get behind the wheel of the automobiles he would be auctioning, especially those he purchased himself and for whom he had no specific collector in mind, to get a feel for how they handled. In this case, however, the cherry-red Jaguar roadster would never see the auction block. It belonged to him and had for the past few years. He kept it at his house in Greece for personal use. In New York, his vehicle of choice was a 1966 Corvette Sting Ray.

"You will get a prize if you know the year this car was manufactured," he said.

"Hmm. Let's see. Streamlined body and covered headlights." She pursed her lips and glanced inside. "Sunken floor pans. Four-speed manual gearbox." Straightening, she said, "I'm going to say it was built in nineteen sixty…five."

"You are close. Sixty-six."

She wrinkled her nose. "What would my prize have been?"

She had to ask. His body tightened, but he managed a casual shrug. "I was going to let you drive it."

"Then it's just as well I got the answer wrong," she told him on a laugh. "The steering wheel is on the wrong side of the car."

"For the United States," he agreed.

"That increases the value, of course, a fact of which I am sure you are aware."

He nodded, pleased by her astuteness and an idea niggled. He pushed it to the back burner. "Fewer than a thousand of the right-hand drive models were produced in 1966."

The restaurant was busy when they arrived. They were shown to their table in a prime location at the window that offered an unparalleled view of the harbor. The day was winding down, the sun starting to set. Boats, both commercial and pleasure craft, were heading in for the night.

"I could sit here all day," she murmured. "What is it about water that is so…compelling?"

Nick lifted his shoulders. He couldn't put it into words, but he understood what she meant. The view drew him. It always had. It was one of the things he missed when he was in Manhattan, and one of the reasons he knew he would never sell his home here, even though he did not spend very much time in it.

A black-vested waiter came by and took their beverage order. Darcie opted for a glass of white wine. Nick ordered the same. A moment later, the man was back with their drinks and a complimentary platter of olives, cheese and dense bread.

"Khristos sends his regards," the waiter said.

"Khristos?" Darcie asked once they were alone.

"The owner. He and I are old friends."

She lifted her glass of wine. "To old friends then."

Nick raised his glass as well, but he had a different toast in mind. "And to new friendships."

She smiled in agreement and clinked her glass against his.

"You know, even though I have only known you a short time, I do consider you a friend, Nick."

In the time it took her to say so, the word lost all of its appeal. "Merely a friend?"

"A very handsome one." She arched her brows. "Better?"

"A little. My ego thanks you."

Darcie selected an olive from the platter and popped it into her mouth. His started to water, only to go dry when she turned the question back around on him.

"What do you consider me? If your answer is a nuisance, feel free to make up something else. My ego will be every bit as appreciative as yours was."

Nick chuckled. "I suppose I should confess that initially I considered you a delightful distraction."

"That was when you offered me a ride from the airport." She nodded, selected another olive. Before popping it into her mouth she added, "Then you saw me as your ticket out of a tight spot with your mother and grandmother."

"A lovely ticket."

She batted her eyelashes comically and murmured her thanks. "And now, after spending the better part of the day touring ancient ruins with me, are we pals?"

Another time, Nick would have laughed. But he weighed her words carefully and then weighed his own. "Not by my definition, but English is my second language. The fact is, Darcie, friendship seems a rather bland term for us. Do you not agree?"

"What other term do you have in mind?"

"That is my dilemma. I have no other term." He sipped his wine. "I was hoping you might."

"Well, if we're being honest, I don't think platonic applies to our situation."

He agreed, of course, but was curious to hear Darcie's reasons. "Go on."

A couple blotches of color worked their way up from her neck until they flamed on her cheeks. "Speaking only for myself, I like kissing you. I'm pretty sure people who are merely friends don't kiss—" she cleared her throat "—like that." She cleared her throat again. "Or enjoy it quite so much."

"We are attracted to one another," Nick agreed. "And I, too, like kissing you."

"My friend Becky would say that what you and I have going qualifies as a fling. Well, a baby fling, really, since we're not…"

Sleeping together went unspoken, but Darcie may as well have screamed it. Nick heard the words loud and clear and finished her thought with a silent *yet*.

He hid his grin behind the rim of his glass and sipped his wine. He liked Darcie's friend's assessment. After all, in addition to sex, *fling* implied impermanence. It bolstered his assumption that Darcie, who had so recently freed herself from her own betrothal, wasn't looking for true love and a lasting commitment any more than he was. She was after excitement, a little fun.

Still, he needed to be positive.

"And, if instead of this baby fling, we were to have a very adult one, what then?"

She moistened her lips. "I'm not sure I understand your question."

"What would you expect?"

The waiter picked that inopportune moment to return and take their dinner orders. Nick clenched his teeth and waited to hear Darcie's response.

"This is all very hypothetical," she began once they were alone again. "I'm not really the sort of woman who goes around having flings, especially of the adult variety."

"I never assumed otherwise," he hastened to assure her. "In fact, you might say that is the reason I am seeking clarity on the matter."

Her expression turned thoughtful. "First and foremost, I would expect the truth. I won't tolerate lies."

Her response surprised him a little. Even though it was none of his business, he asked, "Did your fiancé lie to you?"

"I'm sure he would say no." She pursed her lips, as if considering. "I think Tad lied to himself much more than he lied to me. He said I was the one he wanted to spend the rest of his life with, but, in the end, it wasn't going to be just the two of us."

Nick's brows shot up at that, but he kept his voice neutral when he asked, "What do you mean?"

"I wouldn't have been marrying just him. I would have been marrying his mother, too." The shiver that accompanied her words appeared involuntary rather than manufactured for effect.

"I gather that his mother did not like you."

"I wasn't good enough for her son. Tad's quite the catch. A *doctor*, you know." She emphasized the word in a way that Nick imagined other people had in speaking to Darcie. "But that doesn't change the fact that he's a world-class mama's boy."

"Obviously, I do not know Tad or his mother, but my guess is that no one would have been good enough for her son, even a woman as wonderful as you."

"Thanks." Darcie smiled. "And I know what you mean."

Did she? If so, Nick thought that might have been a recent development. Her uncertainty would explain why Darcie had been flustered by a simple compliment when he first met her.

She was saying, "Evelyn's fault-finding might not have been such a big issue if we hadn't spent so much time with her. Dinner practically every evening, church on Sundays. The last straw was when Tad started talking about adding another master suite on to her house instead of continuing to look for a house of our own after we got married."

"Pieter and Selene will live down the street from my parents, who, as you know, live next door to my grandmother."

"Next door and down the street are not the same as under

one roof with shared main living spaces. I always felt on guard around Evelyn. I couldn't slouch without hearing her comment on my poor posture."

"Tad allowed this?"

"He has a blind spot a mile wide where his mother is concerned."

"Then he got what he deserved," Nick said. "He lost you, but gets to keep his mother."

Her lips twitched. "And don't forget Rufus. He's keeping the cat, too."

"Good riddance, spawn of Satan."

Darcie laughed.

They were both quiet for a moment. Then Nick said, "I am sorry that things didn't work out."

Sympathy was expected, though Nick actually felt no such thing. If Darcie were now a married woman, they never would have met, and he still would be dodging his family's matchmaking attempts. His relief was selfish, his reasons rooted in his current situation, he assured himself. They had nothing to do with that tug of attraction and something less definable that he felt when he was with Darcie.

"Well, I'm not sorry. I mean, I'm sorry that I let things go on for so long and that Becky wound up shelling out good money for a tangerine gown that she isn't going to be able to wear anyplace except maybe a costume party." Darcie shook her head on a laugh. "God, I must sound so cold."

"Not at all. More like honest," Nick said.

He appreciated honesty. And he appreciated her situation. A woman who had recently ended her engagement would not be looking for another relationship so soon. But…

"Getting back to our possible fling, in addition to honesty, what else would you expect?"

"I don't know. This is an awkward conversation."

"It is all hypothetical, remember?"

"Hypothetical or not, it's still awkward. As worldly and sophisticated as I'd like you to think I am, I'm...just not." She shrugged.

When she said things like that, his protective instincts kicked into high gear. For all of her bravado and flippant comments, she was vulnerable and uncertain. She could be hurt. Hell, she already had been by a man who claimed to love her, but had allowed his own mother to belittle her.

Darcie shifted in her seat. "Maybe you should tell me what you would expect."

"Fair enough." He picked up his glass and took a drink, allowing the crisp white wine to bathe his tongue as he searched for the right words. "I would expect to have more dinners such as this one. I enjoy our conversations."

"And?"

"Well, like you, I would expect honesty."

"Of course." She nodded. "And?"

"Whatever were to happen naturally between us, it would be mutually agreed upon and enjoyed."

"A very diplomatic answer," she said.

"Something for both of us to think about."

Their entrées arrived then and the conversation turned to benign topics. Nick was eyeing the dessert menu, if only to prolong their evening, when Darcie said, "That was almost as good as the dinner your mom and grandmother made."

"I will be sure to pass along your compliment. You have room for dessert tonight, yes?"

She grinned. "I'm on vacation. I get to indulge." When he lifted a brow, she clarified, "In sweets."

They ordered coffee and two pieces of chocolate cake layered with a decadent mousse filling. The cake was delicious, but what made his mouth water was watching Darcie savor each bite.

He set his fork aside and, after taking a sip of coffee,

asked her, "Have you decided where I will be taking you tomorrow?"

"I was thinking the Temple of Zeus and Hadrian's Arch. That is if you have the time."

"I will *make* the time."

Darcie had blown her diet big-time with that delicious dessert, so it was a good thing the scrumptious man she'd spent the evening with came calorie-free. Still, if one of them had to go straight to her hips, she would rather it be Nick.

"You are smiling," the man in question noted as they returned to the hotel. "Care to share your thoughts?"

"No." She pressed her lips together tightly afterward to keep from smiling again.

"Ah." He nodded.

"*Ah* what?"

"There is no need for you to say anything now. I know." He glanced over, winked. The accompanying smile was smug.

"What is it that you think you know?"

"You want to invite me in for a drink."

"I want to—"

He cut her off with a *tsking* sound. "But I must refuse." The hotel was just ahead. Its sign lit up like a beacon.

"You're saying no?" Forget that Darcie hadn't asked or, for that matter, having a drink with him wasn't what had caused her to smile in the first place.

"I was, but all right. One drink. Since you insist."

Nick winked again and turned the car to the right. Just that quickly, he was pulling into the valet parking lane at the front entrance.

"You're something else," she murmured with a shake of her head.

"I will take that as a compliment."

Inside the hotel, he steered her to the lounge. At her questioning glance, he said, "I will not claim to be a saint. A drink in your room poses too much temptation. And we have not yet defined our expectations of our hypothetical fling. Let us move slowly."

"Take our time."

"Drive ourselves insane," it sounded like he said.

So they had a drink in the lounge. Afterward, Nick not only walked her to the elevator, but he also insisted on accompanying her all the way to her room.

"I am not coming in," he assured her when the doors of the elevator slid open on her floor.

"Testing your restraint?" she teased.

He snorted, and it was her restraint that was on the line when he told her, "I want to picture where you will be sleeping tonight."

She opened the door and switched on the light. The room was small with just enough space to accommodate a double bed, dresser, writing desk and television. Housekeeping had been by, so the duvet was turned down, the pillows freshly plumped. A foil-wrapped square of chocolate sat in the center of the one closest to the door.

It wasn't the treat that had her mouth watering.

Darcie's gaze cut to Nick. He was studying her as well, his expression seductive. She had to remind herself that it wouldn't be wise to hop into bed with a man she barely knew, even if what little she did know about him she found very appealing.

"I must go." His tone was brusque.

"Yes."

He gave her a quick kiss on the forehead, pushed her inside and shut the door himself.

"Engage the security chain," she heard him order from the hallway.

With their talk about flings and expectations swirling in her head, it was well after two before Darcie finally fell asleep.

The next day, as promised, she and Nick visited the Temple of Zeus and then Hadrian's Arch. It was a small consolation that he appeared as ill-rested as she was. She had her guidebook out and was reading about how the arch, which was built in 131 AD, had marked the boundary between ancient Athens and the new Roman city of Hadrian, when her cell phone rang.

Thinking it might be Tad, she considered ignoring it, but when she saw that it was Stavros, she flashed Nick an apologetic smile.

"I need to take this."

"I will be just there." He pointed to a nearby street vendor's cart and headed off. Darcie unabashedly enjoyed the view as he walked away. She was smiling when she answered. By the time the call ended five minutes later, however, she was fuming and feeling dejected. It didn't come as a surprise that Stavros would not refund her money. Still, she'd hoped.... She went to join Nick.

"I took a chance that you would like chocolate." He handed her an ice cream cone.

"Gee, big risk," she teased. "Where's yours?"

"Ice cream will melt quickly in this heat. I thought we could share." With that, he ran his tongue over the top scoop, all while keeping his gaze on her.

When Nick said things like that, when he looked at Darcie the way he was looking at her right now... She'd never felt like this. Ever. So wound up. So wanted. Wouldn't it just figure that she would be leaving soon?

"It is your turn now." Nick nodded to the ice cream.

Unfortunately, when she went to lick the ice cream, the

top scoop fell off the cone. It plopped on the pavement between their feet.

"The story of my life," she muttered, closing her eyes. She wanted to scream, cry. She settled for sighing.

"It is only ice cream. There is no need to be so upset."

She opened her eyes. "It's not just the ice cream."

His expression sobered. "The phone call, has something happened? Your family?"

"All fine as far as I know. That was Stavros. He finally got around to returning my call."

"And?"

"Well, he was very apologetic when I asked for a refund, but…" Her shoulders lifted. "He did offer to personally drive me to several of the locations on my itinerary, but I declined. He didn't exactly sound sober."

Nick threw the empty ice cream cone into a nearby waste container and plucked his cell phone from his back pocket. "I will call him. I will make him see reason."

"Thank you, but no." She placed a hand over his. "You've already left messages on my behalf. Besides, you said it yourself that first day. He doesn't have the money to refund."

"What will you do now?"

"I can't stay the full two weeks." Even if she wanted to—and oh, yeah, she really wanted to—she couldn't afford it. As it was, her three nights in Athens were going to set her back half a week's pay.

"How long?"

"Another couple of days." And even that was going to stretch her financial limit. It would be worth eating mac and cheese for a month, though, if it meant spending more time with Nick.

"But you cannot leave so soon. You have barely seen any of the sights. You have barely been outside of Athens."

"Believe me, I wish I could afford to continue my vacation, but I can't."

"If you had a place to stay, one that would cost you nothing, would you postpone your return to the States?" he asked slowly.

"What do you mean *if* I had a place to stay that would not cost me anything?"

"I know of such a place, a house that is not far from where we had dinner last night."

"A house?" He had to be joking. A house near the harbor that would not cost her a dime? Her tone light, she asked, "Does it boast the same spectacular view as the restaurant?"

"The view is even better."

"You're serious."

"I am. Do you want to see it?"

"I…"

He took her hand and started toward where he had parked the car. "I will take that as a yes."

Darcie expected the house to be nice. Nick didn't strike her as the sort of man who would recommend anything even remotely substandard. Nor had he exaggerated about the view. The house was farther up the hillside than the restaurant and its windows were placed to make the most of the stunning scenery.

The foyer opened into what she assumed was the main living space. It was spacious, well-appointed.

"Is this really a rental property?"

He didn't answer. Instead, he pointed toward an arched doorway across the room.

"The kitchen is through here," he said.

The home's kitchen was bigger than the one Darcie had glimpsed at Nick's grandmother's house. Even though it was equipped with state-of-the-art appliances, it appeared less used. The stainless steel pots and pans that dangled from the rack over the butcher-block island showed little sign of wear, and there was not so much as a grease splatter on the tiles on the wall behind the cook top. That seemed odd and she said as much to Nick.

He shrugged. "Some people prefer to eat out."

They returned to the living room. She glanced around again. The furnishings were modern and leaned toward masculine with their no-frill lines and muted colors. The massive plasma-screen television would appeal to a man, too. And all of the magazines spread out over the coffee table were geared toward sports and the automobile enthusiast.

"The bedrooms are upstairs," Nick said.

He was three treads up when Darcie's words stopped him. "That's all right. I think I've seen enough."

He turned on a frown. "It is not to your liking."

"Oh, I like it. How can I not? This home is gorgeous." She folded her arms. "It's also no rental. It's yours, Nick."

At least he didn't insult her intelligence by trying to deny it. "I am so rarely here that I could rent it out. In fact, my accountant has suggested I do just that."

Oh, she didn't doubt that. The location was prime, the view stunning, its amenities and furnishings were top-of-the-line. He could lease it by the week or even by the month. It would fetch an outrageous sum.

"You could, but you don't. You're making an exception for me. And my stay would be complimentary."

He dipped his chin. "Yes."

"But there's a price, right?"

She wanted to be irate, maybe even insulted. She was having a hard time getting past flattered and turned on. And that was before he smiled. Heat shimmied up her spine like a brush fire out of control.

"I assure you, it is not what you are thinking."

Arms still crossed, for self-preservation more so than out of pique, she asked, "And what is it that I'm thinking, Nick?"

"That I am trying to take advantage of both you and your current situation."

"Are you?"

"As tempting as I find that, I am a man with scruples, remember? You said so yourself."

"So, what you are saying then, is that if I agree to stay here you would be sleeping on the couch."

His laughter was sharp. "I have scruples, Darcie. But I will not claim to be a saint. If I were to spend the night under the same roof as you, sleeping on the couch would not be an option for either of us."

A disturbingly erotic image of the pair of them—sweaty, sated and tangled up in bedsheets—swirled through her mind. She swallowed hard and managed to say, "Then what do you have in mind?"

He took a step toward her, and even though he was still more than arm's length away, her body began to hum like the plucked strings of a harp.

"I will stay with my family. My mother will be glad for the intrusion. She complains that she does not see me enough when I am in Athens." He took another step forward. "You would have this entire place to yourself. How does that sound?"

Lonely. "Lovely."

"Is that yes, then?"

Darcie gave herself a mental shake. "Nick, your offer is very generous, a little too generous for me to accept."

"I am only repaying your kindness. You did me a favor," he persisted.

"Repayment wasn't necessary. I enjoyed dinner with your family. Besides, you have taken me sightseeing and out to dinner last night. You have more than repaid any debt you feel you owe me."

"Perhaps you will consider staying here in lieu of payment for a job?"

That caught her interest. "What sort of job?"

"You are a trained journalist, yes?"

"I'm a fact-checker."

"You *were* a fact-checker. Regardless, you are a journalist and, most importantly, you know an astonishing amount about vintage automobiles."

"I do," she agreed, still unable to figure out where this was heading.

"In exchange for writing background information for my auction catalog, a service for which I currently pay someone in New York, you can stay in my home for the remainder of your vacation and I will continue to act as your tour guide. We may not be able to hit all of the sites on your original itinerary, but we should be able to manage many of them."

Darcie ran her tongue around her teeth. What he was proposing sounded reasonable. It sounded fair. And, God knew, she didn't want to cut her trip short and fly home to the mess that awaited her. There was so much more she wanted to see and experience in Greece.

And then there was Nick…

"Um, the person who usually does this sort of thing for you, will they be out of work if I agree?"

Nick shook his head. "I have no one on my payroll, if that is what you mean. I contract with a couple of freelance writers in Manhattan whenever the need arises. In this case, I simply would be contracting with you instead."

"And my payment would be free lodgings here."

"And sightseeing. You will have a car at your disposal, should you need one. And I am happy to accompany you."

The smile that spread across his face caused heat to curl

in her belly. As much as she wanted to agree right then and there, Darcie hesitated. "That seems like such an imposition. I can't help but feel like I'm getting the better end of the deal."

"Hmm," Nick murmured thoughtfully as he closed the distance between them. His hands found Darcie's waist and he said, "Then perhaps I should apply conditions."

"Oh? What might those be?" she asked, and gave herself a mental high five for not hyperventilating on the spot. Indeed, for someone who had already confessed to being unsophisticated when it came to matters such as this, Darcie thought she sounded downright blasé.

"You will have to accompany me on my business trips. I have four lined up between now and the day you are to return home." He leaned in after saying so. She felt his lips brush the curve of her neck. "We can combine my business with your pleasure."

"I—I suppose I could fit those into my schedule." She tipped her head to the side, giving him greater access to her neck. While he took advantage of that, she closed her eyes and murmured, "Anything else?"

"You will help me research the vehicles in question. I usually do this on my own, but I would appreciate your insight." His breath tickled her ear.

"Mmm. 'Kay. I have no problem with that."

"No?" He kissed her cheek.

"None whatsoever."

"Good."

"It is good." Bordering on incredible, she decided, as his hands moved up her sides and his thumbs brushed the underside of her breasts.

"So, that is yes?" His voice was low, strained. "You will stay?"

Darcie wrapped her arms around his neck and kissed him. "I'll stay, Nick."

CHAPTER SEVEN

"WE HAD BETTER GO."

Nick made that pronouncement with no small amount of regret. But if he and Darcie stayed in his home much longer, the sparks he was experiencing were bound to ignite into an all-out blaze. And he had just convinced her that he was not, in fact, offering her a place to stay in exchange for a bed-mate. He still had no doubt that Darcie and he would move beyond the hypothetical when it came to having a fling, but he'd meant what he said last night—he wanted both of them going into it with open eyes and clear expectations.

That and he couldn't explain exactly why, but he didn't want the flash and burn of spontaneous sex. With Darcie, when it happened, he wanted to take his time. He wanted to make it last, make it count. Something told him she deserved that. So, he collected his keys from the kitchen counter and steered her out the door as quickly as possible. She didn't object.

On the drive back to her hotel, he said, "I will be by to-morrow morning at nine to collect you. We can move your belongings to the house and then spend the afternoon wandering near the seaside, if you would like."

"That sounds fine, but what about work? Do you have a car you need to go see or one that you want me to start researching online?"

Nick shook his head. "I think tomorrow will be a day off for both of us. Work can start the following day."

"Oh, my God! You're moving in with Nick!"

Becky didn't sound as scandalized as she did jealous. And no wonder. After Darcie had sent her friend a photograph she'd snapped of Nick at the Parthenon, Becky had emailed back that she would be on the next flight to Athens if Nick had a friend she could meet who was even half as good-looking.

No friend. Only a brother and he's getting married, Darcie had emailed back. She'd left out all of the nuances to that particular story, not sure what to make of them herself.

Now, she told Becky, "I'm not moving in with Nick. I'm moving into his house."

"You say potato…. Is there really a distinction?"

Darcie couldn't help but laugh. Nor could she help but be grateful that she'd called Becky before calling her family. She could only imagine what her parents were going to make of the latest twist in her trip itinerary. They hadn't exactly been thrilled about her going on her honeymoon solo. Even though she was a grown woman, she knew they worried. She'd promised to check in a few times during her trip. Her conversation with Becky qualified as a test run, so Darcie strove to clear up any misconceptions. She needed to have her story down pat before relaying it to her mom and dad.

"There's a big distinction. Nick will not be there. He is going to stay with his parents."

She went on to explain the rest of the arrangement to Becky—the work she would be doing for Nick in exchange for the free lodgings. By the time she finished, it sounded like a perfectly platonic business deal, especially since she didn't mention the skill with which Nick kissed or the way she responded to those kisses. No sense pouring kerosene on a fire that was already burning cheerfully all on its own.

"So, it's a business arrangement," Becky said slowly.

"Exactly. Who knows? Nick says he uses freelancers to put together his auction booklets. Maybe I'll be able to snag some of that work when I get home, too. It's not exactly full-length feature writing, but it's a start. I can get my feet wet, begin collecting clips."

"You want to write again?"

Darcie had never stopped *wanting* to write, but as a practical matter, while working full-time as a fact-checker, she hadn't had the wherewithal to seek out freelance opportunities. Besides, Tad had not been encouraging. A journalism career, especially one that eventually might take her to New York, wasn't in the cards for his future wife.

"My life is in chaos anyway. Why not try new things? You know, take some chances."

"Oh, you won't get any argument from me. I always felt you gave up on your dream job much too easily. That's another reason I never liked Tad. He wasn't supportive when it came to your goals. It was all about him. His happiness. His career. His mother," she added drolly. "I'm glad to see your backbone returning."

"Greece has been good for me," Darcie replied. "A new start."

"Yes, and a hot man who treats you like a goddess doesn't hurt, either."

They both laughed, but Darcie knew there was some truth to her friend's words. In the short time she'd known Nick, she had started to feel more confident, more desirable, more in control of her future. Maybe those changes would have occurred regardless once she'd called off her engagement. Still, she credited Nick for accelerating the process.

But did that mean she could handle a no-emotional-strings-attached fling with him? Darcie didn't know. Sure, she flirted a good game, but she'd also confessed her un-worldliness to Nick. She was pretty sure that was what had him holding back.

After Darcie hung up, she called her mom and dad.

Neither of her parents had a problem with her new living arrangements, especially since Darcie left off the part that Nick owned the house where she would be staying. In fact, she left out a lot of details where Nick was concerned, only mentioning that he'd offered her a freelance opportunity.

Like Becky, her father was thrilled that Darcie was re-turning to writing.

"That's the best news I've had in a long, long time," he told her. The pride she heard in his voice made her eyes sting. He'd never stopped believing in her.

"Thanks, Dad." Since her mother was on the extension, Darcie asked, "And you, Mom? What do you think?"

"I'm happy if you're happy." But her voice didn't hold pride as much as trepidation.

"But?"

"I don't know." Then, apropos of nothing, she said, "Tad stopped by today. He dropped off some wedding gifts from our side of the family that had been mailed to the condo."

Not sure what else to say, Darcie replied, "That was nice of him."

"He also brought a box of miscellaneous things you left behind when you moved out."

"Oh." Again, she was at a loss for words.

"I know you often felt second in line to his mother, but by calling off the wedding, well, I think you've made your point. I think things would be different now if you got back together. He…he really loves you."

Darcie swallowed, wishing it were as simple as that.

Wishing she could want the same suburban life her married sisters had so happily embraced.

"But I don't love him, Mom. Not the way I should if I am going to spend the rest of my life as his wife."

"He said he's been trying to reach you but that you haven't returned any of his calls."

Four on her cell. All of which Darcie had let go to voice mail. "I know. And I will."

"When?"

"When I get back."

"Honey—"

"Mom, please. It's over. You need to accept that and so does Tad. He and I, well, we want different things in life."

"What is it that you want, Darcie?" Her mother's tone had turned impatient. "What is it you *think* you're looking for?"

It was her father who answered. "Stop badgering the girl. She simply wants more than what Tad can offer."

Darcie closed her eyes. Bless her dad. He got it. He understood. Her mother, meanwhile, remained perplexed.

"Are you sure it's not just a case of cold feet?" she asked. "A lot of brides get them. It's natural."

"I'm positive, Mom."

And Darcie was, especially when she thought about Nick and all of the heat the man could generate inside of her with a single, simple smile.

The move to Nick's house the next morning was accomplished easily. Darcie had only the one, forlorn-looking bag after all. She'd still heard nothing from the airline about her missing piece of luggage. With her luck, it would show up in Greece about the time she was to return home. Whatever. She was making do and, now that she didn't have to worry about paying for lodgings, she'd decided she was entitled to make a few more wardrobe purchases. Already Nick had mentioned having dinner again. She couldn't very well keep wearing the same dress. And she was starting to feel a little too touristy outfitted in T-shirts, shorts and sneakers. She might as well hang a camera around her neck and strap on a fanny pack to complete the cliché.

Once they arrived at Nick's house, she stood in the driveway and breathed in the sea-scented air, looking forward to the stroll through town that he promised her. The day was warm, but the breeze kept the temperature from being unpleasant.

That was until they went inside and Nick offered a tempting smile and said, "We never got to the bedrooms yesterday."

They hadn't gotten to a lot of things while in his house the day before, Darcie thought, not sure whether it was relief she felt or something more damning.

Even so, she smiled in return and made a sweeping motion with one hand. "Lead the way."

Three bedrooms opened up off the hallway at the top of the stairs. Each had its own bath. Two of the rooms, including the master, faced the harbor and sported private balconies. The master was large enough to accommodate a small sitting area in addition to a king-sized bed. The chairs were upholstered in a luscious aquamarine, which, when combined with the deep blue duvet cover, mimicked the colors of the harbor. The art on the walls featured nautical themes, although the works themselves were more abstract in nature. Darcie was no connoisseur, but the pictures appeared to be signed originals or numbered prints, all of which were expertly matted and framed.

Nick came up behind her as she gazed out at the harbor. She swore she could feel the heat from his body warming her back even though he stood a respectable distance away.

"This is a very, um, restful view," she said.

"You would think so." Dry humor tinged his voice. "Right now, I am feeling very restless, especially when I think of you sleeping in my bed."

"About that." She cleared her throat and turned. "I think I will take one of your guestrooms."

"Are you sure? I spared no expense on that mattress. I think you would be more comfortable in here."

She didn't agree. Indeed, she had a feeling that she would toss and turn all night on the mattress in question, tortured by detailed fantasies and the lingering scent of his cologne. She wasn't quite ready to slip into Nick's bed—alone or otherwise.

Darcie chose the guestroom next door. It offered the same stunning view as the master and could hardly be considered small, even if it only had one chair rather than an actual sitting area. If she wanted to sit at all up here, she would do it on the balcony in one of the cushioned chaises.

It only took her a few minutes to unpack her clothes and toiletries, and then she met Nick downstairs, where he showed her around his home office. Like the rest of the house, the furnishings were modern with clean lines. The wooden desk was stained a deep brown. The bookshelves just behind it were glass and metal. Every electronic gadget one could wish for—tablet, laptop, digital printer and copier—would be at her disposal.

He showed her how to log on to the internet using his laptop, as well as how to access her own email account. With a few clicks of the mouse, he also brought up a raft of research sites that he used to locate collectible cars and determine their value. Given her current job, she was familiar with several of them. Then he opened a file on the laptop and pulled up a catalog from a previous auction at his warehouse just outside Manhattan. It had been created using software Darcie knew well. In addition to color photographs of the automobiles and the prices they were likely to bring at auction, the catalog included several paragraphs describing the vehicles.

Nick tapped his index finger against the screen. "This is the sort of thing I will need you to write for me. Facts tend to be bland. Bland does not generate interest, let alone bids. People need to be persuaded to part with their money, especially in such vast sums. The catalogs are sent out in advance and help generate not only interest, but excitement."

She grinned. She knew where he was heading. "Trust me. The facts won't be bland or boring when I get done with them. I'll make those cars sound so sexy and irresistible that even you will be tempted to bid on them when they come up for auction."

"That is exactly what I was hoping to hear."

Darcie's gaze fell on a framed picture of a younger Nick standing with another man in front of a race car. His uncle, she surmised, recalling their conversation from the day they met. This was the man who had kick-started Nick's passion for cars and, ultimately, set into motion his career.

"Does your uncle still race?"

"No. He is retired. But racing is in his blood. He sponsors other drivers now." Nick pointed to the photograph. "He still owns that car. He won a Grand Prix with it. He retired not long afterward and the car retired with him. He said he couldn't part with it."

"Is it difficult?" she asked.

"Is what difficult?"

"Parting with the cars that you like?" She sent him a grin. "It's obvious that you have a weakness for a finely engineered automobile."

"I do, but they are not my only weakness." His gaze was on her mouth.

"Nick," she said pointedly.

"What were we talking about again?" he asked.

"Cars. Selling them. Even the ones you would like to keep for yourself."

"Ah. Yes. I remember now." He shook his head and shrugged. "I enjoy the automobiles while they are in my possession. That is enough." His gaze was on her mouth again. "I do not need to own something to enjoy it. Not everything is meant to last."

His words, the intensity of his gaze, caused a shiver to run up her spine. A vacation fling was the perfect example. Meant to be enjoyed. Meant to end. Darcie found the thought unsettling, but she shouldn't have. If it was permanence she sought, she should have stayed with Tad. He was the man who'd offered for her hand. No, Darcie had other ambitions, newly revived ones that were just begging to be explored, exploited. Nick was giving her that chance. Anything else that transpired between them came without strings.

"Well, it had better be enough, because you'll never see them again once I give them a write-up."

He stroked the hair back from her face. Where a moment ago his expression had been intense, it was thoughtful now. "I heard it said once that writers are artists who paint pictures with words. So, you are an artist, Darcie Hayes."

How long had it been since she'd seen herself that way? Since she'd last dared to see herself that way? Confidence—new and heady—swelled inside her.

"Thank you."

"I do not want your gratitude."

"But you have it," she argued. He couldn't possibly know what he'd done by giving her this opportunity. To lighten the moment, however, she rubbed her hands together and said, "I can't wait to get started."

"So eager." He took her hands in his. "But tomorrow

will be soon enough. Today we will enjoy ourselves. Are you hungry?"

"Starving. I skipped breakfast," she admitted.

"That is no good. You should never deny yourself."

The man had a point, Darcie thought. She had denied herself a lot the past several years—not food, but other things that, in some ways, were every bit as vital to her well-being. He still had her hands in his. He turned one over, brought it to his mouth for a kiss. A moan escaped. Who knew the palm was an erogenous zone?

Nick leaned toward her, their mouths met. Not far away was a bedroom, one with a mattress for whose quality he had already vouched. She edged back on a sigh.

"Lunch?"

He rested his forehead against hers. "I thought we had just established that you should not deny yourself."

"You're tempting me."

"I should hope so." His laughter was gruff as he stepped back. "But you are not ready and I promised that whatever happened between us would occur naturally and be mutually agreeable. The timing is not right. You need more romance, I think."

She swallowed, liking the sound of that. "So, lunch?"

He swept a hand toward the door. "After you."

They ate near the harbor, in a small bistro that Nick frequented when he was in town. The owner was a big man with craggy features and a booming laugh. He knew Nick by sight if not by name, so he smiled in welcome when they entered.

Lunch was a busy time, but since it was later in the afternoon, the crowd already had thinned. They took a table near the back of the small restaurant.

"Do you know everyone in Greece?" Darcie asked once they were seated.

"No, but I make it a point to get to know the people I like." He reached for her hand. "Take you, for example. I find myself wanting to know everything there is to know."

He said it lightly, but he meant it. He hadn't felt this interested in anything besides automobiles in a very long time. But there was no denying he was curious about Darcie, not to mention intensely curious about the man to whom she so recently had been engaged.

"You want to hear the story of my life?" she asked on a laugh.

"Yes. I believe you promised to tell it to me that first day."

"You already know I'm a magnet for disaster and cursed with bad luck. The rest, I'm afraid, is rather boring."

"I will be the judge."

"All right. But you go first." When he blinked in surprise, she added, "It goes both ways, you know. I have a lot of questions I wouldn't mind having answered, too."

"So, we should satisfy each other's curiosity. Is that what you are saying?"

"It's only fair."

"Ask then."

Nick knew Darcie had chickened out when she inquired, "What's your favorite color?"

"Red. My turn." And he went for the jugular. "How long did you know your former fiancé?"

"Too long."

"That is not an answer," he chastised.

"Get comfortable then," she teased. "And, don't worry. I'll wake you up if you fall asleep."

The server came for their order. When they were alone again, Nick motioned with his hand. "Go on. I am wide-awake and promise to stay that way. For the record, I am always interested in what you have to say."

Darcie swallowed. While it was a bit disconcerting to have Nick's full attention focused on her, she liked that about him. He didn't just pretend to listen to her. He really did, making it impossible to hide behind her usual flippant replies and offhand remarks. Who knew, maybe telling him about Tad would be cathartic rather than merely embarrassing. Maybe it would make it clear not only to Nick, but also to herself that the past was behind her and it was time to grab the present by the horns.

"Well, I met Tad during my senior year of college. I had a really bad throat infection and went to the clinic on campus to get it checked out. He was a first-year intern and working that afternoon."

"He was your doctor? Kinky." Nick arched his eyebrows.

"No! Well, I guess technically he was for that one visit, but I kept my clothes on. Remember, tonsils." She pointed to her throat. "They're up here."

"I am well-versed in a woman's anatomy."

"I'm sure you are." She cleared her throat. "Anyway, the two of us got to chatting. My tonsils were enlarged, something that happened quite often. He thought they might need to come out."

"You talked about enlarged tonsils and somehow still wound up going on a date?"

Darcie pulled a face. "It must have seemed romantic at the time."

"If you say so. Go on."

"There's not much more to tell. Tad and I started dating and then, six years ago, he proposed."

Nick's eyes widened at that. "The two of you were engaged for six years? Did you live together the entire time?"

"No. I moved in once he agreed to a wedding date. That

was two years ago. Tad didn't want to get married until he was done with his residency and ready to start a practice of his own. Evelyn thought it would be too distracting."

"His mother."

Darcie frowned. "I tried to be understanding. She's a widow and Tad is her only child. He's all the family she has. But the closer our wedding came, the clingier and more demanding of Tad's time she became."

"What did your family think of him?"

"Ah-ah-ah. It's my turn to ask a question."

He bowed his head.

"Do you…like scary movies?"

Nick stashed his grin. She'd chickened out again. "No. What did your family think of Tad?"

She exhaled, clearly irritated. "My sisters liked him. I think they liked the idea of me being engaged and heading toward the altar even more than they liked Tad. My mom is still hoping this is just a case of cold feet. Tad was very sweet to her, always full of compliments."

"And your father?"

She rubbed her chin. "Dad never really said anything one way or another while Tad and I were engaged, but I get the feeling he isn't all that upset I called it off, even if he's on the hook for a lot of nonrefundable deposits now."

"Let me guess, you gave up pursuing your career around the time you and Tad got engaged? Your father did not like Tad because he wanted you to follow your dream, and he knew you would give up on it forever if you married someone like Tad. You had taken a job checking facts rather than writing pieces whose facts other people would check for you."

It made sense to him now how she wound up in a career for which she had no passion.

"That about sums it up," she said.

"And so you ended things."

"One week before 'I do.'" Both her tone and her expression were grim. "Not exactly my classiest moment."

"Better one week before than one week after."

"I guess that's one way to look at it." The server returned with their drinks. "My turn again."

"All right."

He figured she would wimp out again. So, he nearly spit out the mouthful of sparkling water when she said, "What are your feelings for Selene?"

"I have no feelings for her. She is marrying my brother. End of story."

"Okay." Darcie accepted the cryptic answer with a nod. Then she hit him with both barrels by asking, "What are your feelings for your brother?"

"I miss him," Nick replied honestly, surprising himself.

CHAPTER EIGHT

NICK WOKE IN his boyhood bedroom to the smell of fresh bread—the crusty variety that his mother and grandmother routinely made in an outdoor wood-burning oven that straddled the property line between their two houses. The scent wafted through the open window, drawing him upright.

He'd spent the past four nights under his parents' roof after spending his days with Darcie. As promised, they divided their time between sightseeing and work. He was enjoying both and he thought she was, too.

Already, she'd presented him with research on three vehicles, including estimated values for the vehicles based on what similar models had brought at recent auctions. She was thorough, conscientious and professional, and damn if he didn't find that all very sexy.

He wanted her. Had since that first glance in the airport. But he was treading carefully for reasons that he couldn't quite explain, since nothing about their relationship called for permanence. Darcie was newly single, finding her way, spreading her wings. He admired her for that. She wouldn't be looking to settle down so soon again. Especially with a man who lived so far away. Besides, Nick had no personal capital to invest in a relationship. He hadn't since Selene.

So why was he finding the idea of sleeping with Darcie and then saying goodbye less appealing by the day?

They were taking things slowly, more slowly than he'd ever moved with a woman. Nick supposed Darcie's candor where her ex-fiancé was concerned was among the reasons he was treading with care. She had been marginalized, made to feel unimportant by the man who was supposed to love her. Recalling the conversation at the restaurant, Nick could admit she had been painfully honest about her past relationship, whereas he had not divulged much at all when it came to Selene. The only secret he'd shared was that he missed his brother.

Admittedly, the revelation had come as a surprise to Nick. But it still didn't come close to all of the soul-baring Darcie had done, and he regretted that.

Meanwhile, he and Darcie continued to play it safe, flirting with abandon, even as they tiptoed around the land mines of their pasts. Safe. Sure. As long as he didn't recall how heated their flirtation turned at times.

On a groan, he got up and took a shower—the cold variety—before wandering to the kitchen. He came up short when he saw Pieter seated at the table. Nick had managed to avoid him since that evening at Yiayia's.

"What are you doing here?"

"Do I need a reason to visit our parents?" Pieter shot back. "Besides, the better question is what are you doing sleeping here when you have a bed elsewhere?"

"It's occupied at the moment."

Pieter smiled. "Precisely my point."

"Is there more coffee?"

Nick motioned to the *briki*. His mother had been brewing coffee in the traditional, long-handled pot for more than three decades. He had a *briki* at his house, too. The copper pot was as bright and shiny as the day it was made since it never saw any use. The same could be said for his electric coffeemaker—both the one here and the one back in New

York. What did it say about him, Nick wondered, that he owned a house and an apartment, but neither felt like home?

In answer to his question, Pieter got up and poured the last of the coffee into a demitasse cup and handed it to Nick.

"Thank you," he said stiffly. Although he was tempted to leave, he took the chair opposite his brother.

"It looks like you had a rough night." Pieter didn't bother to hide his grin.

Until just a few years ago, such good-natured teasing between the brothers had been common. Nick didn't want to miss it. He didn't want to miss Pieter. But, just as he'd admitted to Darcie, he did. He sipped the coffee. It was strong and very sweet. That was how their mother always made it, but it did little to improve his sour mood.

Head bent over his cup, he grumbled, "I don't remember that mattress being quite so lumpy."

The mattress wasn't why he'd slept so poorly, though, and they both knew it.

"I never realized how chivalrous you were. Yiayia even commented on it."

Nick grunted and took another sip of coffee.

"She is sure this is a sign."

"Yiayia and her signs," Nick mumbled. "Everything is a sign to her."

"But is she right in this case?" Pieter set his cup back on its saucer. He was no longer grinning when he asked, "Have you found someone…special?"

Nick stared into his coffee. "Darcie is special."

"Is it serious?"

"It is…complicated," Nick replied truthfully, uncomfortably.

The evasive answer had his brother nodding. "Love is always complicated."

"And you would know!" Nick challenged.

Pieter didn't take the bait. Instead, he replied, "I am happy for you. All of us are. Mama and Yiayia can talk of nothing else."

That should have pleased Nick. It was why he had introduced Darcie to them, after all. With his supposed girlfriend as the topic of their conversations until the wedding, he would no longer have to worry about them trying to set him up. But he felt uneasy.

"What are they saying about Darcie?" he asked.

"It's not so much what they are saying about her, although obviously they like her. It's more the effect Darcie has had on you. You seem like your old self again. Mama and Yiayia are happy you have found someone. As am I."

Emotions crowded in. Nick pushed away all but anger. Arching an eyebrow, he said sarcastically, "So we can be one big happy family again? Do you really think that possible, Pieter?"

His brother swallowed. "It is what I hope, what I want."

"And you get whatever you want. Or you take it, as the case may be."

Pieter looked gut-punched. "You are not being fair."

"Fairness, brother? Really?" His voice rose. Nick rose along with it. Palms planted on the tabletop, he demanded, "You want to talk about fairness?"

Pieter was on his feet as well. "You made your choices, Nick. You are the one who decided to leave Greece, to set up a business in New York, far away from family. Far away from Selene."

"And you were here to offer comfort and company," he added caustically.

But Pieter didn't back down. "You chased *your* dream without bothering to ask her what she wanted. You just expected that she would drop everything, leave everyone behind and follow you."

Nick's conscience stung. Was that what he'd done? Darcie came to mind. She'd sacrificed her dream of feature writing for her fiancé, settling for a fact-checking job at a small trade publication instead. Ultimately, what she'd given up had only fed her dissatisfaction and resentment. Had Nick done the same thing to Selene? If she had followed him to New York, would their relationship have survived?

Because he did not care for the face staring back at him from the mirror in his mind, his tone was harsh when he told his brother, "That is not what I expected, dammit!"

"Then what?" Pieter challenged. "What did you expect?"

Darcie, Selene—both women were forgotten now. Nick saw only Pieter, his brother and, at one time, his very best friend.

"I did not expect you to betray me!" He pounded his fist on the tabletop with enough force to rattle their coffee cups. There it was, the crux of the matter. The one big stumbling block Nick could not surmount, regardless of the number of times he'd tried. "While I was gone, I asked you to look after Selene for me. I knew she would be lonely. I did not think—"

Pieter's fists were clenched at his sides. "How many times must I tell you that is not how it happened? Selene and I did not betray you!"

The brothers glared at one another across the table.

"I do not care about Selene." And it was true, Nick realized. His feelings for his childhood sweetheart were over. "But you! My own brother. I *trusted* you."

"I did nothing to betray you or your trust. God knows! I fought the attraction I felt for her, and I felt it since we were all teenagers. Do you know what it was like to have her choose you?"

Nick blinked. He hadn't known. Had not even suspected. Would he have cared if he had? His anger now, however, was greater than any concern he felt for Pieter's feelings in the past. "So, you got even? Is that it?"

"No." The fight had gone out of his brother. Pieter slumped down in his seat. His voice was quiet, but his words were no less potent when he said, "I love her, I have always loved her, but I never imagined...I never dared to hope... You have to believe me that it was long after the two of you had parted ways that anything developed between us. Even so, we both tried to deny it." Pieter shoved a hand through his hair, his eyes bright with pain, frustration and resignation when he added, "Some things cannot be denied."

The door opened and their mother rushed into the kitchen from the yard. Her face was flushed, her expression one of worry.

"What on earth has happened? Your raised voices can be heard all the way to the coast!"

"Nothing happened," Nick told her, feeling more shaken than he wanted to admit. He crossed to the sink and tossed the remainder of his coffee down the drain.

As he stalked from the room, he heard Pieter say wearily, "He cannot forgive me."

Darcie was at the computer in Nick's home office working on some research when she heard a car pull up the driveway. Her mouth curved into a smile as she recognized the purr of the Jag's powerful motor. Then she glanced at the clock, puzzled. He was almost two hours early for their drive to Trikala. They had an afternoon meeting with a potential buyer for the Porsche he'd been driving the day they met.

Was that really only a week ago? It was hard to believe given all that had occurred since then. Indeed, over the past two weeks Darcie's entire life had been turned upside down. She'd gone from being an uncertain and disenchanted bride-to-be to a single woman who was determined to hammer out a new future for herself. And having a fine time doing it, thanks to Nick.

Her heart skipped a beat when she heard the door open. She turned, intending to tease him about being so eager, but her own smile died upon seeing his dire expression.

"Are you ready to leave?" he asked.

"I, um…" She glanced back at the computer, where she had several files open. "Can you give me another fifteen minutes? I just need to check a couple more things and print this out."

He nodded. "I will be on the terrace."

When she finished, she joined him there. He was so preoccupied that he didn't even hear her approach. When she laid a hand on his shoulder, he turned abruptly, almost as if he expected to find someone else standing there.

"Nick, is everything all right?"

"Yes. Of course." But his eyes remained dark and fathomless and at odds with the smile that turned up the corners of his mouth. "I am looking forward to our trip."

After Trikala, they were going to continue on to Meteora, where they would stay the night in a hotel. Even though Darcie had not asked him to, Nick had booked separate rooms for them, and of course he had insisted on paying for both. First thing in the morning, the plan was to tour a couple of Meteora's remaining six Greek Orthodox monasteries that were built atop rocky sandstone towers. Then the two of them would head back to Athens.

She had been looking forward to the trip as well. But now…?

"What's wrong?" She laid a hand on his arm. "And please don't tell me 'nothing.' I want to help."

"I thank you for your concern. But you cannot help me."

"Nick," she pleaded.

"I had an argument with my brother this morning." He

waved one hand in dismissal. Even so, Darcie's stomach took a tumble.

"Selene?" she suggested.

Nick's gaze returned to the sea. In profile, Darcie watched his jaw clench. "It is an old wound, but it has not healed properly." He sighed wearily then. "I do not know if it ever will."

"Sometimes talking to a neutral third party helps. I've been told I'm a good listener." When he turned, she offered an encouraging smile. Even so, it was a full minute before Nick said anything.

"I have been so angry. And I have felt entitled to that anger."

"But now?"

He swallowed and shoved a hand through his hair, leaving it as messy as his emotions. The expletive that followed—and she didn't doubt it was an expletive—was spoken in Greek.

"Why don't you tell me what happened between you and Selene?" Maybe by taking a step back in time, he would be able to move forward.

"Selene and I had been seeing one another for a couple of years when I went to New York for the first time. I had saved up some money, and my uncle had a contact in the United States. I planned to attend a few auctions, gain some understanding of the business and return to Athens to build my company here."

"But you stayed."

"Not at first, but eventually. The market for classic automobiles is so much larger in America. It made sense!" He was less emphatic when he added, "Selene did not see it that way."

"Were the two of you engaged at the time?"

He shook his head. "I never proposed, but I thought we had an understanding."

"And moving to another country, was that part of the understanding?"

He frowned. "She did not want to leave Athens."

"Of course not. Everything familiar to her is here," Darcie said. "It was a lot to ask."

"I know." He pinched his eyes closed. "We argued about it more than once, each trying to sway the other. I tried to find a solution. The best I could manage was a compromise. I came back to Greece as often as I could." He lifted his shoulders in a shrug.

"Did she ever come to New York?"

"Once. It was right after I took an apartment there. As much as I love Manhattan, that is how much she hated it. Still, I told myself that eventually…" His words trailed off and he shook his head.

"How long have Pieter and Selene been together?"

"Officially, they have been engaged for the past year. They dated for a year before that. Unofficially? I do not want to know, although they have both assured me repeatedly that I was long out of the picture when they started seeing one another."

"You don't believe them?"

"I am not sure what I believe." He sighed heavily.

Darcie glanced out at the harbor. The water was calm now, as was Nick, but when storms blew in, she imagined that the surface would turn choppy and become dotted with whitecaps that could wrest a small boat from its moorings and swamp it. That must have been how Nick had felt when he'd returned to Athens to find his brother courting Selene.

"You feel betrayed."

"Pieter and I are—were—more than brothers. There is barely a year between our births. We did everything together. We were always the best of friends. There was no one I trusted more."

"That must make this situation all the more difficult," she said softly and rested a hand on his arm. "You lost your best friend and...and the woman you loved."

"Did I?" Nick uttered the question softly. His dark eyes were full of pain when he added, "Did I truly love her? Did Tad love you? Is that how love works?"

Darcie frowned. "I'm afraid I don't understand what you mean."

"Real love would not take more than it gave. It would not be selfish," Nick said. Darcie thought of the Bible verse from First Corinthians that she'd asked one of her brothers-in-law to read at her wedding. *Love is patient. Love is kind... it is not self-seeking....* She always felt it underscored love's many good qualities.

"But Tad was selfish with you. From what you have told me, he put himself, his needs and his wants first. And I was that way with Selene. I knew from the beginning that she did not want to move to America. I knew that she wanted a life here, a life like the one she now will have with Pieter."

"Are you sorry?" Darcie swallowed.

"I hurt her. Yes, for that I am very sorry."

But that wasn't what Darcie meant, so she tried again. "Knowing everything that you know, do you...do you wish you had made a different set of choices?"

"I cannot rewrite history."

"Tad wants to." She hadn't meant to say that.

"What do you mean?"

"Nothing."

"Darcie," he pleaded.

"He's left several messages on my cell." She shrugged.

"And?"

"There is no *and*. I'm just saying that even if we cannot

rewrite history that doesn't mean we don't have regrets. So, do you?" She returned to her original question, afraid of what the answer might be.

"No."

But his expression remained so pained that she wondered. Could he still love Selene? The possibility left her uncomfortable, but why? She had no claim on Nick. No right to expect exclusivity when it came to his affection. They hadn't slept together, even if Darcie could admit that was the direction they were heading, albeit at a slow and measured pace. And when they did, she knew it would be casual. Mind-blowing, but casual. So why did it matter?

Because Darcie feared she was trading one emotionally unavailable man for another.

CHAPTER NINE

NICK SWAPPED HIS Jag for the 1963 Porsche 356 that was parked in the garage and they were on their way. If all went as planned in Trikala, his client would buy the Porsche and they would drive away in a 1956 Austin-Healey roadster that, depending on its condition, would knock off most of the Porsche's asking price. The Austin-Healey, meanwhile, would be featured in Nick's next auction.

It took them just over three hours to make the trip to Trikala. Nick remained preoccupied and introspective the entire way, even though Darcie tried to draw him out in conversation. It was a relief when they finally arrived at their destination, but they were more than two hours early for their meeting.

"We can take a walk through Trikala's scenic old town, if you would like?" Nick said.

Since it would kill some time and might just help shake him from his mood, she readily agreed.

Fifteen minutes into their stroll, she was fanning herself. The heat was stifling and the light breeze's effect on it negligible. They stopped at a café and he bought her *Kliafa*, a refreshing orange drink that was perfect given the day's heat.

After taking a sip, she gravitated to the window of a nearby shop. She couldn't help herself. Shoes were on display and all but calling her name.

"Would you like to go inside?" Nick asked. He was smiling, the first real smile she'd seen all day.

"You don't know what you're saying," she warned with mock sternness.

"Pardon?"

"No man in his right mind encourages a woman to shop."

He took her drink and sipped it straight from the straw. All the while his gaze was on her. "I have a condition."

The simple statement managed to raise gooseflesh on her skin despite the day's heat.

"And that is?"

"Everything that you try on you must model for me."

She glanced back at the shoes. "I'm game."

It was an easy enough deal to keep in a shoe store, but then Nick steered her into a shop two doors down.

"Remember our deal," he said, pointing to a display of lingerie.

"I am *not* trying that on," she said resolutely of the bustier. "But I will try on these." She selected a pair of stone-colored capri pants from one of the racks. "And this."

Nick fingered the soft fabric of the turquoise tunic-style blouse in her hands. "The color will complement your complexion and bring out your eyes."

Darcie tried not to glance at the price tag, which she knew would not complement her bank account. For kicks, she added to the growing selection a white halter dress that made her think of Marilyn Monroe.

"I would really like to see you in this."

Clipped to the hanger he held was a tiny bikini that would leave even more of Darcie exposed than the lingerie.

"Right." She snorted indelicately. "I haven't worn a two-piece swimsuit since I was six years old."

He thrust the hanger into her hands. "Then I would say you are overdue."

"Nick."

"Ah, ah, ah. We had a deal." He nudged her toward the changing room in the back of the store. "Keep in mind that on many European beaches it is perfectly acceptable to go topless."

Laughing, she ducked into the small room. She lined up the hangers, leaving the bikini for last and far from certain she would honor their bargain. The first thing she stepped out in was the white halter dress.

"Ta-da!" In her bare feet, she executed a twirl for him and then posed with one hand on her hip. With the other she primped her hair. "I'm channeling Marilyn Monroe."

"Very sexy. Perhaps the store has an air-conditioning duct you can stand over top of. I would not mind seeing a little more of your legs."

Darcie hiked up the hem of the dress's skirt by a couple of inches to accommodate his wish, but he wasn't satisfied.

"Make no mistake, you have very nice knees. However, I was thinking about your thighs." His smile held a dare.

She glanced around. The shop was busy, but the dressing rooms were at the back. A couple of sale racks helped to shield her from view.

She inched up the dress more slowly this time.

"I will tell you when to stop," Nick said quietly.

"I bet."

The hem was not quite to the middle of her thigh when Nick uttered a gruff, "Enough!"

"You don't want to see any more?"

"Not out in public."

Darcie didn't smile, but she wanted to. The same went for pumping her fists in the air. Eat your heart out, Marilyn, she thought, feeling every bit as desired as the famous sex symbol.

Nick stood. "I'm going to buy another *Kliafa*."

"Right now? I was going to model the bikini next," she teased ruthlessly.

After muttering something she couldn't quite catch, he said, "I will wait for you outside."

So it was that Nick never got the chance to see Darcie wearing a clingy wine-colored dress that an ambitious saleswoman slipped into the changing room along with some sexy satin undergarments that the young woman claimed were essential to ensuring the dress's proper fit.

Darcie had to admit, they definitely smoothed out certain areas while lifting others, which was why she purchased them. As for the bikini, she wasn't sure why she bought it. She didn't need it. Wasn't sure she had the guts to wear it out in public. But she looked good in it. Damned good. A little voice that sounded suspiciously like her friend Becky told her she should buy it.

At the cash register, she wound up charging enough to her credit card to leave her feeling guilty and a little giddy.

"You are flushed," Nick noted as they made their way to the restaurant.

"Yes, well, spending more than I earn in a week has been known to have that effect on me." She chuckled weakly.

Despite their shopping trip, the man they were to meet had not yet arrived when they reached the restaurant. Nick requested a table in a shady part of the patio that offered a lovely view of the Litheos River.

"While we're waiting, why don't you tell me a little about Ari Galanos," Darcie said.

"Ah, Ari." Nick chuckled fondly. "I should warn you, he will flirt shamelessly with you. The man goes through cars almost as quickly as he goes through wives."

"Thanks for the warning." The waiter came by for their beverage order.

"A glass of wine?" Nick asked.

"Why not? I'm not driving."

"You could, you know. If you wished."

"No, no." She shook her head. "With or without a glass of wine, that wouldn't be a good idea."

"The roads can be a little treacherous if one is not familiar with them," he agreed.

"Yes, not to mention the fact that it's been a decade since I last drove a manual transmission." She tilted her head to one side and asked, "Are you familiar with the expression, 'If you can't find 'em, grind 'em'?"

"I am not."

"Well, suffice it to say, that was my motto whenever I was trying to shift from one gear to the next."

"Ah." He grimaced as understanding dawned. And they both wound up chuckling.

"This is nice," Darcie said on a sigh a few minutes later, as she sipped her wine and gazed at the river. "I feel very relaxed."

"That is the point of a vacation, yes? To relax, rejuvenate one's spirit."

She nodded. But they both knew this wasn't a normal vacation for Darcie. The trip had been booked as her honeymoon. After calling off her wedding, she had intended to use it as a getaway, a timeout from her post-breakup reality. Now, it was turning into a job opportunity and so much more.

"Thank you."

"For what?" he asked, surprised.

"For helping me get my life back in order."

"Your gratitude is not necessary. You have done that all on your own."

But she persisted. "No, you had a hand in it, Nick. If not for you, I would be on a plane headed home right now, and going back to a job that I'd talked myself into believing was good enough since it pays the bills."

He reached across the table for her hand, giving it a squeeze. "You sell yourself short, Darcie. You would have reached for your dream again, with or without my help. I gave you a gentle push in the right direction. That is all."

Her smile told Nick she didn't quite believe him. Her gratitude made him uncomfortable. Another man might have used it, exploited it even, to maneuver her into his bed. Nick was too scrupulous for that. He wanted Darcie there, and the waiting was taking its toll, but he did not want her to say yes because she felt she owed him something. He meant it when he told her she would have sought out her dream again on her own, even without his prodding. If her passion for writing was anything like his passion for cars, it wouldn't be denied.

Ari arrived as they were finishing their wine. He ordered a second round of drinks, although this time Nick switched to sparkling water. Not only would he be driving later, but he also preferred to keep a clear head in business. Ari was shrewd and he was used to getting his way.

As predicted, the older man's eyes lit with appreciation when Nick introduced him to Darcie.

Still holding her hand, he said in Greek, "Nick did not mention hiring an assistant. Or is your relationship more personal in nature?"

Smiling, Darcie glanced helplessly at Nick.

"Darcie does not speak Greek," he said. "She is an American."

"I apologize," Ari replied in heavily accented English. "I was asking about your relationship with Nick."

"My re—"

"Darcie is a writer," Nick explained. "I have hired her to prepare feature articles on some of the automobiles that will appear in my next auction brochure. Already she has done some research on your Austin-Healey."

Ari didn't appear convinced. His tone was just shy of condescending when he asked, "What have you managed to learn about my automobile, my dear?"

"Let's see, I know the 1956 model is worth more than other 100M Roadsters." She ran a fingertip around the top of her wineglass as she spoke. "That was the only year they manufactured the performance-enhanced model, which tops out at a speed of one hundred and fifteen miles per hour. The car was marketed to customers who wanted to compete or who just plain liked to go fast, which is why it has a tighter front suspension, added louvers to keep the hood in place at high speeds and a fold-down windshield."

Ari's bushy brows shot up. "Beautiful *and* smart. I apologize."

"Darcie is not to be underestimated," Nick agreed with no small amount of pride. And he knew a moment of panic as he wondered if he had underestimated the impact she was having on his life.

Earlier, she had thanked him for helping her to get her life back in order. For helping her find passion again where it long had been missing. It dawned on Nick that she had returned the favor. He always had enjoyed business. It was his personal life that had been lacking. Oh, he'd dated plenty of women, one or two of them for several months before breaking off the relationship and moving on.

None of those women had affected him the way Darcie was. None had made him envision a future with a family that he'd taken for granted when he was a young man.

The drive from Trikala to their hotel in Meteora would have taken less than half an hour, but Nick wanted to put his newly acquired Austin-Healey through its paces.

"Satisfied with the car?" Darcie asked when traffic finally forced him to slow down.

"I am, yes. Ari has taken good care of her. She runs like a dream." He rubbed the leather seat. "And other than this one small tear in the upholstery, her body is in mint condition, as well."

"Why do men refer to cars with female pronouns? I've never understood that."

"It seems more natural to be riding in a female than a male." Nick grinned. "Maybe it is simply the way we are wired."

"So, you're saying it's in your genes?" Darcie rolled her eyes. "Please."

His grin turned wicked. "A different kind of jeans then."

Darcie crossed her arms over her chest and rolled her eyes a second time, but she looked more amused than exasperated. He wasn't sure how she'd managed it, but over the course of the day, she'd drawn him out of his foul mood. Indeed, Nick was actually enjoying himself, whereas he often found buying trips tedious.

He reached for her hand, forcing her to unfold her arms, and then gave her fingers an affectionate squeeze. He was still holding her hand when they reached their destination.

The hotel where Nick had booked their rooms was nicer than anything Darcie would have chosen had she been picking up the tab herself. It went without saying that it was nicer than anything Stavros would have provided as part of the all-inclusive tour.

Their rooms were on the third floor, which like all of the floors, was open to the atrium on the main level. They made plans to meet for a late dinner, which would give them both a chance to unpack and unwind.

"Wear the white dress to dinner," he suggested as he handed her a key card.

"I didn't buy the white dress."

"What is in there then?" He pointed to two bags she carried that were printed with the shop's logo.

She smiled benignly. "I guess you'll just have to wait and see."

When Darcie said it, she was referring to the sexy wine-colored dress. But that changed when she slipped into her room and realized that it joined with Nick's via an interior door. Because she could quite vividly picture him on the other side of it, undressing, she decided to go for a swim. The hotel had a nice pool in a courtyard outdoors. A quick dip and a little lounging on one of the chaises might be the perfect distraction.

She eyed the tank-style one-piece in a bland shade of blue that she'd brought with her from Athens before deciding to slip into the red bikini. She wouldn't wear it downstairs. Probably. But…

She had just finished tying the top's knot behind her neck when a tapping sounded on the interior door. She grabbed her robe, hastily pulled it on before going to answer it. Her mouth went dry at the sight that greeted her. Nick's shirt was open, the buckle of his belt hung to one side of his unbuttoned trousers. The man was built like a god, with ripped abs and the kind of chest that it seemed a sin to cover with a shirt. This was why she'd decided to go for a swim. This was exactly how she'd pictured him looking.

"I interrupted you," she said.

"I believe I am the one who knocked." He sounded amused, but his expression was intense, aroused.

"R-right. I knew that."

"Is this what you plan to wear to dinner?"

She shook her head and managed to drag some air into

her lungs. She had one hand on the doorjamb and plunked the other one on her hip. "Terry cloth is a little too casual, I think."

"You will not hear me complain."

She laughed softly.

"But I am disappointed."

"Oh?"

"I see red." He reached out and plucked at the bow that peeked from the collar of the robe. "You promised to model *everything* for me."

"I offered. You left."

"Because we were in public," he reminded her. "Will you keep your promise now?"

She swallowed. Nodded. And nearly forgot how to breathe when he loosened the robe's belt.

"Do you like it?" she found the courage to ask.

"Take off the robe."

She did as instructed. The robe slipped from her shoulders and pooled at her feet.

"Well?" She tilted her head to one side and managed a smile.

Nick, however, did not smile. Nor did he say anything. He acted, swiftly and decisively. One minute Darcie was on her side of the door, posing provocatively in the itty-bitty red two-piece. The next she was in his room, pinned between his hard body and the wall while his mouth devoured hers.

"I'm taking this to mean you like what you see," she told him on a breathy laugh when the kiss finally ended.

"I do indeed."

"I was thinking about going swimming. You know, in the hotel pool. Um, that's why I'm wearing my bathing suit."

"Is that why?" he asked. He had maneuvered her away from the wall and was now slowly walking her backward toward the bed.

"Why else?" she asked innocently, even as the edge of the mattress pressed into the back of her thighs.

"I think you put on your bikini to torture me." He stepped back far enough so that he could do a slow inspection of her body. A groan of approval vibrated from his throat.

"I didn't know you were going to knock on my door," she pointed out. "So, that's merely a bonus."

Darcie was amazed at her boldness. Not only did she feel comfortable standing nearly naked before him, but she also felt sexy and confident. She planted her hands on her hips and turned slowly side to side before presenting him with her back and glancing flirtatiously over one shoulder.

"So, you like my suit, hmm?"

His gaze skimmed down a second time and he let out a low whistle. "The suit, what little of it there is, is nice. I like the way you look in it, Darcie. You are beautiful."

Better yet, she felt that way. Smiling in earnest, she asked, "So, are we going?"

"Wh-where?" he stammered.

In addition to looking turned on, Nick looked off balance. Darcie's confidence shot up another notch.

"Swimming." She grinned. "You remembered to pack a pair of trunks, right?"

"I did."

"Good. Put them on."

She slipped around him and started for the door, but only managed two steps before his hands clamped on her waist and she was hauled back against his rock-hard chest, abs and…

In the mirror that hung on the opposite wall, their gazes met. Neither one of them was smiling now. The time for humor and teasing had passed. Nick brushed her hair aside and nuzzled her neck a moment, then his hand came up, his fingers fiddled at the nape of her neck. The knot in the bikini's halter went slack.

"It appears that your top has come loose," he murmured huskily.

He gathered both sides in his hands, holding them at her collarbone. If he were to let go...

"So I see, although I believe it had a little help."

"I can retie it," he offered.

She met his gaze without blinking. She thought she might have stopped breathing, too. "Have you got any other suggestions?"

His hands moved lower, slowly exposing more of her skin inch by inch. They both watched his progress in the mirror.

"I can stop. I *should* stop." His eyes pinched closed a moment and he uttered an oath before pulling the straps taut and retying them. At her questioning gaze in the mirror, he said, "My grandmother thinks I am chivalrous. This is a moment that calls for such old-fashioned thinking."

"It is?"

He turned her to face him, framed her face with his hands. "I want you, Darcie. But I...we..." He pulled his hands away and started stalking around the room. The rest of his explanation was in Greek. Oddly enough, she thought she understood what he meant.

"I only have another week left in Greece."

"Yes. But it is more than that."

A lump formed in her throat. It was?

"Remember when we spoke of your life being at a crossroads?" he asked.

"I said it was more like a busy intersection without a working traffic light."

"In other words, dangerous. Which is why we are going slowly."

There was slow and there was snail-like. "I thought you

saw me as adventurous for wanting to rush across and hope for the best."

"I have changed my mind."

"Worried I could get hurt?" she asked with a tilt of her head.

He didn't answer her question, at least not directly. Instead he said, "The stakes have gotten higher. For both of us. Do you understand?"

Her heart gave an unsteady thump. She knew she had been developing strong feelings for Nick. Real feelings. Feelings that could make walking away from a casual fling in a week very difficult. But until now she hadn't thought Nick might feel the same way. Or that having those feelings might be a problem for him. She knew Nick didn't do more than casual, not since Selene. Darcie sighed. "I think so. Now what?"

He expelled a gusty breath and asked, "Do you still want to go for a swim?"

"Sure. You?"

"Yes." He kissed her cheek before adding, "If I am lucky, the pool will be very, very cold."

Nick got his wish. The water was chilly, especially compared to the hot afternoon air. He and Darcie had the pool to themselves and they stayed in it for nearly an hour. Even so, it wasn't long enough to counteract the effect simply being near her was having on him.

It wasn't only lust he felt when it came to Darcie, which was why he begrudgingly had retied her bikini top and hustled her out of his hotel room. Other emotions were involved that made the prospect of a mere holiday fling less and less appealing.

He liked her. He respected her intelligence, her drive, her resilience. The last thing he wanted was to be responsible for her returning home filled with regrets. That was where chivalry had come in. But self-preservation, he could admit, played a role, too.

So much had happened between the pair of them in such a short time. The feelings Darcie inspired were not unwelcome, but they were unexpected. He'd meant it when he said the stakes had gotten higher for both of them.

Now what?

The question Darcie had asked earlier haunted him. He had no clear answer.

CHAPTER TEN

DARCIE YAWNED AND stretched as she lay on the bed in Nick's guestroom. The sun had crested the horizon a few minutes earlier, but she had been awake for more than an hour listening to the distant sound of fishing boats heading out of the harbor.

Since her and Nick's return from Meteora, time had passed much too quickly for her liking. She blamed it on their busy schedule, which was a combination of business and pleasure. Lots and lots of pleasure, even if it stopped just short of actual sex. In addition to doing research on the internet and writing articles for the auction brochure, she and Nick had met with a deep-pocketed repeat client who was eager to add a 1950s-era, American-made muscle car to his already expansive collection of automobiles, and a new client looking to score his first vintage Porsche.

They also had managed a couple more sightseeing day trips on Greece's mainland, and they'd spent one glorious afternoon lazing on a beach on the island of Andros. She'd worn the bikini again. And she'd known from Nick's expression that he loved seeing her in it, whatever the cost to him personally.

Darcie was having the time of her life. It didn't matter what she and Nick did. She enjoyed being with him and talking to him, whether about the automobiles she was researching or movies they'd seen or current happenings in the world. It amazed her, really, how much they had in common for two people who had grown up in different cultures on different sides of the world.

As for their relationship, she wasn't quite sure how to categorize it. *Fling* didn't fit since the word implied sex. She and Nick hadn't had sex, although she swore that every moment she spent in his company qualified as foreplay. She enjoyed kissing him, the exquisite torture of feeling his mouth and hands on her skin. But she wanted more.

On a frustrated sigh, she rolled to her side and hugged a pillow to her chest. She'd never met another man who made her feel more desirable or quite so aware of her femininity. Yet since Meteora and their brush with physical intimacy in his hotel room, Nick had shown the kind of restraint possessed by the monks who lived in the terra-cotta-tile-roofed monasteries they'd toured the following day. No matter how far things progressed between them physically, he always stopped just short of taking her to bed. Now their time together in Greece was almost over.

Part of Darcie acknowledged that maybe it was just as well they hadn't had sex. Physical intimacy would complicate things, at least on her end. As she'd told Nick, she wasn't the sort of woman to fall in bed with a man simply to scratch an itch.

But another part of her ached to be with him in every sense of the word, no matter how short their time together.

She wasn't on the rebound, as her family might assume. Nor was she confused or vulnerable over her breakup with Tad. Indeed, Darcie had never felt clearer on her reasons for ending her engagement, despite her ex's continuing messages, the most recent of which had been surprisingly conciliatory in tone. Tad wanted her back. He wanted to work things out. But Darcie knew no matter how much he was willing to change, she already had changed more.

There was no going back, even if in a matter of days, she would be flying home to Buffalo. She wouldn't be returning to her old life. The old Darcie was gone. The new Darcie wasn't going to settle and make do. That almost made up for the fact that her idyllic vacation with Nick was coming to an end.

Would they see each other again? That was the million-dollar question, and it weighed heavily on her mind.

Not long after she returned to the United States, he would as well. From what she knew of his schedule, he would leave Greece the day after Pieter's wedding. But even without an ocean to separate them, she and Nick would hardly be neighbors. Besides, he had made no mention of getting together once they were both back in America.

Sure, at one point early in their acquaintance he had offered to show Darcie the sights should she ever find herself in the Big Apple again, but the offer had been more polite than anything else, and he hadn't made a similar one since then, much less issued a formal invitation.

In fact, the more involved they had become the less was said about what the future held for the two of them. Personally, at least. Nick made it plain how pleased he was with the features she'd written for his upcoming auction brochure.

"Use my name as a reference if you think it will help," he'd told her.

He'd also given her the contact information for the editor of an online car collectors' blog that sometimes used freelance writers. Why not? she thought. Clips were clips and the more experience under her belt the better.

Overall, Darcie was pretty satisfied with the work she'd done while in Greece. It wasn't going to win her any Pulitzers, but it was a start, a first step in a new and exciting journey.

She had one last feature to write for Nick for an upcoming auction brochure. The car was a 1914 Packard 4-48. The owner lived in New Jersey and was selling it to finance his daughter's college tuition. Nick had inspected the Packard prior to his trip to Greece and estimated it could bring in up to half a million dollars. He agreed with Darcie that, with the right buyer, the sixty-horsepower touring phaeton might bring in even more since many of its parts were original. That was what made her articles every bit as important as the photographs included in the brochures that would be sent out in advance of the auction.

Darcie tossed the pillow aside and rose. She might as well start to work on it. She was nearly finished with the article and was making a second pot of coffee when the doorbell rang. Nick's appearance was unexpected, even though they had plans for later in the day.

When she opened the door, his gaze swept down to her toes before returning to her face.

"You are dressed."

"And you were hoping otherwise."

He didn't bother to hide his smile. "I was. It's why I didn't call first."

"Sorry to disappoint you then."

"Did I say I was disappointed?" He yanked her into his arms for a hard, fast kiss. While she was still recovering from it, he said, "I have a favor to ask."

"After kissing me like that you can ask me anything."

He made a humming sound and she swore his pupils dilated. "Anything?"

Darcie was playing with fire, but she no longer cared. She wanted to feel not just the heat, but the burn. "Anything."

The devil was in his eyes when he asked, "My grandmother has invited us for coffee. Do you want to go?"

The mention of his *yiayia* threatened to put a damper on seduction. She thumped his chest with the back of her hand. "*That's* the question you come up with? Seriously?"

His lips quirked. "Not the only one, but I would like to know your answer." Darcie was wearing the turquoise tunic she'd purchased in Trikala. It had a peasant-style neckline that closed with a ribbon tie. Nick fiddled with the ends of the ribbon as he added, "First."

Her brows shot up. First sounded promising.

Still, she asked, "Will the rest of your family be there? I want to know exactly how large of an audience to expect for this command performance."

He shook his head. "My mother is with Selene and her mother—some last-minute wedding preparations. My father and Pieter are working today. It will just be Yiayia."

"All right," she said slowly.

"We will not stay long," he promised. "Afterward, I thought we could ride the cable car to the top of Lycabettus. The view from the hilltop is even better than that from the Acropolis."

It would be the last touristy thing Darcie did in Greece, but that wasn't why she frowned. "Nick, about spending more time with your grandmother, I really like her, which makes me feel—"

He stopped her with another kiss. This one was slower, deeper, sweeter. By the time he finished, they were fully inside his house with the door closed behind him and the foyer wall against Darcie's back.

"If it helps, I am as uncomfortable as you are with the charade, but it is not all an act now." He tipped her chin up. "Is it?"

"It was never *all* an act."

"Exactly. We might not have met when and where we said we did, but I have not lied to them about my feelings. I have always been attracted to you physically, but it is more than that now. Yes?"

"For both of us," she agreed.

"Which brings me to my other question," he said softly.

Darcie could barely breathe, but she managed to say, "And that is?"

Nick tugged on the tunic's ribbon until it gave way. The neckline gaped open, offering a tantalizing glimpse of cleavage.

"May I please make love to you?"

A chorus of *Hallelujah!* rang in her head, but she couldn't keep from asking, "Right now?"

He flicked open the button on her capris. "Right now. I can wait no longer."

They arrived at his grandmother's house two hours later. Darcie was still tingling all over from the best orgasm she'd ever experienced. At one point she hadn't known whether to laugh out loud or start to cry. She'd done neither, thank goodness. Nor had she burst into song, though the lyrics to U2's "Beautiful Day" had been on the tip of her tongue.

As Nick shifted the car into Park, she checked her reflection in her compact mirror for the third time.

"You look the same as you did five minutes ago. In other words, perfect," he assured her, leaning over to give her a kiss.

"I feel…conspicuous," Darcie replied. "Like your grandmother is going to take one look at me and *know* what we were doing less than an hour ago."

"There is no need to worry. She might suspect, but she will not *know*." Nick winked.

"Gee, thanks. That puts my mind at ease."

* * *

"Something about you is different," Yiayia said to Darcie the moment she and Nick walked through the door.

Darcie felt her face flame scarlet and she shot Nick a panicked look.

He put his arm around her shoulders and said mildly, "Greece agrees with her."

Yiayia's expression was shrewd. "Something agrees with her." Then she motioned with her hand. "Come. We will eat outside. The day is too nice to sit in the kitchen."

They followed her through the house and out to the veranda. Darcie took a seat in the shade of the pergola. The midday air was heavy with the scent of roses.

"I made *koulourakia portokaliou* just this morning. I have the recipe for you." She sent Darcie a wink.

"Thank you," Darcie said.

"Are you excited for the wedding?" Yiayia asked as she poured the tea. "Selene and Pieter's wedding, that is."

The older woman's smile turned wily.

"Weddings are exciting," Darcie evaded. She nibbled a cookie.

"What color is the dress you will wear?"

"My dress. Oh, um…" She glanced at Nick for help.

"Darcie wants it to be a surprise."

Yiayia frowned at that, but couldn't resist offering a little unsolicited advice.

"You should wear a bright color. Do not be afraid to stand out. When I was a young woman, I favored red. I was wearing red the night Nicolas's grandfather saw me at a dance. He said the color caught his attention even before I did. For every anniversary my Alexandros gave me red roses." She sighed.

"How long were you married?" Darcie asked.

"Thirty-seven years. It has been twenty-three years since

I lost him. But it feels like yesterday that I was a young woman planning my own wedding." She patted Darcie's hand. "Time passes too quickly. Now my grandchildren are falling in love and getting married."

Falling in love…was that what was happening to Darcie? The assessment felt alarmingly right. Her gaze connected with Nick's. His expression was one she could not read.

"What about you, Yiayia?" he asked then. "What color will you wear to the wedding?"

Now a smile lurked around the corners of his mouth. Darcie knew it was because his grandmother always wore black.

Yiayia pointed a finger at him and smiled. "It is to be a surprise."

They all laughed.

Then Yiayia asked, "Have you ever been to a Greek wedding?"

Finally, a question Darcie could answer with complete honesty. "No. Never."

"Ah, then you are in for a treat. It is too bad you will not see Selene ride the donkey to church, but there will be video to watch later."

"A donkey?" Darcie tried to picture the lovely young woman she'd met perched atop an animal in her wedding day finery. The image simply wouldn't come.

"It is a tradition that represents the bride leaving home," Nick explained. "Her family and friends will walk with her."

"It sounds like fun."

"You wait until you have your turn on the donkey. You will not think so," Yiayia warned. "The donkey I rode, he wanted to run. My father had to hold the rein tight to make him go slow. My mother said it was because the animal knew how eager I was to get to the church."

Once again, they all laughed. The good humor didn't last

long. It vanished as soon as the older woman asked Darcie, "Has Nikolos told you about the *koumbaro*?"

"Yiayia." His voice was uncharacteristically sharp.

But his grandmother was undeterred. She briefly explained it to Darcie, including the custom with the switching of the crowns.

"It sounds lovely," Darcie replied, unsure what else to say. Meanwhile, Nick's expression had grown pinched. If Sophia noticed, she chose to ignore it.

"It also is a special honor that Pieter has asked of Nikolos, but he refuses."

"Yiayia," he said again. This time, his tone was not sharp, but sad, pained.

"After we met you, Darcie, and we saw with our own eyes how you and Nikolos are together, we all hoped…" Yiayia's shoulders rose in a shrug as her voice trailed off.

"I will not do it. I cannot," Nick said. "I would feel… foolish. I feel foolish as it is given all of the talk surrounding Pieter, Selene and me."

"Pride, Nikolos? That is what keeps you from saying yes? Even now that you have found love again yourself, you will not relent? You choose to keep your pride and begrudge Pieter and Selene their happiness?"

"Yiayia—"

But she wasn't through. "Have you no forgiveness in your heart for your only brother?"

"I…" He frowned, unable to finish.

The tension that followed was so thick a machete would have had a hard time hacking through it. It was just as well that Darcie and Nick left soon afterward. The tea and cookies had begun to churn in her stomach.

She said nothing on the drive to where they would catch the cable car to Lycabettus, and during their tour of St. George's Chapel she kept the conversation focused on archi-

tecture and history. At that point, it was really more mono-
logue than conversation. Nick contributed very little. Even
when they stopped at a tavern for a cold drink before heading back down the hillside, he remained unnaturally quiet
and circumspect. It was like the drive to Trikala, only worse.

Obviously, he was troubled by what his grandmother
had said. Was it merely Nick's pride that was injured? Did
he still feel so betrayed by his brother that he was unwill-
ing to act as his *koumbaro*? Or did Nick continue to harbor
tender feelings for Selene?

They were in the cable car, descending from the hilltop,
when he surprised her by bringing her hand to his mouth
and planting a kiss on the back of it.

"What was that for?"

"An apology. I have not been very good company today."

"You have a lot on your mind."

"Yes." He nodded, then added, "Thank you, Darcie."

She blinked at that. "For what?"

"For not pushing me on this matter the way my family is."

She managed a smile. Those questions she had would go
unasked and unanswered.

For the second morning in a row, a knock sounded at the
door as Darcie was making a pot of coffee. Nick. Her heart
picked up speed and her body temperature shot up by several degrees as she recalled the tenderness with which he'd
made love to her the night before. Where that first coupling
during the day had been frenzied and rushed, Nick had been
exquisitely slow and thorough the second time.

As for those questions that had troubled Darcie earlier
in the day, they were forgotten. Surely, the man who made
such sweet love to her could not still love someone else.

She was smiling as she opened the door, a comment

about being insatiable ready on her lips. But it wasn't Nick who stood on the stoop. It was Selene.

"Forgive me for being so rude and not calling first," the other woman said in halting English. She smiled nervously as she clutched her handbag to her chest. "I hope I did not catch you at a bad time."

"No. Not at all," Darcie replied, trying not to feel self-conscious in a pair of jersey cotton shorts and a tank top that doubled as her sleepwear.

Thank goodness she had at least dragged a brush through her hair and rubbed the sleep from her eyes. Meanwhile, Selene looked picture-perfect in a cotton skirt and sleeveless blouse. Even in a pair of high heels, she barely came to Darcie's shoulder. The old Darcie would have slouched. This Darcie squared her shoulders and settled her hands on her "good birthing hips."

"May I come in?" Selene asked.

"Of course." Darcie stepped aside. It seemed odd to be welcoming Nick's former girlfriend and soon-to-be sister-in-law into his house, but neither woman commented on it. "I just poured myself coffee. Would you like some?"

"Please."

They made their way to the kitchen, where Darcie got a cup down from one of the cupboards.

"I don't know how to use a *briki*. I hope this is okay," she said, pouring from the carafe of the automatic coffeemaker.

"This is fine. Thank you." After stirring in an obscene amount of sugar, Selene took a delicate sip. To her credit, her grimace was barely detectable.

Darcie sipped her own coffee. Silence ensued as the women eyed one another.

"So…" Darcie expelled a breath.

"This is very…"

"Awkward."

"Yes. You must be wondering why I am here."

"Um, a little," Darcie admitted. She didn't ask if Selene had ever been in Nick's home before. Quite honestly, she didn't want to know.

"As you must be aware, there is a...strain between Pieter and Nick. It goes back years to when...when Pieter and I began to date."

"Because you used to date Nick," Darcie added, figuring it best not to tiptoe around the big white elephant sitting in the center of the room.

Selene closed her eyes briefly, nodded. She looked miserable. Ridiculously put-together and gorgeous, but miserable all the same.

"Pieter is...I do not know the English word to describe it." Selene set her coffee down on the counter and paced to the window. "He loves his brother very much."

"I'm not trying to be rude, but *you* loved Nick at one time, too."

"I did or at least I thought so. Nick and I, we were so young when we began seeing each other. I was a teenager, barely one year out of school. I thought I knew my heart, but my feelings for him changed as time passed."

Darcie was in no position to cast stones. After all, she'd thought she'd loved Tad. She'd accepted his proposal of marriage and then had spent six years making wedding plans, a couple of those years living under the same roof. She'd been a lot older than Selene at the time, too.

"You didn't want to relocate to another country."

Selene shook her head. "I love it here. Greece is...home."

"It must have been difficult when you realized how you felt about Pieter."

Selene nibbled her lower lip. "It happened...slowly. At least for me. Pieter and I have known each other for so long. We started as friends. After Nick moved to New York and we broke up, Pieter would call. Checking up on me, he said." Her expression turned soft and her smile was nostalgic. "We started meeting at a café in town after work for coffee. Then it became drinks at a tavern in the evening. At first, we talked about Nick. How much we both missed him. Then we just talked. About everything."

"And you realized how much you had in common," Darcie said, her thoughts turning to Nick.

"Yes. We liked the same things. We *wanted* the same things in life."

"You were falling in love." Darcie wanted to ignore the voice whispering that she was in the same predicament. Could this really be the Big L?

"The first time Pieter kissed me, I had never felt that way before. Then he told me he loved me and confessed that he had been in love with me for a very long time. We both cried, because by now I was in love, too. But…" Selene pinched her eyes shut. When she opened them, they were bright with unshed tears. "I never meant to come between brothers."

Darcie didn't doubt the other woman's sincerity. Selene's pain was nearly palpable. Still, she felt the need to point out, "All the same, Nick felt betrayed. He trusted Pieter."

"Pieter never betrayed Nick's trust. Nick and I were no longer a couple. Even though we had done nothing wrong, we both felt guilty at first. We even stopped seeing each other for several weeks, but…" She lifted her shoulders. "Eventually, we could not deny what was in our hearts."

"I'm happy for you." How could Darcie be otherwise? "But I'm not sure I understand what this has to do with me."

"Pieter's mother and grandmother have tried to bridge the gap between the brothers."

"By trying to set Nick up on dates," Darcie mused. "He told me."

"They did not know about you at the time," Selene hastened to add.

"I know." How could they?

"They want him to be happy. That is what we all have wanted for him. And now he is. He has found love again."

Selene smiled. Darcie nearly choked. She rested a hand on her chest. Her heart beat unsteadily beneath it.

"About that, I don't know that I can claim the credit." Could she?

"I do not understand what you mean."

"Nick and I haven't been seeing each other for very long." As in less than two weeks. And even though they'd made love, neither of them had attached a label to their feelings.

"The length of time does not matter. He *is* happy. Anyone who knows him can see that."

Okay, Darcie would give her that. And she had to admit, she was pretty darned happy, herself. But… "It's not like you and Pieter."

And it wasn't. Not by a long shot since they would be saying goodbye soon, and their future, assuming they even had one, was far from determined.

Selene was nodding. "I understand. Pieter and I denied we were in love at first, too."

"Oh, hey. Look, I'm not denying anything. It's just that… and Nick and I aren't…he hasn't said…" She swallowed.

Selene's smile was serene. "He loves you, even if he has not said so. Yiayia is right about the two of you."

Darcie squinted at Selene through one eye. She was going to regret it, but she had to know. "What is Yiayia saying?"

"She has seen the way Nick looks at you. The way you look at each other. She says it is a good sign."

Even as Darcie's heart kicked out a few extra beats, she was protesting, "But I'm not Greek!"

"And *still* Yiayia likes you!" Selene chuckled softly before sobering. "Our wedding is in just two days. The only gift Pieter and I want, the only one that truly matters, is Nick's blessing."

Uh-oh. "I don't know what you expect me to do, Selene."

The young woman reached across the table and took Darcie's hand in both of hers. "If you could just talk to him. Please."

"It's not my place." And hadn't Nick already thanked her for staying out of it and not pushing? But Selene looked so heartbroken, Darcie found herself softening. "What would I say to him? What could I possibly say that Pieter and the rest of the family haven't already?"

"I do not know," Selene admitted on a ragged sigh. She let go of Darcie's hand and rose. "I am sorry to have bothered you."

"It was no bother. Really."

They were at the door when Selene said, "At least Nick will be at the wedding. For a while that seemed doubtful. Even with you at his side, I know this will not be pleasant for him."

Darcie swallowed. She wouldn't be there. He would be on his own.

Selene was saying, "Perhaps I am being selfish in wanting more for Pieter's sake."

Her words struck a chord in Darcie. *For Pieter's sake.* Not her own.

"Love isn't selfish," Darcie murmured when the door had closed.

Nick had told her that very thing after his argument with Pieter. At the time, he'd seemed to be examining his old reasons behind the brothers' feud. She had an idea.

Darcie hadn't pushed, but she cared about Nick too much not to offer a little nudge.

CHAPTER ELEVEN

Something was on Darcie's mind, but Nick couldn't figure out what. Women were rarely a mystery to him. But then, Darcie had been from the very beginning. Not mysterious in the way some of the women he'd dated back in New York tried to be. Darcie wasn't one to play games. For her, seduction wasn't an art that she practiced. She came by it naturally.

Nick would be lying if he said he hadn't enjoyed the little pieces of herself she'd revealed in their short time together. Or if he said he wasn't looking forward to seeing, learning more. All of which made her looming departure from Greece more disconcerting. Their time together had been amazing and sweet, and was proving all too brief. Already he was trying to think of ways to prolong it. But to what end? The answer he kept coming up with left him staggered.

Was he falling in love?

For her last night in Athens, Nick had made reservations for dinner at one his favorite restaurants, determined to show her a wonderful time and, as a side bonus, to keep his own mind off the fact that his brother's rehearsal dinner was that same evening. Nick had no official role in the wedding, but he'd still been invited. Both he and Darcie had.

"That sounds nice," Darcie said when he had called to confirm their plans. Then she'd thrown him completely when she added, "But you need to cancel the reservation. I've decided I'm going to make dinner for you here."

"You are? And what will be for dessert?" he'd asked.

"I think you know."

She'd sounded a little breathless. And Nick had been torturing himself ever since with fantasies of her prancing about his kitchen, wearing a little white apron and nothing else.

When he arrived at the house just after five o'clock, however, the kitchen was missing both a cook and a meal. Darcie was on the terrace, reclining on one of the chaise lounges with a glass of chilled wine in her hand. Her eyes were closed, her face tilted toward the sun. She was wearing a tank top and shorts that ended high on her thighs and her tanned legs looked ridiculously long. Her feet were bare. Her toenails painted a festive shade of tangerine.

"I thought you were making dinner?"

"That was just part of my ploy to lure you here."

He leaned over and captured her smiling lips for a long, thorough kiss. "Should I be worried for my safety?" he asked as he straightened.

In answer, she set aside her wine, grabbed his tie and tugged him back for a second kiss.

His breathing ragged, he said, "Perhaps we should take this inside and skip ahead to that dessert you promised."

"Sorry." She sounded seriously contrite. "I'm afraid there's no time. You'll be late."

"For?"

"Dinner."

He couldn't think straight with his hormones staging a riot. A common occurrence around Darcie. "I canceled our reservations, remember?"

She inhaled deeply before letting out her breath. "I'm not

talking about the restaurant. I'm talking about Pieter and Selene's rehearsal dinner."

He snagged the wine she'd set down and took a sip, stalking to the terrace's rail. "I am not going."

Darcie stood and joined him at the railing. "I want you to reconsider. In fact, I am asking you to."

"Why?"

"Because if you don't go, Nick, you're going to regret it. Just as you will regret not playing a meaningful role in their wedding."

"It is not as simple as that!" he shouted.

But Darcie was undeterred. "I'm not saying everything will magically be all better. But it's a start. This rift between you and your brother, it will never truly begin to mend otherwise."

"And to think I thanked you for not interfering," he said dryly as his temper began to simmer. He shoved a hand through his hair. "I know you mean well, but this is not your business, Darcie. You are a tourist here on holiday. This is my life!"

She didn't back down, even if just for a moment she looked as if she'd been slapped. "I may only be a tourist, Nick, but your family thinks otherwise, which is why Selene came to see me."

Nick didn't bother to mask his surprise. "Selene was here? What did she want from you?"

"From me? Nothing." Darcie waited a beat. "What she wants is something only you can give. She wants you and Pieter to be brothers again. In short, what she wants, Nick, is your blessing on their marriage. Not for her sake, mind you. For Pieter's. Love isn't selfish, remember?"

Nick swallowed. He recognized the lump lodged in his throat as guilt, and that was before Darcie said, "Selene asked if I would talk to you. She thought you might listen to me since we're supposedly a couple. You know what?" Darcie poked a finger in his chest. "I got the feeling that she would have gotten down on her knees and begged if she felt it necessary. It is that important to her. To both of them."

Nick closed his eyes as emotions tumbled fast and furiously inside him. His anger of a moment ago had drained away. As for the betrayal he'd felt for so long, that was gone, too. It had been ebbing for a while now, he knew, the last remnants disappearing as he'd gotten to know Darcie. The emotion that remained was undiluted shame. He hung his head as it crashed over him like a rogue wave.

"I'm sorry." Darcie's hand was on his back, her touch tentative. Where a moment ago her tone had been confrontational, it was apologetic now as she said, "I don't mean to cause you more pain, and I know I have no business whatsoever interfering in your personal life, but I said what I said because I care about you. Deeply. I want you to be happy. And, frankly, Nick, in addition to having regrets, you'll never truly move on with your own life until you let go of the past." Her voice hitched when she added, "And you haven't done that."

He turned. "You think I still love Selene?"

"No. Well, maybe I've sort of wondered," she admitted softly. She made her tone light when she added, "I know you're insanely attracted to me and all, but—"

Was that all it was? He didn't think so, but what he really needed Darcie to know right now was the absolute truth. "I do not love Selene."

"Oh. Good. That's *really* good." A smile fluttered briefly on her lips before she added, "But you've held so tightly to the past, Nick, that you're robbing yourself of a future with your brother and the family you clearly adore."

She understood him so well, better than any woman ever had. His conscience flared as he thought of how only a moment earlier he'd called her a tourist just passing through. He owed her an apology, but he didn't trust his voice enough to speak. Darcie apparently took his silence to mean something else and continued.

"You've helped me start over these past couple of weeks. I only wanted to return the favor. For what it's worth, I believe Selene when she says that she and Pieter did everything they could to deny their feelings for one another."

"I know."

"Did you also know that when they realized they were in love they even stopped seeing each other for a while?"

"No." The news didn't sit well with Nick's conscience now that he no longer saw himself in the role of the injured party. He said softly, "I think I always knew Pieter had not set out to betray me."

Just as he knew he had been selfish in his expectations of Selene. Nick had disregarded her feelings to follow his dream. Then, even after they had parted ways, he'd somehow still expected her to change her mind, to—what? Pine for him? Because it would have soothed his pride. He didn't care for what that said about his character.

He turned, caught Darcie's hand in his. His smile reflected the remorse he was feeling.

"My grandmother was right. I have let my pride get in the way of what truly matters. And you are right as well, Darcie. I already have regrets where my brother is concerned. I do not want to have more."

She squinted at him. "So, you're not angry with me for butting in?"

"No. I am angry with myself for many things, including what I said to you just now. A tourist just passing through." He winced as he repeated it. "It was insulting to you and an outright lie. You are so much more than that to me, Darcie. Can you forgive me?"

She kissed him in answer. Afterward, she asked, "Does this mean you are going to the rehearsal dinner?"

"No. It means *we* are going." When she opened her mouth to protest, he said, "Do not even think about backing out. I want you with me. I…*need* you there."

She smiled. "I'm so happy you will give them your blessing. It is the only gift she said they want."

Nick had already swallowed his pride, now he searched his heart and reached a decision.

"I will give them my blessing, but I can think of an even more meaningful gift to offer."

The rehearsal dinner wasn't at a restaurant. Rather, it was at the Costas home. More specifically, in his parents' yard, which had been decorated with white streamers and flowers to fit the occasion.

Even though the actual wedding party was quite small, Nick's mother and grandmother had been cooking for the past two days in preparation of the feast. In addition to his parents and grandmother, the bride-and-groom-to-be, and Selene's parents, of course, only a few friends and close relatives would be in attendance. The size of the audience would make it easier to humble himself, Nick decided.

The house smelled of lamb and simmering vegetables when he and Darcie arrived. She'd been quiet on the drive over, but she'd rested her hand over his on the gearshift and had never let go. Nick appreciated her support. He appreciated *her*. If not for her interference… No, it went further than that. If not for her appearance in his life, what he was about to do would not be occurring. Nick would have jetted back to New York and remained locked in his bitter disillusionment, isolated from his family, angry with the brother who had always been his best friend.

Love is not selfish.

Now, as they walked through the door that opened into the yard, he held her hand tightly, not only because he needed her support, but because he also didn't want to let her go. Ever.

God help him. Nick fully understood his brother's predicament now. Love happened. Even when one didn't go looking for it. Even when the timing was all wrong. It was terrifying and wonderful all at the same time. And denying it served no purpose.

His mother and grandmother were in the kitchen, arguing over the doneness of the roast.

"Nick!" Thea cried out when he and Darcie entered the room.

"Mama." He kissed her cheek, wiped the tears that had started to leak from the corners of her eyes.

"Please tell me you and Darcie will be staying," she whispered hoarsely, hopefully.

"If it is not too much trouble."

She huffed out a breath that served as her answer. "I will set the extra plates on the table."

While Thea bustled to the cupboard and got to work, Yiayia stood rooted in place, her hands clasped in front of her as if praying. She nodded, opened her mouth but said nothing. It was the first time Nick could recall his grandmother being speechless. He kissed her cheek as well.

"I know," he said softly. "I know."

"Do you want me to send Pieter inside so you can speak to him in private?" his mother asked.

It was tempting, but too easy. "No. I will go to him." Taking a deep breath, he extended a hand to Darcie. "Will you come with me?"

"You don't need to ask."

Conversations dried up midsentence when he and Darcie stepped out into the yard. Selene's parents, who he had not seen in years, looked horrified at first, as if they feared Nick was there to make a scene.

"Nick!" Selene called. Then her hand shot to her mouth, as if she wasn't sure she should draw attention to his arrival.

Nick's gaze cut to his brother, who was standing beside her. Pieter's eyes grew wide in surprise. Afterward, he neither smiled nor frowned. His expression remained wary, although Nick told himself he saw hope flicker in his brother's eyes as he closed the distance that separated them.

"Hello, Pieter. I hope I am not too late."

"Dinner has not yet started."

"That is not what I mean," Nick said quietly. "I hope I am not too late to repair the damage my stubbornness has done."

The stiffness left Pieter's shoulders. His mouth curved in a smile. "You know better than to ask."

In an instant, he had made his way around the table and was embracing Nick.

"Thank you," Pieter whispered.

"One more thing," Nick said afterward. "If you still want me to act as your *koumbaro*, I would be honored."

"There is only one thing to say to that," Pieter replied before shouting, *"Opa!"*

"I am sorry, Pieter." Nick transferred his gaze to Selene then. Long ago, he'd thought he would spend the rest of his life with her. Even after their breakup, after he'd understood how ill-suited they were, he'd refused to accept how perfectly suited she was to Pieter. When he started to apologize, however, she stopped him with a shake of her head.

"The past is the past, Nick."

For once, they were all in agreement.

"Pieter and Selene are so happy," Darcie commented as Nick drove her back to his house later that evening.

She got misty-eyed just thinking about how the brothers had embraced and the joy on Thea and George's faces after Nick agreed to act as Pieter's *koumbaro* at the service. She wished she would be there to see it.

As if he could read her mind, Nick said, "I know you are scheduled to fly back to the States, but I would like for you to attend the wedding with me."

It's what his family was expecting. What they had been expecting since the first time they met Darcie. Only she and Nick had known that her flight was scheduled to depart before the nuptials ever occurred and that he had intended to attend on his own.

"My family will be disappointed if you are not there to share in the celebration. They credit you for making me come to my senses, you know." He cast a smile in her direction, and then sobered. "I do, as well."

Something about his expression was different. Darcie couldn't quite put a finger on it. "I think you would have eventually."

"Perhaps. But not in time for their wedding. Not in time to ease their hearts with my blessing or to act as my brother's best man. So, will you come with me, Darcie?"

"I want to, Nick," she said slowly.

He studied her a moment. "Saying that you want to is not the same as saying you will. Please say yes."

Darcie took a deep breath and gave herself over to fate. "Yes."

"You're staying in Greece?"

"Sheesh, Becks, you make it sound like I'm moving here for good," Darcie replied on a laugh. "It's only for an extra couple of days. You and I will still meet for coffee and gossip when I get back. It will just have to wait until Tuesday now."

Darcie had already called her father with similar news since he had volunteered to pick her up at the airport. He'd taken the change to her itinerary in stride, probably because Darcie had left him with the impression it was the result of the airline overbooking her return flight. She felt a little guilty about that, but figured the white lie was better than having him worry.

Becky, however, wasn't buying it.

"What's really going on? And, no, I will not wait until Tuesday for an explanation. I want to know right now."

"Okay." Darcie sighed. "You know how I mentioned before that Nick and his brother were estranged, and the rift between them was a source of friction for the entire family?"

"Uh-huh. You said that was why his mother and grandmother kept trying to set him up on dates," Becky said.

"Right. So, he was pretending to be dating me so they would cease and desist."

"Uh-huh. His family wanted Nick to find happiness himself so he would— Oh, my God!"

An ocean away, Darcie could see her friend jumping to conclusions. "Becky, no. It's not—"

But her friend was shouting excitedly, "He's in love with you! That gorgeous Greek man is in love with you!"

"No." Despite the denial, Darcie's heart took off at a gallop. She swallowed and forced it to slow down. "He hasn't said anything about love. He's patched things up with his brother, and now he's asked me to stay and attend the wedding. It's his way of saying thanks, I think. Because…I don't know…I helped him put aside his lingering feelings of betrayal and move on."

"And how do you suppose you managed to do that?" Becky asked, her voice laced with triumph. "The man has moved on…to you! Are you in love with him?"

"I just broke off my engagement." Darcie's protest sounded weak even to her own ears.

"The timing sucks, I'll give you that. But your breakup with Tad was a long time coming, and we both know it."

"Nick and I hardly know one another," Darcie said, well aware that the explanation carried little weight. True in terms of time, they had only just met. In other ways...it was as if she had known him forever. He understood her so well.

"My mom and dad met on a blind date, eloped a month later and have been going strong for thirty-five years."

"Becks—"

"You knew Tad for years, Darcie. *Years!* And you still weren't sure in the end. Doesn't that tell you something? When it's right, it's right. And you just know it. The amount of time doesn't matter."

"I've got to go."

"Darcie—"

"See you Tuesday," she said and quickly disconnected.

She didn't want to talk about it. She didn't want to *think* about it. What Becky suggested was preposterous, outrageous and very, very probable, at least on Darcie's end. As for Nick...well that was a whole other matter.

Rain was forecast for Pieter and Selene's big day. The sky was thick with fat dark clouds when Darcie and Nick entered the church, but nothing could dampen the excitement of the guests assembled in the church's pews. When the bride started up the aisle, all eyes were on her, and even the insistent tapping of rain against the stained-glass windows was ignored. Selene made a gorgeous bride. And she was so obviously in love.

Darcie had never attended a Greek wedding, but in many ways it was not so different from the American ones she had attended, even if she didn't understand much of what was being said. Love and commitment, such things were universal. At Nick's family's insistence, she was seated in the front row, wedged between his mother and grandmother. Even before the ceremony started, Sophia had stuffed a lace-edged hankie into her hand.

"You will need this," the older woman predicted.

Thea had nodded, dabbing her eyes.

Nick, of course, was on the altar with the bride and groom during the exchange of vows. He looked as handsome as ever in formal attire, his dark hair tamed for the event. As the *koumbaro*, he placed the crowns on their heads at the appointed time, and then switched them back and forth three times to symbolize their union.

Darcie might not have understood the words being spoken but the emotions translated perfectly. She found herself sniffling and dabbing at her eyes right along with Thea and Sophia, grateful for the hankie.

"Thank you," Nick's mother whispered to Darcie as the bride and groom shared their first kiss as husband and wife. "You have given me back my sons."

"I...oh. Actually, Nick—"

"Nick is so happy." Thea smiled. "Maybe soon Pieter will be switching the crowns on your heads."

Darcie's eyes filled and the tears spilled over. As Thea squeezed her hand, Yiayia wiped them away with a knowing smile.

By the end of the ceremony, the storm had passed. As they left the church for the reception hall, patches of blue were visible in the sky. It was fitting given all that had happened.

Darcie had never enjoyed herself at a wedding reception more, especially when the dancing began. Nick and his family showed her some of the basic steps to traditional Greek dances.

"I'm afraid I have two left feet," she told him after one dance, during which she had stepped on his toes at least half a dozen times.

Now they were seated at a table, enjoying a glass of wine. Darcie had sworn off the ouzo after the first toast. The inside of her throat still felt as if it were on fire from the strong spirit.

"You were doing well for just learning. It takes time."

Time that she didn't have. "I can't believe I'll be going home soon."

"Let's not speak of that now." The band began to play a new song. The melody was familiar, if old. Darcie placed it by the time Nat King Cole started to sing "Unforgettable." Nick stood, held out his hand. "I requested this one especially for you."

"Am I unforgettable?" Darcie found the courage to ask.

"What do you think?"

Gazing into his dark eyes, she chickened out. "I think I have had the best vacation ever, and I'm going to be really sorry to see it end."

On the dance floor, Nick gathered her closer and rested his cheek against hers. It was just as well that he could no longer see her face, because despite Darcie's best efforts, her eyes began to tear.

CHAPTER TWELVE

"Is THIS GOODBYE or is it 'see you later'?" Darcie asked Nick as they sipped coffee in a crowded Newark airport café.

The question had been weighing heavily on both their minds, but Darcie apparently was the only one brave enough to give it voice. Another time her newfound courage might have made her smile. After all, mere weeks ago, she had been a go-along-to-get-along girl. Right now, her transformation took a backseat to heartache.

Her connecting flight to Buffalo wouldn't board for another hour yet. She'd insisted he didn't need to wait with her, but Nick was just as insistent that he would—prolonging the inevitable.

Neither of them had slept on the long flight from Athens. They'd spent the time talking, each sharing details of their lives from the mundane to the profound. Even so, they had scrupulously avoided making any reference to their relationship and the future.

Until now.

"Is there a difference?" he asked.

"You know there is." She gathered up the empty sugar packets and crushed them into a ball. Her gaze was fixed on her fist when she continued. "I'm only asking because if this is the last time I'm likely to see you, I'm going to want to make my kiss count."

"They have *all* counted," he assured her.

"True. Some more than others," she added thinking about their lovemaking.

Back at his home after the wedding, Nick had undressed Darcie slowly, hands caressing her skin as if memorizing her body's every dip and curve. The exquisite tenderness of his touch, the soft cadence of his voice as he spoke in his native tongue, both had been in stark contrast to his fierce expression and ultimate possession.

Afterward, he'd gathered her close.

"Tonight, I will stay," he'd told her. "I want to watch you wake."

True to his word, when Darcie opened her eyes early the next day, Nick had still been beside her and already awake. Indeed, given the shadows under his eyes, she'd wondered if he'd slept at all.

"Just as I suspected," he'd said quietly.

"What?"

"You are even more beautiful in the morning."

So, now, she had to know. "Will we see each other again, Nick? Whatever the answer is, I promise I can handle it. I'm not fragile."

No, Darcie wasn't fragile, but that didn't mean she couldn't be hurt or manipulated. She had been in the past. Nick was determined to do neither. Unfortunately, he found himself in a predicament. The past two weeks had been amazing, so much so that he didn't want them to end. They made for a great beginning. But...

It would be much easier if they lived in the same city. Then they could fully explore their feelings and decide over time where they were heading. But Darcie lived on the other side of the state, which was better than being on the other side of the ocean, but still not close enough for a relationship to develop naturally. As it was, what had occurred between them in Greece had been shaped by outside forces, not the least of which were her broken engagement and his strained family ties.

Now that they were returning to their everyday lives, what would happen? In the light of a new day, would she look back on her time in Greece and see it as a romantic holiday dalliance and nothing more? That was how it had started. That was all it was supposed to be.

Nick didn't wonder how he would feel once he was back in his old routine. He knew. He loved Darcie.

So, he said, "I want to see you again."

"You don't sound happy about that."

"I am being cautious, I suppose. For both of our sakes."

"Are you worried that I'll suddenly realize I still love Tad or that I want to go back to my old job as a fact-checker?" she asked.

"No, but you have choices to make, Darcie. And I don't want to put any added pressure on you."

"I think I've already made those choices."

Nick nodded, somewhat mollified, but he still felt the need to point out, "Darcie, your life is in a state of upheaval. It has been since we met. In a way, you are starting over. I was selfish once. I expected someone else to bend her life to suit my needs. I don't want to do that again. You have so much to sort out right now."

"I need a new address and to revamp my resumé. The rest…" She shrugged. "It will sort out itself."

"Your plane leaves in less than an hour for Buffalo. That is where you live. I am in Manhattan."

"And if I lived in Manhattan, too?"

His heart took off like a shot at the idea. That was Darcie's dream, he knew. To move to New York City and work as a serious journalist. Even as he wanted to offer to help her pack her bags and move that very day, he also knew she needed money to do so, and she wouldn't accept his financial assistance. He'd had a hard enough time convincing her to accept it in Greece, and even then she had insisted on a *quid pro quo* arrangement. But without a reliable source of income, she wouldn't be able to swing New York's high cost of living.

"I want you in New York. Make no mistake about that." He swallowed hard then as he pushed what he wanted behind what would be best for Darcie. "But the city is very expensive, and I am trying to be realistic. Also, your entire family is in Buffalo. When everything is said and done, you may…you may decide that is where you want to stay. I would understand."

It would kill him, but he would understand.

Darcie's smile was reassuring. "I'm not Selene, Nick. I'm not going to change my mind. I *will* come to New York." The smile disappeared then. "But it's going to take a little while, before I have established myself as a writer and can afford to move."

"A little while," he repeated.

They both fell silent.

"And in the meantime?" she asked.

"It is a short flight. I can be in Buffalo every weekend."

"That's a lot of frequent flyer miles," Darcie murmured.

"It won't be forever. Eventually, we will be together in the same city." Even as Nick said it old memories swirled like vultures. He did his best to ignore them, but some of his concern must have shown on his face.

"You're wondering if while we are apart I will reach the conclusion that what happened in Greece was simply meant to stay there," she said softly.

He didn't care for Darcie's assessment, but he couldn't argue its accuracy. "I would understand."

"Because I'm supposedly vulnerable and confused and

we only just met?" She arched an eyebrow. "Oh, please. I spent years with Tad and I never felt for him what I'm starting to feel for you, Nick."

He knew what he was starting to feel, too, but, as much as Nick wanted to give voice to the words, he was afraid. "Absence does not always make the heart grow fonder. Sometimes…feelings change."

Her eyes were bright, but she nodded. "And you think mine will."

"No!" God help him, he hoped not.

"All right. Let's put it to the test."

"What do you mean?"

"We won't see each other until I can afford to move to New York," she said baldly.

Her suggestion caught him off guard. "How long will that be?"

"I don't know," Darcie admitted on a frown.

"Six months," he declared. "That is all the time I will give you." It might take longer than that for her to build her resumé, but half a year was all the time Nick was willing to be apart.

She nodded. Exhaled. "And during that time, we won't see one another."

"No." He swallowed before adding, "Nor will we speak to one another on the telephone."

She nibbled her lower lip. "I assume texting and emails will be out of the question then, too, huh?"

He chuckled in spite of himself. Mirth didn't last long before he sobered. "We will have no contact at all. If I am in contact with you, I will want to *be* with you. My resolve will weaken."

"And that would be bad?"

"Not bad, but…selfish." It kept coming back to that.

"You need time, Darcie. You may not think so, but I want you to have it."

And he wanted her to be sure of her feelings for both of their sakes.

She exhaled slowly and nodded. "Okay. No contact at all. And then what?"

"If after six months we both still feel the same way we will meet."

"Where?" She chuckled as she added, "On the observation deck of the Empire State Building?"

"If that is where you wish."

"That was a joke, Nick. Sorry. Obviously you've never seen *An Affair to Remember* or *Sleepless in Seattle*."

She quickly explained how the couples in both movies had made plans to meet at the New York landmark.

"I like the idea of a neutral site so there is no pressure, but too many variables appear left to chance," he said. "I do not want to leave anything to chance where you are concerned."

She smiled. "Then where?"

An idea came to him. "Are you familiar with Tidwell's?"

"The big auction house in Brooklyn that is your main competitor?"

He nodded. "The first Saturday of each month, it auctions classic automobiles. We can meet there in January."

"The start of a new year." She smiled. "I like it. Very symbolic."

If all went as he hoped, it would be the start of much more than a new year. He jotted down the pertinent information on a paper cocktail napkin and handed it to her.

"Remember, we will not be in touch between now and then, so do not lose this."

The smile she gave him now was wobbly. "I've already got it committed to memory."

"If…if you do not come—"

"I'll be there. I'll wear red in honor of your grandmother. If you change your—"

Nick stopped her from finishing the thought with a kiss. Then, with time ticking down until her flight boarded, he walked with her as far as the airport allowed.

"This is not goodbye, so there is no need to make it count," he reminded her as he drew her into his arms.

"That's right. It's see you later. Or, more accurately, see you in six months."

Still, the kiss counted. When it came to Darcie, everything did.

CHAPTER THIRTEEN

DARCIE HAD BEEN back in Buffalo a full week when she saw Tad. She had called him upon her return to the States and left a brief message to let him know she was home safe and sound, and appreciated the concern he'd expressed in his many voice mails. She'd tried to make it clear in her tone that she didn't want to rehash the past, but he showed up at her parents' house one evening anyway.

Becky had been nice enough to let her move in after the breakup, but Darcie couldn't keep imposing on her friend, nor could she afford to pay half the rent if she wanted to save up for New York, which meant she'd moved back in with her parents.

"Tad, it's so good to see you. Isn't it good to see him, Darcie?" Her mother beamed a smile in her direction as they stood in the foyer.

"Come on, hon. Let's leave them alone," her father said. He sent Darcie a wink of encouragement as he led her mother to the kitchen.

"I probably should have called first," Tad said. He smiled weakly. "I guess I didn't want to take the chance that you would tell me not to come. I think we need to talk."

"I think we've said all there is to say."

His expression made it clear he didn't agree.

"I ran in to Becky while you were in Greece. She told me

you'd met someone. A smooth-talking local who was squiring you about Athens because of a little misunderstanding with the tour company."

A little misunderstanding?

"Tad, the company you booked our honeymoon trip with was all but bankrupt. If not for Nick I would have been stranded at the airport and then booking a return flight to Buffalo within two days."

"I'm sorry about that. I'm sorry about a lot of things, Darcie." He reached for her hand. Because it would have been rude to tug it away, she let him hold it while he went on. "When you didn't answer any of the messages I became worried that something had happened to you."

How sweet, she was thinking, until he added, "Or that you'd done something stupid."

"Stupid?"

"You haven't been acting like yourself, Darcie. Your mother mentioned that you're thinking of quitting your job. You love that job."

"I've *tolerated* that job," she corrected. How could he still not understand that? "I've always wanted to be a serious journalist and live in the city."

"I thought you outgrew that dream."

"No."

Tad went on as if she hadn't spoken. "When your mother told me that you'd postponed your return from Greece, I almost booked a flight to Athens."

That came as a surprise. Tad had never been the sort to do anything spontaneous. "Why would you do that?"

"To save you from doing something rash. Given your fragile state of mind and what Becky had said about your tour guide…"

She did tug her hand away now and then crossed her arms over her chest. "My fragile state of mind?"

"You weren't thinking clearly. I hoped by giving you time, you would come to your senses and then we could sit down and have a rational discussion about our future."

She shook her head. Her smile was sad, even if she knew she had made the right decision. "We had plenty of time to talk, Tad. We were engaged for six years. I thought I wanted to be your wife, but—"

"I know you were upset about moving in with my mother. You've made your point. I'm willing to compromise. We can buy our own house. We won't build the addition onto Mother's. She understands." Of course he would have run it by Evelyn first to gain her approval. "Besides, she's only sixty-six and in good health yet. We can revisit our living arrangements in a few years."

"No!" Darcie screamed before moderating her tone. "Look, Tad, I don't want to hurt you, but we aren't getting back together."

The Taylor Swift song played in her head and she nearly added a few *evers* just for emphasis.

"It's the man you met in Greece. He turned you against me," Tad muttered sourly.

Of this much Darcie was certain. "Nick doesn't have anything to do with our breakup. I made that decision before he and I met."

"You're stressed out, confused," Tad insisted. "You don't know what you want. You don't know what you're saying."

"But I do know, Tad. I can't marry you. I'm sorry. I don't love you."

She loved Nick.

Nick's apartment was quieter than he recalled it being, and some of the delight he found in Manhattan definitely was missing. He went about the business of living and working, but the days ticked by slowly and it was a constant struggle not to pick up the phone and call Darcie. He wanted to talk to her or even just hear her voice saying his name.

The brochure she'd helped him with went to the printer. He popped a few copies of it in the mail to her when he got them. That was business and as a contract employee she was entitled to them. As much as he wanted to, he didn't include a personal note, only his business card paper-clipped to the first page of one of the copies. In addition to no phone calls, they were to have no correspondence of any kind. He cursed himself a fool for coming up with the idea.

How was she? What was she doing? Such questions haunted him. Most of all, he tortured himself wondering: would she change her mind? Come January, would she be at the auction house? Six months was starting to feel like a life sentence.

Darcie felt the same way, but she was using the time wisely. Since her return to Buffalo, she'd nailed down several more freelance jobs. The articles she'd written for Nick's auction brochure helped open some doors. Others she unlocked with sheer persistence. Interestingly enough, it was her work as a fact-checker at the trade publication that proved to be the deal sealer when it came to finding full-time employment in New York.

The week before Thanksgiving she interviewed with three magazines in the city, coming into town early on a Friday morning. She'd been tempted to seek out Nick after the interviews were over. His business card was in her purse. But they had a deal. She flew back to Buffalo the following morning, watching the city grow smaller from the plane's tiny window.

Regardless of what happened with Nick, she would be back. Two of the magazines had offered her a job on the spot. Darcie had already called to accept one of them. The pay was low, and she wouldn't be doing as much writing as she'd hoped. At least not at first. But the potential was there in the future not only for assignments, but also for a monthly column in the print magazine as well as in the online version.

In the meantime, she would be living her dream.

Nerves fluttered like a dozen butterflies in her stomach the morning of the auction in January. If all went as she hoped that day, Darcie would be with Nick, and they would be kicking off a new chapter as a couple. In anticipation of that, she made sure to put on her sexiest underwear.

And if he wasn't there?

She pushed the thought away and finished dressing. When she was done, she eyed her reflection in the full-length mirror that was attached to the back of the bathroom door in her tiny Brooklyn efficiency. She had purchased a new dress for the occasion. Red, as she'd promised him. It scooped low in the front and fitted snugly across her hips. When she'd tried it on at the store, she'd snapped a picture with her cell phone and sent it to Becky for confirmation.

Her friend had texted back: Va-va-va-voom.

It was a bit much for a daytime auction, but Darcie didn't care. She wanted to make a statement. And, truth be told, she couldn't wait for Nick to slip it off and then work his way through her sexy undergarments.

The day was cold and it had snowed the night before, leaving the sidewalks covered in slush. After she got out of the cab, she sloshed her way to the auction house's main door in a pair of impractical high heels. Her toes were frozen by the time she got inside the large, cavernous building. She was early by an hour, but the place was already crowded with would-be buyers, car enthusiasts and others who just enjoyed the spectacle. Even though she didn't plan to make any purchases, she had to sign in and received a numbered paddle. Then she made a loop of the main room, hoping to spot Nick. With just minutes to spare before the first automobile went on the block, she hadn't had any luck.

What if he had changed his mind?

She hadn't wanted to consider the possibility, but now, with her nerves working overtime, she could think of little else. Before they'd said goodbye at the airport, he'd seemed so concerned that Darcie would be the one to have second thoughts, given all of the upheaval in her life, but what if he had? What if after six months apart, he'd decided he didn't want to pursue a relationship with her after all?

"Ladies and gentlemen, we'd like to get started. If you could please take your seats," a man's voice said over the public address system.

Darcie found an open spot in the middle of a row halfway up the main aisle.

The first automobile up for bid was an Austin-Healey similar in age to the one Ari had traded to Nick as part of the Porsche deal in Trikala. It needed some body work and the upholstery on the driver's side was in poor condition. It came as no surprise when it went for a song to a man with a handlebar mustache seated three rows behind her.

"Come on now, ladies and gentlemen. You can do better than that," the auctioneer teased the crowd. "These cars are classics. Even the ones that need work are diamonds in the rough."

By the time the fourth automobile came up for bid the crowd was primed. Paddles were shooting into the air all around her, but Darcie had stopped paying attention. She was too busy glancing about for Nick and trying to keep her hopes from deflating.

Maybe she had misunderstood their conversation in the airport. For the third time since arriving at the auction, she looked at the cocktail napkin she'd saved from six months earlier and read the information. There was no mistake. This was the right place. The right time. But where was Nick? Even as she tried to deny it, the answer she kept coming up with was that he'd changed his mind.

Finally, the last vehicle listed in the program came onto the block. It was a 1962 Maserati Spyder. The cherry-red convertible was in mint condition. The auctioneer opened the bidding at seventy-five thousand. It quickly shot up to twice that and kept climbing even as Darcie's spirits started to free-fall.

"I have one-ninety, one-ninety, can I get two? Can I get two?" The auctioneer's chant was rapid-fire. The two in this case referred to two hundred thousand dollars.

The auctioneer got his wish and then some. The vehicle ultimately sold for a quarter of a million dollars. And that was it. The auction was over. Nick wasn't there.

Darcie could barely swallow around the lump in her throat. Her eyes were stinging, her nose starting to run. In a few minutes, she was going to look every bit as wretched as she felt. She wanted to be anywhere but where she was. Unfortunately, leaving wasn't going to be accomplished quickly given the crowd. She rose along with the other people packed in the auditorium. The first tear was sliding down her cheek when the auctioneer's voice boomed over the loudspeaker again.

"Hold on, folks. Hold on. Take your seats again, please. We have one last item up for bid today. It's not listed in your programs. It's something very special."

A murmur of surprise went up from the crowd as people returned to their seats. Darcie swiped at her damp cheeks. Unless she wanted to draw attention to herself by stepping over the half-dozen spectators in her row that were between her and the aisle, she had no choice but to take hers as well.

Once the audience had quieted down, the auctioneer continued. "This item is a little unusual. It's going to require a special buyer, which is why the seller has set a reserve."

Darcie was hunting through her purse for a tissue and only half listening, but she knew that meant the seller had requested a minimum bid be met in order for the sale to go through. Such a strategy could prove risky, but it also ensured that an item of great worth didn't wind up selling way under value simply because the right buyers weren't in attendance.

Must be some car, she thought, momentarily halting her quest for a tissue to glance at the stage. She didn't see an automobile. Instead, she saw Nick saunter out.

The women in the crowd went wild, cheering and clapping and whistling shrilly. Darcie would have joined them had she been capable of making noise. But at that moment, even breathing was proving difficult.

He was here!

And looking gorgeous in a classically cut tuxedo with a snowy white shirt and black bow tie. His dark hair was neatly combed. Just wait till she got him alone. She was going to run her fingers through it, leaving it mussed and sexy.

"I've got a platinum credit card!" a curvy blonde near the front hollered. "Whatever the reserve is, I'm sure I can meet it."

Other women began shouting out dollar amounts then, even though the auctioneer had yet to start the bidding.

"Ladies, ladies. Quiet down. As I said, this is a special auction item. Nick Costas is offering a personal tour of Manhattan and dinner at his favorite Greek restaurant to the woman who meets his reserve."

"What's the amount?" someone called out.

"Nick and I have known one another for a long time.

We're competitors in business, but friends, too. Still, he hasn't told me. All he has said is that he will let me know when or if the terms of the sale have been met."

When the audience began grumbling, the auctioneer silenced them. "It gets more bizarre, folks. Nick will pick up the tab for the winning bid and give the amount to the charity of the winner's choice."

"So, there's no risk?" a woman asked.

"Only to your hearts. So, ladies, get ready to raise those paddles. Bidding starts at one thousand dollars."

It escalated quickly from there, hitting ten thousand before Darcie could process what was happening. He was selling himself, but not to the highest bidder. That was where the reserve came in. Nick was waiting for her. If she loved him, he was, quite literally, hers for the taking.

Darcie set her paddle on her seat. She didn't need it. She had a better idea.

"Excuse me," she said to the gentleman seated to her left. She had to repeat the process five more times before she made it to the aisle and was heading toward the stage. She no longer cared about making a spectacle of herself.

Nick spotted her when she was halfway there. His mouth curved into a grin that set her heart bumping irregularly.

"I believe the reserve has been met," he told the auctioneer. His gaze never wavered from hers.

She climbed the steps and met him center stage. The huge crowd fell silent. For Darcie, at that moment, they simply didn't exist.

"I was getting a little worried that you weren't here," she admitted, wrapping her arms around his neck.

His hands found her waist. "I apologize for that. I wanted to make a statement."

"You certainly did. I was going for that with this dress, by the way."

"So I see. I can't wait to take it off you. Six months is very long."

"Felt like a lifetime," she agreed. "But I've kept busy."

"Writing?" he asked.

"And plenty of it. Did I mention I moved here to take a job at a magazine? I just started last week."

His smile was wide and tinged with pride. "I knew you could do it."

"Kiss him already!" the woman who'd offered her credit card at the beginning of the auction shouted.

Darcie grinned. "How do you feel about public displays of affection?"

In answer, Nick lowered his mouth to hers.

"I love you, Darcie Hayes," he whispered afterward.

"I love you, too."

EPILOGUE

BECKY FUSSED WITH the satin folds of Darcie's wedding gown as they stood at the back of the church. Although the denomination wasn't Greek Orthodox, much to Yiayia's dismay, Darcie had insisted that some of the elements of a traditional Greek ceremony be incorporated into their wedding.

One year to the day after they'd met in the Athens airport, Nick had gotten down on one knee and proposed. Now, Darcie was minutes away from becoming his wife.

The music began. Her sisters, wearing dresses the same shade of blue as the Aegean, started up the aisle one at a time. As Darcie's maid of honor, Becky went last. Then it was just Darcie and her father standing at the back of the church, a white runner strewn with rose petals the only thing between her and Nick.

"Slow down," her father whispered, as they began to walk as the wedding march began. "Make him wait a little longer."

It might have been good advice if Darcie had not been so eager herself. She already felt as if she'd waited a lifetime for this moment, even if by many standards her romance with Nick had been a whirlwind.

Finally at the altar, she smiled at Nick, took his hands. Vows were spoken. Rings were exchanged. A unity candle was lit. Then Pieter, grinning broadly, placed crowns on their heads and switched them three times.

"You may kiss your bride," the priest said.

Nick's eyes were bright. His expression mirrored the sheer joy Darcie felt.

"At last," he murmured just before their mouths met.

* * * * *

UNDER THE BRAZILIAN SUN

CATHERINE GEORGE

CHAPTER ONE

THE Oporto concourse was crowded, but as Katherine made her way through it with her luggage trolley she finally spotted a man holding up a sign with her name on it.

She smiled politely as she approached him. 'I'm Dr Lister of the Massey Gallery in England.'

The man stared for a moment in blank surprise, then hurriedly took charge of her trolley. '*Bem-vindo, Doutora*. Senhor Sousa sent me to welcome you. My name is Jorge Machado. Please to follow me to the car.'

Katherine was only too pleased to let the man take over. Installed in a sleek limousine she relaxed against the butter-soft leather upholstery as they left the airport to head north into the heart of the Minho, an area of Portugal she'd learned was still deep-rooted in tradition. Once they left the motorway for a slower winding route along the River Lima they passed a cart drawn by plodding oxen oblivious of passing traffic, with two black-clad women pacing alongside, and Katherine smiled in delight. Real Portugal!

Originally, Katherine had intended hiring a car to sandwich in a brief holiday somewhere in the region once her mission was completed, but in the end she had taken her employer's advice and accepted the transport provided. She would simply take a taxi to Viana do Castelo afterwards, and find a hotel for whatever time was left over from her mission. But for now it was good just to sit back and watch this picturesque part of the world go by as she speculated about what waited for her at journey's end.

Some work was necessary, for a start. The unknown Mr de Sousa required an art expert to authenticate a recently acquired painting, and had paid all expenses and fees necessary to fly her boss to Portugal. James Massey was renowned and highly respected in the art world for searching out unrecognised works by major artists, and Katherine considered herself fortunate not only to work at his gallery, but for the benefit of his invaluable experience as he'd taught her how to differentiate between the genuine article and the fake. But James, to his chagrin, had gone down with influenza shortly before he was due to leave for Portugal and had asked Katherine to take his place. Elated that he trusted her to deputise for him, she'd dropped everything to make the flight.

The new man in her life had objected strongly when she put their embryo relationship on hold to take off for Portugal, not least because she turned down his offer to go with her. Katherine had been immovable. A client paying so generously for her services deserved her total concentration. The painting would probably need some cleaning before she could even begin to venture any kind of opinion and, dependent on its age and condition, this might take time. Andrew Hastings had taken the rejection so badly Katherine had been surprised to receive his text at the airport demanding she contact him as soon as she arrived. She shrugged, preferring to think about Mr de Sousa instead. James Massey knew surprisingly little about the client, other than his possession of a painting he believed to be of some importance, and his willingness to pay generously to find out if he was right. She fervently hoped that he *was* right. If the client's find was a dud or, worse, a fake, she didn't fancy breaking the bad news. That was a side of the business normally dealt with by James Massey.

'We have arrived, *Doutora*,' said her chauffeur, and Katherine sat to attention at the sight of high walls with a gated archway surmounted by a stone cross. He aimed a remote control at the wrought iron gates, which swung open to reveal a landscape so beautiful she asked him to drive slowly through acres of rolling verdant gardens ringed with mountain views. When the house itself finally came into view it outdid its surroundings. White-walled and red-roofed, two wings fanned out from a central stone tower wreathed in greenery. Before the car came to a halt in the circular courtyard the massive door in the tower swung open and a plump little woman came hurrying out, her surprise obvious as she set eyes on the visitor.

'Here is Doutora Lister, Lídia,' said Jorge Machado with emphasis on the title as he helped Katherine from the car.

'*Bem-vindo*—welcome to Quinta das Montanhas, *Doutora*,' the woman said, recovering quickly.

Delighted to hear more English, no matter how heavily accented, Katherine smiled warmly. 'How do you do? What a glorious house.'

The woman smiled, pleased. 'Senhor Roberto regret he is not here to greet you but arrives very soon. I take you to your room, *Doutora*.'

Jorge followed behind with the luggage as the friendly, bustling Lidia led Katherine through a vast cool hall with a high vaulted ceiling, and on up a curving stone staircase with a balustrade of wrought iron as delicate as black lace. The smiling woman showed Katherine into a big high-ceilinged room with louvred blinds at tall windows, and an armoire and massive white-covered bed in dark carved wood. And, best sight of all to Katherine at the moment, a tray with an ice bucket and mineral water on a table between the windows.

Jorge followed them to wheel Katherine's luggage to the chest at the foot of the bed, then turned to leave. 'When you are ready, *Doutora*, please to come down to the *varanda*.'

Lidia showed Katherine a door which opened into a bathroom. 'You need, yes?'

'I do indeed. *Obrigada*,' said Katherine in relief, her thanks so fervent the woman smiled in sympathy.

'I bring food now?' she offered, but Katherine shook her head.

'No, thank you; I'm too hot right now. I just need some water.'

Lidia promptly filled a glass for her. 'I come back soon.'

Not sure what "soon" might mean, Katherine downed the water and made do with a wash rather than the shower she would have preferred. She brushed out her hair and pulled it back into a ruthlessly tight twist, and then exchanged her T-shirt and jeans for tailored black linen trousers and plain white shirt. Then with a wry little smile she added the dark-rimmed spectacles she wore for computer work. The efficient look would hopefully impress a man who was bound to be of a certain age if he owned a fabulous house like this *and* had money to spare for valuable paintings. Katherine sent brief texts to James and her friend Rachel, and last, guilty because it was an afterthought, another to Andrew, then began to unpack. Before she'd finished the roar of a car engine shattered the peaceful afternoon and Lidia hurried in, shaking her head in disapproval.

'I do that, *Doutora*. You come now. He is here.'

Katherine followed the woman down the curving staircase and out onto a long veranda with a gleaming floor and carved stone pillars entwined with greenery. A man in A casual linen jacket and jeans leaned against one of them, looking out over the gardens. He was tallish and lean, with a mane of black curling hair and a profile any movie star would have envied. When Lidia spoke he turned quickly, with a smile which died abruptly at the sight of Katherine, his dark eyes narrowed in surprise.

'Doutora Lister,' announced Lidia with a touch of drama and withdrew, leaving total silence behind her.

'*You* are Dr Lister?' the man said at last.

At last, rejoiced her hormones. You've finally found him. 'I'm Katherine Lister, yes,' she said, proud of her composure as she smiled politely.

He sketched a graceful bow. '*Encantado*. Roberto de Sousa. I regret I was not here to welcome you when you arrived.'

'Not at all. Your people made me very welcome.'

The client was a far cry from the elderly businessman Katherine had pictured—at a guess, only a few years older than her own twenty eight. And she could have sworn she'd seen him before somewhere. The overlong hair and dark eyes tilted above knife-edge cheekbones were puzzlingly familiar; unlike the eye-catching scar slashed down one side of his face, which was the once-seen never-forgotten kind. When the silence continued Katherine decided to break it.

'Is there a problem, Mr de Sousa?'

'I was expecting a man,' he said bluntly.

Katherine stiffened. 'I thought Mr Massey explained that he was sending me in his place.'

He nodded coldly. 'He did. But he did not inform me that the expert Dr Lister is a woman.'

'Even so,' said Katherine, every hackle suddenly erect in protest, 'I'm fully qualified to make the inspection you require, Senhor de Sousa. Not with as much experience as Mr Massey, it's true, but with more than enough, I assure you, to give you an informed opinion of your painting.' She waited, but no response was forthcoming. The attraction, it seemed, had not been mutual. 'Of course, if you insist on a male expert I'll leave at once. Though I would be glad of a cup of tea first.'

Roberto de Sousa looked appalled. He clapped his hands, and as if by magic Jorge Machado reappeared, bearing a tray. 'Why has Dr Lister received no refreshment?'

'*Desculpe me, Doutora,*' said the man to Katherine. 'I waited for the *Patrao.*'

'You should have served my guest without waiting for me,' said his employer, frowning. 'Please sit, Dr Lister.'

Jorge filled one of the fragile cups with tea, the other with black coffee, and offered Katherine a platter of cakes she refused with a friendly smile for him as she sat down.

Roberto de Sousa sat opposite, smouldering in silence again across the table. This time, he could just sit there, lip-zipped for ever as far as she was concerned, decided Katherine irritably. Gorgeous he might be, but once she'd drunk the tea she'd ask for transport to Viana do Castelo.

'Please tell me how well you know Mr James Massey,' he said at last.

'All my life,' she said briefly.

'He is a relative?'

'No, just a close friend of my father. How do *you* know him, Mr de Sousa?'

'By reputation and by information I acquired on the Internet. I contacted Mr Massey after my research showed he is the best man to authenticate my painting. I bought it for relatively little—a song, as you say.'

'But you think it's valuable?'

Roberto de Sousa shrugged indifferently. 'The value is unimportant. It is not for resale. My interest is the identity of the artist and, if possible, the subject.' He was silent again, as though turning something over in his mind. 'If you would consent to stay to examine it,' he said at last, 'I would be most grateful…Doctor.'

Her first instinct was a flat refusal. But, conscious that she represented the Massey Gallery, also deeply curious about the painting, Katherine changed her mind about a quick getaway. For pride's sake she paused as though considering her answer, and finally nodded graciously. 'Since you've paid so generously for my time, I have no choice.'

'*Obrigado*, Dr Lister. You shall see the painting in the morning in the full light of day, and tell me your requirements. Mr Massey warned there must be cleaning before any opinion is possible.' He glanced at his watch. 'But now you must be tired after your journey. Please rest before joining me for dinner.'

So she was to have the honour of dining at his table. And the mere mention of dinner reminded her that now her thirst was gone she was hungry. 'Thank you, Mr de Sousa.'

'*De nada.*' He paused. 'A small thing. If I am addressed correctly it is Mr Sousa.'

'I see. I'll remember that.' She got up.

He escorted her across the hall. '*Ate logo*—until later, Doctor.'

She nodded politely, and mounted the curving stairs with back very erect.

Roberto de Sousa watched her out of sight, then returned, deep in thought, to the veranda. He sat down, absently rubbing the leg which gave him hell if he stood too long. His surprise at finding that Dr Lister was not a man had obviously—and unfortunately—offended his guest. But if she were fully qualified to give an informed opinion on his painting, in theory he had no problem with a female expert. His lips tightened. In practice, however, he deeply resented the need to welcome a woman to his home now he was disfigured; even an efficient intellectual in spectacles like Dr Lister, with her scraped back hair and masculine clothes. At the Quinta the only females in his life were on his staff, whereas at one time he had been surrounded on all sides by beautiful, willing women. His face set in harsh lines as he ran a finger down his scar. All that, and many other things, had changed forever the day his luck had finally run out.

Katherine's equilibrium was in normal working order again by the time she settled down on the bed with a book. Roberto de Sousa's reaction to her had been more of a blow than she cared to admit. Her mane of brown hair and opalescent green eyes were assets which generally did her no harm with the opposite sex. But from the reaction of her client she'd obviously disguised her assets too well in an attempt to minimise the figure which curved a little too much in some places for her own taste, but had never been a drawback where men were concerned. She bit her lip. The client's preference for a male expert was another blow. If she informed Roberto de Sousa that his painting was a fake, or of no intrinsic value, he might refuse to accept her findings. She shrugged. Not the end of the world; she would simply rely on backup from James. Photographs of the painting would be emailed to him for his verdict—and earn her undying gratitude from Judith Massey for keeping her bored, convalescent husband in the loop.

Katherine had wondered beforehand whether she would be invited to join her host's family for the meal, but so far no mention had been made of a wife, or of any other relative. Indeed, James had known so little about the client Katherine had speculated quite a bit about Roberto de Sousa during the flight, but nothing had prepared her for her reaction to him, which was a first in her life when it came to men. She had also been unprepared for his hostility too, which was as surprising as his relative youth and scarred, darkly handsome face. She shrugged. He might have wanted a man to pass judgement on his painting but she would soon show him she was more than equal to the task. Nevertheless, the prospect of dinner was a bit daunting.

Katherine had fully intended wearing a sleeveless leaf-green shift with a clever bit of draping to flatter her curvier bits, but she put it back on its hanger, her eyes glittering coldly as she chose minimising black linen instead. With no jewellery to soften the starkly plain dress and only the merest touch of make-up, tonight she would play the intellectual role to the hilt to dine with a man whose aura of sardonic melancholy was so intriguing—and surprising. She would have expected someone of his age and race to be more outgoing. Perhaps he had been before the scar.

A minute before eight the slightly panting Lidia arrived to announce that Senhor Roberto awaited his guest. Katherine put the glasses on and gave a last look in the mirror to make sure no strand of hair had escaped from its ruthless twist. At last, feeling like Boudicca going into battle, she followed the woman down the curving staircase to the hall, where Jorge was waiting to escort her out on the veranda, which looked even more inviting with soft lights glowing in the greenery wreathing the pillars.

Roberto de Sousa rose slowly from one of the cane chairs and stared at her in total silence, his spirits sinking at the sight of his starkly elegant guest. He recalled himself hurriedly and bade her good evening.

Did he ever say anything without thinking it over first? Katherine wondered.

'Lidia is not pleased because I wished to dine out here,' he said, leading her to a table. 'The *sala de jantar* is big for two people. I thought you would prefer this.' But in truth the preference was his, in the hope that his scar would look less prominent in the soft lighting.

'I do,' she assured him, noting that the table was laid for only two. No wife in evidence then; at least not here.

He pulled out a chair for her. 'What will you drink? Gin and tonic, perhaps?'

Katherine glanced at the frosted bottle sitting in a silver ice bucket. 'May I have a glass of wine?'

'*Pois e.* This is the vinho verde of the Minho.' He removed the cork with a twist of his wrist and filled two glasses. 'I will join you.' He gave her a glass and, reminding himself that she was his guest, touched his own to it. 'What shall we toast?'

'A successful outcome for your painting?'

He nodded. 'To success.'

The cool wine went down like nectar, the perfect accompaniment to the dish of hot appetisers Jorge set in front of Katherine.

'The national dish,' Roberto informed her, '*bolinhas de bacalhau*. You have tasted these before?'

'No, but they smell delicious.' She popped one of the miniature cod balls in her mouth. 'And they taste even better. I'll remember my first food in Portugal with pleasure.'

Roberto sat facing her, his scar stark in his dark face against the white of his shirt, soft lighting or not. 'You have eaten nothing since you arrived?' he said, frowning.

She shook her head. 'Lidia offered, but I was too hot and thirsty.'

'Then you must eat more of these.' He pushed the plate towards her.

'No, thank you,' she said firmly. 'Otherwise I shan't need any dinner.'

'You must eat well, or the chef will take offence.'

The chef! Katherine digested that, along with the *bolinha*, and set out to be a polite dinner guest. 'Have you lived here long, Senhor Sousa?'

'I do not *live* here, Doctor.' He smiled crookedly, the scar much in evidence. 'The Quinta das Montanhas is the retreat I escape to for a holiday alone from time to time.'

Some holiday home! 'This is such a beautiful part of the world,' she remarked, 'but totally unknown territory to me. Unlike the majority of my fellow Brits, I've never been to Portugal before.'

'Then it is most important that you enjoy your first visit.'

Roberto de Sousa, however reluctant, was an attentive host, but Katherine found it hard to relax as they ate crisp grilled chicken fragrant with herbs.

'Is the food to your taste?' said Roberto, refilling her glass.

She nodded politely. 'My compliments to your chef. He's a genius.'

He eyed her in amusement. 'I was joking. Jorge's wife, Lidia, is cook here.'

'Then she's the genius,' said Katherine, and smiled warmly at Jorge as he came to take their plates. 'That was utterly delicious. Please tell your wife.'

He bowed, gratified. '*Obrigado, senhora*. You would like *pudim*?'

Katherine smiled regretfully. 'I can't eat another thing.'

Jorge returned the smile with warmth that won him a wry look from his employer. '*Café, senhora?* Or tea?'

'Not even that, thank you.'

'*I* would like coffee, Jorge, *por favor*,' said his employer sardonically. 'And bring *agua mineral* for the lady.'

'*Agora mesmo, Senhor.*'

Once Jorge was assured later that nothing more was needed, Katherine sat back, gazing out at moonlight which added magic to the scene. 'It's so peaceful here,' she commented. 'I see why you think of it as a haven.'

His eyes shuttered. 'Because I have never stayed here long enough to tire of such peace—until now.' He looked up at her in enquiry. 'I trust that taking Mr Massey's place so suddenly caused no problems for you?'

She shook her head. 'None that I couldn't solve, Mr Sousa.'

'*Muito bem.* I am most interested in your work. What, exactly, do you do at the gallery, Doctor?'

Katherine seized on the subject in relief. 'My job mainly involves searching the Internet for sleepers,' she began, 'the unidentified or wrongly catalogued works that slip through the net unnoticed. It can be very exciting.'

'I hope that my painting is equally so.'

'So do I,' she said with feeling.

'That was a most heartfelt remark!'

She smiled wryly. 'When paintings are brought to us at the gallery, James breaks the bad news when they're copies or fakes.'

He nodded, enlightened. 'And you do not welcome the task of giving me such news.'

'No. I don't.' She looked him in the eye. 'But I will if I have to.'

'Have no fear, Dr Lister. I will not blame you if my painting is a fake. Or doubt your findings,' he added.

'Thank you. I admit that worried me when—' she stopped, flushing.

'When?' he prompted.

'When you were so taken aback because I was a woman.'

'Only because I had been expecting a man,' he said smoothly. 'But if Senhor Massey trusts you to pass judgement on my painting I shall do the same.'

'Thank you!'

'*De nada.* Let me give you more wine.'

'Just water, thank you. I need a clear head for my detective work in the morning.'

His sudden smile altered his face so much it cancelled all impression of familiarity. A smiling Roberto de Sousa was so breathtaking he was definitely like no man Katherine had ever seen before.

'You regard your work as solving a mystery?' he said, intrigued.

'In a way. It's hugely rewarding—and exciting—to reveal the true identity of a lost work of art.'

'Perhaps my painting will be one of these.'

She hoped so. Fervently. 'Do you have any idea who the artist might be?'

'It is more hope than idea. But I shall say nothing until you give me your opinion. Do you rise early?' he added.

'During the working week, yes. I'll start on your painting as early as convenient in the morning.'

Conscious that his initial reception of his guest had been anything but warm, Roberto steeled himself to make amends. 'Before you begin tomorrow, perhaps you would like to explore the gardens—a short walk before your mystery-solving.'

Recognising an olive branch when she saw one, she nodded, smiling. 'I'd like that very much indeed. And now it's time I said goodnight.'

'Your breakfast will be brought to your room. I shall await you here later at nine. Sleep well. *Dorme bem*, as we say in my country.'

She smiled politely. 'My first day in Portugal has been so full I'm sure I will. Now I'm here, I can't imagine why I've never been to your country before.'

'Ah, but Portugal is not *minha terra*, the land of my birth,' he informed her. 'The Quinta das Montanhas is my retreat here in the Minho from time to time, but my family home is in Rio Grande do Sul in the south of Brazil.' He gave her the graceful bow again. 'I am a gaucho.'

She had an instant vision of pampas grasslands and cattle herded by men in flat hats and leather breeches. 'You live on a cattle ranch?' she asked, secretly impressed.

He nodded. 'My father is *patrao*. I rode as soon as I could walk, but long hours in the saddle are not possible for me right now.' His face darkened as he collected a walking stick to cross the hall with her. 'You have noticed I limp?'

'No, I haven't,' said Katherine, surprised, with such obvious truth his face relaxed slightly. 'An accident?'

'A car crash.' He shrugged. 'But, as you see, I survived. *Boa noite*, Doctor.'

It took a long time to fall asleep in the wide bed. Katherine blamed the bright moonlight for keeping her awake, but the real culprit was Roberto de Sousa. She would have been a lot happier about his electrifying effect on her hormones if her impact on him had been anything remotely similar but, mortifyingly, it had not. She felt deeply curious about the accident that had scarred his face and left him with the limp she hadn't noticed until he mentioned it. Other than the scarred, handsome face, her first impression of him had been coordination and grace—plus his obvious displeasure that a mere woman had come to pass judgement on his precious artwork. She sighed, praying that the painting was in reasonable enough condition for any kind of identification, let alone the one he hoped for. In one way she wished James Massey had come here to do it.

But if he had she wouldn't have come here to Quinta das Montanhas and met Roberto de Sousa, the most attractive man she'd ever met in her life, scarred and hostile or not.

She smiled suddenly, imagining the reaction if she described the charismatic client and his glorious house to Andrew Hastings. She'd known Andrew only a short time, but already he was displaying character traits which made it unlikely that their relationship, such as it was, would last much longer. Katherine enjoyed male company, but so far in her life had managed to keep her relationships light and undemanding, firmly secondary to her work. Orphaned in her teens, she was long accustomed to full autonomy over her life. Loneliness was no problem because she shared the house inherited from her father with two former college friends, both of them male. The three of them lived separate lives on separate floors of her three storey town house, and Hugh and Alastair paid their landlady good money in rent, but Andrew strongly disapproved of the arrangement and had lately begun urging her to share his house instead. Her obdurate refusal was an ongoing bone of contention between them, and her sudden dash to Portugal on the very day that he had tickets for Glyndebourne had been the last straw. But helping James out had been far more important to Katherine than a performance of *The Marriage of Figaro*, gala or not. Besides, she had no intention of moving in with a man whose outlook on life was so different from her own.

In spite of her restless night, Katherine woke early. She had showered and dressed in her usual working uniform of jeans and T-shirt and yanked her hair back in its twist by the time a knock on her door heralded the entry of Lidia with a tray.

'*Bom dia, Doutora*,' Lidia announced, beaming. She put the tray on a small table at the window and drew up a chair.

Katherine returned the smile warmly. 'Good morning, Lidia. *Obrigada*.'

'Is enough breakfast, or you like bacon? Eggs?'

Katherine laughed and assured Lidia that the array of crisp rolls and fruit was more than enough. 'It's perfect. Thank you.'

The woman smiled, pleased. 'Eat well. I come back at nine.'

'Could you ask Jorge to come with you, and take the tripod and work box downstairs?'

'*Pois e*. I tell him.'

With time for the kind of breakfast she never bothered with at home, Katherine sat at the open window to eat at her leisure as she looked out on the acres of beautiful gardens. No matter what happened about the painting, she was glad she'd been given the opportunity to see this heavenly place—and make the acquaintance of Roberto de Sousa. The Gaucho, no less. Very sexy.

The man waiting for her on the veranda later, however, looked weary rather than sexy. The shadowed eyes below the tumble of damp curls conveyed pain to Katherine.

'*Bom dia*,' he said as she joined him. 'You slept well?'

'Very well, thank you.'

Roberto eyed her tripod and work box with interest. 'These are for your work?'

She nodded. 'I take photographs of the painting to record its original condition, and then more shots as I go along. The box contains the various tools and solvents for the preliminary cleaning. This can be a messy process, so I shall need a place to work where I won't spoil anything. And with bright daylight rather than strong sunlight, if possible.'

He nodded. 'I shall arrange it. Do you still wish to walk for a while before you start?'

'Yes, please. I've been gazing out over your gardens while I ate breakfast. I'd love to see more.' And postpone the stress of her first encounter with the painting.

'*Vamos*, then.' He picked up the walking stick leaning against a pillar.

'Are you sure you feel like a walk today?' she asked, and regretted it when his mouth tightened.

'I assure you I can hobble—if that is the word—for a while without falling, Doctor.'

She flushed. 'I'm sorry—'

'No! It is I who am sorry.' He forced a smile. 'Forgive me. I swam too much this morning and now I pay for it. Come. I will show you the pool.'

On the leisurely stroll they encountered two gardeners, elderly men who looked up with smiles as their employer stopped to have a word with them each time.

'They were very pleased to see you,' commented Katherine.

'They have known me all my life,' he informed her. 'Quinta das Montanhas was my mother's childhood home. Now it is mine.'

Katherine was impressed. 'Your mother left it to you?'

'She gave it to me. My mother is still very much alive. But since their marriage, when my father stole her away to live in Rio Grande do Sul, she does not come here often. She dislikes the long flight.'

'I sympathise with her! The flight from the UK to Oporto was more than enough for me. Oh!' she said with sudden pleasure, as they turned down another path. 'A tennis court.'

'You play?'

'Yes, though not very well.'

'Better than I—now,' he said bitterly.

'Forgive the personal question,' she said with caution, 'but can nothing be done for your limp?'

His mouth twisted. '*Deus*, yes! I do the punishing exercises, a physiotherapist tortures me, I swim and walk every day, and every day it is improving. Eventually, I am assured, I shall be normal. Whatever normal may be,' he added savagely. 'To achieve that I shall even endure plastic surgery on my face, so I do not give little children nightmares.'

Mentally kicking herself for bringing the subject up, Katherine was glad to reach the swimming pool, which was big enough to give any man a workout on his daily swim. 'What a wonderful setting, with those trees in the background and the mountains beyond,' she said brightly.

He nodded in brief agreement, but said nothing more until they reached a summerhouse on the way back to the house. 'Before we return, let us inspect the *estufa*. Would this suit for your work? Here you have daylight, no one to disturb you, but you are near the house. Also,' he added, 'it revolves, for you to follow the light.'

Katherine ran up a shallow flight of steps into an octagonal room with a table and wicker chairs, a tiled floor and as much natural light from the windows as she could wish for. She beamed at Roberto. 'This is perfect! All I need now is the painting, plus a large blanket and my equipment and I'll get started.'

'Coffee first,' he said firmly, and waved his stick in the direction of the house. 'We shall drink it on the *varanda*, where the painting awaits.'

It was frustrating for Katherine to keep to Roberto's slow pace. Excitement and apprehension filled her now the moment of truth had finally arrived. Even if the painting was all he believed it to be, she might fail to identify the artist, which would be disaster after insisting that she possessed the necessary expertise. As they mounted the veranda steps the sight of the swathed package on the table accelerated her pulse.

'Shall I unmask him?' asked Roberto.

Katherine nodded, swallowing. 'Yes, please.'

With care, he removed the wrappings from the unframed canvas, then stood back. 'A little dirty, *nao e*?'

'Normal if there's any age to the painting,' she agreed, nerves suddenly gone as she looked down at the canvas, which showed a young dark-haired man in sober eighteenth century clothing. 'Certainly no dandy,' said Katherine slowly, 'though he would look a lot more elegant without the layers of overpaint. The jacket is just a blob and there's too much neck cloth.'

'What does that mean?' demanded Roberto, face tense.

'The overpaint may be hiding a repair in the canvas, or an addition by another artist,' she said absently, her eyes glued to the subject's face, which had suffered less than the body. Itching to get started, she smiled absently at her client. 'If you'll have my gear sent over to the summerhouse—with a thick blanket to lay the painting on, please—I'll get to work straight away.'

'First you must drink coffee,' he insisted as Jorge appeared to place a coffee pot on the waiting tray. Roberto gave him some quick-fire instructions, and the man bore the tripod and work box off to the summerhouse. 'I shall carry the painting there myself when you are ready,' he told Katherine, pulling out a chair for her.

Wishing she could get straight on with the job, she began pouring coffee. 'After I've cleaned the painting with white spirit, I can remove some of the overpaint with solvent, if you wish. By then I might even have some idea about the artist.' She had a pretty wild idea already, but had no intention of dropping names at this stage. Further investigation might prove her horribly wrong, and Roberto de Sousa's faith in her opinion would be gone for good.

He sat down beside her. 'You must not work too long without taking a break. Jorge will fetch you when lunch is ready.'

'I won't be able to face a meal in the middle of the day,' she warned.

'You must eat for energy. A small sandwich, at least,' he said firmly. 'I will join you here at one.' He looked up as Jorge returned. 'All is ready?'

'Sim, senhor.'

Katherine found that the summerhouse had already been dusted and swept, and a second table brought in to hold a tray with glasses and bottled water in an ice bucket, also a large metal bell with a wooden handle and a thick brown blanket.

Katherine positioned the blanket where the light was brightest and Roberto laid the painting down on it. He stood back, his eyes on her face as she subjected the painted face to a close scrutiny.

Katherine took her time, her excitement mounting. He looked familiar. Could she possibly be right about the artist?

She turned to smile absently at Roberto. 'Right. I'll make a start now.'

He smiled wryly. 'You wish me to leave you to your detecting, *nao e*?' He touched the bell. 'Ring if you need anything. Jorge will come. I shall see you at lunch.'

Alone with the portrait at last, Katherine took off the spectacles to peer through her magnifying glass. 'Right, young sir. Time for your close up.'

She went over every inch of the painting, then took a photograph to record its original state. Her instinct was screaming at her to start cleaning, but she doggedly kept to her usual routine. Once she'd taken everything she needed from her box, she pulled on a builder's mask and her binocular headband, drew in a deep breath and moistened the first cotton bud with white spirit.

CHAPTER TWO

KATHERINE could have sworn that only minutes had passed when Roberto himself arrived to say lunch awaited her on the veranda, by which time the bin liner at Katherine's feet was piling up with swabs and she was in no mood to break off to eat. But she smiled politely and straightened her back as she exchanged the binocular lenses for her spectacles, aware of his obvious disappointment that she had so little to show for her labours.

'I'm just taking off the dirt. You'll only see a difference when I get to the overpaint.'

'I did not expect him to look worse than before,' he admitted.

'I look worse, too,' she said ruefully as they walked back to the house. 'I need a scrub.'

'I shall wait on the *varanda*,' Roberto said. 'There is no hurry.'

'Yes, there is,' she contradicted. 'I must get back to work.'

His lips twitched. 'You enjoy your detecting so much?'

'I do.' She could have added that in this case it was almost unbearably exciting, but said nothing in case she was wrong.

Over lunch, Roberto told Katherine that he would be out for most of the following day. 'Be sure to stop and rest often. I shall tell Lidia to see to this.'

'Oh, I will,' she assured him.

'Have you any thoughts yet about the hand that painted our young man?' Roberto asked, filling their coffee cups.

'At this stage it's hard to tell. After I've cleaned the canvas I'll remove some of the overpaint to look for signature brush strokes. They function like fingerprints to identify the painter. But I'll only do enough to form an opinion. If the painting is valuable I'll leave the rest to the restorer James uses most, a lady with the necessary experience. Unless there is someone else you have in mind, of course.'

'I have not. It was my intention to leave all in Senhor Massey's hands. But I would trust you to do all, Dr Lister,' he added with formality.

That was a relief! 'It's very kind of you, but I'm an art historian, not a professional restorer. Besides, I can't stay here that long.'

'You are so eager to return to England? You have a lover waiting there for you?' His eyes gleamed as colour rose in her face at the sudden descent into the personal.

'I have a *friend*, yes. But I was referring to my job,' she said frostily.

He raised an eyebrow. 'I am sure Mr Massey would allow you to stay if I asked.'

Katherine finished her coffee and stood up. 'That's up to him.'

'If he agreed, it would cause problems in your private life if you stay here?' Roberto got up more slowly, jaw clenched at the effort.

'None at all.' None that mattered compared to the painting, anyway. She looked at her watch. 'Time I got back to work. I'll just run up to my room for my laptop.'

'I shall see you at dinner. I will not walk with you to the *estufa* because I know well I am too slow for you,' he said sardonically.

Guilty because he was right, Katherine managed a smile. 'I'll look forward to reporting to you at dinner.'

Not as much as I shall, thought Roberto, as he watched her racing up the stairs. His initial hostility towards her was receding rapidly, leaving him with a growing desire to know the efficient Dr Katherine Lister better. The Quinta was a beautiful, peaceful haven, but lonely. He smiled bitterly as he limped back to his rooms. At one time he had longed for privacy and time to himself. His mother had told him many times to be careful what he wished for in case the wish was granted. And, as always, she was right. He would gladly pay James Massey whatever he asked for more of Katherine's time, if only to look forward to conversation with her over dinner. She was a rare type of woman in his experience, expert in the subject which interested him so greatly. And if his scar repelled her she hid it well. He smiled a little. It was unusual to meet a woman who made no effort to use her physical assets to attract him—a novelty compared to the old days. And she had obviously never heard of him, though this was not surprising. His career had been cut short before it reached the heights once hoped for.

Katherine remembered to have a word with Lidia on her way out again, and learned that there was a bathroom on the ground floor for visitors, which would be kept for her sole use during her stay.

'*Perfeito!*' Katherine said, smiling, having looked the word up in the pocket dictionary acquired for the trip. She settled down to work with new zest now the first stage of cleaning was over.

With a canvas in dirtier condition Katherine would have repeated the cleaning process, but due to the time factor she moved straight on to the next stage. Beginning on a section on the subject's coat, she set down a piece of card with a small window cut in it, then dipped a cotton wool bud in acetone and set to work within the aperture. The effect was electrifying. The overpaint had obviously been applied well within the past fifty years or so because it dissolved like magic within the tiny frame, revealing much lighter pigment underneath. Katherine went on moving the cardboard frame fraction by fraction, applying acetone as she went, and then took a photograph to email to James for his verdict, and sat back in one of the chairs for a break.

James rang her almost at once. 'You *are* having an interesting time. That's genuine eighteenth century pigment by the look of it. But ten to one you're going to find damage somewhere. Ask de Sousa whether you should carry on.'

'He's already talking about my staying on here to do that, if you're agreeable.'

'Is he now?' There was a pause. 'As a matter of interest, how old is he, and is there a Senhora de Sousa?'

'He's thirty-something, and if there is a wife she doesn't live here. Bye for now.'

A shadow fell over the steps as she disconnected and Katherine turned, to find Roberto watching her.

'*Perdoa-me*, it was not my intention to listen, but—'

'You heard what I said.' Her face heated.

He nodded. 'Your lover is jealous that you are living in my house?'

'I was talking to James Massey!'

His face relaxed slightly. 'Your employer was asking about me?'

'Yes. Sorry about that.'

'*Por que?* It is natural he feels responsible for you.' Roberto turned as Jorge arrived with a tray. 'I shall join you here for tea.'

She raised an eyebrow. 'And check on what I've been doing?'

'*Exatamente*,' he agreed.

'It's not a lot. I go very carefully at this stage.'

Roberto leaned to inspect the small area she indicated. 'You photographed only this small section?' he said, astonished, and sat down next to her to look over her shoulder. 'I can see that the paint is lighter there. That is important?'

'Crucial. James agrees that it looks like genuine eighteenth century pigment.' Katherine filled both cups as she began. 'So do you wish to ship the painting to James's restorer right away, or shall I carry on until I have a clearer idea of what's under the overpaint before you send it away for repair?'

'Repair?' he said sharply.

She nodded. 'There may be damage of some kind, rips in the canvas, even holes.'

Roberto blenched. '*Deus!* If so, is repair possible?'

'Oh, yes. The restorer James uses is a miracle worker.'

'But if you remove this overpaint, Katherine, could you then give your opinion on the artist?'

'I could probably do that much, yes. But it would

just be an opinion,' she warned. 'So do you wish me to carry on?'

'Yes. It would please me very much if you continue until our young man is revealed in his true colours. Further decisions can be left until then.' Roberto got up. 'I shall leave you to your detective work.' He turned at the top of the steps. 'When your Mr Massey rings again, tell him the only Senhora de Sousa in my life is my mother. I once had a wife for a short time many years ago it is true, but alas no longer.'

Katherine winced. 'I'm so sorry—'

'No, you mistake me,' he said coolly. 'Mariana is not dead. She divorced me.' His eyes locked on hers. 'Also tell Mr Massey that you are safe here. No harm will come to you in my house.'

Face still hot after he left, she found it hard for a while to resume her usual concentration. Next time James rang she would make sure no one was in earshot. But, to her intense annoyance, it was Andrew who rang a few minutes later.

'Why the hell haven't you called me, Katherine?' he demanded. 'Surely you knew I would be worried?'

'I texted to say I'd arrived—'

'Then obviously forgot all about me!'

'You could have rung me if you were that concerned.'

'It was your place to ring *me*, Katherine, in the circumstances. You took off with barely a word of apology about spoiling the trip to Glyndebourne!'

She gritted her teeth. 'For heaven's sake, Andrew, James was ill and needed me to take his place. It was an emergency! We can go to Glyndebourne any time.'

'I see,' he said stiffly. 'James is obviously far more important to you than I am.'

Enough, thought Katherine. 'I haven't got time for this—'

'No! Please. Don't ring off,' he broke in, his tone suddenly conciliatory. 'I'm sorry, darling—'

'Can't talk any more now; I must get on. Bye.' Before he could interrupt again, she switched off her phone.

Katherine felt so annoyed it took a while to get back into her groove again, but at last she began working at her usual speed, until a combination of fading light and a message from Roberto via Jorge brought her to a halt.

'Senhor Roberto says perhaps finish now, *Doutora*,' said the man tactfully.

Katherine looked at her watch and sat back with a sigh as she removed her goggles and mask. 'I'll just clear up and cover the painting. Can you ask where it should be stored overnight, please?'

'*Sim, senhora*. Then I come back for your equipment.'

'You can leave the work box and tripod here overnight. I'll just take my camera and laptop.' She grimaced as she indicated the overflowing bag of swabs. 'Sorry about the mess.'

He shook his head, smiling. '*Nao importa*.'

Katherine put her solvents and tools back in the box, then put her glasses on and turned back to the painting with mounting optimism. Tomorrow, she promised the young man silently, I'll know for certain who painted you. Maybe—though this is a long shot—I'll even know who you are.

'Dr Lister,' said Roberto, coming up the summerhouse steps, 'you have worked too long—' He stopped dead as he saw the painting.

'Don't worry. I know it looks a mess like that, but by the time I've finished your boy will look a lot better, I promise,' she assured him and began to wrap the canvas very carefully. 'Where will you put him overnight?'

'In the *sala*. Come, I shall show you.' Roberto took the canvas from her so reverently Katherine had to hide a smile.

'When you first saw the painting, what appealed to you about it?' she asked as they crossed the hall. 'It's not everyone's cup of tea.'

'Something about the subject's face called to me very strongly, even through the medium of the Internet. I always visited art galleries whenever I could because painted portraits fascinate me. These days, I visit them through my computer.' He paused before double doors at the end. 'If you will open them, *por favor*, Katherine.'

She went before him into a large, formally furnished drawing room, where the painting to one side of the fireplace caught Katherine's eye. The subject, a young girl in a gauzy white dress, smiled dreamily from the canvas. 'Who is she?'

'I do not know her provenance,' said Roberto with regret. He crossed the room to lay his canvas down on an escritoire. 'The label was "Portrait of a Young Girl", artist unknown, and therefore cost little. She is charming, but to me she looks lonely.'

'So you bought the young man as company for her?'

He nodded. 'He would look good facing her, no?'

'He will do when he's been restored. Have you never researched your pretty lady?'

'No. When I bought her I was *ocupado*—busy—and had no time.'

'Whereas you've gone to great expense as well as time to find out more about your young man!'

Roberto nodded. 'Because I hope I know the artist.'

'Who?' Katherine demanded.

His eyes danced, lighting up his face to an extent which made her blink. 'Ah, no! I await your opinion before I risk mine, *Doutora*.'

'Fair enough—you're paying.'

'Because this is true, I insist you rest before dinner.' He gave her a commanding look. 'Jorge goes with me tomorrow, but I have told Lidia to make sure you do not work too hard while I am gone.'

Had he indeed! 'I get totally absorbed and forget the time,' she admitted. 'But when you see your young man again tomorrow he should look very different. Will you be away all day?'

He shook his head. 'I shall return in time to dine with you.'

'This is a beautiful room,' she remarked as they moved towards the door.

'But formal, no? I prefer my *apartamento* at the back of the house. I can be untidy there without risking Lidia's wrath.'

She laughed. 'That's hard to imagine!'

Roberto nodded in wry agreement. 'I am fortunate such good people care for me.' He paused as he held the door open for her. 'While you are here they will care for you also, and not just because it is my wish. Both Jorge and Lidia think you are a very charming young lady.'

To Katherine's surprise, she felt her face flush. 'How very sweet of them.'

Roberto regarded her with pleasure. '*Que maravilha!* A lady who can blush!'

'Not something I do very often,' she assured him, embarrassed.

'Perhaps it is because you are tired. Rest now. You wish to dine on the *varanda* again?'

'Yes, please.' She walked quickly up the stairs, but this time turned to look down before heading for her room and, to her annoyance, found her face heating again as he gave that graceful bow of his before turning away.

In her room, Katherine stripped off her clothes impatiently. This blushing business had to stop right now. Overpoweringly attractive though her client might be, she was here purely on business. She ran a deep bath instead of a shower and lay back in it, frowning. It was only twenty-four hours since her first encounter with Roberto de Sousa. He had been put out at first because she was a woman, yet now, unless she was mistaken, he was beginning to enjoy her company. Of course that might not be such a big deal from her point of view. Maybe he'd not had much contact with women since his accident, due to the scar he was so bitter about. Yet she was so used to it, already she hardly noticed it. He must have been outrageously handsome without it— probably had to beat women off with a stick. But she was here purely to do a job. And tomorrow, by the time he came home from wherever he was spending the day, she should know whether her instinct was right about the artist. If it was, her job would be done and she could ask for transport to Viana do Castelo as her reward, a prospect which was not nearly as pleasant as it should have been.

A rest on her bed during the day was a novelty to Katherine. A lie in on Sundays was the nearest she ever came to one. But life here at the Quinta das Montanhas was dangerously addictive. It would be all too easy to get into the habit. She wondered if Roberto did the same. He'd mentioned an apartment at the back of the house so perhaps he had a ground floor bedroom—easier for his leg than tackling the beautiful stairs all the time. She was deeply curious to know what had happened, but it was pointless to get too interested in him. Once she'd finished here she would never meet Roberto de Sousa again. Besides, a man who came from a cattle-ranching background in Brazil, with a holiday home like Quinta das Montanhas at his disposal, lived on a different planet from Katherine Lister, art historian and researcher.

This conclusion did not rule out looking a bit more appealing to have dinner with Roberto. Katherine considered the sexy green dress, but in the end went for ivory linen trousers worn with heels and a bronze silk tunic. She let her newly washed hair hang loose to her shoulders, added a touch more make-up than before and, after a moment's hesitation, decided against her glasses. She was ready and waiting when a pretty dark girl knocked on her door.

'Pascoa,' she announced, smiling shyly as she pointed to herself. 'Senhor Roberto waits, *Doutora.*'

'*Obrigada,* Pascoa,' said Katherine, smiling, and followed the girl downstairs to the hall, where Jorge was waiting. 'Good evening,' she greeted him.

'*Boa tarde, Doutora.* Lidia is cooking the *carne de porco,*' he explained as they crossed the hall to the veranda. He opened the doors and ushered her outside. Roberto was leaning in his usual place at a pillar, his eyes on the garden. He turned quickly as she joined him, his eyes wide in involuntary shock which acted like balm on her bruised ego.

'You look…most charming, Doctor,' he said when he'd regained the power of speech. 'It is hard to believe you have been working all day.'

'Not all day. I've been lazing on the bed in the guest

room for the past hour.' She smiled. 'Something I never do at home.'

Roberto pulled out a chair for her and gestured to the wine resting in its silver bucket. 'You would like this again?'

'I would. Thank you.'

'So how do you spend your evenings in England?' he asked as he filled their glasses.

'At home alone, I make supper, do some ironing, watch television or read.' Katherine pulled a face. 'Nothing very exciting.'

'And other times someone takes you out to dinner?' he asked, easing himself down in the chair across the table.

'Yes. Or I go out with friends—female gender,' she added.

'But one of your friends is a man, *nao e*?'

'More than one.' She grinned. 'I share a house with two of them; an arrangement much disapproved of by the man who currently takes me out to dinner.'

Roberto's lips twitched as he offered her morsels of toast spread with paté. 'He is jealous?'

Katherine thought about it. 'Andrew wants me to move into his house instead.'

His eyes gleamed between enviable lashes. 'Do you wish to do that?'

She shook her head. 'Absolutely not. My house really is mine. My father left it to me. And my tenants pay me good rent to share it, and the three of us get together with other friends occasionally for a drink or a meal, which I enjoy very much. Great paté, by the way,' she added.

'*Pate de sardinha*. Lidia made it, so eat more.'

Roberto leaned to top up her glass. 'You say your father left the house to you? He is dead?'

Katherine nodded soberly. 'Yes. My mother died when I was little. Dad brought me up single-handed and did a fantastic job of it.' She cleared her throat. 'Then, just after my eighteenth birthday, he had a major heart attack, which killed him.'

'*Que tragedia*,' he said softly. 'You have other relatives?'

'Dad's younger sister came to live with me at the time, but eventually Charlotte met Sam Napier, the architect she's married to now.' Katherine smiled warmly. 'They wanted me to make my home with them, but though I was deeply grateful to them I preferred to stay on at the house. Two of my fellow students were looking for somewhere to live so, with fantastic help from Sam, modifications were made to create three separate flats. The arrangement works so well Hugh and Alastair are still with me.'

'And you do not wish to leave to join your lover,' he remarked.

'He's just a *friend*,' she said irritably, then caught her lip in her teeth.

Roberto eyed her in wry amusement. 'You do not offend me, Doctor. It is I who do so with my talk of a lover. But that is how this man regards himself, *nao e*?'

'I met him only a short time ago,' she protested.

'It takes only a moment to fall in love!'

She frowned, taken aback by the sudden descent into the personal. 'From impartial observation I've noticed that it takes only a moment to fall back out again, too!'

All talk of love was abandoned as Jorge arrived to

set down a platter of succulent pork slices flanked by
an array of vegetables and a side dish of sautéed potato
slices.

'This smells heavenly!' Katherine said reverently.

'We shall serve ourselves, Jorge,' said Roberto, and
smiled at him. 'Thank Lidia for the *batatinhas*.'

'What are they?' asked Katherine as she helped
herself.

'The potatoes.' He smiled. 'They are my weakness
prepared this way, but at one time I could not eat as
many as I wished.'

'You had to diet?' she said, astonished. 'That's hard
to believe.'

'I had to take care with what I ate,' he assured her.
'Now, I do not.'

Katherine longed to know more as she went on with
her dinner. 'I always have to watch my weight,' she said
sadly.

'*E verdade?*' he said, surprised. 'Why?'

'Otherwise, my clothes don't fit. So, as a basic matter
of economy, I try not to eat chocolate, and puddings,
and so on.'

Roberto leaned to refill her glass. 'The wine will do
no harm, I promise. Not,' he added, 'that I think the
doces would harm you either, Katherine.' He shot a look
at her. 'You allow me use of your name?'

'Of course,' she said quickly, annoyed because she
felt flustered. 'I was a bit overweight as a teenager, right
up until my father died, when I found that grief was far
more effective than any diet.'

His eyes softened. 'You were close to him.'

'Yes. I even followed his career choice. He lectured
in art history. He met James Massey when they were at
university.'

'And now you work for your father's friend.'

She stiffened. 'Which is absolutely nothing to do with nepotism—'

'I am sure it is not,' Roberto assured her hastily. 'But it would please your father to know that his daughter works in safe keeping with his old friend, I think.'

'True. But I earn my salary, Senhor Sousa.'

He sighed. 'Now I have offended you. *Perdao!* It was not my intention. *Agora*, please eat more or Lidia will also be offended.'

Katherine went on with her meal for a moment or two, then decided to take the plunge. 'May I ask about your accident?'

Roberto tensed as though about to refuse, then shrugged, his eyes bitter. 'I was in a car crash, and fortunate to survive. But for a while it was hard to convince myself of that.'

'Because you were in such pain?'

His smile was sardonic as he refilled their glasses. 'Also because of vanity.'

'Vanity?'

Roberto nodded. 'My broken leg was in full length cast, I had bad concussion, black eyes, broken nose and teeth, and half my face held together with stitches. Frankenstein's monster was prettier.'

'Sounds as though you were lucky to be alive,' said Katherine with a shiver. 'Did you have any passengers?'

'I was the passenger, Katherine. When the car swerved off the road on a bend the driver leapt clear. The car did not burst into flames as in the movies, *gracas a Deus*, but it suffered much damage as it crashed down a hillside into trees.'

'What happened to the chauffeur?'

His eyes hardened to obsidian. 'The driver was a woman, Katherine. I learned later that she had only a sprained wrist, also *contusoes*—bruises because bushes broke her fall. She ran from the scene in panic. It was left to a passing motorist to ring for help. I knew nothing of this. I woke up in hospital, with my parents by my bed.'

'What a horrible shock for them to see you so badly injured.' Katherine's eyes were warm with sympathy, which hardened to something else entirely at the thought of the woman who'd left Roberto to his fate. 'And the lady driving the car?'

'She rang me eventually at the hospital, begging me to say *I* was driving,' he said without expression. 'But the answer was negative because the police already knew I was not driving. It took much time to free me from the passenger seat of my car.'

'Why would she ask you to do that?'

'We had a disagreement over dinner, and because of it we had taken more wine than was wise, so I insisted on ringing for a taxi. But she was in a great hurry to get away and snatched my keys.' He looked suddenly grim. 'We were still arguing in the car because she would not fasten her seat belt.'

'So she was able to jump clear and leave you to your fate.' Katherine shook her head in disbelief. 'After that, she actually expected you to say you were driving?'

'Yes. But even if I had been fool enough to agree, I could not lie because the police knew the facts, also that Elena had spent the evening with me from the publicity shots taken on our way to dinner. When the truth came out she was fired from a television soap she was appearing in. She had a minor role as an innocent young girl desired by a married man.' He smiled sardonically.

'When it was known that Elena Cabral had not only been drinking but jumped from the car to leave me to my fate, the press crucified her.'

'Where did this happen?'

'Near Porto. There were horrific pictures of me in the press.' His mouth twisted. 'My parents wanted to fly me straight home, but living at the Estancia would have meant much travelling for treatment, so I preferred to remain here to recover in the Minho. My father could stay only a short time with me, but my mother left only recently.' He smiled. 'My parents do not like to be separated for long, so finally I insisted I was well enough for her to leave me.'

Katherine gazed at him in silence. With an Estancia as the family home, the Quinta for holidays, and soap-actress girlfriends in the mix, Roberto de Sousa lived a very different life from hers—or from anyone she knew. 'Thank you for telling me,' she said at last. 'I hope it wasn't painful to talk about it.'

'Not to such a sympathetic listener.' He smiled suddenly, the effect like a light going on in a darkened room. He looked up as Jorge appeared to clear away. 'Tell Lidia the meal was *gostoso*, as usual.'

Katherine nodded in fervent agreement and the man smiled, pleased.

'You would like dessert, *Doutora*?'

'No, thank you,' she said with regret. 'Could I have some tea, please?'

'*Pois e!* I will also bring *café* for the *Patrao*.'

Roberto smiled wryly as the man left. 'I must take the back seat with Jorge now you are here, Katherine.'

She laughed. 'I don't think so. Both Jorge and Lidia obviously think the world of you.'

'My mother told them to take good care of me—and

they do.' He sighed. 'Lidia feeds me well, and Jorge is a slave driver when I exercise, also he will drive me to Viana do Castelo tomorrow for a check-up with a doctor and session with the physio. I prefer to drive myself but for hospital visits Jorge insists he does,' he added loudly as the man came back with a tray.

Jorge smiled. 'Dona Teresa *mandou*,' he said simply.

'He said my mother ordered him to do it, so nothing I say will make any difference,' said Roberto, resigned.

'Thank you.' Katherine smiled warmly at Jorge as he set the tray in front of her.

'*De nada, Doutora. Boa noite.*'

'So, Katherine,' said Roberto when they were alone, 'will you solve our mystery tomorrow?'

'I certainly hope so, or you'll have spent a lot of money for nothing in getting me here!'

'And will pay more for you to stay longer!' He rolled his eyes. 'That does not sound good, I think. You must make allowances for my English.'

She shook her head. 'You speak it very well. So do Lidia and Jorge to a lesser extent, though with much stronger accents than yours.'

'We sound different because I am Brazilian and I was taught at school. Also I have travelled much. They are Portuguese and have not, but they have learned some basic English to deal with visitors to the Quinta das Montanhas. It is rented out for holidays for part of the year—the reason why I built the pool and the tennis court,' Roberto added.

Katherine stared at him in astonishment. 'You can actually bear to let the general public use your home?'

'When I am not here, yes.' He shrugged. 'I am a practical man, Katherine. People pay very well to stay here, and it provides work for my *empregados* and money for the maintenance of the house. But not so many visitors are booked this season because I stay at the Quinta myself.'

'Does Lidia cook for the guests?'

'I do not allow this. Breakfast only is provided. There are good restaurants in the area.' His jaw clenched. 'For obvious reasons, I do not patronise them.'

'I'm not surprised with someone like Lidia to cook for you!'

He smiled crookedly. 'You do not allow me self-pity.'

'No, indeed,' she said briskly. 'You could so easily have been killed in the accident, yet here you are in this beautiful place, waited on hand and foot.'

'*E verdade*,' he mocked. 'I lack nothing—except company.'

She eyed him warily. 'Surely you could have help with that?'

He shook his head. 'Until now, I felt no lack. I did not realise how lonely I had been until I gained the privilege of *your* company.'

Katherine's eyes narrowed.

'Do not misunderstand,' he said swiftly. 'I am trying to say—very badly—that I would not be human if I did not enjoy the company of a woman who is expert in the subject which interests me most. Who is a most attractive woman,' he added. 'You cannot deny this, Katherine.'

'I'm passable,' she admitted warily.

'But you restrain that beautiful hair and wear severe clothes as disguise.' The dark eyes fastened on hers with intent. 'Have no fear. I expect nothing more than your expertise and your conversation, Katherine.'

'I know that, Senhor Sousa!' she retorted, furious that he imagined she'd thought otherwise.

'Now I have angered you again,' he said, resigned.

Katherine pulled herself together, and returned to safe common ground. 'Reverting to the subject that interests you so much, I find something very familiar about your young gentleman.'

Roberto's eyes lit up. 'You have seen him before?'

'I must have. I certainly know him from somewhere.' She sighed in frustration. 'If James were here he'd probably take one look and instantly tell you the identity of both the subject and the artist, and when and where it was painted.'

He chuckled. 'I am sure Senhor Massey is a most interesting man, but I cannot be sorry that he sent you to me instead, Katherine. Tell me,' he went on, with an abrupt change of subject, 'does this friend of yours ring you every night?'

She blinked. 'No. No, he doesn't. Andrew's not very happy with me right now. I cancelled a night at the opera with him at Glyndebourne so I could help James out by coming here to look at your painting.' Her eyes flashed. 'He feels I let him down.'

Roberto frowned. 'He is a fool, this man.'

'I'm beginning to agree,' she sighed. 'He's charming and good company, but he got hugely stroppy when I insisted that helping James out was far more important than a trip to the opera.'

'Stroppy is angry?'

'Yes, but in a childish way. *Most* unappealing,' she added, eyes kindling.

'So you will not marry him, then.'

'Good heavens, no!' Katherine stared at him, astonished. 'I've never had the least intention of that. Neither has Andrew. My insistence on running my own life would be far too big a problem for him, for a start. And because most men are like him, I don't see marriage in my future at all.'

Roberto nodded morosely. 'Marriage is difficult enough when both partners want the same things. When they do not it is disaster. My wife begged me to give up my way of life for her. When I refused she left me.'

'She didn't like living at your ranch?'

'No.' His eyes shuttered. 'Katherine, will you have a little cognac for a nightcap?'

She shook her head, and refilled her teacup. 'No, thanks. I'll just drink this tea, then I'm off to bed. Shall I give you more coffee, or would it keep you awake?'

'I am not good at sleeping, whether I drink coffee or not.' His mouth turned down. 'And that is fact, not self-pity, Doutora Lister.'

She frowned as she poured. 'Does your leg keep you awake?'

He nodded. 'But it is improving. When I first came here I relied on the *muletas*.' He thought for a moment. 'Supports—crutches, yes? Later, I walked with two sticks, now I need only one. Soon,' he said with confidence, 'I shall walk unaided.'

'Amen to that,' said Katherine gravely, and got up. 'Goodnight, then.'

He rose to his feet with effort he ignored. '*Boa noite*, Katherine. *Dorme bem*.'

CHAPTER THREE

A HARD, exciting day's work, followed by dinner with a host who was no longer so hostile, resulted in such a good night's sleep Katherine woke next morning to find her breakfast had arrived.

Pascoa smiled apologetically as she deposited the tray. '*Bom dia, Senhora*. I wake you?'

'A good thing you did,' Katherine said ruefully, looking at her watch. 'I'm late.'

The girl pulled out a chair. 'Enjoy,' she said shyly.

'I shall. *Obrigada*, Pascoa.'

While Katherine was eating the limousine come into view below her windows and went gliding down the drive. Roberto, it seemed, was already on his way. She felt a pang of sympathy as she pictured the day in front of him. He might not even be up to dining with her tonight, which would be a shame. If her work went really well today, there might not be any other tête-à-tête suppers before she left. Which, for obvious reasons, was probably just as well.

'Senhor Roberto say not work too hard,' said Lidia firmly when she came to collect the tray. She smiled. 'But you will, *nao*?'

'Probably,' admitted Katherine, smiling.

'He left painting on *varanda*.'

'*Obrigada*, Lidia.'

'*De nada.*'

Later, Katherine frowned at the face in the portrait as she laid the painting on the blanket. 'Where *have* I seen you before?' She gathered her tools and settled down to work, her excitement mounting as she gradually revealed folds in the man's coat. She let out a whistle when she removed the overpaint from the cravat and discovered not only a more modest neck cloth, but a series of small rips, roughly sealed with filler. Confident that James' favourite restorer would deal with those, Katherine carried on undeterred, eager to get to the face. Lidia brought her back to earth with a jolt a few minutes later when she arrived with a coffee tray.

'Rest now, *Doutora*,' she said firmly.

Katherine stretched, feeling guilty when she looked at her watch. 'Is that the time already?'

Lidia smiled as she poured coffee. 'You love your work.'

'I do indeed.' She drank gratefully. 'Wonderful. I needed that.'

'Lunch *numa hora*,' said the woman, holding up one finger.

A phone call from Andrew interrupted Katherine soon afterwards.

'Hi,' she said briefly.

'Ah, the elusive Dr Lister herself,' he said with sarcasm. 'You've actually deigned to answer your phone.'

'I had forgotten to turn it on—sorry.'

'So you should be. I was worried, woman!'

Woman? 'Absolutely no need, Andrew. I'm just caught up in the work I'm doing here.'

'Revealing a lost Rembrandt to the world, I suppose!'

Her eyes flashed coldly at the sneer in his voice. 'No. Not a Rembrandt—but something very interesting, just the same, both to me and the client. Look, I'm at a rather tricky stage right now.'

'Ring me later then.'

'All right. Half seven?'

'Fine. I'll make a point of hanging on before going out tonight.'

Later, Katherine was so eager to start on the painted face she swallowed most of her salad lunch without tasting it. She worked with mounting anticipation, and felt a warm tide of relief flood through her as she identified unmistakable brush strokes. Lighter tones began to appear in the dark hair clubbed back from the face, and at last she gave a crow of pure triumph as a signature flash of light on a stray hair provided the last piece of the puzzle.

'Well?' she demanded, when James rang in response to her update.

'One of his minor early works, of course,' he said jubilantly, 'but even without seeing it in the flesh, I'm sure it's Gainsborough.'

She let out a deep heartfelt sigh. 'Hallelujah, so am I!'

'Of course you are. Have you told the client?'

'No. He's away for the day, so I'll break the glad news when he gets back.'

'Well done. And once you've done that, Katherine, there's no need for you to hang on there any longer,' he pointed out.

'No. No, there isn't,' she agreed quietly, feeling suddenly flat. 'Actually, James, unless it's going to cause problems at the gallery, I'd like to stay until my scheduled flight on Sunday. I fancy a day or two in the sun.'

'Fine by me. You finished the job sooner than I expected. Besides, Judith's finger is firmly on the pulse at the gallery.' He chuckled. 'I'm such an impossible patient she's glad to get away from me, poor darling.'

'Then hurry up and get well! Thanks, James. I'll let you know when the painting's on its way.'

Katherine closed her phone and sat staring at the face in the painting. She was pretty sure it hadn't turned up during past research, so why did he look so familiar? He was young. No more than twenty, at a guess. She jumped as Lidia rattled a tea tray behind her.

'You stop now, yes?'

Katherine nodded. 'I'm dying for some tea.'

Lidia put the tray on the other table and came to take a look. She shook her head in surprise. '*Engracado*—he look like Senhor Roberto.'

Katherine's eyes opened wide in sudden comprehension. 'Of course! You're right, Lidia. That's why he looks so familiar. I should have seen it before—the eyes and those eyebrows. Not the mouth so much, and the hair is straight, but there's definitely a resemblance. When will Senhor Sousa be home, do you think?'

'*Cinco horas*, maybe.' Lidia held up five fingers. 'Jorge telephone when they leave.'

'In that case I'll drink this tea, then have a bath. I'll take the painting upstairs with me.' Katherine smiled sheepishly. 'I want it to be a surprise.'

Lidia laughed. 'A very nice surprise!'

Katherine carried the painting upstairs later and laid it on the chest at the foot of the bed, too tired afterwards to risk staying long in the bath. She wrapped her wet

hair in a towel so she could stretch out on the bed, and
went straight to sleep.

She shot upright when her phone rang, rolling her eyes
as she saw the time. 'Hi, Andrew,' she said, resigned.

'Do you know what time it is?' he said furiously. 'I'm
due at a legal dinner tonight!'

'Then you'd better be on your way. Sorry. I've been
working so hard I fell asleep after my bath.'

'For God's sake, how hard can it be, dabbing at a
painting all day—?'

Katherine cut him off mid rant. Andrew had always
claimed he found her work fascinating. Not any more,
apparently. She got up quickly and, after a moment's
hesitation, zipped herself into the green dress which did
such good things for her shape. She brushed her hair into
a shining bell and did her face, fastened gold studs in
her ears, then switched on her phone again. No point in
cutting herself off from the world just because Andrew
was being a pain. It rang immediately, but this time her
caller was Rachel Frears, her room mate at university
and close friend ever since.

'What's up with Andrew?' Rachel demanded. 'He
just rang me in a right old tizz. Says you hung up on
him. Has he been a naughty boy? He even asked me to
apologise for him.'

'That's new!' Andrew and Rachel had not taken to
each other. 'He's annoyed because I took off to Portugal
without him, and I've been working too hard since to
ring him.'

'Does he demand regular phone sex, then?'

Katherine hooted. 'He'd be lucky! How's it going in
the world of breaking news, Miss Hotshot?'

'I wish! I've just done a riveting features item on the
ten hottest dress shapes for autumn. By the way, how

come your work takes you to the beach, while mine keeps me here in an office?'

'I'm not at the beach. I'm in the Minho in the north.'

'So who's this man who's paying you to have a holiday, then?'

'Hey—I'm working my socks off!'

'Which doesn't answer my question, Dr Lister.'

'I'll give details when I get home—' Katherine broke off at a knock on the door. 'Got to go—dinnertime. I'll ring you before I leave.'

Katherine left Pascoa at the foot of the stairs and made for the veranda unescorted. The click of her heels on the polished stone floor brought Roberto into the hall to meet her, a look in his eyes which sent her pulse into overdrive.

'Good evening, Katherine. You look very beautiful.' So beautiful it was hard to remember that this goddess was the intellectual historian he'd found so daunting at their first meeting.

'Thank you,' she said, outwardly composed.

'How was your day?'

'Very busy.' She eyed him closely in the soft lighting on the veranda, but he looked no more tired than usual. 'How did you get on with your doctor?'

'He was pleased with my progress,' he said with satisfaction, and filled two wine glasses. 'And the *fisioterapia* was not such torture today.' He touched his glass to hers and smiled. 'Perhaps because your company this evening is my reward.'

Not sure how to answer that, Katherine sat in the chair he pulled out for her. 'I'm glad you had a good day. I did too.'

Roberto sat beside her, his eyes bright with anticipation. 'You have made progress?'

She nodded and jumped to her feet. 'I should have brought the painting down with me—I'll just run up and get it.'

Roberto got up more slowly. 'Please do not run, Katherine. Jorge is not here, and if you fall I cannot pick you up.'

And this, Katherine could tell, bothered him enormously. 'I'll just walk quickly,' she promised and hurried out into the hall.

Roberto followed and crossed to the foot of the stairs, watching as Katherine mounted them as though she had wings on her heels, the clinging fabric of her dress outlining her shape so exactly his mouth watered. His lips tightened. If she had finished work on the painting she would soon leave. He must find some way to persuade her to stay longer. He smiled as he saw her reappear, moving slowly now, as though she carried the Holy Grail. She descended the stairs with care, her eyes glowing over the canvas.

'Here he is. Shall we take him into the *sala* under the lights right away? Otherwise Lidia will be serving dinner.'

'*Sim senhora!*' Roberto limped rapidly across the hall to turn on the overhead lights in the *sala*. Katherine unveiled the canvas and put it on the desk, Roberto's indrawn breath as they leaned over it all the reward she needed.

'I've cleaned him up as much as I could,' she explained. 'Our top restorer will remove the stubborn bits with her scalpel. Then she'll make the necessary repairs and top the whole thing off by replicating—as near as possible—the original glaze finish. There's no signature, which was quite common, but James shares my opinion. Even from just the photograph I sent him he thinks there's no doubt about the artist.'

'Dare I guess?' he said huskily, his eyes glued to the canvas.

'Please do.'

Roberto took in a deep breath and turned to face her. 'Thomas Gainsborough?'

Katherine's radiant smile was all the answer he needed. He let out a shout of triumph and caught her in his arms and kissed her. His arms fell away at once and he stood back, a wry smile on his lips.

'I beg your pardon, Katherine.'

'No problem,' she assured him breathlessly. 'I could have kissed someone myself when James confirmed it.'

For a moment she thought Roberto would kiss her again, but he turned away to look at the picture.

'Lidia thinks he looks like you,' Katherine told him.

'*E verdade?*' He eyed the portrait in surprise. 'You agree with her?'

'I do now. At first I just thought he looked familiar, and couldn't think why. I was sure I'd never turned him up during my research, so it was only when Lidia commented on it that I saw the resemblance.'

Roberto smiled crookedly. 'He is much prettier than me.' He looked closely at the painted face. 'But he is familiar, *com certeza*. The first time I saw him I felt this, even disguised with such dark paint.' He shook his head. 'Come. We must return; Lidia will not be pleased if dinner is spoiled.'

Katherine hardly knew what she ate in her excitement, which Roberto shared, all vestiges of his normal melancholy gone as they discussed the painting.

'Will you keep it?' asked Katherine at one stage.

He shook his head. 'Now the provenance is confirmed I cannot hang it here because of security. Instead, I shall give our young man away as a very special Christmas present.'

'So your maiden will have to languish alone in the *sala*.'

'No, Katherine, she will be part of the same present. I will hang some other painting in the *sala*.'

Some present! Katherine hotly envied the lucky recipient, and looked up with a smile as Jorge came to clear away.

'Would the *senhora* like dessert?' he enquired.

Since the *senhora* had barely noticed the excellent fish she'd eaten, Katherine nodded, smiling. 'Yes, please.'

'You have not eaten dessert before,' observed Roberto when Jorge had gone.

'Tonight I'm in the mood to celebrate,' she told him, eyes sparkling.

Roberto looked at her in silence for a moment, his euphoria dimmed.

'What's the matter?' Katherine demanded. 'Are you in pain?'

He shook his head. 'I realise that now your work is done you will leave.'

There was a pause while Jorge appeared with a custard tart for Katherine, and then left them to a silence so intense it was tangible.

'Actually,' said Katherine, when she could bear it no longer, 'I'm not going home just yet. It was always my intention to go on to Viana do Castelo for a couple of days once my mission here was accomplished.'

Roberto's eyebrows rose. 'You are staying at a hotel there?'

'I'm not booked anywhere. I had no idea how long I'd be here at the Quinta. But if there was time afterwards I planned to ask for transport to Viana do Castelo and chance finding somewhere for the rest of my stay.'

'When is your flight?' he demanded.

'Sunday.'

He gave her the rare illuminating smile that lit up his entire face. 'Do you have a reason for staying in Viana?'

She shook her head. 'Only that it's not far from here, and from the guidebook it seemed like a pleasant place to recover. I've concentrated so hard on the painting I fancy a couple of days doing nothing but swim and sunbathe before getting back to the gallery.'

'But you could do those things here!' He leaned forward. 'Katherine, stay here at the Quinta until you fly home.'

She gazed at him in silence, her pulse racing.

'All I ask is your company, I swear.' He waited, but when she said nothing he slumped back in his chair. 'Forget I asked. Jorge shall drive you to Viana whenever you wish.'

She cleared her throat. 'Couldn't *you* drive me there tomorrow?'

His eyes narrowed. 'Why?'

'To ship the painting to James.'

'Unnecessary. A courier will collect it.'

'Pity.' Katherine smiled at him. 'I thought we might have lunch somewhere afterwards.'

Roberto's eyes narrowed. 'Is that a condition for your stay here?'

'No. Of course not.' She looked at him very directly. 'I thought it might do you good to get out for a while.'

'I do get out—to the hospital.' His smile was grim. 'I have faced danger many times in the past, but now I look like a monster I am not brave enough to eat in public, Katherine.'

'You look nothing like a monster,' she said flatly. 'But I understand how you feel.'

His eyes locked with hers. 'Then stay, Katherine.'

She looked at him in silence for a while and at last nodded, smiling wryly. 'Yes, I will. Though I'm not sure I should. Life will seem very humdrum back at home afterwards.'

'But you have a lover there.'

'Once and for all, Andrew is not my lover.' Her eyes flashed. 'And after the fuss he's made about my coming here, I'm not sure I even think of him as a friend any more.'

'Yet he wants you to live with him, no?'

'Because he thinks it's a sure way to get me to sleep with him,' she said; and regretted the words the moment they were out.

Roberto smiled broadly. 'Almost I pity this man. Because you will not do as he wishes, will you, Katherine?'

'No.' As she looked into Roberto's gleaming, heavily lashed eyes it was clear that the relationship Andrew wanted was never going to happen.

'He cannot be the first man eager to be your lover,' Roberto said, taking some cheese with sudden appetite.

'True. But there've been relatively few relationships in my life.'

Roberto eyed her questioningly. 'Why, Katherine?'

It was not a habit of hers to discuss her personal life, but he seemed genuinely interested in her so why not? Once she left Portugal she would never see him again. 'I need to like and respect a man before I get physically close to him. So when I was a student I was considered weird because I was selective, rather than a serial bed hopper.'

His eyes lit with laughter. 'The men you selected were greatly envied, no?'

'There weren't that many! I was just as happy with friends of my own sex, one of whom, Rachel Frears, is now engaged to Alastair, my tenant.' She sighed. 'They will naturally want to move somewhere else together, so I'll soon be looking for someone to replace him.'

'This is necessary for you, financially?'

Katherine nodded matter-of-factly. 'I love my job, but the salary isn't huge, and to keep my house I need the rent from the flats.' She ate some of the tart, eyeing him curiously. 'Did you enjoy life as a student?'

'I did not go to college.' He waited. 'You do not ask me why?'

She shook her head. 'I feel privileged to know the truth about your accident, Roberto, but you don't have to tell me anything else.'

'At last you say my name!' He leaned nearer to touch her hand. 'You must surely wonder how I live here, in luxury, yet do nothing that entitles me to such a life.'

She sat very still as his fleeting touch sent her pulse haywire. 'I assumed that your parents are wealthy enough to make that possible.'

'This is true,' he agreed. 'But until the accident I worked hard on the Estancia. Then I came here to a friend's wedding and met Elena, who almost killed me.' He smiled mirthlessly. 'Fate is a cruel mistress, *nao e*? For the time being I am no help to anyone. But I am striving to get fit as quickly as my body will allow and soon,' he added fiercely, 'I shall go back to Brazil and relieve my father of the work involved in running Estancia Grande. It is my heritage,' he added simply.

It was later, after Jorge had bidden them goodnight, before Katherine asked the question she'd wanted to ask the moment Roberto brought the subject up.

'The danger you faced in the past—was it anything to do with the work you did on the Estancia?'

'No, it was not.' He smiled sardonically. 'But I worried my mother greatly.' He paused, eyeing her closely. 'Are you tired, Katherine?'

'Not in the least. I had a nap earlier on, so sleep won't come easily tonight.'

'Then will you walk with me in the moonlight?'

'I'd love to,' she said eagerly, and got up, holding out her hand to him.

Roberto took it in his as he got to his feet. As they passed the pillar at the top of the veranda steps he flicked a switch, and lamps lit up throughout the gardens.

'How lovely,' she said, delighted. 'If you'll consent to take my arm, Senhor Sousa, you won't need your stick.'

'It will be my great pleasure,' he assured her as they set out on the beautifully kept paths. 'I come here alone at night when I cannot sleep. But it must surely annoy you to walk so slowly?'

She chuckled. 'I admit that it did when I wanted to get back to work, but tonight it's good just to stroll in the night air. I'm in no rush to get to bed.'

While Roberto, with Katherine's fragrance surrounding him, suddenly burned to pick her up and rush her to *his* bed. With no hope of achieving this, he schooled his clamouring libido and concentrated on the feel of her arm linked in his and the pleasure of the moment instead. It was some time since he had been in such close proximity with a woman. Not that the women he'd known in the past, other than his mother and his young wife, had ever walked further than from his car into some expensive restaurant.

'Why did you chuckle?' asked Katherine, looking up at the profile outlined by the moonlight.

'It is not polite to talk of women I've known in the past, but it occurred to me that none of them would have agreed to a walk in the dark—or even in daylight.'

'Were there very many?'

'Enough.' He shrugged. 'I had money to spend. And until the accident I was not bad to look at.'

A bit of an understatement, thought Katherine, resisting the urge to move closer. 'Were they all actresses like the lady who crashed your car?'

'There were also models.'

No surprise there. 'But how did you meet them? You said your Estancia was a long way from the nearest town.'

'I was many years working away from home before I returned to work on the Estancia.'

'You're very mysterious about what you did in those years away,' remarked Katherine.

'It was nothing criminal,' Roberto assured her, and smiled as she exclaimed in delight as they reached the pool.

'How lovely it looks in the moonlight!' She made for a wrought iron bench at the far end. 'Shall we sit for a moment to admire it?'

'You are tactful and think I need to rest, no?' he said as they sat down.

'Not at all. The rest is for me in these heels.' She leaned back with a sigh of contentment. 'Do you have a pool on the Estancia?'

'Yes. My father is enlarging it, ready for when I go home. As you say,' he added wryly, 'I have much to be thankful for—more than I deserve.' He turned to look at Katherine. 'When my mother agreed to leave me here to recover she did not know that fate would send you to me.'

She looked away. 'It was James who sent me, not fate.'

He laughed softly. 'I prefer my version.'

'You speak very good English, Roberto.'

He shrugged. 'It was necessary for me to learn. But I can do nothing about my accent.'

'Nor should you—it's very attractive.' So attractive it sent shivers down her spine.

'I am pleased you think so,' he said, in a tone which made the shivering worse. 'You are cold, Katherine. We must return to the house.'

She stumbled as she got up and Roberto leapt to steady her, but his leg gave way and they fell back on the bench in a tangled heap, laughing breathlessly. His arms tightened. 'I must let you go,' said Roberto with regret. 'If I do not you will run away tomorrow, no?'

CHAPTER FOUR

IF SHE had any sense she would! 'Probably,' Katherine said lightly, 'so let's walk back to the house.'

Roberto got to his feet at once and held out his hand. As they walked slowly back, she would have given much to surrender to instinct and melt into Roberto's arms for the kiss she had wanted just as much as he had. But one kiss would inevitably lead to more than that, and this time, with this man, her resistance was at an all-time low. He was right. It took very little time to fall in— what? Love or lust? Either way, it felt very dangerous in this moonlight.

When they reached the house Roberto bowed over her hand very formally in the hall.

'*Boa noite*, Katherine. *Dorme bem*.'

'Goodnight, Roberto. I hope you sleep well too.'

He gave a short, mirthless laugh. 'I doubt that.' He smiled suddenly. 'But if I lie awake I will take pleasure in thinking of the day I spend with you tomorrow.'

'No exercises?'

'I will finish early, and wait for my swim until you can join me. If you will?'

Katherine smiled up at him. 'I'll look forward to it.'

'I also.' He raised her hand to kiss it, and then

walked with her to the foot of the stairs. 'Ate amanha, Katherine.'

She said goodnight and went up the stairs without looking back. She was in bed later, looking at the moonlight filtering through the slats of the blinds, before she remembered that Roberto had not explained the danger of his past life after all. She hesitated, cast a look at her laptop on the dressing table, and then gave way to temptation. She could find out right now. Something she could have done the moment she'd learned his first name, if she hadn't been so preoccupied with the painting. Katherine slid out of bed to switch on the laptop, and sat transfixed when her search led her to a shot of a younger unscarred Roberto. It was hard to tear her eyes from the handsome, laughing face to read the caption below.

> *Roberto Rocha Lima Tavares de Sousa, the racing driver professionally known as Roberto Rocha, was often compared during his budding career to his compatriot, Ayrton Senna, who died so tragically years previously on the Imola racetrack in Italy. But after only a few successful seasons, when the world championship seemed a probability rather than just a possibility in his future, Roberto Rocha retired from the track and returned home to Brazil.*

Katherine's fascinated eyes stayed glued to the screen as she read about Roberto's progress from winning almost every race he entered as a youngster in his karting days, then went on to success at every stage on his way to the top. Her lips twitched when she found he'd made the headlines as much for his playboy lifestyle as for his prowess at the wheel of a racing car.

She stared at the laughing, handsome face for so long it was late when she switched off the machine and got back into bed. Hugh and Alastair were ardent fans, but her interests lay with rugby and tennis. Motorsport had never had the least appeal, though occasionally she'd read about its biggest stars in the papers; the slim young men in jumpsuits and helmets which gave them a Martian uniformity as they diced with danger to earn their spectacular money. She smiled wryly. With success in such a glamour sport, a parade of actresses and models had been inevitable for someone with Roberto's looks and money. Yet he'd given it all up to return to the Estancia. She wondered why. And, now she came to think of it, his interest in paintings seemed an odd combination with his past career. She would ask him about it tomorrow.

Katherine was ready in shorts and T-shirt over a jade one-piece swimsuit when her breakfast arrived, but felt too keyed up to eat much of it because the sun was shining outside, and Roberto might already be waiting for her. She ate half a roll, swallowed a cup of tea and, armed with a towel, managed to make it through the house unescorted for once. She sprinted through the gardens to the pool, where parasols were already open to shade the steamer chairs ranged alongside it. She shed her outer clothes, left them on the iron bench and lifted her face to the sun for a moment before diving neatly into the water. By the time she'd completed two lengths Roberto appeared, holding a pile of towels, and she hoisted herself out, smiling.

'Good morning.'

As she stood up his eyes lit with something which made her want to dive for cover.

'*Bom dia, sereia linda!*'

'I know *bom dia* is good morning,' she panted, wringing water from her braid. 'What was the rest of it?'

'It means beautiful mermaid, Katherine. How are you today?'

'Much better for my swim—aren't you coming in?'

'I will soon.' He handed her a couple of towels. 'Let us sit in the sun for a while first.'

Katherine wrapped herself in a large towel sarong fashion and mopped her face with another as she followed him to a deckchair. 'What a heavenly morning.'

Roberto eased himself down beside her. 'Did you sleep well?'

'Not that well.' She braced herself. 'In fact I have a confession to make. Last night, Roberto, I invaded your privacy. I looked you up on the Net.'

He shrugged, unperturbed. 'Such information is open to all who care to look, Katherine.' He raised an eyebrow. 'So. Now my past is the open book to you.'

'A very glamorous past!'

'It was not all glamour,' he assured her. 'To achieve success in motorsport, a driver must make sacrifices. I devoted many years of my life to it, and left home and family when I was young to do it.'

'That must have been hard!'

'It was. I missed my family and felt great *saudade* for my home.' He smiled reminiscently. 'But every time I got in the car and closed my helmet ready to race, it was the only place in the world I wanted to be.'

'Yet at the height of your success you gave it up and went home.'

'I had no choice, Katherine.' He let out an unsteady

breath. 'My older brother Luis was my father's right hand at the Estancia. Like me, he had ridden as soon as he could walk. But in a storm when he was out with the herd his horse was frightened by lightning and threw him. The fall would not have been fatal, but the horse's hoof struck my brother's head and killed him instantly.'

Katherine gazed at him in horror. 'Oh, Roberto, how tragic!'

Roberto nodded sombrely. 'I returned home immediately to support my parents in their grief, intending to stay for a while before returning to the track. I knew well it had been hard for them to let me follow my dream, constantly afraid that I would die on the track like Senna. Yet I had no serious accidents during all the years I was racing.' His mouth twisted. 'The only time I came near to death was driving from a restaurant.'

'But that was because your friend Elena was at the wheel,' Katherine pointed out.

'*E verdade*. But she was no friend of mine.'

'You don't speak to her now?'

His jaw clenched. 'She blames me for the loss of her career.'

'Because you couldn't lie for her?'

'*Exatamente*. She rang so often to say I had ruined her life I changed my phone. When she could not reach me she rang the number here at the Quinta, which was a big mistake because my mother answered.' He gave an evil chuckle. 'I don't know what *Mamae* said to her, but Elena has not contacted me since.'

'Did you care for her?'

'Not at all. I hardly knew her.' Roberto pushed his sunglasses into his hair to look into Katherine's eyes. 'At my friend's wedding Elena introduced herself to me to beg a great favour. She offered to pay for a meal if I would take her out in my car. Good PR, she told me. It would get her more screen time and therefore more money. I was amused by her honesty and agreed to drive her to the restaurant of her choice in my Maserati, but declined payment for my dinner. She had arranged for a photographer when we arrived, but fortunately he did not stay to witness our violent argument when we left.'

'An argument, even though you'd known her such a short time?'

'She offered sex in exchange for the large sum of money she was desperate for.' His mouth turned down in distaste as he put the glasses back on. 'She flew into a rage when I refused. The sum was nothing to me, she argued, but it would mean everything to her.'

'If she was in regular work in a television series, even in a minor role, surely she earned good money herself,' said Katherine, surprised.

'These are the words I said to her, but she refused to tell me why she needed such money. When I said no she snatched my keys out of my hand and ran for the car, screaming that now I *must* give her money to get it back.' His mouth twisted. 'I was a fool. I should have let her take it. But it was my beloved Maserati, you understand, so I wrenched open the door to dive into the passenger seat as she took off. She had no experience of such a powerful machine and failed to control it. I grabbed the wheel as we hit a bend but could not prevent the crash which ended all hope of returning to my career on the track.' He shrugged. 'My parents blame Elena, but she did not force me to get in the car. A man who values a piece of machinery more than his own safety has only himself to blame, *nao e*?'

Katherine was silent for a moment, eyeing him thoughtfully. 'She isn't hugely clever this lady, is she?'

He smiled. 'Why do you say that?'

'From what I read about you last night, she tried to sell you something women stand in line to give you for free,' she said bluntly.

He hunched a shoulder. 'If they did, they do so no longer.'

'Probably because you're hiding from them,' said Katherine practically. 'Come *on*, Roberto. Be positive. You've got a scar and a limp, but both of them will improve. You could have been killed but you're alive—' She bit her lip, flushing when Roberto gave a shout of laughter.

'It is good you did not choose a career in nursing!'

She grinned. 'I'd make a good Nurse Ratched in *One Flew over the Cuckoo's Nest*.'

He shook his head. 'You are not capable of such cruelty, Katherine.'

Her eyes dropped. 'I think I'll have another swim. Are you coming in?'

'*Pois e.*' He stood up to strip off his shirt and jeans. He held out his hand to her, but drew back, smiling wryly. 'It is best you get up unaided, or we have a repeat of last night, no? I would enjoy it, but you would not.'

'I wouldn't say that,' she said demurely, then ran along the side of the pool and dived in. When she turned at the end, laughing as she trod water, he was standing at the edge of the pool, shaking a finger at her. But he was laughing again, she saw with satisfaction, noting that lean though he might be, Roberto had the powerful legs of a man used to a life on horseback, plus a muscular torso for the same reason, or maybe as the result of the fitness regimes all racing drivers endured to stay at the top of their game. One look at that taut bronzed body and no woman in the world would care a toss about his facial scar. 'Come on in,' she called. 'The water's lovely.'

So are you, *linda flor*, thought Roberto as he dived in. He reached her in a few powerful strokes and exerted stern self control to keep from snatching her close as she smiled up at him. *Deus*, it had been too long since he held a woman in his arms.

'I won't challenge you to a race because I don't do much swimming these days,' she said with regret. 'But I'll try to keep up with you for a while.'

'We shall take it easy,' he promised, but after a couple of lengths she grinned at him and put on speed and he laughed, accelerating to keep up with her. But soon Katherine began to lag behind.

'I'm done,' she spluttered as he towed her to the steps.

'You swim well, Dr Lister.'

'But I'm seriously out of practice. You, on the other hand,' she gasped, 'are not even out of breath.'

'Because I am not out of practice,' he agreed, thrusting his wet curls back. 'But now I must do more lengths to complete my daily workout. When you go in tell Jorge we need coffee in half an hour, *por favor*.'

'Will do.' Katherine wrung the water out of her braid, wrapped herself in a towel and as she dried off stood watching Roberto power through the water before she went back to the house.

Katherine gave the request for coffee and ran upstairs to shower. As she hurried into jeans and a scarlet T-shirt, she reminded the niggling voice of caution in her head that all too soon she would be back in her normal everyday life which, satisfying though it was from a work point of view, and even from a social one, there was nothing in it to compare with this halcyon period spent with Roberto de Sousa in his beautiful house. She would be unlikely to make a discovery as exciting as the Gainsborough again, for a start. Even when her research did turn up something promising, James always took over from then on. This period at Quinta das Montanhas was a one-off experience in every way, and she would savour every fleeting moment of it.

Roberto was gazing out into the garden from his usual post at the veranda pillar when she rejoined him. Her espadrilles made no sound on the shining floor and he turned sharply as she reached him, smiling in approval.

'You were quick!'

'I suppose the women you know take more time—and effort—to get themselves together!'

He eyed her with appreciation as he led her to the table, where a coffee tray waited for them. 'You need no such effort, Katherine. Lidia says you ate no breakfast, so break your rules about *doces* and take some of her little cakes.'

'I will. I'd forgotten how hungry I get after swimming. And you don't have to diet to fit into a racing car any more.'

'It is one advantage,' he agreed dryly. 'Though it was not dieting in the usual sense. I merely kept to those foods which made me strongest for the task. Part of which was mental as well as physical.'

'Did you get depressed if you finished low down in the points?'

'It was not depression exactly, but...what is the word?' He thought for a moment, then snapped his

fingers. 'Obsession! Because tenths of a second quali-
fying time meant better start position on the grid.' He
shrugged philosophically. 'I have no such obsessions
now.'

'Except for believing that your scar makes you into
a monster,' she said before she could stop herself.

Roberto drank some of his coffee, eyeing her thoughtfully over the rim of his cup. 'You do not think this,
Katherine?'

'You know I don't. In fact—' She managed to stop
herself this time, and coloured at his look of intense
interest.

'In fact,' he prompted.

Oh, well, in for a penny. 'When I saw you at the pool
it was obvious that no woman who saw you without your
clothes would care a toss about the scar.'

He gave a delighted laugh, shaking his head as her
colour heightened. 'You are so good for me, Katherine
Lister. I thank you for the compliment. But surely you
noticed that one leg is not as straight as the other?'

'No, I didn't.' She drained her cup hastily.

'You are blushing again! I embarrass you so much,
Katherine? *Disculpeme*; it is not my intention.' He eyed
her objectively. 'Though you look most beautiful when
you blush.'

'And you exaggerate, Senhor Sousa!'

'Roberto, *por favor!* And I tell the truth, Katherine.
Yours is a beauty not only of looks but of brain.' He
grinned. 'A powerful combination!'

She laughed. 'You're in a good mood today.'

He leaned to take the cup she'd filled for him. 'I have
thought much about what you said yesterday. You say
the truth, Katherine. I have my family at home in Brazil,
also this beautiful house here in the Minho and, unlike

my beloved brother, I am alive, with good honest work waiting for me at the Estancia when I am fit. I should be thanking God for this, not complaining about the scar and my leg—' He looked up as Jorge came to say the *Patrao* was wanted on the telephone.

'The lady refused to give her name,' he added in apology.

Roberto's eyes narrowed. '*Com licenca*, Katherine.' He snatched up his stick and limped away quickly.

When Roberto returned to the veranda his eyes were dark with fury he masked quickly as Katherine looked at him in question.

'*Que descaramento!*' He tossed his stick away and sat down. 'You have the phrase talk of the devil, *nao e*? The mystery caller was the subject of our conversation, Katherine.' His eyes hardened. 'Elena Cabral rang to beg for money again.'

'Did she say why this time?'

'She says she owes money for gambling debts, and has been threatened with violence if she does not pay. She tried to soften me with tears and much sobbing.'

'You don't believe her?'

Roberto shrugged. 'She is experienced actress, Katherine. Tears are easy for her. When I refused she made threats, screamed she would make me sorry.' He squared his formidable shoulders. 'There is no further harm she can cause me so let us forget about Elena and think of pleasanter things. A courier is coming to pick up the painting this afternoon.'

'I'll pack it for you, if you trust me with it,' Katherine said promptly.

'*Pois e*—you're the expert!' He stretched cautiously in his chair. 'I have been thinking,' he went on.

'About the painting?'

'No. About you, Katherine. I asked you to stay here at the Quinta instead of in Viana do Castelo, but I am sure it must be boring for you.'

'It's been anything but boring this morning!' She waved a hand at the sunlit vista outside. 'And what hotel could possibly offer more than this!'

'The company of other guests, perhaps, also a beach, and shopping in the town.' His lips twitched. 'All women like shopping.'

Spare cash for shopping was in short supply, due to the unromantic need for plumbing repairs back home, so Katherine laughed and shook her head. 'This one can survive without it, I promise.' She paused. 'But I would like to see a little more of the Minho.'

'You would like Jorge to take you on a drive after lunch?'

He had to be joking! 'I hoped you would be kind enough to drive me yourself, Roberto Rocha,' she said challengingly. 'After all, you're supposed to be a good driver.'

To her relief, he threw back his head and laughed. 'I am not just good, I am brilliant. And I would be most delighted to take you out this afternoon.' He looked at his watch. 'I kept the crate for the painting, so if you would now help me pack it, Katherine, we have just enough time before we eat.'

She sealed the crate out on the veranda, taking great care to make the painting secure for its journey to England. 'Where it was probably painted some time between 1752 and 1759,' she told Roberto. 'Gainsborough was based in a town called Ipswich about then before going off to find fame and fortune in London.'

He smiled with deep satisfaction. 'It is so good to talk with someone who shares my interest in such things.

Except for my mother, all women I have known were bored with the subject.'

'You obviously spent time with the wrong women,' said Katherine, grinning—then bit her lip. 'Sorry. I forgot you'd been married.'

He shrugged. 'Mariana had no interest in art. She wanted a home and children and a husband who wanted those things, too. At that time I did not.'

'You must have been very young when you met?'

'Much too young to marry. But Mariana was very pretty and sweet and because I had to leave for Europe to race I married her only a few weeks after we met. She was expecting my child by the time I left. She went back to her family, but soon afterwards she lost the baby. Because I could not get home right away she turned to a childhood friend for consolation. In time, she divorced me and married him.' His mouth turned down. 'Mariana's treatment hurt my pride—though I did not lack attention from other women.'

'So I discovered during my research!'

'Ah, but I did not act on it while I was married,' he said virtuously.

Katherine eyed him curiously. 'I had a vague idea divorce wasn't legal in Brazil.'

'At one time it was not,' he agreed, 'but in the seventies the law was changed, and these days divorce is a very simple matter. I am speaking in legal terms, you understand. To the devout, like my parents, marriage is for life.' He shrugged. 'Their only consolation about my divorce was my freedom to marry again and give them the grandchildren they long for. Our family is unusual in our country. Now Luis is gone, I am the only child.'

She nodded sadly. 'I have no siblings either.'

He looked at her very directly. 'You would like children, Katherine?'

She put the finishing touches to the packing case and straightened. 'Yes. But I would need a husband to father these children first, and I've never met anyone I could imagine in the role. And I'll have to get a move on because I'm already twenty-eight,' she added.

'So old,' mocked Roberto. 'I am years more than that—'

'Which is totally different. A man can go on fathering children for decades longer than Mother Nature allows a woman to be a mother.' Katherine patted the crate. 'When is the courier coming to collect him?'

'Later this afternoon, but we need not wait. Jorge will be here to send our young man on his way.'

CHAPTER FIVE

KATHERINE ran back downstairs after lunch to find Jorge hovering in the hall, looking anxious.

'Senhor Roberto must not drive too far, *Doutora*.'

'I'll see that he doesn't,' promised Katherine. 'In fact, I could say I prefer you to drive us, if you think he's not up to it today.'

Jorge looked horrified. '*Nao, Doutora!* Say nothing, *por favor*. He has much pride, you understand.'

'I do, perfectly,' she said, and patted his arm. 'Don't worry. I'll make sure he doesn't overdo things.'

'*Muit' obrigado*.' He smiled apologetically. 'Lidia is anxious.'

So was Jorge, thought Katherine with sympathy. She went outside to wait, wondering what car Roberto drove now the Maserati was gone. It was a surprise to see Roberto at the wheel of a gleaming black Range Rover. She ran round to the passenger door, smiling as she hopped up onto the seat.

'I was expecting a sexy sports car,' she said, breathing in the scent of leather and new car.

'It *is* a sports car, Katherine. A Range Rover Sport with a V8 supercharged engine,' Roberto said with relish.

'Of course it is,' she said, laughing.

'You may laugh at me,' he said with dignity, 'but this model is also automatic, which is easier for me right now.'

'And it's wonderfully comfortable!' Katherine secured her seat belt and sat back with a sigh of pleasure. 'Right, let's hit the road.'

Instead of driving at top speed as she'd expected, Roberto took her on a leisurely journey along the River Lima, pointing out places of interest as they went. Although, as Katherine told him, everything she saw in this part of the world was interesting to her.

'It's so green. It's quite different from how I imagined it,' she told him as they passed hilly fields edged with stone and greenery on smallholdings where agriculture, Roberto informed her, was sometimes still carried on in the traditional way, with use of oxen rather than machinery.

'You think only of the Algarve, with the cliffs and sandy beaches and Mediterranean climate which make a holiday playground. Here in the Minho, life is different. Slower, some say backward, but I say peaceful and traditional. And it is green here because it rains a lot,' he added. 'We shall drive to Viana do Castelo, which has good shops. You will like it.'

'Because I'm a woman and can't possibly exist without shopping,' she teased, and Roberto laughed.

'As in most of Portugal, you will find good shoes there, and all women love shoes.'

Katherine was no exception. 'I would enjoy some window-shopping,' she admitted. 'But you wouldn't, so I'll pass.'

'I have the dark glasses, also the hat,' he pointed out, tilting his straw Stetson over his eyes. 'And with you at my side no one will look at me, so it is no problem.'

He peered at her over his sunglasses. 'I would like to window-shop with you, Katherine.'

'Then we will,' she said, smiling at him.

'If you permit this I can manage without my stick,' he said, and tucked her arm in his as they left the car later to stroll in the town. He glanced down at her as she sighed. 'You are not happy to do this?'

'Of course I am.'

'So why do you sigh?'

'Because I know perfectly well I should have gone home as soon as I'd finished work on the painting.'

'Yet you stayed when I asked. Because you pitied me?' he demanded abruptly.

'Certainly not,' she retorted, and felt him relax. 'I feel sympathy, not pity.' She smiled up at him, winning such a dazzling smile in response her heart contracted.

'As I have said before, you are good for me, Katherine.'

'You can repay me by acting as tour guide.'

'*Sempre as seus ordems,*' he said promptly, and gestured grandly with his free arm. 'Here we are in the Praca da Republica, with fountain constructed in 1553. You are attending, *Doutora*?'

'Hanging on every word!'

'*Muito bem*. The Praca is the hub of daily life here in Viana, where the historian may find many types of architecture to admire.'

'This one's full of admiration,' she assured him.

'I am most pleased to hear it. The Renaissance building at the far end, the *Misericórdia*, has magnificent—' He stopped, frowning at the arcades supported by female figures. 'I do not have the word.'

'Caryatids,' supplied Katherine.

'*Obrigado, Doutora Historiadora.*'

'Good heavens, is that what I am?'

'Amongst other things, yes, Katherine.' He grinned down at her.

'Please carry on with the tour, Senhor Guide. Or are you getting tired?' she asked anxiously.

'With your arm in mine, how could I be tired?' He led her round the square, pointing out the Baroque living in harmony with the Manueline in the architecture styles of the mansions whose wealth, Roberto informed her, had been derived from trade with Brazil as well as the rest of Europe. 'Enough history,' he said abruptly. 'Now we look at shoes.'

Katherine laughed, only too happy to gaze at the tempting wares in the shop windows, but remained steadfast in her refusal to buy anything at all, even the pair of slender-heeled nude beauties which made her mouth water.

'You like those?' said Roberto.

'I'm just looking,' she said firmly, and turned away. 'And now, Senhor Sousa, it's time we went home, or Jorge will scold me for not looking after you.'

'First we buy the shoes.'

And, short of causing a disturbance in the Praca da Republica, Katherine had to accompany Roberto into the shop. A few minutes later they emerged with the sandals, which fitted so perfectly and looked so fabulous Katherine had decided to forget about plumbing for once and splurge. But there was a nasty moment when she found that Roberto had already paid for the new shoes while she was resuming her old ones.

'Tell me how much they were and I'll pay you when we get back,' she insisted outside, and then eyed him anxiously as his limp became more pronounced. 'You're tired. We should have stopped sooner. Do you need a rest before we go back?'

'*Nao, 'brigado*,' he snapped. 'Let us get back to the car.'

'Don't be afraid to lean on me,' she told him, and slid her arm more securely through his, dismayed that he was so offended.

Once they were in the car on the way back to the Quinta, Roberto obviously more comfortable seated at the wheel, Katherine returned to the subject of shoe payment.

'They are a gift,' he said flatly.

'I can't accept them,' she said, equally flatly.

'*Deus me livre*, they are not diamonds,' he growled, and stared straight ahead in smouldering silence for the rest of the journey.

'Roberto, please try to understand,' she said miserably as they turned in at the gates of the Quinta. 'You've already paid handsomely for my services—' Damn, that came out all wrong. 'I mean—'

'I have enough English to know what you mean,' he snapped, and drove up the sweeping curves of the drive at breakneck speed to bring the car to a stop with panache at the great main door. 'If you cannot bring yourself to accept such a trifling gift from me, *nao importa*—throw them away.'

Before Katherine could reply, Jorge came hurrying to open the car door to help her out, and Roberto drove away round the house at a speed which left Jorge staring after him in consternation.

'He is in pain, *Doutora*?' he asked anxiously.

'Probably.' Also angry. Roberto Rocha de Sousa, it was plain, didn't take kindly to opposition.

'You would like tea?' asked Jorge as they crossed the hall.

Not if it meant an awkward encounter on the veranda while she drank it. Katherine smiled at him. 'I thought I'd just go up to my room for a while.'

'Tea will be brought to you,' he said firmly.

'Was the painting collected?'

'*Sim, senhora*. It is on its way to London.'

As she should be, too. Katherine sighed, feeling depressed after her altercation with Roberto. Dinner wouldn't be much fun tonight.

Lidia brought the tea up, which added guilt to Katherine's gloom.

'I should have had this downstairs and saved you the trouble,' she told the woman in remorse.

'Is no trouble,' said Lidia, surprised. 'I come myself because it is Pascoa's day off. You have nice trip?'

'Yes, indeed. I liked Viana do Castelo very much.'

'*Muito bem*. Now you have rest before dinner.'

Which was more than Lidia was likely to get without Pascoa's help. Katherine drank her tea, but concentration on her book proved so difficult she had a long shower instead, and afterwards spent more time than usual on her hair and make-up to boost her morale.

When Lidia arrived at dinnertime to announce that Senhor Roberto waited on the veranda she handed over the smart carrier bag containing the shoes. 'Senhor Roberto say you left this in car.'

Katherine went downstairs with considerable reluctance, wishing she could have eaten in her room. Which was stupid. She would have to face Roberto some time.

He came to meet her in the hall, a wry twist to his lips

when he saw she was wearing the shoes. '*Desculpe-me*, Katherine. I lost my temper.'

'I noticed!' She smiled. 'Are we friends again now?'

'Of course.' He ushered her out onto the softly lit veranda, filled two wine glasses and took the chair opposite, eyeing her challengingly. 'I thought perhaps you would not dine with me tonight.'

'No danger of that,' she assured him.

'Because you forgave my bad temper?'

She shook her head, grinning. 'Because I'm hungry.'

He grinned back, looking suddenly younger. 'You tease me! And I like it very much.' He sobered. 'I shall miss you so much when you leave, Katherine.'

'Won't you be going home to Brazil soon?' She smiled as Jorge appeared with a dish of *bolinhas*. 'Yummy! I love these.'

Roberto laughed. 'It is good to see a woman eat with such appetite.'

'I suppose the ladies in your past all existed on carrot sticks and fresh air!'

'It is possible they did in my absence,' he said cynically, 'but in my company they chose the most expensive dishes on the menu.'

'How did they get on with Lidia's cooking?'

Roberto shook his head. 'None of them came here. The Quinta is my retreat. I kept an *apartamento* in Lisboa while racing in Europe, and the rest of the season I was competing too far away to think of anything but the next race. I have always had complaints from women, starting with Mariana, that my concentration on my sport was so intense I had no emotion to spare for relationships.'

'You miss racing?'

'Very much. But as you told me, Doctor, I have much

to be grateful for. Including,' he added, as Jorge came in with a tray, 'Lidia's wonderful cooking.'

'Amen to that,' said Katherine reverently.

They kept to less emotive subjects over the meal, Katherine gratified by Roberto's interest in her work at the gallery. They were so absorbed in her account of one of James's major discoveries they looked up in consternation when Jorge rushed in looking worried and, with a word of apology to Katherine, spoke to Roberto in Portuguese as he handed him a letter.

Roberto studied it, his face grim. 'Jorge found this taped outside one of the *sala* windows,' he told Katherine. 'He did not find it until now when he was checking that all was secure for the night, as usual. I must look for myself; I will not be long.'

As he hurried off with Jorge, Katherine collected the dishes and carried the tray across the hall to the kitchen.

Lidia relieved her of it in dismay. '*Doutora*—I take that.'

'Jorge was busy with Senhor Roberto, so I made myself useful. May I look round?'

'*Pois e.*'

Katherine followed her into a large kitchen with state-of-the-art appliances living in harmony with an old cooking range which had obviously been left in place for its aesthetic qualities. 'What a marvellous room,' she exclaimed, and Lidia did her best to smile as she loaded the dishwasher.

'I feel much guilt because letter came when Jorge take me shopping.'

'It wasn't your fault,' soothed Katherine, and gave Lidia something to keep her busy. 'Could I possibly have some tea—and coffee for Senhor Roberto?'

The woman instantly sprang into action, then exclaimed in dismay as she loaded the tray. 'I did not serve *sobremesa*. I made *pudim de arroz*—rice pudding.'

'We'll have it later.'

Katherine took one look at Roberto's face when he rejoined her, and poured coffee for him. 'Did you find anything else?"

'No.' He discarded his stick and sat down, accepting the coffee gratefully. He showed her the note, which was written in large printed capitals. 'It threatens harm to me, my house and all who live in it if I do not pay the money.'

Katherine frowned. 'The person who delivered it must have seen Jorge and Lidia leave to go shopping. You think Elena is involved?'

He shrugged. 'I hope that no one else is after my blood.' He drained the coffee and stood up as the bell rang. 'It will be the *Guarda Nacional*. I rang them to report this.'

CHAPTER SIX

KATHERINE waited uneasily as Roberto went into the hall, wishing she could understand the rapid interchange as he made his report to the police. The wait seemed endless before she heard goodnights exchanged and the bolts rammed home on the great main door.

When Roberto rejoined her he apologised for the long wait. 'They wished to question Lidia and Jorge, also to inspect the *sala* and the window where the note was left. They have taken the note with them.' He sighed wearily. 'I need a drink. Join me in a brandy, Katherine. We must talk. Will you be too cold on the *varanda*?'

'Not at all.' She felt depressed. In the circumstances, she'd have to leave right away to save additional worry for Roberto by staying.

He poured brandy into glasses and handed her one. 'We both need this, I think.'

Katherine took a fiery sip and put the glass down. 'A good thing my flight is on Sunday, Roberto.'

'I know this,' he said grimly and drained his glass, shuddering as the fiery spirit hit its target. 'But do not be frightened, Katherine. I will not allow harm to come to you.'

'I'm not frightened for myself—at least, not much,' she added honestly. 'I'm more worried for you, Roberto.'

He glared at her. 'Because I am crippled and cannot defend myself?'

'For heaven's sake, cut the drama, Roberto, this is serious,' said Katherine impatiently and then bit her lip, eyeing him warily as he gave her a wry smile.

'*Desculpe-me*, Katherine. What are you trying to tell me?'

'The truth, Roberto.' She held his eyes. 'You're *not* physically capable of fighting off an attacker right now.'

He shook his head in scowling amazement. 'We have so little violent crime here I cannot believe this.'

'I find it hard to believe myself, but it's only sensible to take precautions.'

'You are right, *sem duvida*.' Roberto glanced out into the night. 'And to start such precautions, it is best we go inside. I shall turn off the lights here and lock the doors then take you upstairs.'

'You don't have to do that—'

He eyed her impatiently. 'Of course I do, Katherine. No one else sleeps on the upper floor. I will not rest until I know you are safe inside your room.'

Secretly very grateful for his escort, she waited while he locked up and then offered her arm for support.

Roberto gladly abandoned his walking stick for the slow ascent, but in such close, tempting proximity to her body he felt himself harden in fierce response. He clenched his teeth against the force of it, telling himself he would take her only as far as her room. His mouth tightened. But then she would be totally alone up here should the unthinkable happen and some *meliante* break in.

Katherine slid her arm from his and took his hand

as they reached the landing. 'What's troubling you, Roberto?'

Many things, he thought savagely, not least the desire to seize her in his arms and kiss her senseless. 'I worry because you will be alone up here tonight.'

'I've been alone up here every night since I arrived,' she pointed out.

'But until today you were in no danger—'

'You surely don't think someone would actually try to break in?' Katherine stared at him in consternation.

He thrust a hand through his hair, his eyes bitter. 'Yesterday, I would have laughed at such an idea. Tonight, who knows? I cannot endure the thought of you alone and vulnerable, so far away from me.'

Katherine wasn't very happy about it, either. Even if by some miracle she managed to sleep, the mere possibility that someone might try to climb in through her window would give her nightmares. She opened her bedroom door and crossed to the bedside table to switch on a lamp. 'Could you lock the windows, please? As one of those precautions, I'll keep them closed tonight.'

He shut the door behind him and crossed the room to secure the tall windows, his eyes raking the moonlit gardens. 'Do not worry, Katherine. It is bright as day outside. Only a fool would try to get in on a night like this.'

'I hope you're right,' she said doubtfully.

'You are afraid?'

'A bit.' She hesitated. 'Are you tired, or could you stay and talk for a while?'

Roberto turned to face her. 'I am not tired, but I will not stay.'

Katherine gave up. 'Goodnight, then.'

Roberto closed his eyes in desperation, and then

opened them again, abandoning all effort to hide the hunger in his eyes. 'If I stay I will want more than just to talk. And I promised to keep you safe, *nao e*? That must mean safe from me, also.'

She moved closer, meeting the look head on. 'Stay, just the same. Please?'

Roberto gave a despairing groan and seized her in his arms, his lips devouring hers in a kiss which went on so long they were both shaking when he raised his head at last to look into her dazed eyes.

'You see?' he said through his teeth. 'One kiss and we set the world on fire.' His eyes burned into hers. 'I am entranced by your mind and your knowledge of art, *e verdade*, but also by your beautiful body, Katherine.'

'I am by yours, too, Roberto,' she said candidly, her colour rising.

He swallowed convulsively. 'You mean that?'

'Every word.'

He let out a deep, ragged sigh and drew her down beside him on the bed. '*Deus*, I thought no woman would ever look at me with pleasure again.'

Katherine leaned against him, exulting in the rapid thud of his heartbeat against hers as she breathed in the scent of his heated skin. 'In the past you were accustomed to a great many women looking at you with pleasure?'

'Yes,' he said simply. 'Pretty playmates were part of the life I led after Mariana divorced me.' He raised her hand and pressed a lingering kiss in her palm. 'And you have no wish for marriage either, *nao e*?'

She shook her head. 'Not true. I just haven't met a man I want for a husband.' Nor even for a lover in the true meaning of the word. Until now.

He caught her by the chin and looked deep into her eyes. '*Agora*, Katherine, tell me you want me.'

'Of course I want you. I asked you to stay!'

'Because you are frightened.'

'And because I want you to make love to me, Roberto. Are you going to, or are you just going to talk about it?' She scowled at him crossly. 'I won't ask again!'

'You need not!' He kissed her in passionate assurance as they fell back on the bed together, the seduction of his seeking, smoothing hands so ravishing they took Katherine's breath away.

'*Eu te quero, amada,*' he whispered, his breath burning her skin.

No translation was necessary. Roberto's words sent such heat flaming through her Katherine pressed even closer to him, which only made the heat worse—or better. She would be gone soon and if she sent him away now she would regret it for the rest of her life. To make this clear, she kissed him in such explicit invitation he growled in delight against her parted lips, his hands caressing her to such a pitch of longing she helped feverishly when he undressed them both with urgent hands. She tensed as Roberto laid her on her back but, instead of immediately crushing her body with his, as she expected, he propped himself on an elbow and lay there just looking at her, his eyes moving over every inch of her as though he wanted to eat her up. She moved restively, unable to lie still under the glittering, hungry gaze.

'No. Do not move. For a little while just let me look at you, Katherine,' he said huskily. 'I want a picture of you in my mind, so that I can look back on this moment and remember.'

To her embarrassment, her nipples hardened in

response to his words, and he drew in a sharp breath and bent his head to tease and torment them with wickedly skilful lips and grazing teeth, while his hands made love to every curve and hollow of her responsive body. When they moved lower at last, his skilled, seeking caresses brought her up off the bed; her hands urgent on his back and, with a deep, relishing sigh, he slid over her. Her mouth dried as their bodies came into full, naked contact, the rasp of hair-roughened muscular thighs between the smoothness of hers so erotic her heart hammered in her chest.

'You told me,' he reminded her in a tone that made her breath catch, 'that you allowed such closeness only if you had feelings for the man. Do you have such feelings for me, Katherine?'

As if she was going to say no in this situation! She nodded wordlessly.

He gave her a glorious smile and kissed her mouth as he entered her body with a smooth, slow thrust which stunned them both by the sheer tactile pleasure of it until Roberto surrendered to the urging of his body and began to move, his lovemaking enhanced by the words he whispered in her ear until he had no more breath for talking as their bodies surged together in urgent rhythm that blotted out everything other than the pleasure they were giving each other, a frenzied joy so intense it was almost pain as completion finally engulfed them in a throbbing wave of rapture so intense it brought tears to Katherine's eyes.

Roberto held her tightly, his face buried in her hair. When he raised his head at last he frowned as he saw her tears. 'You are crying, *amada*?'

She shook her head, blinking the moisture from her

lashes. 'Just tears of wonder. I've never experienced anything so…so overwhelming before.'

His eyes gleamed with such blatant male satisfaction Katherine laughed as he kissed her tears away.

'Why are you laughing at me?' he demanded, raising his head.

'You looked so smug!'

'What is smug?'

How was she supposed to search for vocabulary in these circumstances! 'Pleased with yourself.'

'What man would not be pleased when his woman finds joy in his arms?'

His woman. Katherine thought that over with disquiet. 'Roberto—'

'Do not ask me to move, *querida*—unless I am crushing you?'

Now the subject had come up, she had to admit that he was, a bit. The lean, graceful body was surprisingly heavy. 'I was going to remind you about my flight.'

Roberto groaned, his arms tightening like steel bands. When she protested he rolled over, taking her with him to lie on top of him. He smiled up into her eyes, smoothing the hair back from her face. 'Better, *nao e*?' He pulled the sheet up to cover her and brought her head down to fit into his shoulder. 'Stay, Katherine,' he said, and kissed her. 'We have hours of tonight to enjoy together before we must part.'

Dawn came too soon for Katherine next morning. But her first thought as Roberto kissed her into warm, throbbing life again was the threat he received yesterday.

'What troubles you, *querida*?' he demanded. 'You do not want to make love again?'

Incredibly, she found she did, which astounded her

after the night they'd just spent together. He kissed and caressed her into such rapid response she postponed discussion of the problem until she could think and function again normally.

At last Roberto slid reluctantly out of bed. 'I wish we could shower together, but until my leg recovers this is not possible. It will be something to look forward to in future,' he whispered, and leaned to kiss her. 'While I take my lonely shower hurry through yours, Katherine,' he ordered, and began pulling on his clothes. 'Join me for breakfast on the varanda today. I am hungry.'

'So am I,' she admitted.

Roberto gave her a grin which brought such quick colour to her face he bent to kiss her pink cheeks. 'You are so beautiful when you blush. Be quick, *por favor.*'

'How about your exercises?'

He laughed. 'After such joyous exercise last night I will take a holiday from the painful kind today. So hurry.'

When Katherine joined Roberto the look on his face rang alarm bells. 'What's wrong?'

'There was an intruder here last night. An attempt was made to force the door to my part of the house. It was unsuccessful because I recently installed a new security system. Jorge checked all the outer doors, but he found nothing else.' He smiled into her worried eyes. 'They could not attack me because I did not spend the night in my room, *nao e*?'

'Thank God you didn't!' She bit her lip. 'Did Jorge wonder where you were?'

'I told him I slept in one of the rooms upstairs to ensure your safety.' He grinned. 'I did not say which one.'

She grinned back, but quickly sobered. 'I was right, Roberto. You're in danger from someone, Elena or not.'

'*E possiviel*,' he agreed reluctantly. 'I have informed the *Guarda*.'

'Good,' she said fervently, and smiled as Jorge appeared with a tray. 'Good morning.'

'*Bom dia*. Senhor Roberto says you also leave tomorrow, *Doutora*.'

'If possible, yes.'

He looked relieved and cast a look at his employer. 'Senhor Roberto should leave, also—'

'I am hungry, Jorge,' said Roberto gently. 'Perhaps you will leave us to enjoy our breakfast? We will leave discussion until later.'

'*Pois e*,' said the man, and hastily withdrew.

Katherine raised a disapproving eyebrow. 'You were a bit short with him, Roberto. The poor man is obviously worried about you.'

'I know he is. But I am eager to enjoy every moment of our first breakfast together, *carinha*.' He raised her hand to his lips.

But knowing it would also be their last, Katherine found it hard to enjoy the food, famished though she was. A direct result, apparently, of spending most of the night making love. A first in every possible way.

'What are you thinking?' asked Roberto.

She coloured slightly. 'I never realised how hungry one gets after a night of...of...'

'Love?' He grinned. 'It is plain you have not had the right lover until now.'

Wasn't that the truth! 'While we're on the subject, Roberto,' she said, pouring coffee for him, 'what happened last night was not...not usual for me.'

'Or for me,' he assured her, a look in his eyes that curled her toes. 'I have never experienced such rapture before.'

She gave him a wry smile as she filled her teacup. 'I bet you say that to all the girls, Roberto Rocha.'

His eyes flashed coldly. 'You are wrong, Katherine. I do not.'

'Then I apologise. I just want you to know that one-night stands are not a habit of mine.'

With intense concentration, he slit open a roll and filled it with ham. 'You think,' he said slowly, 'that I will think less of you because you made love with me last night?'

'It crossed my mind,' she admitted. 'Could you do one of those for me, please?'

He smiled. 'You may have this one. I will do another.'

'Thank you.' She munched on the roll for a while, thinking hard. 'What I'm trying to make clear is that last night was wonderful, unique, and totally outside my experience. But will never happen again.'

'*Por que*? I was not a good enough lover?' he demanded.

Katherine glared at him. 'Typical male reaction!'

'What else? I am a man, also *Brasileiro*—and *Gaucho*. I demand to know why we cannot repeat such pleasure, Katherine.' Roberto fixed her with a look which turned her heart over, then looked up impatiently as Jorge hurried onto the veranda.

'*Telefone*, Senhor Roberto. Dona Teresa.'

'My mother at this hour?' Roberto grabbed his stick and got up. '*Com licença*, Katherine. Please eat more.'

She watched him hurry away, stick tapping. 'How is Lidia this morning?' she asked Jorge.

'She feels bad that we were out when the letter was delivered.'

'Far better you were both out than either of you got hurt, Jorge.'

He smiled gratefully. 'It is wise that you leave tomorrow, but it has been a pleasure to meet you, *Doutora*. Perhaps you will return soon.'

Katherine smiled non-committally, and with a bow Jorge took away the tea and coffee pots to replenish them. She wandered over to one of the pillars to gaze out over the garden, so lost in thought she was startled when Roberto's arms slid round her.

'You look sad, *carinha*,' he whispered in her ear.

She turned, smiling valiantly. 'Only because I'm leaving soon. But I'm glad you're leaving too.'

He smiled exultantly. 'We shall leave together. But not on a flight to England.'

Katherine tipped her head back to look up into his face. 'What do you mean?'

'I was a long time on the telephone, not only because my mother wished to talk. She had a sudden desire to know all was well with me.' He smiled. 'When I told her about our adventures she called my father to the phone. He said that I must leave at once. He is a very practical man, and suggested a most simple solution to this threat. I close the house, hire a security firm to guard it for a week or two, and give Lidia and Jorge a holiday.' He kissed her hard. 'And here is the best part. My parents invite you to accompany me to the Estancia, Katherine. So we are leaving from Lisbon tomorrow. After much telephoning, I have found two cancellations for a flight to Porto Alegre.'

Katherine stared at him aghast. 'But I've got to

get back to work—I can't just take off for Brazil, Roberto!'

His arms tightened. 'Why not? I will pay for more of your time, and Senhor Massey will give you leave.'

She pulled away, shaking her head vehemently. 'You can't just pay for me, Roberto. Money doesn't solve everything.'

'In this case it can buy me more time with you,' he said flatly. 'Come with me. Just for two weeks if that is all you wish, Katherine, to make up for the stress these threats are causing you.'

'It's not your fault, Roberto!'

'Of course it is my fault! When my friend returned from honeymoon he told me that Elena had been what you call a gatecrasher at his wedding. She got in with the photographer.' He shrugged. 'She saw me there and thought I would be an easy…mark is right?'

Katherine nodded.

'And I was,' he said bitterly. 'No one forced me to get in the car with her, so I know well I am responsible for what happened to me, but not for the loss of her TV job. Yet now she is beginning her *bobagem* over money again.'

Katherine shivered. 'It's such a good thing you're off to Brazil. You're out of her reach there.'

Roberto's eyes glittered hotly. 'But now things are changed between us, Katherine, I do not want to let you go. So come with me to the Estancia, *querida.*'

She shook her head sadly. 'I really can't do that, Roberto.'

His dark eyes locked with hers, willing her to say yes. 'Two weeks is all I ask, Katherine—for now.'

She pulled out of his grasp and turned away to look out over the garden. A fortnight in Brazil was a tempting idea. She had taken very little in the way of holidays lately. James was probably fit enough to take over the reins again by now, and his wonderful Judith would help out. An opportunity like this would never happen again in her lifetime. Her mouth tightened. Nor could she let it happen now. It had been against every principle she possessed just to let him pay for the shoes, so a fortnight's holiday in Brazil at his expense was right out of the question. And even if she were mad enough to give in to him it would be hell afterwards to fit into her normal way of life again. A life without Roberto Rocha Lima Tavares de Sousa.

The period before Katherine left the Quinta das Montanhas was dominated by constant persuasion from Roberto, who never let up with his demand that she fly to Brazil with him even though she was equally immovable with her refusal.

The plan to close up the house was carried out with military precision. As soon as the security firm had set up its base at the Quinta the following morning, Lidia's brother would arrive to take her with Pascoa to stay at his house in Braga. Jorge would then drive Roberto and Katherine to Porto for her flight to the UK, and afterwards take Roberto to Lisbon for his flight to Porto Alegre. During that eventful last day, while Roberto was involved with the cancellation of his medical and physio appointments, and giving notice of his intention to the *Guarda Nacional*, Katherine spent time on her own phone, informing those who needed to know that she was returning as scheduled.

When Katherine reported to James that she would be back in work on Monday she asked him about the Gainsborough. 'How does it look now, boss?'

'Nearly finished and looking good. It would arouse huge interest at auction, but de Sousa is adamant that I just ship it off to Brazil when it's ready.' He paused. 'Katherine, take a day off to recover and start on Tuesday. You sound tired.'

Due to sleep deprivation, amongst other things. 'It's been an eventful few days here.'

'Was the client a problem? I was a bit worried once I looked him up. Did you know he's actually Roberto Rocha, one-time glamour boy of the racing car circuit?'

'Not until I looked him up. Why were you worried?'

'Judith saw the shot of the chap in his glory days on my computer. My unimpressionable wife was bowled over.'

'Well, I wasn't,' she lied. 'See you Monday.'

CHAPTER SEVEN

ROBERTO elected to occupy the room next to hers that night instead of sharing her bed again, but after Katherine had tossed and turned for an hour her door opened and closed again softly and Roberto slid into bed with her, his naked body hot and hard against hers.

'I could not sleep,' he whispered.

'Neither could I.'

'I lay awake, wanting you very badly, Katherine.'

Since she had been doing the same, she responded with passionate fervour to his kisses as he slid her beneath him.

'I have been longing for this—for you—for a whole hour,' he said against her parted lips. 'I can wait no longer, *amada*.'

Neither could Katherine. No foreplay was required or necessary. Her body had been ready for him the moment it came into contact with his, and she gave a visceral little groan of satisfaction as he thrust home into her tight, welcoming warmth. The sorcery of her clenching inner muscles incited him to a wildness which left her revelling in the surprise of her own power, then regretting it when culmination left them shaking in each other's arms all too soon, stunned by the force of it.

'*Desculpe-me, querida,*' Roberto panted, raising his head a fraction. 'I was too fast.'

She shook her head vehemently. 'Tonight I wanted fast.'

'Our loving will always be fast when you caress me in such a way!'

She smiled up at him jubilantly. 'Never knew I could do that!'

He chuckled and kissed her nose, then turned her in his arms. 'Perhaps now we can both get some rest.'

Dazed by the force of their lovemaking, Katherine slept heavily in the warmth and security of Roberto's arms and woke early and heavy-eyed in the morning.

Roberto, however, looked annoyingly chipper. '*Bom dia, linda flor.*'

She shuddered, feeling nothing remotely like a beautiful flower. 'Are you always this cheerful in the mornings?'

'No. But how could I not be happy after last night?' His arms tightened, his eyes bright with sudden demand. 'Now you will change your mind, Katherine, *nao e*? You will come with me today.'

She eyed him suspiciously. 'Is that why you stole into my bed last night? To change my mind?'

He shook his tousled head. 'I came because I could not exist another moment without you.' He gave her a kiss so soft and sweet she wanted to cry. 'Hurry through your bath. We shall breakfast together before the security people arrive.'

Lidia arrived with tea while Katherine was dressing. 'I cook hot meal today,' she said in a tone that brooked no argument. '*Dez minutos,*' she added, holding up her hand twice.

'Thank you, Lidia.' Katherine smiled warmly. 'Are you happy about staying in Braga for a while?'

'It make Senhor Roberto happy, so I am happy,' said the woman simply. 'I help pack?'

'Almost done, thanks. I won't be long.'

Ready for travel in the black trousers and white shirt of their first meeting, Katherine hurried down to join Roberto.

'Ah!' he said with appreciation as he drew out her chair. 'Last night you were temptation in my arms, this morning you are severe *Doutora* again. I like this look, it is very sexy!' He sniffed the air as Jorge brought their breakfast. 'Lidia has made a hot meal this morning. She goes to Braga after you eat?'

'Her brother comes at eight,' Jorge informed him, and took the covers from the dishes. 'Lidia says please to eat everything.'

Katherine was only too happy to. Who knew when she'd be eating another meal? Up to date she'd never managed to eat much on a plane. At the mere thought of leaving Roberto to fly in the opposite direction, her heart contracted. 'Is yours a non-stop flight?'

He shook his head. 'There is a brief stop in Paris, then a longer one in São Paulo, where I must change to Congonhas Airport for the rest of the journey to Porto Alegre. There I board a smaller plane to reach the Estancia.'

She eyed him with sympathy. 'That's a very long time for you to stay immobile. How far is the road journey to Lisbon?'

Roberto moved his chair nearer and took her hand. 'Two hundred and forty or so of your British miles.'

'It's a lot of driving for Jorge today, too,' she said anxiously.

'He will have a break at Porto, since you insist on leaving me there. Afterwards, if I can persuade him, I will drive to Lisbon. You are thoughtful, Katherine Lister, but do not worry. Jorge enjoys driving as much as I do.' His eyes shadowed. 'Or I used to.'

'And still do, Roberto! The minute you're behind the wheel of your car you're a happy man.'

He smiled. 'You are right. I would drive all the way today from choice, but it would not be wise before a long flight.'

Katherine winced. 'When you get home, what will you do about your physio and exercises?'

'The pool is ready, and I know the exercises—*Deus*, how well I know them! I shall continue with them when I get to Estancia Grande.'

Knowing how constricted she felt on a plane with two legs in good working order, Katherine eyed him anxiously. 'How will you manage with your leg during the flight?'

'In first class, I will have room to stretch out.' He smiled. 'And I will be so brave the attendants will pay much attention to me.'

She could just imagine it, and busied herself with filling cups to hide a pang of jealousy.

'If you were with me,' he said softly, 'I would not mind the pain. Change your mind, Katherine. Come with me.'

'I can't!' She mopped quickly at a stray tear as Lidia came to say goodbye.

She gave Katherine a sharp look. 'You are sad to leave, *Doutora*?'

'I am indeed.' Katherine got up and kissed the woman's cheek. 'You've been so kind.'

Lidia smiled shyly and squeezed her hand. '*O prazer*

e meu, Doutora. Come back soon. My brother waits, and Pascoa is in the car, so I go now. Adeus.'

'She said the pleasure was all hers, Katherine,' said Roberto after he returned from seeing Lidia off. 'She says you must come back for another holiday one day.'

'I came to work, not for a holiday,' she reminded him.

He nodded in satisfaction. 'And I am most grateful to Mr Massey for sending you to me.'

'You weren't very pleased about it when you first saw me!'

'*E verdade.* You looked so daunting in your severe clothes and spectacles,' he demanded, taking her hand.

'Normally, I only wear those for computer work, but I thought they might impress you with my competence.' She smiled. 'Did it work?'

'*Sim, senhora.* It worked perfectly.'

'You weren't very friendly.'

Roberto looked her in the eye. 'I had no wish for a woman in my house while I look like this.'

Katherine leaned forward and planted a series of little kisses along the ridged flesh of his scar, and received a series of kisses on her mouth as response.

'You soon changed your mind,' she pointed out when she could speak.

His eyes gleamed. 'I was seduced by your intelligence!'

'Were you indeed?' she said wryly.

He raised her hand to his lips, his eyes suddenly very serious. 'So change that informed mind of yours, Katherine. Come to Brazil with me.'

This wasn't fair, she thought in despair. Roberto was making it harder by the minute to say goodbye to him.

It was almost a relief when the doorbell clanged and he went to speak to the head of the security firm.

While he was gone, Katherine took a wistful look over the gardens, then went upstairs to get her belongings together. She checked she'd left nothing behind and carried her suitcase downstairs.

'You should have waited for Jorge to do that,' Roberto said with displeasure.

'I've left the heavy stuff to him. Is everything arranged?'

He nodded. 'The men will keep a low profile by day and make regular rounds by night. Any intruder will meet with a nasty surprise.' Roberto picked up his stick. 'Now there are men to guard us, will you walk with me in the garden for a while, *carinha*? It will be good to exercise my leg before the journey.'

'I'd love to. I'll take my camera.' Katherine gave him a worried look as they went down the veranda steps. 'Will you manage some kind of exercise on the plane?'

'I will annoy the other passengers by much walking in the aisle.' He slanted a gleaming look at her. 'Perhaps a female flight attendant will hold my hand.'

She raised a cynical eyebrow. 'They'll be falling over themselves for the privilege.'

'You are so good for me!' He caught her in his arms and kissed her. '*Querida*, it is so hard to part with you.'

Katherine's throat was too thick with tears for speech. Get a grip, she told herself. Behave like a grown-up.

They both fell silent as they made their slow way back. Katherine paused to take some shots of the beautiful house, and asked Roberto to pose for her.

'And don't turn your good side to me,' she ordered. 'I want you just the way you are.'

She took several shots of him, and then let him take some of her, feeling as though her heart was being torn in half. Roberto was right. It took no time at all to fall in love. She'd managed it the first time she'd set eyes on him, something she'd previously believed happened only in fiction. But it was no reason to go haring off to Brazil with him. Roberto wanted her, she knew only too well. But whether his heart was in tune with his body was a different matter. Roberto Rocha was long accustomed to girls who took one look and fell in love with him. Or at least fell into bed with him.

When they finally set off Katherine craned her neck to take one last look at the house as the car moved down the winding drive. Her time at the Quinta das Montanhas had been short, but it had changed her life.

Roberto slid an arm around her and drew her close. 'Do not look so sad, *amada*. I will bring you back here one day, I promise.'

Not going to happen, thought Katherine miserably.

'When you reach Heathrow, please seek help with your luggage,' he ordered.

'I'll take a taxi and text Rachel. She'll be waiting as I get home.' Katherine smiled brightly. 'She's a journalist, by the way, so she'll want every last detail about my stay here.'

'Will you tell her about me?'

'Of course. But only about your home and past career, and the painting, not—'

'That I am your lover?' He put a finger under her chin to bring her face close to his. 'Because that is exactly what—and who—I am, *linda flor*,' he whispered against her parted lips, and kissed her with a heat she returned in kind. 'I will not make a spectacle of you at the airport,' he said unevenly, 'so this must be our goodbye. When I get home to the Estancia there are things I must do. When I have achieved them, I will come to you.'

The drive to Oporto ended all too soon for Katherine. When they arrived at the Francisco Sá Carneiro Airport Jorge stacked her luggage on a trolley and shook her hand very formally.

'*Boa viagem, Doutora.*'

She smiled warmly. 'Goodbye, Jorge. You and Lidia have been so kind.'

'*Sempre as seus ordems,*' he assured her, and with tact left them alone together.

Roberto took Katherine's hand, his eyes holding hers. 'I may come no further with you, *amada*, so go. Go *now*, before I drag you back to the car and take you to Brazil.'

She chuckled, as he intended her to, and laced her fingers with his. 'Goodbye, then.'

He raised her hand to his lips to kiss it, then with a sudden groan pulled her into his arms and kissed her mouth as though his life depended on it. '*Ate logo*, Katherine. I refuse to say goodbye.' Roberto put her away from him, breathing hard. 'Now go, *por favor*. And do not look back.'

Katherine obeyed blindly. The sheer physical pain of parting with Roberto left her feeling numb, not only during the longueurs of Security and Check in, but throughout the entire time she sat pretending to read a book while she waited to board the plane. It was only when she accepted tea later from a stewardess as the plane cruised towards Heathrow Katherine realised she'd sat through takeoff and the climb to altitude without even noticing. She shook her head in astonishment, surprising the man sitting next to her. Falling in love had strange side effects. But now she'd done so at long last, why couldn't she have fallen for someone who at least lived on the same continent?

Rachel came hurrying out of the house in Parsons Green when the taxi arrived and took charge of some of the luggage as Katherine paid the driver. Once everything was hauled inside the flat, Rachel gave Katherine a hug, eyeing her closely.

'I'll put the kettle on. Alastair's playing golf with Hugh, so we can chat in peace over tea and cakes.'

'Thanks, Rachel. The unpacking can wait.' Katherine yawned. 'I feel very lazy.'

'You look shattered. Surely you're not going straight back to work tomorrow?'

'I'll see how I feel in the morning.'

'But exactly how *do* you feel?' demanded Rachel. 'I'll make tea before you tell all. And I do mean all!'

Katherine curled up in a corner of the rubbed old leather sofa of her childhood while Rachel was busy in her kitchen and gratefully accepted the tea, but turned down the pastries. 'Could I postpone those until later?'

Rachel smiled in sympathy and sat opposite in the matching armchair. 'Bad flight?'

Katherine shook her head. 'Just tiring.'

'You look done in,' accused her friend. 'Was it hard work restoring the painting?'

'No.'

'Just no?' demanded her friend. 'Come on, Dr Lister. Give. What's wrong? If you don't tell me I'll explode.'

'I had such a lovely time it was a wrench to leave the

Quinta das Montanhas,' said Katherine with perfect truth.

'The house of the mysterious Mr de Sousa! What's he like?'

'Charming.'

Rachel's eyes narrowed. 'Come on, I want more than that. I take it he has money if he paid for your services, Doctor, but is he young, old, single or attached, thin, fat, bald—?'

'Divorced. Early thirties, slim, dark curling hair.'

Rachel was small and delicate-looking, but with a shrewd brain under her stylish blonde bob, and she'd known Katherine since they were teenagers. 'You liked him a lot.'

'Yes.'

Rachel's blue eyes narrowed in frustration. '*Talk* to me. Tell me what happened to make you look so down. I'm worried!'

Katherine obediently gave an account of her stay at Roberto de Sousa's glorious house, beginning with the first encounter.

'He was expecting a man?' Rachel chuckled. 'You must have been a nice surprise, then.'

Katherine shook her head. 'Not at all. Roberto didn't want a woman. Particularly a starchy art historian in glasses, with hair scraped back and so on.'

'You were on first name terms from the start?'

'Almost. He insisted on it.' Katherine went on to describe her excitement as she identified an early Gainsborough, followed by excitement of a different kind when she discovered that her host was better known as Roberto Rocha, one-time star of the racing circuit. 'But motorsport is not my thing, so I'd never heard of him.'

'*What?* You're kidding!'. Rachel's eyes widened. 'I once had a fling with a sports journalist who wept when Roberto Rocha retired so young. Damn it, Katherine, I wish I'd been there with you to interview him—sorry, love, keep going.' She listened without interruption until Katherine finished, and then shook her head in wonder. 'It's happened, hasn't it? You've fallen hard for a man at last. Are you going to see him again?'

Katherine smiled bleakly. 'Not easy when we live on different continents. Besides, he'll probably forget all about me once he's back on the ranch.'

'As if!' said Rachel scornfully. 'I must look him up on the Net. I want to see this man for myself.'

'I've got some photographs on my laptop. Boot it up if you like.'

Rachel leapt to the desk to switch on the machine, and let out an inelegant whistle as the first shot came up. She turned the laptop screen towards Katherine.

'Is this the house?'

'Quinta das Montanhas, his holiday home in Portugal. The family home is on a ranch in Rio Grande do Sul, in Brazil. And that's Roberto,' said Katherine, her heart contracting as the next shot came up to show him smiling at her from the screen. 'I had to persuade him to let me take the photograph.'

Rachel eyed the image in silence for a moment, then turned to her. 'He's hot! And from the look in his eyes, Roberto's pretty hot for you, too.'

'We only met a few days ago.'

'What difference does that make?'

Katherine watched as Rachel slowly scrolled through the rest of the photographs, then, unable to bear looking at them any longer, asked her to switch the machine off.

'You do realise,' said Rachel, complying, 'that your

holiday snaps could be a nice little earner for me if I wrote a feature to go with them.'

'Yes. But you won't.'

'Sadly, no.' Rachel smacked her lips. 'Pretty lad, your Roberto.'

'He thinks his scar makes him ugly.'

'Wrong! It's hugely sexy. And those eyes smouldering as you snapped him! No wonder you fell for him. Who wouldn't?'

Katherine laughed for the first time, and Rachel nodded in approval.

'That's better. Alastair and Hugh are bringing food home, and I've laid the table for four upstairs.' She held up a hand. 'Don't say no. You'll sleep all the better afterwards.'

Katherine actually wanted nothing more than to crawl into bed. 'Just for an hour. But before I scrub myself I'd better do some unpacking.'

'Hurry up, then,' said Rachel promptly. 'See you upstairs about seven.' She turned at the door. 'Did you let the legal eagle know you were coming home today?'

Katherine stared at her in dismay. 'Oh, Lord, I forgot—I'll text him now.'

She was wielding a hairdryer when her doorbell rang later.

'Welcome home!' Andrew boomed through the intercom. 'Let me in.'

She released the lock and opened her sitting room door, standing back as Andrew strode in, brandishing a sheaf of flowers, sleek of hair, smartly dressed, and just slightly overweight. Or maybe that was just the contrast with Roberto. She stood still, bracing herself for an unpleasant few minutes.

'Hello, there,' he said, smiling, and waved a hand in front of her face. 'Earth to Katherine.'

'Hello, Andrew,' she said without warmth. 'I'm afraid you've caught me at a bad time. I'm getting ready to go out.'

He frowned. 'But surely you've just got home.'

'I have.'

He handed her the flowers. 'I brought these as a peace offering.'

'Thank you.' She put them down on a table.

He eyed her askance. 'What the hell's wrong with you, Katherine? You can't be jet-lagged after a flight from Oporto!'

'I'm just tired.'

'So how come you're going out?'

'I'm not. I'm having supper upstairs.'

'With the usual suspects, of course,' he sneered, but hastily changed tack in response to her glare. 'Katherine, if I was out of order before you went away, I'm sorry. But I feel I had every right to be annoyed when you took off the very day I had gala tickets for Glyndebourne.'

'I disagree,' she said coldly. 'Your behaviour was unpleasantly immature, Andrew.'

His light blue eyes opened wide in sudden fury. '*Immature?* That's rich. If anyone's immature it's you, Katherine. It's time you left this student squat of yours and shared my house.'

'This is no squat, it's my family home. Besides, you just want me to share your bed,' she retorted, and could have kicked herself when heat leapt in his eyes.

'I'll share yours, if you prefer!'

She shook her head. 'Not going to happen, Andrew.'

His eyes turned ugly. 'Oh, yes, it is.' He seized her

by the shoulders, shaking her slightly when she winced in distaste. 'I've had it up to here with your teasing.'

'Teasing?' she hissed in outrage as his fingers bit into her flesh, then flushed in hot embarrassment as Alastair and Hugh burst into the room with Rachel close behind. Andrew dropped his hands, staring defiantly as both men, fit muscular six-footers, stood shoulder to shoulder to face him.

'Did he hurt you, Katherine?' asked Hugh in a deadly quiet voice.

'Say the word and I'll throw him out,' ordered Alastair, his Scots accent more pronounced than usual.

'Absolutely not,' she said irritably, and turned to Andrew. 'Time you were leaving, I think. It's not the way I would have chosen to say goodbye, but goodbye it is. It would never have worked out for us.'

He made a move towards her but stopped in his tracks at the look Alastair gave him. 'All right, all right, hold your horses. Look, Katherine, I'm sorry if I hurt you. I apologise, abjectly. Will you forgive me?'

'Yes.' She managed a bleak little smile. 'But it's still goodbye, Andrew.'

CHAPTER EIGHT

'MY GOD,' said James Massey when Katherine arrived at the gallery the next day. 'You look terrible. Not my flu, I hope!'

'No. There was a welcome home party last night, so I got to bed a bit late. Are you recovered, James?'

'Yes, thank God.' He smiled warmly. 'I owe you big time for stepping in for me, Katherine.'

'I was only too glad to help. Now, where's my young man?'

Katherine's heart gave a thump as she looked at the painting. Fully restored, the likeness to Roberto was unmistakable. 'When are you sending it off?'

'I'll wait to hear from the client.' James eyed her over his spectacles. 'So how did you get on with Roberto Rocha de Sousa?'

'Rather well,' she said sedately. 'He was very kind. So were the people who work for him.'

'You're not sorry I sent you to him, then,' he said slyly.

'No,' said Katherine with perfect truth. 'It was a very interesting experience.'

A day back in routine was oddly comforting after the emotional highs and lows of the past week. Katherine immersed herself in work so completely James had to remind her it was time to go home. Panicking at the thought of missing Roberto's call, she ran for the Underground, joined the crush of commuters on the train home and rushed into the house with just time enough to make some coffee while she waited for the all important phone call.

But the phone remained silent. As the evening wore on with no word from Roberto Katherine's emotions ranged from desperate disappointment to white-hot anger, which finally died into the cold ashes of bitter resignation. It was the oldest story in the book. After the accident, Roberto had been without female company and fate had sent her to him just when he needed a woman most. Probably any reasonably attractive woman would have done. But Katherine Lister had just happened to possess that certain something extra—insider knowledge of the subject that interested him most. Plus a response to his lovemaking that clenched her fists in fury at the thought of it. She'd even owned up to feelings for him! Though looking at it with the cold clarity of hindsight, she suspected that had been for her own sake as much as Roberto's. After all, she had a reputation to uphold. Other people might fall into bed with changing partners with joyous abandon, cerebral feelings or not, but never the famously choosy Katherine Lister. Who now knew that choosy had been nothing to do with it. With others, up to and including Andrew Hastings, she just hadn't been sufficiently attracted. Whereas one look at Roberto Rocha de Sousa had fired up the pilot light under her hormones, igniting a response she had never experienced before. And never would again.

It was a long, long week. Katherine's absorption in the work she loved passed the daytime hours at reasonable speed. But the evenings were bad. Rachel was the only one who knew just how bad. The weekend was bearable, courtesy of an invitation to Sunday lunch with Charlotte and Sam, where Katherine's trip to Portugal was the main topic of conversation over the roast. But however empty the evenings during the following week, Katherine felt no regrets about giving Andrew his marching orders.

'He said I was a tease,' she told Rachel.

'Because you said no?'

'Apparently.' Katherine scowled. 'I should have said no to Roberto, too.'

Rachel's eyes widened. 'You mean you actually… um…slept with him?'

'Yes. Literally. I was the only one on the upper floor of the house, and after the threatening letter came he refused to let me sleep alone and unprotected up there. So Roberto shared my room. And my bed.'

'To protect you. New approach!'

'At the time I was very grateful. I didn't fancy lying awake all night, afraid someone might climb through the window and mug me.' Katherine shrugged. 'It was no big deal.'

Rachel gave her a troubled look. 'Is that true?'

'No, damn it, it's not. For me it was a great big deal.' Katherine's eyes glittered coldly. 'But obviously not for him. And that, Rachel Frears, is the last time I mention his name, I promise.'

Two weeks to the day of Katherine's return, the phone rang while she was picking at a solitary supper.

'Katherine?'

She stiffened. 'Who is this?' Though she knew very well.

'Roberto. Roberto de Sousa,' he added when she made no response.

She rubbed a hand over the heart turning cartwheels at the first sound of his voice. 'Why, hello. You got home safely, then.'

'A week ago,' he informed her.

A *week* ago? 'You sound tired.'

'Just a little. Tell me, Katherine, how are you?'

'I'm very well,' she said untruthfully. 'How are you? Did your leg stand up to the flight?'

'No. *Infelizmente*, it gave me hell. When my father met me at the airport he insisted on taking me straight to the hospital, where work was done on it which much improved it, *gracas a Deus*.'

'That's good news. I'm glad for you.'

'I stayed at the hospital for treatment for a while. I did not ring you while I was in the hospital because I am well known there, you understand, and I was never alone. There was much to say to you that could not be overheard. So. *Escuta*—listen, Katherine.'

'I'm listening.'

'I had much time to think in the hospital, even more now I am back at Estancia Grande. You know that when Luis died it was my intention to stay at the Estancia only until I could leave to resume my career. But the crash changed that.'

'And now you're resigned to knuckling down to life on the Estancia?'

'*Exatamente*—as I always intended to one day. My father has bought my mother an *apartamento* in Porto Alegre, so that once I am fit enough to take over from him, they can spend time together in the city occasionally.'

'How do you feel about that?'

'I am glad for my parents, but I will be lonely here

without them. I miss you, Katherine,' he added with sudden urgency. 'Have you missed me?'

'I wondered why you hadn't rung,' she admitted, her mouth twisting at the understatement.

'You thought I no longer cared?'

'You never said you did care, Roberto.'

'*Como*?' he said, amazed. 'You did not hear the things I said as we made love?'

'They weren't in English so I assumed they were just the usual things men say.'

'They were not,' he said hotly, and paused for a moment. 'You said you had feelings for me. Were they just these usual things, also?'

'Whatever they were, they changed when I didn't hear from you.'

'You thought that once we parted I forgot you?' he demanded.

'Something like that, yes.'

'How could you think such a thing? I have never felt such rapture in a woman's arms before, Katherine.'

'That's hard to believe when you subject me to a fortnight's silence before informing me of the fact,' she snapped, suddenly so angry she wanted to hit something. Preferably Roberto de Sousa, bad leg or not.

'You are angry with me, *querida*,' he said with satisfaction. 'So you still care a little, yes?'

She took in a deep breath. 'Why didn't you get in touch?'

'I was…not well for some time,' he admitted, so reluctantly Katherine smiled a little. Roberto the gaucho obviously hated to confess to weakness. 'I wished to feel better before I spoke to you. Also, I have had much to think about before I talked to you.'

'So talk.'

'You sound like *Doutora*, not my Katherine.'

'Probably because I'm not your Katherine!'

'You have gone back to your lover?' he demanded.

For a moment she was tempted to say yes. 'No,' she said shortly.

'*Por que*? Why, Katherine?'

'You know why.'

'Because you love me!'

'Because I didn't want to leave my house to live in his.'

'You must leave it one day, when you marry,' he said, surprising her.

'Not necessarily. The lucky man could just live here with me.'

'You would insist on that?'

'Probably. But since I'm not about to marry anyone, the question doesn't arise. The painting's ready, by the way,' she added, to change the subject.

'That is good...*momento*.' He broke off to speak to someone in the background. 'Forgive me, I must go, Katherine. I will ring you tomorrow. Is this time of day good for you?'

'Yes, but not tomorrow,' pride forced her to say.

'Then I will ring the next day. *Ate logo*, Katherine.'

'Goodbye,' she said politely.

She spent the rest of the evening alternately elated because Roberto had rung at last, and furious because she'd postponed another call for an entire day, just to save face. To pass the time the following evening, she did some late night grocery shopping before going home, then ground her teeth in frustration when she got back to a message on her phone from Roberto.

'I wanted to speak to you before you went out, Katherine. I shall ring again tomorrow. *Dorme bem*.'

Rather to her surprise, Katherine did sleep well and got to work earlier than usual so she could leave on time with a clear conscience. She was determined to be at home early enough to sit calmly with a sandwich and a cup of coffee when the phone rang, which it did, prompt to the minute.

'Katherine?'

'Yes, Roberto.'

'*Otimo*, I do not like speaking to a machine.'

'I told you I wouldn't be at home last night, so why did you ring?'

'To hear your voice, Katherine. And I did, but only on the message on your telephone. You have had a busy day?'

'Yes. I think I've found something interesting for James to follow up, a possible sketch by Etty. Have you heard of him?'

'No. Tell me about him. What is he famous for?'

'Nudes,' she said reluctantly.

Roberto cleared his throat audibly. 'I will look him up. But no woman he has painted could be more beautiful than you, Katherine.'

'How kind of you to say so,' she said primly.

He laughed softly. 'That was Dr Lister speaking, *nao e*?'

'And, still speaking as Dr Lister, shall I tell James to ship the painting right away?'

'Yes, Katherine. Then it will arrive in good time for my parents' wedding anniversary at Christmas. I shall also give them the unknown young lady in white to make the pair.'

So his parents were the lucky recipients. 'I'll tell the shippers to take extra care,' she promised. 'How many years have your parents been married?'

'Thirty-five, Katherine—a triumph compared to my record! I shall arrange a *festa* to celebrate such an achievement, with all our friends and neighbours invited to a traditional *churrasco*.'

'Sounds like fun,' she said, feeling wistful.

'How do you celebrate Christmas, Katherine?'

'Very quietly.' It was the time she missed her father most of all. 'Beforehand, there's a lot going on socially, but I spend the day itself with my aunt and her husband.' And then return home in the evening to a house more than usually empty because Rachel, Alastair and Hugh would be with their families.

'My mother is most interested in the lady who identified my painting,' said Roberto. 'Therefore, it would please her very much if you came to stay with us at Christmas.'

Katherine's eyes widened. 'To Brazil?'

'It is where I live,' he said dryly. 'Come to me and see how we gauchos live here in Rio Grande do Sul. Say yes, Katherine.'

It was a tempting thought, but impossible, of course. 'It's good of you to invite me, but I can't take any more time off, Roberto.'

'If you could have this time, you would come?'

'I suppose I might,' she said cautiously.

'You do not wish to see me again?' he demanded. 'I was just a…how do you say…a fling?'

'I don't do flings,' she snapped.

'Then come,' he ordered. 'I will give you time to think about it, then ring you tomorrow.'

Katherine thought about it so much she had a restless night, unable to get round the fact that Roberto had taken two whole weeks to get in touch with her. Whatever treatment he'd had, or thinking he had to do, surely he could have just rung to say he'd arrived, if nothing else. But then, she reminded herself, she didn't know Roberto de Sousa well enough to understand the workings of his mind.

She learned a little more about those workings when she arrived at the gallery the next morning. James called her into his office to inform her that he'd received a request from Roberto de Sousa to allow Dr Lister two weeks holiday over Christmas to travel to Rio Grande do Sul. First class travel expenses would be provided.

Katherine eyed him narrowly. 'What did you tell him?'

He grinned. 'I said yes, of course. You'd be mad to turn down a free holiday in Brazil!'

Rachel said the same when Katherine rang her at lunch time. 'Just go, girl. You know you want to!'

Katherine did want to, but couldn't bring herself to let Roberto know that. Yet. 'You went over my head,' she accused when he rang.

'*Como*? I do not understand,' he said, surprised.

'You contacted James about giving me time off before I'd even agreed to come.'

'But you said you would consider it if you had the time off, Katherine, so I contacted Senhor Massey to… to expedite matters. This is right?'

'The word is right, yes.'

'My mother will write to you to invite you formally, if this is your problem, Katherine.'

'How kind of her.'

'So you will come?' He paused as though waiting for her answer. At last, in a harsh tone she'd never heard from him before, he said, '*Muito bem*, if you do not wish to see me again, forget it.'

'Hold your horses,' she said, panicking.

'*Como?*'

'I do want to see you again,' she said, climbing down. 'But if you want the truth, Roberto, I'm still hurting because you took so long to ring me.'

'I wanted to be strong again before I spoke to you,' he said harshly. 'Can you not understand that, Katherine?'

'Is that because you're a gaucho?'

'No, *querida*, because I am a man!'

'As I well know,' she assured him, and he laughed softly.

'So make me a happy man, and say you will come to me at my home, Katherine.'

Suddenly she wondered why she was dragging her feet. Of course she would go. Life was too short to pass up a chance like this. 'Since you put it that way, yes, I will, Roberto. Thank you very much for inviting me. I'll be happy to spend Christmas at your Estancia.'

There was silence for a moment. '*Gracas a Deus*,' said Roberto huskily. 'I shall be counting the days until you arrive. Tomorrow you must tell me which day you can leave and I will arrange a plane ticket.'

Once everything was settled after a prolonged and satisfactory talk with Roberto the following night, Katherine asked Rachel to an impromptu meal with Alastair and Hugh, and to their astonishment served champagne with rare fillet of beef.

'I know it should be red wine with this, but who cares?'

'This is obviously a special occasion,' said Rachel. 'What's up?'

'I'm going away for Christmas,' Katherine informed them.

'That's a few months away,' Alastair pointed out.

'True, oh, obvious one.'

'Are you going back to Portugal?' asked Hugh.

'No, to a cattle ranch in Rio Grande do Sul,' said Katherine with drama.

'To stay with Roberto Rocha!' Rachel announced, and then howled with laughter at the look on the men's faces. 'That's the mysterious client who paid Katherine to identify his painting.'

'Hold on!' said Hugh. 'Are we talking about the Brazilian racing driver here? The glamour boy who retired young?'

'The very same,' said Katherine, and smiled demurely. 'He's interested in my kind of work.'

'From what I remember, it's probably not only your work he's interested in, Dr Lister,' said Alastair, grinning, and then sobered. 'You'd better watch your step.'

'I'm staying with his parents, so it's all very respectable,' she assured him. 'And I'm travelling in style. Roberto's arranged a first class airline ticket.'

Once the urgent matter of the Christmas visit was settled with Roberto, during their regular phone conversations they caught up with everything that had happened in their lives since the parting at the airport in Oporto.

'The night we left the Quinta the security firm caught Elena's photographer friend searching my room,' Roberto told her. 'He swore on his mother's life that he was working alone, but I cannot believe that.'

'So once again the charming Elena gets off scot-free,' said Katherine.

'Let us speak no more of her. My interest is in you, Katherine Lister.'

Sooner than she would have thought possible, Roberto told Katherine he'd begun spending regular periods on horseback with the herd now his leg was so much improved. 'It will mean less frequent phone calls,' he warned. 'You sound tired, *querida*.'

'Life's a bit hectic right now, but I don't mind that. It makes the time pass more quickly until—' She stopped abruptly, not sure it was wise to show how much she longed to see him.

'Until we are together again? Tell me you share my impatience, Katherine!'

Of course she did. So much so she changed the subject in case he guessed how much. 'Roberto, have you any idea about your mother's dress size?'

'*Como*? How could I know that?'

'Think of me—'

'I do, constantly. Night and day!'

'Be serious.'

'I am very serious.'

'Concentrate. Is your mother something the same size as me? Is she dark, or fair, her eye colour and so on?'

'She is not quite as tall as you, and is just a little more…how shall I say…rounded? Her eyes and hair are dark like mine. Why?'

'I'm doing some Christmas shopping tomorrow.'

'You need buy nothing for me,' he said promptly. 'All I want for Christmas, Dr Katherine Lister, is to see you again!'

CHAPTER NINE

KATHERINE was seen off by Rachel and Alastair at Heathrow to catch her plane to São Paulo for the connection to Porto Alegre. The weather, which had been stormy for days beforehand, had relented to provide a still, frosty December evening for the flight.

'You'll get a bed in first class,' Alastair informed her. 'Or so my boss says. Never had the pleasure myself.'

There was a tearful hug from Rachel and a hearty one from Alastair before Katherine plunged into the long process of getting through Security on her way to her first experience of first class travel, the main advantage of which seemed to be fewer people and more space. When she finally boarded the plane she was surprised to find only fourteen passengers in first class. The flight would obviously be more comfortable than others she'd experienced, but for nights beforehand Katherine had been kept awake by increasingly cold feet about actually meeting Roberto de Sousa again. She had known him for such a short time that serious doubts had begun to creep in about the wisdom of flying halfway round the world to him. When they met again they might not feel the same intensity of emotion which had sent them into each other's arms so quickly at the Quinta das Montanhas.

But now she was here, fastened into her comfortable

seat, it was too late for doubts, and, once they had taken off and a meal was served, Katherine settled down to watch a film, with a Portuguese/Brazilian dictionary to study as backup.

She dozed, rather than slept, during the endless night and woke very early to visit one of the bathrooms to freshen up and change her clothes ready to disembark at seven at Guarulhos Airport in São Paulo. Leaving London in winter to travel to summer in Brazil had posed a problem about what to wear on arrival, and she had fallen back on jeans and matching jacket, plus a new scarlet T-shirt, to make sure Roberto spotted her straight away.

Over breakfast, Katherine learned she would have a good two hours to make the connection to Porto Alegre, and was glad of it later as she plunged into the noisy, colourful chaos of the airport to pass through Customs. The process was so bewildering and took so long she eventually reached the TAM check-in desk with very little time to board the plane.

When it touched down in Port Alegre later, Katherine took in a deep breath as she entered the great vaulted interior of Salgado Filho Airport. She'd made it! In spite of language problems, she managed to get to the baggage carousel, but because she was impatient it seemed to take forever before she was in possession of her luggage. Breathless with excitement, she decided to carry her bags and, having memorised the word for exit, made as fast a beeline for it as she could, laden with luggage. She came to a full stop when she reached it, her heart sinking when there was no sign of Roberto. Instead, with a feeling of déjà vu, she saw a stranger scanning the crowd as he held up a placard with her name on it. But this time there was no surprise when she presented herself. The man smiled, bade her welcome, showed her some identity and introduced himself as Geraldo Braga of Estancia Grande. He relieved her of her luggage and held out a letter. 'This will explain all, *Doutora*.'

Katherine read swiftly:

My son begs your forgiveness that he cannot come himself to greet you. He has been held up out with the herd. He asks that you trust yourself to Geraldo Braga, who will fly you here to Estancia Grande. My husband and I eagerly wait to welcome you. With kindest regards,
Teresa Rocha Lima de Sousa.

Katherine returned the letter to the envelope and smiled valiantly to hide her disappointment. '*Obrigado*, Senhor Geraldo.'

'If you will follow me, *Doutora*.'

Within a dizzyingly short time she found herself in a light aircraft with Geraldo Braga at the controls, and her excitement was intense as they soared up into the blue and left the city behind. When they eventually flew over vast grasslands her pilot gave her an approving smile as he saw her pleasure.

'Please to look down. We are now over Estancia Grande land, *Doutora*.'

She could see that the green of the rolling grassland had given way to something brown. 'What crop is that?'

'It is cattle. Estancia Grande cattle,' he added with pride.

'All that!' She stared down, amazed, at the great stain of brown on a landscape which eventually turned back into green grassland as they flew on.

'Soon you will see the house,' she was informed, and Katherine took in a deep breath, her excitement intense as he reduced speed to begin their descent. As they flew lower she saw a runway leading to a building that obviously housed the plane and, some distance beyond it on a rise, a large white house sheltered by trees, with other buildings nearby. The plane was set down so skilfully she could hardly believe they were on the ground when Geraldo got out of his seat to release her.

When he opened the door Katherine saw a man and a woman waving as they hurried towards the plane.

'*O Patrao* and Dona Teresa,' announced Geraldo, and leapt out with an agility she devoutly hoped she could copy. But the moment she was set on her feet Katherine was taken into a scented embrace as Teresa de Sousa bade her welcome with warmth that set some of her fears at rest.

'It is a great pleasure to meet you, Dr Lister,' she said in an attractive, husky voice. Elegant in tailored linen, Teresa de Sousa smiled warmly as she released her guest. 'This is my husband.'

He took Katherine's hand and, to her surprise, kissed it instead of shaking it. 'António Carlos de Sousa,' he announced. 'I add my welcome, Dr Lister.'

'Katherine, please,' she said, feeling absurdly shy.

'And I am Teresa,' Roberto's mother informed her and smiled at Geraldo. 'You will take the luggage, *por favor.*'

'*Agora mesmo*, Dona Teresa,' he assured her.

'I apologise for my son's absence,' said his father. 'He was much concerned when he was delayed.'

'He comes now,' said Teresa, the dark eyes so like her son's gleaming with anticipation as she turned to her guest. 'Watch, *cara.*'

Katherine looked in the direction of Teresa's pointing hand and realised that the noise she could hear in the distance was the thunder of hooves. As it grew nearer, her eyes widened in delight as a cloud of dust resolved itself into a group of riders who reined in their mounts in a sudden theatrical standstill. Antonio laughed softly behind her as one of the riders spurred his mount ahead of the rest, and sat easily in the saddle as he inclined his head in greeting. Like all the men behind him, he wore a flat hat with a chinstrap, a bandanna tied at the open collar of his loose linen shirt, balloon-pleated breeches and loose pleated leather boots with spurs. He swung down with lithe grace from the saddle, a revolver in a holster swung at one side of his silver-studded belt and a string of wooden beads and gleaming silver-sheathed knife at the other.

He swept the hat from his black curls and bowed, spurs chinking. 'Bem-vindo, Doutora. Welcome.'

Katherine's heart thumped as she gazed at him. Was this gorgeous creature the man who'd limped his way round Quinta das Montanhas? 'Thank you,' she said quietly, and held out her hand.

Roberto bowed over it and raised it to his lips, gave her a look which turned her knees to jelly, and then turned to introduce her to his men. 'Doutora Lister de Inglaterra.'

As one man they swept off their hats and smiled at Katherine, then one of them took the reins of Roberto's horse and, at his nod, the group wheeled round in a precise move and galloped away.

Teresa de Sousa smiled at her husband. 'Come, querido, we will hurry ahead and order tea while Roberto accompanies Katherine to the house. Do not linger too long, Roberto.'

The moment his parents were out of earshot, Roberto seized Katherine's hands. 'You came.'

She smiled slightly. 'As you see.'

'Until this minute, when I see you in the delectable flesh, I had doubts.'

'I said I would, Roberto.'

'After I used much persuasion!' His eyes glittered under the brim of his hat. 'Forgive me for my absence at the airport. I cursed the delay to high heaven. But I knew Geraldo would bring you safely to me.'

'And here I am,' she agreed, still afflicted with ridiculous shyness.

'*Gracas a Deus*,' said Roberto with feeling. 'I want very much to kiss you, Katherine, but I will not until we are alone.' He peered down into her eyes. 'Or do you not want to kiss me?'

'Not if it will give offence of any kind to your parents.'

'That does not answer my question,' he said huskily, and quickened his stride until she tugged on his hand to stop him.

'You're not limping!'

He smiled. 'At last you notice. I am better, no?'

'Better, yes.' She looked up into his face. 'And the scar is quite faint now.'

'But I am still not pretty enough to kiss?'

Katherine laughed and took his hand as he led her up the drive towards the big white building she could now see had two single-storey wings branching from the main house.

'You like our home?' asked Roberto, watching her face.

'It's beautiful.' Katherine was impressed. When Antonio de Sousa stole his bride away from her

Portuguese home he had brought her to a newer, but no less imposing house in Rio Grande do Sul. Roberto led her across a long colonnaded veranda into a large hall with a sweeping staircase and a tall, brightly decorated Christmas tree. He showed her into a comfortable room furnished with hide sofas and smaller, more feminine pieces upholstered in velvet and chintz faded enough in places to give the room a welcoming, lived-in look.

Teresa was waiting for them. 'You would like tea or coffee, Katherine?'

'I'd love some tea,' said Katherine gratefully, 'but first I'd like a very quick tidy up.'

'*Pois e*. Come. Antonio has gone to the *curral*. He will be back later.'

Katherine followed her hostess to a bathroom under the sweep of the curving staircase in the hall. After a quick session with the contents of her handbag, Katherine went back across the hall, smiling wryly as she passed the great tree. This was all a long way from her preconception of a cattle ranch. Teresa de Sousa smiled warmly as Roberto led Katherine to a seat beside him on a sofa.

'Are you very tired, Katherine?' he asked.

'A bit.' She smiled wryly. 'I feel as though I've been travelling for days.'

'I know this feeling!' Teresa shuddered in sympathy as she gave her guest a cup of tea. 'I changed planes twice on flight from Lisboa. Roberto did this also. When he arrived he was in great pain.' She smiled proudly at her son. 'He looks different man now.'

'But Katherine says she liked me before, even with my scar,' Roberto informed her.

'Because she is woman of intelligence.' Teresa smiled at her guest with gratitude. 'It was good fortune that

Senhor Massey sent you to the Quinta, Katherine. You liked my old home?'

'Very much. It's a glorious house. But so is this, in a different way, *Senhora*.'

'*E verdade*, but, please, I am Teresa.' Her eyes sparkled. 'I have so much to tell you about my recent discoveries. But not yet. First you must recover from your journey. And Roberto must go to his rooms for a bath. He smells of horse.'

He shot a gleaming look at Katherine. 'Did you enjoy the little demonstration I put on for you?'

'Immensely. It was superb horsemanship. Do the men here really dress like that all the time?'

Roberto nodded. 'To ride with the herd, yes, because it is the most practical dress. But otherwise the younger men wear jeans, ride motorcycles and drive pickups as in the rest of the country.'

'It was good of them to put on a show for me!'

He laughed. 'They were most happy to impress you.'

'And they did,' Katherine assured him. 'I'm honoured.'

Teresa got up. 'Come, Katherine. I take you to your room.' She shook her head at her son, who promptly rose to accompany them. 'You have your bath. I will take care of your guest, *meu filho*.'

With a wry smile, Roberto gave his graceful little bow. 'Be quick, then.'

Teresa de Sousa led Katherine up the curving staircase to a landing which ran the length of the upper floor. 'I hope you will like your room, Katherine.' She ushered her into a large bedroom at the far end. It was furnished in similar style to the Quinta, but in lighter wood which echoed the burnished coppery-gold of the polished floor.

To Katherine's surprise, the windows looked down on a flower-filled garden enclosed by tall hedges.

'How absolutely lovely,' she exclaimed, and smiled at Teresa. 'I didn't expect a garden like this at a cattle ranch!'

'It is all my work,' her hostess said, plainly delighted. 'When Antonio brought me here as a bride it was just grass and trees and the *curral* with the horses.'

'You've done it all yourself?' said Katherine, astonished.

Teresa laughed. 'I have help, but I am designer and *chefe*, and I work in it most days.'

'The flowering hedge is magnificent.'

'Hibiscus does well here. *Agora*, we must hurry, Katherine. There is your bathroom through that door, but now we return to my impatient son.' Teresa paused as they left the room. 'You like Roberto?' she said bluntly.

Katherine nodded. 'Very much.' Just to see him again had made it plain that 'like' didn't even begin to cover her feelings for Teresa de Sousa's charismatic son.

Teresa smiled mischievously. 'It is plain he likes you very much also, Katherine.'

Antonio de Sousa was chatting to his son over glasses of beer when they went down. As they got to their feet, Katherine saw that now Roberto was dressed in similar clothes to his father their physique was similar, but he had inherited his looks from his mother rather than from his equally handsome sire.

They had drinks on the veranda, but afterwards Antonio went off to his office to do some work, and suggested Roberto show his guest around the Estancia.

'Katherine might wish to rest on her bed,' Teresa protested.

Roberto got up quickly. 'Then I shall take her up to her room. Later, Katherine, we shall explore outside.' He took Katherine's hand to hurry her up the stairs. When they reached her room he closed the door behind him and took her in his arms, rubbing his cheek against her hair. 'Now we are here in private I can kiss you at last, if you wish, *amada*.'

'Of course I wish,' she said with a sigh, and surrendered to the mouth that devoured hers with such hunger she felt dizzy, her breath tearing through her chest as she inhaled the scent of Roberto's skin. As she felt him harden against her she pulled away, gasping. 'You'd better go now.'

'I know I must,' he groaned. 'Ah, *querida*, it is so good to have you here.' He trailed a hand down her flushed cheek as though convincing himself she was real. And then said the last thing she expected. 'Can you ride?'

She blinked. 'Ride?'

'A horse.'

'Oh. Yes. Though not recently.'

'*Otimo.* We shall ride together in the morning.'

'It's Christmas Eve tomorrow. Won't your mother mind if we take off?'

He shook his head. 'My mother is so delighted to have such a clever, charming guest she will not mind, I promise.'

When Roberto had torn himself away after demanding, and receiving, one last kiss, Katherine decided that the first thing on the agenda was unpacking. And found that the suitcases on the chest at the end of the bed were empty. She ran to the wardrobe, where every stitch of clothing she possessed was either hanging from the rail, perfectly ironed, or neatly folded on the shelves. She raised her eyebrows as she stripped off her jeans and shirt. The de Sousa family led a very different life from hers! They were obviously conventional when it came to relationships too, if Roberto had to kiss her in secret. But since he had invited her here for Christmas, the de Sousas must surely realise that there was more between her and Roberto than just his gratitude for her work on his painting. Katherine sighed as she leaned back against the pillows on the pristine white bed, wishing he could share it with her later.

Katherine shook her head in wry wonder. This was something new in her life. Before meeting Roberto, her attitude had been a take it or leave it view on the rare occasions she'd found a man she liked enough to let him make love to her. She'd had no idea how wonderful the experience could be, given the right partner. Except that Roberto, in almost every other way, was exactly the wrong partner. He was now ready to put the glamour and excitement of his past career behind him and settle down to his share of running the Estancia Grande, but there was no place in his kind of life for someone like Katherine Lister.

She spent an hour deep in thought, then had a wash and did her face, dug out a perfectly ironed pink shirt and went down to the veranda.

'I sent for tea when I heard you,' said Teresa, and smiled. 'You feel better now?'

'I do indeed. I was all set to unpack, but I found some kind fairy had done it for me.'

Roberto held out a chair for her. 'Did you sleep?'

'No. I'm not one for naps in the day.'

'But you rested. Which was good,' approved Teresa.

'This is Dirce,' said Roberto, as the maid appeared with a tray. 'She unpacked for you.'

'*Muito obrigada*,' Katherine said to the girl, and Roberto explained briefly to the shy, smiling girl.

Knowing that Roberto was impatient to take her outside, Katherine drank down a cup of tea, excused herself to her hostess and went off with him to explore.

'I will not take you to my mother's garden,' said Roberto as they left the house. 'She will want to show you that herself. I will take you to the swimming pool, and then to the *curral* so you can meet some horses.'

'I'd better make friends with one if I'm to do some riding in the morning.'

'It is a long time since you rode?'

'Ages. So we'd better not go too far tomorrow or I won't be able to sit down to eat my Christmas dinner.' Katherine looked around her with interest as they made for a grove of trees which sheltered a sizeable swimming pool.

'You shall swim there later if you wish,' he told her and led her past it to make for the *curral*, a railed enclosure near a cluster of vine-covered outbuildings. She could hear men's voices and the sound of horses whickering, and she smiled up at Roberto in eager anticipation as they reached the group of horses tethered at the *curral* rails. Unlike the stable bred hacks she rode at home, these were the rough-coated descendants of wild mustangs, he informed her, stocky, strong animals with the stamina necessary for the hard work required of them. A group of men with dark, smiling faces came to greet Roberto, among them some Katherine had seen earlier. The head man patted one of the horses and beckoned politely.

'Geraldo is asking you to take a look at this one and see if you approve,' said Roberto.

Katherine climbed on the first rung of the rail so she could reach the horse's ears, and spoke into them softly while she stroked his head, telling him he was such a handsome fellow she'd like to ride him next day.

He whickered softly, and blew on her fingers, and Roberto laughed. 'I think he says he would like that very much. How could he not?' He called the other men over and introduced them. Katherine smiled warmly and greeted Geraldo again, then said *muito prazer* to Jose, Mario, Helio and Jango, and hoped she would remember which was which among the younger men.

'We will have a short ride tomorrow,' said Roberto as they strolled back to the house.

'Good. Other than not getting too stiff, I'd really like to help your mother.'

'Dirce and Maria the cook are already doing so, along with relatives they bring along for the occasion to help,' he assured her. 'Friends and neighbours will be sharing our meal, and preparation has been going on for days.'

She eyed him in alarm. 'I should have brought something grander to wear for the occasion.'

He laughed. 'Ah, Katherine. You may be a historian, but you are all woman also! And for this I am truly thankful,' he whispered in her ear.

'It's no laughing matter, Roberto Rocha de Sousa!'

He kissed her swiftly as they reached the trees near the house. 'It will not be the Christmas dinner you are used to, *amada*. It is a *churrasco* under the trees here, so no ball gown is necessary.'

'That's a relief.' Katherine eyed her feet in their flat

suede loafers as they approached the house. 'There's another problem, though, Roberto. No riding boots.'

'No matter. We will find some for you.'

Dinner that night was an informal affair on the veranda.

'We have simple meals on the days before Christmas, Katherine,' said Teresa. 'But on the day, our friends will join us for an Estancia Grande *churrasco*.'

'I wish you would let me help in some way,' said Katherine.

'After travelling so far, we cannot let you work,' said Antonio, filling her wine glass. 'And Roberto takes you riding in the morning. You ride at home?'

'Not as much as I'd like. When I was young I rode regularly at weekends and went on riding and trekking holidays with my father. These days, I just hire a mount when I have time.' She smiled at him. 'A different breed from your horses here.'

'Do not take her too far, Roberto,' warned his mother, eyeing Katherine with sympathy. 'It is recent that you lose your father?'

'No. Ten years ago, when I was eighteen.'

'He would be proud that his daughter is a *Doutora* of art history,' observed Antonio kindly.

Katherine nodded. 'He'd be delighted. Dad had a doctorate in the same subject, and lectured at the local college. He was at university with James Massey, the man I work for at the gallery.'

'And because of Senhor Massey I met you,' said Roberto with satisfaction.

After dinner Teresa led her guest across the hall into the formal drawing room for the first time, her excitement plain to see as she threw open the doors with a flourish. '*Olha*, Katherine. Here are the gifts Roberto has given us for our anniversary.'

'They arrived!' Katherine smiled in delighted recognition at the pair of paintings hanging either side of the massive stone fireplace. The young girl in her filmy white seemed to smile across shyly at the soberly dressed young man with the gleam in his eye. 'How marvellous! He looks really good now, Roberto!'

'Because you worked so hard on him,' he said, and kissed her hand. 'You are a clever lady.'

'*E verdade*, Katherine,' agreed his father, and smiled at his wife. 'Teresa wishes to tell you a story.'

Katherine was fascinated to hear that after Roberto mentioned his resemblance to the young man in the painting his mother had spent hours at her computer researching her family tree.

'Because of her research, some days we meet only at dinner,' said her husband dryly.

She gave him a sparkling glance. 'Better I am spending time with a computer than a lover, *nao e*?'

'Much better,' agreed her son fervently. '*Pae* would have killed him.'

'*E verdade,*' agreed Antonio, so matter-of-factly Katherine couldn't help laughing. 'Gauchos are jealous husbands,' he informed her with a gleam in his eye, then at an imperious look from his wife begged her to continue.

Teresa de Sousa's research had led her to José Luis Rocha Lima, an ancestor who had been involved in wine shipping in the late eighteenth century. 'He spent much time in England in a town called…how do you say it, Roberto?'

'Ipswich?' said Katherine in excitement. 'Where Gainsborough once lived?'

'*Isso mesmo.*' Teresa smiled triumphantly. '*Infelizmente*, I have no...no...'

'Provenance?'

'*Exatamente*, Katherine. I have no papers which prove the portrait is of a Rocha Lima.' Teresa took her son by the hand and led him over to stand underneath the portrait. 'But Roberto is proof enough, *nao e*? If I tie his hair back—'

Roberto dodged away, laughing. 'No ribbons, *por favor*!'

There was much animated discussion about the painting over coffee later, but at last Katherine had to smother a yawn, and Roberto jumped to his feet and held out his hand.

'You are tired, and if we are to ride in the morning we must go early. You still wish this?'

She nodded. 'If you can find me some boots, yes.'

'I have some which might fit,' said Teresa. 'But to rise early you must sleep now, *cara*.'

'What time must I get up?' asked Katherine, as Roberto took her up to her room.

'I will call you,' he promised, and took her in his arms as he backed into the bedroom door to close it. 'I want so much to make love to you, *amada*,' he whispered, and kissed her with a sudden, overwhelming hunger she responded to with equal heat.

'Me too,' she said breathlessly when she could speak. 'That's not going to happen, so go now, darling.'

Roberto's eyes blazed down into hers. 'I like this word. Say it again.'

'Darling—' Whatever else she'd intended to say was

smothered as his demanding mouth brought them to a mutual fever pitch of longing.

'This is torture,' he said hoarsely, and let her go. 'I will see you in the morning.'

CHAPTER TEN

KATHERINE was ready next morning when a tap on the door heralded not Roberto, as she'd expected—and hoped—but his mother, with two pairs of pleated soft boots, and Dirce following behind with a tray.

'*Bom dia*,' said Teresa, smiling. 'You are up early, Katherine.' She gestured to the girl to put the tray on the chest. '*Obrigada*, Dirce.'

'Good morning. I wasn't sure what time Roberto wanted to set off.'

'Soon, but only after you have eaten breakfast. Try the larger boots, *cara*.'

Katherine slid her foot into one and wriggled her toes. 'With socks, they'll be perfect.'

'*Muito bom*.' Teresa smiled. 'Roberto is impatient, but you must eat first.'

Katherine was as impatient as Roberto to set out on their ride together. After a sketchy breakfast she hurried downstairs in her borrowed boots and found Roberto on the veranda, spurs jingling in tune with his impatience as he talked to his parents. When Katherine joined them he swept off his flat black hat and bowed, looking so breathtakingly handsome in full gaucho dress again she laughed in delight.

'*Bom dia*, Katherine,' he said, preening outrageously. 'You like me in my working clothes?'

'I wish I had some just like them!' she assured him.

Antonio de Sousa handed her a black hat like Roberto's. 'You will need this, Katherine.'

'And do not take her far, Roberto,' warned Teresa. 'Katherine must be well for Christmas Day.' She turned to her husband, looking worried. 'Perhaps you should go with them, *caro*.'

He exchanged a look with his son, and shook his head. 'Roberto will take good care of our guest, *querida*.'

Katherine put the hat on and smiled at Roberto. 'Will I do?'

His eyes gleamed. 'Oh, yes. You will do.' After good-byes and promises to be careful, Roberto seized her hand and hurried her off towards the *curral*. 'How are you today?' he asked, once they were out of earshot. 'Did you sleep well?'

'Not really. It was no effort to get up early.'

'Nor for me. I wanted you in my bed, Katherine.'

She stopped before they reached the *curral*. 'Is that your main reason for asking me here? The bed part, I mean?'

His eyes glittered under the black hat's brim. 'No. How could it be? I knew well that unless we were married, or at least *noivado*, my mother would not expect us to sleep together. I shall exercise much patience until we stay for a time in Porto Alegre before your flight home.'

Katherine eyed him narrowly. 'What will your parents think we're doing in Porto Alegre?'

'Shopping!' He led her to the horses, which were saddled and ready, waiting with two of the men in attendance. Katherine tried a careful greeting in Portuguese which won warm smiles, and went up to her horse to pat him.

'The saddle here is different from the English type,' Roberto warned.

Katherine found it had no cantle or pommel, just a simple sandwich of leather pads and woollen blankets with a thick sheepskin on top. But she would probably soon get used to it. The sun was already so hot she took off her sweater and put it in her saddlebag while Roberto buckled circular spurs to her soft boots. He handed her the reins and gave her a leg up, and she settled herself on the strange saddle, leaning to gentle the horse while Roberto adjusted her stirrups.

'In the past a gaucho rode barefoot,' he informed her, 'gripping the straps between the toes for balance.'

Katherine pulled a face. 'I'm *really* glad I don't have to do that. What's the horse's name?'

'Garoto, which means boy, *mais ou menos*—words you will hear often. They mean more or less.' He motioned her to follow as the other men rode off ahead of them.

'Do we need an escort, then?' asked Katherine.

'No. They go to work.' Roberto waved a gloved hand towards the horizon, where a sea of brown marked the presence of the herd. 'We go with them so you can meet some of the Estancia cattle.'

Soon Katherine was comfortable enough with the saddle and the gait of her horse to gaze in appreciation at the vastness of the landscape. 'What on earth does it feel like to know this is all yours, Roberto?'

'I feel proud! This is *minha terra*, my land,' he said, a possessive note in his voice as he swept a hand to encompass the rolling green of the pampas. 'At one time, when Luis was still here, I had the freedom to go off and prove myself in my racing career. But now I am home to stay. My father is older than he looks, and suffers a little with the blood pressure. So now he can spend time at the apartment in Porto Alegre with my mother, as she so much wishes, while I gradually take over.'

'Is he happy about that?'

'It makes my mother happy, and he would do anything to ensure her happiness.'

Katherine nodded soberly, her eyes lighting up as they grew near enough to hear the bellowing of the herd. She watched, enthralled, battling to control Garoto's excitement as encircling horsemen and dogs drove the cattle on, herding them through gates in the line of fences she could now see demarcating the pastures. 'Amazing! How many in this lot?'

'Several hundred head,' yelled Roberto, his teeth a flash of white in his tanned face as he moved his horse nearer. 'Stay by me!'

Katherine followed him as closely as she could as the last stragglers were rounded up with much flapping of the long white scarves used by some of the men. 'Will they remain here now?'

'Because it is Christmas, yes, for the men to enjoy the *ferias* with their families. Afterwards, they will be driven to more distant pastures.' He cursed suddenly as one of the riders broke away from the rest and came riding hell for leather towards them.

'*Bom dia*,' called an unmistakably feminine voice as the rider reined in her mount. Her eyes flicked over Katherine's shirt and jeans, and dismissed them as no contest for her own gaucho splendour.

'What are you doing here, Gloria?' demanded Roberto.

The huge dark eyes opened wide in innocence. 'I heard you had visitor. I came to meet her.'

'How do you do?' said Katherine. 'I'm Katherine Lister.'

'This is Gloria Soares, daughter of one of neighbours,' said Roberto briefly.

'I brought message from my father for Senhor Geraldo, who now wishes to speak to you, Roberto,' said Gloria. '*Va embora*. I shall share my coffee with Miss Lister.'

'She is Dr Lister,' corrected Roberto. 'Stay right here, Katherine. I will not be long.'

'I look after her,' promised the girl, and took a flask from her saddlebag as Roberto rode off. She unscrewed the cap and filled it with steaming liquid. 'Black. OK?'

Katherine nodded, and gentled her mount with a soothing hand as he sidled closer to the other horse. 'Thank you.'

'You stay here long?' asked Gloria, handing the cup over.

'Until after the holidays.'

'Then you get back to hospital?'

Katherine blinked. 'Oh...no. I'm not a medical doctor. I'm a historian.'

The girl stared at her blankly, then her face lit with a megawatt smile as she saw Roberto returning and she leaned from her saddle to grasp Garoto's bridle with an ungentle hand. 'Roberto is mine,' she hissed.

When Katherine fought to control the fidgeting horse the coffee spilled on the ground. She tossed the cup back to Gloria with a cool smile. 'Thank you. Goodbye.'

'Come, Katherine,' said Roberto, reining in between them. 'We must return. *Ate ja*, Gloria.'

'*Amanha*,' she retorted. 'Christmas Day.'

She saluted them with her whip, then reined her horse up on his back legs in a showy display, which was the last straw for Garoto. He went bolting off in fright, and Katherine bit back a scream and hung on for dear life on the unfamiliar saddle, with Roberto in frantic pursuit as they shot towards a stand of trees.

'*Katherine!*' yelled Roberto in warning.

She ducked instinctively to avoid low branches and the horse, completely spooked by this time, bucked her off and raced into the distance.

Roberto leapt from his horse and looped the reins over a branch, then fell to his knees by Katherine, demanding that she tell him where she was hurt.

'I'm…winded…not…hurt,' she gasped, when she could speak.

Very gently, he ran his hands over her arms and legs and, even more gently, along her ribs. Reassured there was nothing broken, he gathered her into his arms and held her carefully, his heart thundering against hers. '*Deus!*' he groaned at last. 'Gloria is too careless.'

But Katherine was only too aware that the girl had done it deliberately. 'Do I walk back?' she said, when she could breathe more easily.

Roberto shook his head. 'My horse will take both of us.' He kissed her swiftly. 'Can you get up now, *amada*?'

She nodded. 'Yes, if you help me.'

'Do not try to walk. Just raise your arms.' He picked her up and carried her to his horse. He spoke soothingly to his mount as he settled Katherine on the saddle, then swung up behind her. 'Lean on me, *carinha*.'

Katherine did so, gratefully. 'When we get back I'll have a hot bath and I'll be fine,' she assured him.

They had ridden only a short distance when Antonio de Sousa came thundering towards them.

'*Deus*, Roberto, *que foi*?' he demanded breathlessly as he reined beside them. 'When Garoto came back alone Teresa was sure Katherine had bad fall. Are you hurt, *cara*?' he asked, touching Katherine's hand.

'Only my dignity.' She smiled at him ruefully. 'I fell off.'

'You did not,' contradicted Roberto fiercely. 'The horse bolted, then threw you off. Did you examine him, *Pae?*'

Antonio was so upset that, with an apology to Katherine, he lapsed into Portuguese to explain. When he finished, Roberto looked furious as he translated.

'Garoto was bleeding from thorns on his neck when they unsaddled him. Did Gloria get near enough to do this?'

'*Gloria?*' exclaimed Antonio. 'That girl was out with the men again?'

Roberto nodded, and bent to Katherine. 'Did she touch Garoto?'

In no mood to be noble, she nodded briefly.

As they came in sight of the *curral* two young men came running to help. Antonio dismounted and held up his arms to take Katherine, but Roberto shook his head. 'I will carry her. She says she is not hurt, but before I let her walk my mother must examine her to make sure.'

Antonio nodded in agreement as, with great care, Roberto lifted Katherine down. 'My wife has much experience with broken bones.'

'I'm sure there's nothing broken. I can walk,' gasped Katherine, manfully ignoring her sore bottom.

'*Fica quieta*. I need to hold you,' said Roberto through his teeth, and kept on walking.

Teresa came running from the house, her English a little fractured as she demanded details, and Katherine let the stream of Portuguese from the de Sousas flow over her head, interrupting only to mention a bath as Roberto, breathing hard by this time, carried her up to her room, with Teresa following behind.

Roberto laid Katherine on the bed, for which she was deeply grateful. Sitting had no appeal for the moment.

'I will run a bath,' said Teresa, but Katherine shook her head, smiling ruefully.

'I'd rather a hot shower, please. I landed too hard on my behind to sit in a bath.'

'*Nossa Senhora!*' exclaimed Teresa in distress. She looked at her son. 'Go shower, *caro*. I will help Katherine.'

'I will come back soon,' Roberto assured Katherine, and kissed her with a ferocity that made his mother blink. 'When you fell off my heart stopped,' he said hoarsely.

She smiled reassuringly. 'At least I didn't fall on my head—but I'm afraid I lost the hat.'

Roberto said something so rude about the hat his mother protested and shut the door on him as she sent him away. With long experience of her menfolk's bruises, sprains and occasional broken bones, Teresa helped Katherine undress, then ran practised hands over her until she was satisfied nothing was broken.

'I just bruised my bottom,' Katherine assured her.

Teresa nodded, smiling in sympathy. 'We give you cushion to sit at table for lunch.' Her eyes darkened. 'It is time Ildefonso Soares kept Gloria on tighter rein.'

* * *

Once the meal was over time rushed by in preparation for Christmas Day. Teresa gave her afternoon nap a miss and excused herself to go off to the kitchen, and suggested Katherine recline on the veranda to watch Antonio and Roberto supervise the men who were setting up tables and chairs, and stringing lights among the trees. But after watching for a while Katherine went for a walk to avoid stiffening up. She left the veranda to make for the kitchen block and found a hive of industry inside. Teresa smiled in welcome.

'You need something, Katherine?'

'I want to help. Can I join you?'

'*Pois e!*' Teresa ushered her into the large, busy room, which was filled with savoury smells. '*Escuta,*' she said loudly, and the smiling faces turned as she spoke to them quickly in Portuguese. 'I told them you wish to help. You know Dirce.' The girl nodded, smiling. 'Here is her mother, Maria the cook and Lourdes, sister of Maria, and Ana and Zelia her daughters.' All the women smiled and murmured a shy *muito prazer*, then Maria and Lourdes went back to slicing up meat for the *churrasco*, while the younger girls fashioned small savoury pastries.

Teresa eyed Katherine hopefully. 'You can cook, *cara*?'

'Yes, though not on this scale. But there must be something I can do.'

'Another *sobremesa* for tomorrow would be good. Something English, perhaps?'

Katherine nodded, eyeing the fruits Dirce had sliced ready for a *salada de frutas*. 'I could make a couple of trifles.' She listed the ingredients she needed, and was soon whipping up a sponge cake for the base. While it was baking, she went on to the tricky job of making custard, and the time passed so quickly Katherine was in the cold room off the kitchen later, putting her trifles together, when she heard Roberto burst into the kitchen with a flood of questions for his mother.

'*Calma, calma*, she is in there!' said Teresa.

He strode into the room to glare at Katherine. 'I searched the house and could not find you!'

She smiled. 'I was just enjoying myself with the others in the kitchen. I live alone at home, remember.'

Roberto stood utterly still as he looked down into her eyes. 'You need never be alone again.'

They gazed at each in silence until at last Katherine managed a smile. 'I need to finish this.'

He kissed her swiftly. 'Do not be long.'

When they sat down later to a Christmas Eve dinner served early so that the maids could get off in good time, Katherine was deeply touched to find that Teresa had done her utmost to make her guest feel at home.

'Tomorrow we have *churrasco*,' she told her guest as Maria came in with a huge turkey on a platter. 'But tonight we eat British Christmas dinner.'

'You need more cushions, Katherine?' asked Antonio, eyes twinkling as he carved.

'Not right now, *obrigada*,' she said, laughing.

Once the food was distributed the maids were thanked and sent off. 'Tonight we clear away ourselves, because they return early in the morning with their families for the *churrasco*,' said Teresa, and raised her glass in toast. 'We wish you a most happy Christmas, Katherine.'

Katherine raised her glass to them, smiling in gratitude. 'Thank you so much for inviting me here.'

After dinner Teresa refused offers of help from her guest and told Roberto to take Katherine for a walk under the stars. 'This is one night of year Antonio helps me in kitchen,' she said, laughing at her husband.

Katherine hurried upstairs to exchange her heels for flat sandals, and rejoined Roberto on the veranda.

'I switched on the lights in the trees,' he told her, taking her hand.

'It's magical,' she said, then turned to him urgently. 'Roberto, I've brought Christmas gifts for your parents. Should I hand them over tonight?'

'In the morning is better, after breakfast. We eat this together at Christmas. Most other days we leave the house early, either to ride with the herd, or work with the men at the dehorning and castrating.' He laughed as she winced. 'It is a necessary part of life here.' He brought her round to face him as they left the lights behind, his face suddenly very grave. 'Does our life here seem alien to you, Katherine?'

'Different, not alien.' She smiled up at him. 'I've only seen cattle like yours in Western films before.'

Roberto pulled her close to kiss her and, as she responded with unreserved fervour, went on kissing her until they were both trembling. She tore her lips away at last and held his face in her hands.

'Tell me the truth.'

'*Sempre*—always,' he said with passion.

'Are you going to marry Gloria Soares?'

'*Como!*' Roberto held Katherine away by the shoulders, staring down at her in outrage. 'Are you *louca*? You think I would bring you here to meet my family if I was promised to another woman—which is wrong description for a spoilt child like Gloria!' His fingers suddenly bit into her skin through her dress. 'She said this to you today?'

'More or less. Just before she hurt poor Garoto and

did her rodeo act to make him bolt with me,' Katherine said hotly.

His face hardened with sudden menace. 'Tomorrow I will have words with Maria Gloria Soares.'

'You'd better keep her right away from me, Roberto de Sousa,' said Katherine tartly. 'I might be tempted to punch her nose in revenge for my bruise.'

He gave a delighted crack of laughter and pulled her close again. 'If we were alone,' he said in a tone which buckled her knees, 'I would be most happy to kiss your bruise better.'

She swallowed, and buried her face against his chest. 'That's not fair.'

'You have the saying that all is fair in love and war, *nao e*? And this is not war between us.' He tipped her face up to his, the look in his eyes impossible to mistake in the faint light coming from the trees.

'No,' she agreed, and stood on tiptoe to kiss him.

He returned the kiss with fervour, then raised his head as bells pealed in the distance. '*Escuta*. It is Christmas Day. *Feliz natal*, Katherine.'

CHAPTER ELEVEN

THE moment Katherine got up next morning she sent texts to Charlotte, Rachel, Alastair and Hugh, and was ready in good time when Roberto, in best gaucho gear, came to fetch her for breakfast. When she gave him a kiss and wished him a happy Christmas, he took her in his arms and kissed her fleetingly.

'It will be happy because you are here with me,' he whispered, and took her down to join his parents, who were in *festa* dress like their son for the breakfast which was served early so gifts could be exchanged before the maids arrived.

Katherine had given much thought to hers, and felt deeply relieved when Teresa expressed delight as she unwrapped a cashmere sweater and cardigan.

'*Que coisa linda*, cara. Thank you.'

Katherine smiled. 'When I learned that it snows here in winter, I thought this might be useful.'

'Useful? It is beautiful. I shall be so *chique*! You also, Roberto,' Teresa added as he held up the heavy Cambridge blue sweater Katherine had given him.

'I wish it was cold enough to wear it today,' he said and leaned to give Katherine a kiss. '*Muit'obrigado*, Katherine.'

She smiled apologetically as his father took a bottle

of venerable single malt whisky from its box. 'I'm afraid yours is not very inspired, Antonio.'

'It is great treat for me, *cara*,' he assured her, and smiled mischievously. 'But I shall hide it. I refuse to share with our guests.'

'You have not opened your present from Antonio and me, *cara*,' said Teresa. 'Were you so worried that we would not like your gifts?'

'Yes,' admitted Katherine honestly, then blinked, totally overwhelmed when she found her present was a gaucho outfit like the men's, complete in almost every detail—shirt, kerchief, *bombachas*, poncho, even spurs and a silver knife. The only thing lacking was the gun. 'How absolutely wonderful! Thank you both so much.'

'We could not buy the boots, but I think we have right size in everything else,' said Teresa with satisfaction.

'My gift is very small,' said Roberto and slid a tiny package towards Katherine.

She removed gold paper from a small velvet box which contained earrings of oblong emeralds suspended from diamond studs. She swallowed hard. 'Oh, Roberto!'

'You do not like them?' he demanded.

She flashed him a reproachful look. 'Of course I like them, but I didn't expect such…such…'

'Excellent taste?'

'Extravagance!' She got up to kiss him, and went round the table to thank his parents in the same way.

'They are perfect with your eyes, Katherine,' said Teresa, and looked at her son. 'Is why you chose them, *nao e*?'

He nodded. 'But I feared she might not accept them.

She was very angry in Viana do Castelo because I paid for some shoes!'

Katherine felt the blood rush to her face. 'That was different.'

'*E verdade!*' Roberto smiled triumphantly. 'You cannot refuse anything I give you today because it is Christmas. And today is *festa* day so you must wear them now. I will put them in for you.'

Katherine took the plain gold studs from her earlobes and let Roberto replace them with the emeralds, which looked so incongruous with her T-shirt she laughed up at him. 'Cinderella needs to change into her party dress. When do the guests arrive?'

'Any time from noon onwards,' said Antonio, smiling genially. 'Come, Roberto. We must check the fires in the *churrasco* pits.'

'Who does the actual cooking?' asked Katherine.

'Antonio and Roberto begin while Geraldo, husband of Maria, keeps fires burning,' said Teresa, 'then the other men take over.'

'Hurry to change your clothes, *querida*,' ordered Roberto. 'Wear the green dress!'

Katherine looked with admiration at Teresa, who had exchanged her normal tailored look for a full-skirted dress in white-dotted blue cotton. 'I shall look very ordinary in my plain little shift.'

'You will be *muito elegante*,' said Teresa firmly. 'But hurry, *cara*, the girls are here, ready to start frying the *empadinhas* they made yesterday.'

For Katherine the experience was so different from her normal quiet Christmas Day with Charlotte and Sam she had to pinch herself from time to time to make sure she wasn't dreaming. In flat gold sandals instead of heels, and with one of Maria's large white aprons tied over her green dress, she hurried back and forth with the smiling maids to lay the tables and take trays of sliced meat to put in cool boxes alongside Roberto, who looked so blazingly happy as he tended the barbecue pits Katherine found it hard to recognise the embittered, injured man she'd first met. A few minutes before noon Teresa took Katherine away to tidy up before the guests began to arrive.

'You do this every Christmas?' asked Katherine with awe, as they went in the house.

'For many years, yes.' The fine dark eyes shadowed slightly. 'But not last year after Luis died.' Teresa squared her shoulders. '*Agora* we celebrate that Roberto is recovered and happy. Life must go on, *nao e*?'

Normally not the most demonstrative of people, Katherine couldn't help giving her a little hug. 'Absolutely. From experience, I know it does.'

Beforehand Katherine had wondered at the quantity of food being prepared, but as guests arrived with children and, in some cases, grandchildren, along with the families of the men who worked on Estancia Grande, it was obvious why Teresa and her team had prepared for so many. Roberto and Antonio left their posts to greet their colourfully dressed guests, leaving Geraldo and his men to oversee the sizzling meat sending up a wonderful aroma into the air.

Roberto kept her close as his parents presented her to one group after another, his arm tightening round her waist when Ildefonso Soares, the last to arrive, came up with Gloria, striking in a flame-coloured number with more flounces on it than any dress there.

'*Calma, amada*,' murmured Roberto, as he felt Katherine tense. 'No fighting on Christmas Day.'

Katherine flashed him a sparkling look and gave both

the latecomers a radiant smile. *'Muito prazer, e Feliz Natal.'*

Gloria lunged forward, obviously intending to kiss Roberto, but he gave her cheek a pat and shook her father's hand.

'I come to help, Dona Teresa,' the girl announced, but Antonio shook his head, smiling.

'It is not necessary, *cara*. We have Katherine's help today.'

Ignoring Gloria's scowl, Teresa showed her to the place reserved for the Soares family at one of the tables, which were now loaded with festive food and drink.

Antonio de Sousa and his wife sat at the head of a table with the families of their men, with Roberto and Katherine at the foot. At first the women were shy, but as Roberto supplied rapid translations for Katherine's questions they grew more relaxed, and there was much laughter when he handed her his *cuia*, a gourd filled with *mate*, the local herb tea she was instructed to drink through his *bomba*, a silver spoon with a perforated bowl.

'It is a straw to draw up the mate,' he told her.

With expectant eyes on her she obediently sucked some of the hot liquid into her mouth, but as the taste hit her tongue her eyes opened wide, then watered with the effort to swallow the bitter brew instead of spitting it out. She shuddered and very carefully said, *'Nao, obrigada. Agua por favor!'*

Everyone laughed as Roberto passed her a glass of water. 'Well done,' he whispered, taking her hand. Katherine smiled up at him, intercepting a look from Gloria which should have killed her on the spot. 'We're attracting attention,' she whispered, but his grasp only tightened.

'I do not care.'

To Katherine's surprise, she didn't either and smiled as she got up in response to his mother's signal, as Teresa beckoned to Maria and her team to follow them as some of the men struck up music with guitars and accordions.

'We fetch the *sobremesas* now,' Teresa announced as they hurried into the house.

Maria, Dirce and the other women took bowls of fruit salad to the tables, along with ice cream for the children. Teresa took a great crystal bowl of cream-topped trifle to the table where the Soares family was sitting, and Katherine put the other in front of Antonio.

'Would you like to try some?'

Antonio gazed at the inviting confection with anticipation. 'With much pleasure, *cara*.'

Katherine's trifle was greeted with equal enthusiasm by all the adults on the table, including Roberto. Katherine smiled to herself as she saw Gloria deliberately push hers away untasted, much to the satisfaction of her father, who ate both portions with gusto.

By this time children were playing under the trees, with parents interfering only when things grew heated. Then suddenly the music changed, and every child was instantly alert as they heard the familiar strains of *Jingle Bells*.

'*Papae Noel!*' shrieked a small girl, and at once there was a mini stampede as the children flocked towards the white-bearded figure in red seated on a horse pulling a trailer filled with bulging sacks of presents.

As he dismounted with a loud, 'Ho-ho-ho!' the children swarmed around him in vociferous demand.

'*Calma, calma.*' He held up quelling hands and spoke

magic words which sent them scampering back to sit on the grass, gazing up at *Papae Noel* in expectation.

'Heavens, he must be hot,' murmured Katherine, utterly delighted by the scene.

'Not too much. His suit is thin silky fabric,' Roberto told her. '*Com licenca*, I must help my father give out the presents.'

As Father Christmas read out the names on the gifts, either Antonio or Roberto distributed them to the eager recipients under the indulgent eyes of parents and grandparents. When every child had a present, another sack was produced with small gifts which *Papae Noel* handed out to the rest of the guests, including one for Katherine. Roberto resumed his place beside her as everyone at the table opened their gifts, displaying them with cries of pleasure. Then all eyes turned on Katherine as she took the wrapping paper from a velvet box. She needed no translation to know that everyone was begging her to open it, and took out a gold chain with a pendant emerald which matched her earrings. She gave Roberto a startled glance.

'It is Christmas Day,' he reminded her, 'so you must accept it, Katherine.'

'Then I will. Thank you. *Muito obrigado*,' she repeated for everyone's benefit, then bent her head so Roberto could fasten the clasp.

At his signal, the music began again and many of the guests flocked to the space under the trees to dance, including Gloria Soares, scarlet frills fluttering as she commandeered centre stage.

Katherine was only too pleased to concede it to her, though after a while Roberto insisted she partner him in the dance she soon found easy enough, happy to follow his lead to an accompaniment of encouraging smiles from the other dancers. But from then on she sat with Roberto's parents while their son did his duty by some of the ladies, and finally danced with a triumphant Gloria. But her pretty, sultry face was stormy by the time she ran back to her father, and soon afterwards they were first to leave. Roberto stood with Katherine and his parents to say goodbye to departing guests as children were rounded up and sleeping babies carried home to bed.

Much later, after Maria and her team, helped by the Estancia hands, had cleared away all signs of the celebration, Katherine and Roberto said goodnight to his parents and before going to bed went outside for a walk under the lights twinkling in the trees.

Roberto took her hand. 'So, Doutora Lister, how did you enjoy your gaucho Christmas?'

'Immensely. It was such a lovely day.' She raised an admonishing eyebrow. 'Though you shouldn't have been so extravagant. My gift from Father Christmas caused quite a stir.'

He shrugged. 'It was just jewellery, Katherine—not a ring.'

The word seemed to hang in the air in the still, starlit night. She wondered how she would have reacted if it had been a ring, and all the implications that went with it, and experienced a pang of emotion hard to identify.

'So what happens here tomorrow, Roberto?'

'My parents will rest, the servants will have a holiday, and you and I shall spend more time together,' he announced with satisfaction. 'We shall go for a short ride—if a certain delectable part of you is better now.'

'It must be, because I haven't given it a thought all day,' she said, laughing.

He caught her close and rubbed his cheek against her hair. 'To have you here with me today is the best

Christmas present of my life.' He looked into her eyes. 'Until I actually saw you standing by the plane, I had doubts that you would come.'

'I had some myself,' she said wryly. 'It was a big step for me to fly all this way to stay with a man I'd known such a short time, Roberto. It didn't help when you weren't there to meet me, either.'

'I apologise for that, Katherine. I was furious when I got held up with the herd—though it gave me chance to put on my little show for you.' He smiled down at her. 'I wanted to impress my woman.'

Katherine eyed him narrowly. 'Is that how you think of me?'

'Yes,' he said simply. 'I believe fate meant us for each other.'

'Then it's a pity fate hadn't located us closer together,' she said ruefully. 'Sheer geography is a bit of a problem for you and me, Roberto Rocha de Sousa.'

'But we will find a solution.' He took her hand to walk back to the house. 'You must be tired. You have worked hard today.'

'I enjoyed it enormously. By the way,' she added, giving him a sidelong smile, 'what did you say to Gloria? She was not a happy girl after you danced with her.'

'I gave her hell for causing your horse to bolt with you.' Roberto shrugged. 'I also threatened to tell her father, which made her panic. Much as he dotes on her, Ildefonso Soares could not have forgiven her for causing harm to my guest—nor to my horse,' he added, smiling, and took her in his arms. 'Now, let us forget everyone else and enjoy these few moments together before we must go to our separate beds.'

CHAPTER TWELVE

FOR the rest of her stay at Estancia Grande, Roberto ensured that Katherine experienced as much as possible of the gaucho way of life. She went riding with him most days, an activity she enjoyed all the more in her comfortable gaucho outfit. There were invitations to barbecues with friends of the de Sousas, a traditional gaucho dance for the festive season and even, to her great delight, a day at a rodeo.

'They go on for many days, and Luis and I competed when we were young,' Roberto informed her as he drove her home. 'But only one day was possible for you this time, since you leave the Estancia tomorrow. But we have our stay in Porto Alegre before you fly away from me, *amada*.'

'Your mother talks about the city a lot,' Katherine told him, refusing to think about flying away just yet. 'In strictest confidence she told me she likes it almost as much as Lisbon.'

He laughed. 'The highest accolade of all from Teresa Rocha Lima!'

Dinner that night was an extra special occasion, with every local delicacy Teresa could think of since it was Katherine's last night at the Estancia.

'What will you buy when you do your shopping, *cara*?' she asked over the meal.

Shopping? Katherine went blank for a second.

'You mentioned presents,' Roberto reminded her.

She nodded hastily. 'For my aunt, and James Massey and his wife. And a few friends.'

'You will find much choice in Porto Alegre,' said Teresa, and sighed. 'It is sad that you must leave so soon. You must persuade Katherine to return soon, *meu filho.*'

Roberto smiled at his mother. 'I will do my very best.'

'And now,' said Antonio, rising, 'we will drink a toast to our guest. *Boa viagem*, Katherine.'

'Thank you.' She blinked hard and raised her own glass. 'To the de Sousa family for making me so welcome. It has been an unforgettable Christmas.'

There were more farewells next day when Katherine was ready to leave. She went into the kitchen to say goodbye to Maria and Dirce, and then took a walk to the *curral* with Roberto to say goodbye to the men there, and then to Garoto, who pushed his nose against her hand. Then Geraldo and Janio carried her luggage to the plane, where Antonio stood with an arm round his wife as Katherine kissed them goodbye. As Roberto took the plane up and away from Estancia Grande, she looked down through a blur of tears at the two figures growing smaller as they waved in farewell.

'You are sorry to leave, Katherine?' said Roberto.

'Yes,' she said tersely, her throat too thick to say more.

At the airport they took one of the orange town taxis, and Roberto asked the driver to take them on a short tour of the city on the way to the São Rafael Hotel. He helped Katherine into the back seat, slid in after her and pulled her close to kiss her hard the moment the taxi moved off.

'I needed that,' he said gruffly, and rubbed his cheek against her hair. 'I love my parents, you understand, but it is good to have you to myself at last, Katherine.'

'They were very kind to me,' she reminded him.

'My mother was a little nervous before you arrived, *carinha*.'

'Why?'

'Because you are a *Doutora Historiadora*, and therefore very clever. She was expecting someone far more intimidating than you, Katherine. Although,' he added thoughtfully, 'if you had arrived wearing those severe clothes and the famous spectacles you would have frightened her to death.'

Katherine hooted. 'I haven't known your mother long, Roberto, but I can't imagine her feeling intimidated by anyone.'

'*E verdade!*' Roberto laughed. 'She was just a teenager when my father, who was fifteen years older, brought her here, but now she is very much *Dona da casa*, and rules Estancia Grande with a firm hand.'

'Your father adores her, and she him. It's heart-warming to see them together.'

'Heart-warming,' he repeated softly. 'I like that.'

Katherine smiled at him, then turned to look out at the square they were entering. 'Come on then, Roberto de Sousa, do your tour guide bit.'

'*Sempre as seus ordens*,' he said promptly, and began rattling off information. 'We are in the Praça da Matriz, and that building with the large dome is the Catedral Metropolitana. Close by is the Palácio Piratini, the

Governor's residence, and to the north the Teatro São Pedro. There are many such buildings in the city but we shall leave them for another day.'

Not that there would be many more days. Katherine pushed the thought away as she craned her neck to take it all in.

'Now,' said Roberto firmly, 'we go to the hotel. You would like a little rest before lunch, no?'

'Actually, I'd like a shower. I got a bit hot in the plane. The flight was a lot more exciting with you in charge, Roberto.'

He grinned. 'You did not trust me to land you safely?'

She grinned back. 'I suddenly remembered that Roberto Rocha was at the controls!'

'I will have my revenge for such slander,' he threatened as they arrived at the hotel. 'I stay here when I am in Porto, my parents also. It is not as big as some of the modern hotels, but it has much character, also excellent food, and on the top floors there are suites with a view of the lagoon.'

The process of checking in went very smoothly with Roberto in charge. Katherine barely had time to look round a reception lobby with gleaming golden floors and big leather furniture before they were in a lift on the way to their suite, where Roberto led her into a charming sitting room.

'The luggage will arrive soon, but I need another kiss,' he informed her, closing the door behind them. He took her in his arms and kissed her, then raised his head to smile down into her eyes. 'I have dreamed of being alone together like this.'

So had Katherine, but for the moment it seemed unwise to say so. Though for some reason the brief kiss had dispelled the unexpected frisson of nerves she experienced at the glimpse of a large bed through the half open bedroom door. 'So show me this view, then.'

They went to the windows to look down on the great lagoon. 'The Lagoa dos Patos,' he informed her.

'*Patos?*'

'Ducks.'

She grinned. 'I expected something more romantic, like flamingos.'

Roberto shrugged in mock apology. '*Desculpe, senhora*, no flamingos.' He turned at a knock on the door. 'That is our luggage.' He went to tip the porter, then rejoined Katherine at the window and put his arm round her waist. 'Have you recovered from my flying skills enough to eat, *querida*?'

She nodded with enthusiasm. 'As long as I shower first before we go down.'

He tipped her face up to his. 'I suggest we ring room service for our lunch, and then tonight, when you have rested, we shall dine out. You would like that?'

'Of course I would, though maybe not *churrasco* tonight. I've eaten more meat since I came here to Brazil than I've had for months at home.'

'And here we have the best beef in Brazil, also the best way of cooking it.' His eyes gleamed. 'It gives a man strength—his woman also. Which bag do you need first?'

'The smallest.'

'I shall put it with mine at the foot of the bed.' His eyes met hers. 'You approve?'

Knowing he meant more than luggage, she nodded her assent. 'Now, where's this bathroom?'

After her shower Katherine wrapped herself in one

of the hotel robes and opened the door to see Roberto gazing down at the view. 'How long will lunch be?'

He spun round, his eyes eating her. 'I said half an hour. Shall we rest for a while first?'

'You're tired?'

'No, *amada*, I am not.' He gave her a look which melted her bones as he crossed the room in two strides to pick her up, and then stood laughing down at her with such blatantly male satisfaction she laughed with him. 'I can now do this, Katherine.'

'Indeed you can.' She rubbed her cheek against his as he carried her to the bed.

Roberto lowered her gently, then followed her down to kiss her with such sudden, explosive heat robe and clothes were soon tossed away as they came together at last on the wide white bed, her hunger a match for his as he made love to her with words she only half understood but with caresses which needed no translation as they set her body on fire.

'Since the moment I saw you again I have longed for this,' he said against her mouth.

'Then love me. Now,' she ordered huskily, and Roberto gave a stifled elated laugh and united them with a smooth, fierce thrust that thrilled her to the core.

'I hurt you?' he gasped, but she shook her head vehemently her fingers drumming such a wild, demanding tattoo on his shoulders Roberto made love to her with joyous lack of inhibition, kissing her open mouth as he drove her relentlessly towards the summit she flew over at last before him, and he gave a great groaning sigh in the throes of his release and collapsed on her. They lay panting and winded, held fast in each other's arms, until a knock on the door brought Roberto off the bed to dive into the robe he'd torn from Katherine.

She pulled the sheet up to her chin and lay still, listening as Roberto gave instructions to a waiter. A suite which opened into a sitting room had its advantages, she thought with approval. Roberto had merely looked flushed and slightly tousled about the head to confront the waiter while she probably looked like a wreck. She leapt to her feet to escape into the bathroom, but Roberto caught her and swept her up in his arms before she made it.

'It is too late to be shy, *carinha*!'

'I'm not shy.' Well, not much. 'I need another shower.'

'I will share it with you, *linda flor*. I have dreamed of this, also.' He set her down gently in the shower stall, threw off the robe and joined her.

Katherine half expected him to make love to her again once they were naked together, but Roberto merely held her close as the water streamed over them, then stepped out to fetch towels. He wrapped her in one of them, laughing as her stomach gave a sudden rumble.

'I hate to be unromantic,' she said wryly, 'but I'm hungry. I couldn't face much in the way of breakfast this morning.'

He gave her a searching look. 'You were sad to leave the Estancia?'

'Yes. It was hard to say goodbye.'

'I am pleased to hear that,' he informed her with satisfaction. 'Put on a robe while I dress, then we eat, *Doutora*.'

In underwear and robe, Katherine finger-combed her hair and followed Roberto into the sitting room, where their lunch waited on a table under the windows. With a flourish, Roberto removed a cover to display a vast colourful salad embedded with huge prawns.

'Wow!'

'So you see, English girl, we gauchos do not eat meat *all* the time.' He smiled. 'Come. Eat. You must renew your energy.'

Katherine raised an eyebrow and he pulled her close on the sofa beside him, chuckling as he kissed her cheek.

'I meant because you were so brave to fly here with me as pilot,' he assured her virtuously.

They enjoyed their long lazy lunch in front of windows with a spectacular view of the lagoon, the only cloud on Katherine's horizon the prospect that soon she must leave all this behind and go back to her normal life. But looking on the plus side, she reminded herself firmly, she had been given a glorious holiday with Roberto in a country she'd always longed to visit; though her preconception of Brazil had been mostly of Rio de Janeiro and Carnival, with minimal knowledge of the wide open spaces of gaucho country in Rio Grande do Sul, which she had come to love during her short stay. Riding out over his land with Roberto had been a deeply satisfying experience. She had enjoyed the camaraderie of his men, also achieved a close rapport with her horse.

'When you go back to the Estancia will you pat Garoto for me and tell him I'll miss him, Roberto?'

He took in a deep breath and then put their plates on the table and lifted her onto his lap. 'I need to hold you,' he said tersely, smoothing her head against his shoulder. Katherine relaxed against him, happy just to be alone with him in the quiet of the air-conditioned room, while the vibrant city life of Porto Alegre went on around them.

'When you say such things,' he said at last, his voice

husky, 'almost you make me cry. And it is not macho for a man to cry!'

'You take great pride in machismo?'

'*Pois e!* What man does not?' He gave her a crooked smile. 'When you left me in Portugal I wanted very much to cry, and exerted much self-control to avoid disillusioning Jorge.'

'I cried buckets,' she said frankly, and he laughed and hugged her close, but inwardly she shuddered. All too soon it would happen again when she flew home.

'Would you like tea, Katherine?'

She shook her head, stifling a yawn, and Roberto took her hand to pull her to her feet. '*Agora.* Now you rest.'

After the hectic programme of the past few days the idea was suddenly very appealing. 'But what will you do, Roberto?'

'I shall rest with you.' He looked surprised that she'd needed to ask. 'When you wake we shall drink tea and coffee, as we did many times in Quinta das Montanhas and at Estancia Grande, but here is better because we shall be in bed together. Not,' he said, his handsome face suddenly stern, 'that I will make love to you. You need sleep, Katherine. There are shadows under those beautiful green eyes. I will just hold your hand while you sleep, then later we go out on the town.'

She smiled drowsily and leaned back against the banked pillows. 'I loved Christmas at Estancia Grande, Roberto, but I'm so glad to be here alone with you for a while before I leave.'

He slid down beside her and raised her hand to his lips. 'It was a brilliant idea of mine, nao e?' He shifted slightly to look down into her eyes. 'Did your former lover object when you came here to me?'

'I didn't tell him. Andrew and I are no longer friends.' Katherine pulled a face as she described the unpleasant encounter in the flat.

Roberto lapsed into Portuguese to swear violently. 'He meant to force you?'

'I don't think he would have gone that far, but Hugh and Alastair's arrival cut it short. At which point I told Andrew it was over in front of witnesses—good move because he's a lawyer—and said goodbye. I haven't seen him since.'

'I would like to meet him,' said Roberto with quiet menace.

'Unlikely that you will,' she pointed out.

'I will never force you, Katherine.'

She turned to smile at him. 'No need. One look from you, Roberto Rocha de Sousa, and I melt in your arms.'

'*Amada!*' He leant to kiss her swiftly, and then settled beside her, holding her hand. 'Now close your eyes. *Dorme bem.*'

Katherine woke alone later to the soft glow of lamps from the open doorway to the other room. She shot up to look at her watch as Roberto came to sit on the edge of the bed.

'You feel rested now?' He bent to kiss her nose.

'I do, but I'm sorry I slept so long!'

'*Nao importa*, we eat later here in the city. Also you were up very early almost every morning at the Estancia. Tomorrow, you can have breakfast in bed.' He smoothed her hair back with a caressing hand. 'I spoke with my parents. My mother is glad we arrived safely, but feels very sad now you are gone. I am commanded to ask you to come back again soon.'

'How sweet of her.' Katherine felt enormous relief

that Roberto's parents had been so friendly. She had never been invited to meet a man's parents before, mainly because she'd deliberately kept her former relationships too casual for the question to arise. 'It was very good of your parents to invite a total stranger to their home for Christmas, Roberto.'

His eyebrows rose. 'You were my guest, not a stranger, Katherine. They were both eager to meet the clever lady who revealed my painting as a Gainsborough. And because of its provenance, she will always be grateful to you.'

She shook her head in wonder. 'I had no idea when I took James Massey's place that I would not only meet a star of the racing circuit—'

'Who you had never heard of,' he growled.

'True, but due to the joys of technology I soon found out! As I was saying, I had no idea that I would meet a sports celebrity who owned a Gainsborough, let alone that the subject of the painting would be his ancestor.' She met his eyes squarely. 'Nor that my client would be the most attractive man I'd ever met in my life.'

Roberto's eyes widened. 'Is that what you thought that first day? Even though I limped and had a scar?'

'Yes.' Her eyes flashed. 'While you were furious because I wasn't a man, and took one look at my clothes and spectacles and dismissed me as a frump.'

'Frump? What is that?'

'Someone who looked like me that day.'

He grinned and threw out his hands. 'To me, you seemed so blazingly intellectual you scared me greatly, *Doutora*. But you are also beautiful and compassionate and so looked past my injuries to the man underneath.'

Not quite. Dr Katherine Lister had simply taken one

look and fallen head over heels in love with the client just the way he was, scars and all. But until she was sure that Roberto's heart was involved in his feelings for her she would keep that to herself.

Lit up by night, Porto Alegre was even more exciting. Katherine held Roberto's hand in the taxi on the drive to the restaurant, in constant need of his touch as the time drew nearer to leave him. She pushed the thought away as they arrived at the Italian restaurant Roberto had chosen as a change for Katherine. Not that the location mattered to her. Roberto for companion was the important thing. She would willingly have stayed at the hotel and ordered room service again but, knowing he wanted her to experience some Porto Alegre night life, she had worn the green dress again and, with the emerald pendant and earrings to transform it, felt as beautiful as Roberto constantly told her she was.

The restaurant was intimate and sophisticated, the red wine was mellow and Roberto held her hand as much as possible throughout the meal as he outlined their itinerary for the next day before her flight.

'We will go shopping for these presents you must buy, Katherine.' He flung up a hand. 'And do not flash those eyes at me—I will not try to pay for them. Though if I find something you would like for yourself I *will* pay.'

'Roberto, you've gone to enormous expense to bring me here, no more presents are necessary,' she said firmly, and suddenly looked wistful. 'I had such gorgeous Christmas gifts from you and your parents, but I won't get much opportunity to wear them.'

'You must wear jewellery when you go out with friends?'

She laughed, and touched a hand to the pendant and earrings. 'True. But not like these. I shall keep them for special occasions.' She sighed. 'And the gaucho outfit will be just a souvenir. I ride in pretty ordinary gear at home. When I do, which is very seldom these days.'

'It looks very good on you, *amada*.' He raised her hand to his lips, oblivious of the other diners. 'And you should keep up the riding. Did you enjoy riding with me?'

'You know I did, Roberto. The entire holiday has been a wonderful experience.'

'It is not over yet, *querida*.' He summoned a waiter, paid the bill, then stood up and held out his hand. 'Come, Katherine. Let us find a taxi.'

Back at the hotel, it seemed like the most natural thing in the world to get ready for bed together, and then slide into each other's arms as though this was something they'd done every night for years.

Katherine smiled as she told Roberto this and he nodded in full agreement.

'I felt this from almost the first time I saw you.'

'You mean a bit later than that, after I scrubbed up and lost the glasses!'

'*E verdade!*' He laughed and hugged her closer. 'I was determined to have you, Katherine Lister, no matter how many men you'd left behind in England.'

She gave him a dig in the ribs. 'There was precisely one! Whereas you've had countless women in your life, Roberto de Sousa!'

'Mariana was the only one of significance.' He switched on a lamp and looked into her eyes. 'You are different. In my dreams I had always longed to meet a woman who appealed to my mind as well as my body. I had given up all hope of this—then I met you.' He kissed her with sudden, fierce possession, his hands moving in a demanding glissade down her spine to mould her against that part of him that sought entry, and her thighs parted for him in ardent welcome as he united their bodies in the earthy, heart-stopping intensity of rapture she knew she would never know again once they parted.

Roberto raised his head as his breathing slowed, consternation in his eyes as he saw her face. 'You are crying! Why?'

She swiped her tears away impatiently, about to lie, then changed her mind. 'Because I'm leaving you tomorrow.' She bit her quivering lower lip so hard Roberto frowned and placed soft, sweet kisses along her mouth to soothe it, then turned on his side and drew her against him.

'I know too well you are leaving me, so now we talk.'

Katherine looked up into his taut, determined face, and drew in a shaky breath. 'I'm sorry to spoil things by crying. Normally, I don't do tears much.' And all the tears she'd shed recently had been over Roberto de Sousa.

'I know this.' He stroked her hair back from her forehead. 'At the thought of parting with you I want to cry myself.' He sighed. 'But men do not cry, of course.'

She managed a grin. 'Especially gaucho men!'

'That is better, *carinha*. I prefer your smiles to your tears.'

'So do I,' she said dryly. 'So what do you want to talk about, Roberto?'

'Myself, of course—what else would a man want to talk about?' he teased, then sobered. 'I want you to listen very carefully to me, Katherine. And stay close while I talk.'

Katherine had no intention of moving even a hair's

breadth. His warmth and nearness were a vital necessity as she braced herself to listen.

'When Luis died,' he began, 'I naturally returned immediately to the Estancia to comfort my parents. But because I want truth between us, Katherine, I confess that I did not intend to stay very long. Because I had been living away from home for years I had seen my family only on short visits for special reasons like Christmas and anniversaries. Because it was some months since I had seen him, it was a shock to find that my father was looking so much older. Because my mother is many years younger than him, the change in her was not so great.

'So Roberto Rocha, darling of the racing circuit, decided to take a sabbatical from his career and stay at the Estancia to lighten some of his father's load. Because he had been born to it, he was soon so much part of life on Estancia Grande he began taking over from his grieving father more and more. But he never lost sight of the ultimate goal—that once his father had overcome his grief Roberto Rocha would return to his life on the track for a few years until it was the natural time to retire and return to his roots.

'Then I went to a friend's wedding, met Elena, and was moron enough to throw myself into my car to prevent her stealing it,' said Roberto with disgust. 'All thoughts of a career ended. I worked hard to recover physically, but mentally I was…how do you say …wallowing in self-pity. Then fate sent Dr Katherine Lister into my life and changed it for ever.' He turned her face up to his and kissed her to emphasize the point. 'When my father took me to the hospital straight from the airport I was ready to endure anything the doctors could do to help me walk and ride normally.'

Katherine smoothed a hand over his hard chest. 'Was the pain terrible, Roberto?'

'For a while, yes, but I did whatever was asked of me to begin recovering.' He lifted her hand to his lips. 'But I could not ring you until I knew for certain that I would be able to function normally, both in the saddle and on two feet.'

'You could have asked someone to send me an email, so I at least knew you'd arrived safely,' she pointed out.

'I preferred to wait until I could hear your voice, Katherine,' he said flatly. 'I had much time to think about what my life would be once I was home on the Estancia for good. And though I love my parents, and enjoy the company of men, I needed more in my life. I so much missed you, *amada* I asked you here for Christmas, hoping that you would enjoy a stay on the Estancia.'

'Which I did,' she sighed.

'You took to the life like…you have a phrase about ducks?'

'Like a duck to water?'

'*Isso*. To ride out with you on Garoto by my side brought me much joy.'

'Me too,' she said huskily.

Roberto turned her face up to his. 'Then I have a question to ask.' His eyes, darkly brilliant with an emotion which started her heart beating like a drum, locked with hers. 'Do you love me, Katherine?'

It wasn't the question she'd been hoping for, but she burnt some of her boats and answered it anyway. 'Yes. I do.'

He let out a deep unsteady breath and kissed her until

her head reeled. '*Gracas a Deus*,' he said against her mouth. 'How I have longed to hear you say that.'

'Why?' she demanded.

'You must know why!'

Katherine looked deep into the dark, possessive eyes and burnt the last of her boats. 'Is it by any chance because you love me?'

'You have to ask?' he said in astonishment. 'I thought it was written across my forehead for all to see.'

Her eyes fell, as her heart thumped so loudly she was sure he must be able to hear it. 'I knew only too well you wanted me—physically, I mean.'

'And I do,' he assured her with passion. 'I adore your body, but even more I love you with all my heart and soul and always will. So will you marry me and live in the land of the gaucho with me for ever, Katherine? Because if you say yes it must mean until death parts us.'

'I do say yes. To almost everything,' she added, to avoid any misunderstanding.

'Almost?' he said warily.

'I've been on my own for a long time, and I'm used to running my life the way I want it. And although I would enjoy life on the Estancia, Roberto, I'm accustomed to earning my own living. I'd like to carry on with my job. With the wonder of technology, I could work for James wherever I am.'

'I will buy you the ultimate in computers so you can do that, I promise,' he said emphatically. 'And if you miss your life in London you shall invite your friends to stay whenever you wish—but not the lawyer! So, Dr Lister. Will you marry me?'

She smiled at him radiantly. 'Yes, Senhor Sousa, I will.'

Roberto held her close in passionate thanksgiving, and then got out of bed to make for his overnight bag. As he slid back beside her he held out his hand. 'This is not a present, Katherine. This is a token of my love. Will you accept it?'

She looked at the emerald and diamond ring lying on his palm and blinked away tears. This was no time to be crying! 'Oh, Roberto! It's glorious. Of course I'll accept it.'

'I bought it with the other pieces,' he informed her as he slid it on the appropriate finger, 'but before I could offer it to you it was necessary to wait until you had more experience of what life with me would mean.' He raised her hand and kissed the ring, then gave her an imperious look. 'Do not make me wait long before we add a wedding band, *querida*. We have spent too many years of our lives apart. It is time that we were together, as fate intended.'

EPILOGUE

MOONLIGHT bathed the gardens with its usual magic at Quinta das Montanhas when Katherine joined the man leaning against a pillar to wait for her. Roberto de Sousa took her in his arms and kissed her with rather more reverence than she had expected in such circumstances.

'*Minha esposa*,' he said against her lips. 'At last you are my wife.'

Katherine sighed happily. 'We finally made it. Now all we need is a *churrasco* party at Estancia Grande when we get home, to celebrate the deed, and I'll feel we're well and truly married.'

Roberto laughed softly. 'I know easier—and more delightful—ways to convince you of that!'

'I bet you do, Roberto Rocha!'

'*I* was not the one who gave that name to the photographers at our wedding, *querida*!'

She sighed. 'I know. Who knew Hugh would be so sneaky? Sorry about that.'

'On such a day, why would I mind?' Roberto kissed her again, the reverence less in evidence this time. 'But that was yesterday, and my bride was so tired last night I—saint that I am—let her sleep in peace. But now Lidia and Jorge have served us a sumptuous wedding supper and vanished to their quarters, come, *minha mulher*, let us do the same.' He held out his hand. 'I can carry you upstairs if you wish, but it is better I keep my energy for more important activities, *nao e*?'

'Absolutely,' she assured him as they went hand in hand up the familiar staircase. Roberto picked her up to carry her inside the bedroom she'd slept in before, and set her down to undress her with urgent hands before laying her on the bed.

'*Amada*,' he said huskily, as they lay naked together for the first time as man and wife. 'I have so longed for this day—and this night. I need much consolation for all the nights we have spent apart.'

Katherine gladly provided it, putting all the pent up longing of their separation into her kisses as Roberto made passionate love to her with hungry lips and urgent hands until their bodies could no longer exist apart. As they came together as man and wife for the first time, tears hung on Katherine's lashes as Roberto told her in two languages how much he adored and cherished her, and how happy she made him, until at last there was only the sound of their sobbing breaths as they surged together to a climax that left them speechless in each other's arms.

Roberto raised his head at last, his eyes luminous in the moonlight streaming through the window. 'Look at me, Katherine.'

She raised heavy eyelids to gaze up into the taut, handsome face, marvelling that she was really here, in her bridegroom's arms at long last. 'I'm looking,' she whispered.

'I swear I will make you happy, always.'

'I am happy. A happily married woman,' she added in wonder. 'But I had to get through a surprising amount of work to achieve it, not least organising things with the house.'

'It is good your friends are renting it from you,' he agreed, and rolled on his back, pulling her close. 'They wished to buy it, no?'

Katherine nodded. 'But I could never sell it.'

'It would cause pain to sever your link with your father,' agreed Roberto.

She reached up and kissed him, grateful for his perception. 'Yes. But I have the comfort of knowing it's in good hands. Hugh is still renting the top flat, and I was happy to let Alastair and Rachel turn the two lower floors into one for their first home. Sam Napier will make sure the conversion is done well.'

'I liked him very much, Charlotte, too. She is a most elegant lady.'

'But your mother stole the show in that fabulous hat.' Katherine chuckled drowsily. 'I'm so pleased she braved the flight to see us married.'

'I will tell her that when I ring the Estancia after they return home.' Roberto smoothed the hair back from her face. 'James Massey told me he is happy about the new arrangement with you.'

She nodded happily. 'With the aid of my spanking new computer I can work for him from Estancia Grande as easily as I can at the gallery.'

'Do not let the computer take up all your time, *amada*.' He rolled onto his side to look into her eyes. 'Save most of it for me.'

'I will,' she assured him.

'Ah, *querida*, do you know how I felt when you made your vows to me?'

'Pleased? Happy?'

'*De certeza*. But it was more than that. When I was

racing I believed that the only thing important was to be world champion.' He drew her close. 'I was wrong. To win you as my wife is the greatest achievement of my life. Why are you crying, *amada*?'

'How can you expect me not to when you say things like that to me?' She blinked the tears from her lashes and smiled into his eyes. 'If it's any consolation, Roberto Rocha, you'll always be world champion as far as I'm concerned. If we had a bottle of champagne handy I'd spray it all over you to prove it.'

Roberto gave a delighted laugh and hugged her close. 'There is something I would like more than champagne.'

'What is it?'

'This is our wedding night, *querida*, so make a guess!'

'If you mean you want to make love to me again, take me, I'm yours!' she assured him, smiling. Her smile faded. 'I mean that, Roberto. I've been yours from the moment I first set eyes on you, whether you wanted me or not.'

His eyes lit with the smile which always made her heart beat faster. 'Of course I wanted you, *amada*. While I breathe I always will. And now I have you, *minha esposa*, I will never let you go!'

* * * * *

LET'S TALK
Romance

For exclusive extracts, competitions
and special offers, find us online:

MILLS & BOON

THE HEART OF ROMANCE

A ROMANCE FOR EVERY KIND OF READER

MODERN

Prepare to be swept off your feet by sophisticated, sexy and seductive heroes, in some of the world's most glamourous and romantic locations, where power and passion collide.
8 stories per month.

HISTORICAL

Escape with historical heroes from time gone by. Whether your passion is for wicked Regency Rakes, muscled Vikings or rugged Highlanders, awaken the romance of the past.
6 stories per month.

MEDICAL

Set your pulse racing with dedicated, delectable doctors in the high-pressure world of medicine, where emotions run high and passion, comfort and love are the best medicine.
6 stories per month.

True Love

Celebrate true love with tender stories of heartfelt romance, from the rush of falling in love to the joy a new baby can bring, and a focus on the emotional heart of a relationship.
8 stories per month.

Desire

Indulge in secrets and scandal, intense drama and plenty of sizzling hot action with powerful and passionate heroes who have it all: wealth, status, good looks…everything but the right woman.
6 stories per month.

HEROES

Experience all the excitement of a gripping thriller, with an intense romance at its heart. Resourceful, true-to-life women and strong, fearless men face danger and desire - a killer combination!
8 stories per month.

DARE

Sensual love stories featuring smart, sassy heroines you'd want as a best friend, and compelling intense heroes who are worthy of them.
4 stories per month.

To see which titles are coming soon, please visit

millsandboon.co.uk/nextmonth

MILLS & BOON

MODERN

Power and Passion

Prepare to be swept off your feet by sophisticated, sexy and seductive heroes, in some of the world's most glamourous and romantic locations, where power and passion collide.

Julia James

Heiress's
**PREGNANCY
SCANDAL**

MILLS & BOON
MODERN

Jennie Lucas

Chosen for the
**SHEIKH'S ROYAL
BRIDE**

MILLS & BOON

Kim Lawrence

**A WEDDING
AT THE
ITALIAN'S DEMAND**

MILLS & BOON

Sharon Kendrick

The
**SHEIKH'S
SECRET BABY**

MILLS & BOON
MODERN